Eliza eth Garne was born in Chesnire, and now lives in Oxford. She is the author of the acclaimed *Nightdancing*, which won a Betty Trask Award, and was shortlisted for the Authors' Club First Novel Award.

Praise for *The Ingenious Edgar Jones*:

'There are cities where the present fades like a ghost, thinned by swarming visions from centuries of imagination. Like Venice, Paris and St Petersburg, Oxford is veiled in satire and romance, ripe with illusion and disillusion, heavy with power to beguile and then to turn a stone shoulder on the poor fools it has captivated ... Elizabeth Garner's Oxford consumes lives ... The city of bristling railings, closed gates, watchful gargoyles and petty men with lavish pretensions is as atmospheric as it is claustrophobic ... Garner has made – or unmade – her own visionary Oxford in an enjoyable and eloquent novel' Helen Dunmore, *The Times*

'A gothic fantasy full of supercilious academics and forbidden rooms ... creepy and claustrophobic ... Edgar is bold and fearless, naturally resourceful and brimming with imagination ... a sad, sweet tale' *Daily Mail*

'A dazzling novel that takes wing from first page to last' *Saga Magazine*

'The main character in *The Ingenious Edgar Jones* is Oxford. Its gargoyles, greens and gatehouse leap from the page with surprising drama ... there is much to admire in this memorable second novel' *Financial Times*

Also by Elizabeth Garner and available from Headline Review

Nightdancing

THE INGENIOUS
EDGAR JONES

ELIZABETH GARNER

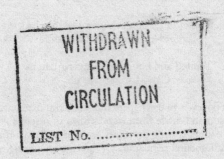

headline
review

First published in 2007 by
HEADLINE REVIEW
An imprint of HEADLINE PUBLISHING GROUP

First published in paperback in Great Britain in 2008 by
HEADLINE REVIEW
An imprint of HEADLINE PUBLISHING GROUP

1

Cataloguing in Publication Data is available from the British Library

F162409   ISBN 978 0 7553 0254 3

£11.00   Typeset in Caslon by Avon DataSet Ltd,
Bidford-on-Avon, Warwickshire

Printed and bound in Great Britain by
Clays Ltd, St Ives plc

Headline's policy is to use papers that are natural, renewable and
recyclable products and made from wood grown in sustainable forests. The
logging and manufacturing processes are expected to conform to the
environmental regulations of the country of origin.

HEADLINE PUBLISHING GROUP
An Hachette Livre UK Company
338 Euston Road
London NW1 3BH

www.headline.co.uk

For Sam

My thanks to:

Joe Garner; George McGavin; Sarah Ballard; Mary-Anne Harrington; my parents; Gilbert Greaves; Rachael Kerr; John Mitchinson; Nicole and Nadav Kander; Jay Leggett; Ben Spencer and Matt Bradbury; Lucy and Loic Webb-Martin.

PART ONE

The night that William Jones's world changed began like any other.

At six o'clock he rose from his bed, made his prayers and his ablutions. At quarter-past six he took tea and toast with his wife, Eleanor, in their front parlour. And at half-past six, to the beat of the bell of the grandfather clock, he buttoned up his coat, pulled his hat down upon his head, kissed his wife and lifted the latch of his front door.

The steady pace of his footsteps marked out the half-hour walk across Oxford. It was a cold February night. The sky was clear and pinpricked with stars. The moon was nothing but a splinter, the curl of a stray feather stuck to the velvet dark of the sky. William pulled up his collar and watched the mists of his breath rope through the air before him.

He always loved the turning from the lanes of Jericho out on to St Giles. It was an invisible boundary between the quiet domestic world where he was a loving husband and the University where he was a watchman at the college gates. Every time he trod this path he would reflect how the change in the streets echoed the differences between his worlds. The roads of Jericho twisted in upon themselves, and a man could get easily lost. It was sometimes thus when he was sitting by the fireside with his wife. The conversation would ebb and flow between them, full of affection, and talk of the daughter that was blossoming in her belly. But there were times when there were shadowed corners in their speech, when a thing might not mean to Eleanor what it meant to him, and he would feel that he had taken a wrong turning down a dark alley, and was sitting in a room that seemed in outwards appearance to be his home, but was not.

Whereas when he emerged on to the University streets, there stood the broad walls of the colleges, set shoulder to shoulder, their domes, spires and battlements pointing magnificently towards the heavens. And here William knew exactly who he was: he was Porter Jones, warden of the nights, the man who watched over great minds as they slumbered. Here William had a place and a function, and no one could shift him from it.

But on this particular evening, the University was retreating from him as he walked through it. It was often thus when the moon waned. The college walls were swallowed by the night, the lamps that hung over the entrances illuminated them in piecemeal: the mouth of a doorway, say, or the curve of a window. As the scholars slept, it was as if the University simply dissolved itself, brick by brick, stone by stone, and drifted off into the night, leaving only a cornice here, a buttress there, and a few curious gargoyles peering down at the shattered world below.

But if William Jones understood one thing in life then it

was the ways of Oxford. He had been at the college his whole life. He had worked his way up from kitchen boy to scout to watchman. He had walked the streets at dawn, dusk, and all the hours in between. He knew every whim of the city and nothing could break his stride. He marched past the expanse of shadow that was St John's College and turned left down Broad Street. There was Balliol at his shoulder, and its companion, Trinity, with its vaulted roof and gated garden. And huddled next to Trinity, the White Horse tavern, with its belly of a window pushing out upon the street. Every night it framed the same tableau: roaring men, jostling against each other, their backs bent by the beams. It was still remarkable to William that it was here, two years previously, that he had found the woman who had made him a husband. But that was the truth, and all he could really conclude from it was that there was opportunity in any corner of this world if only one had the wits and the will to look for it.

William was by the crossroads at the bottom of Broad Street when the sky split open. He did not register the start of it. A single star fell from its fixture, flared through the sky and was gone, leaving a trail of gold, as if the velvet damask of the heavens had been sliced open. No sooner had it passed than another fell in its wake, and another, and another.

William was striding up Hollywell Street when he noticed the change in the elements. The road before him had a golden sheen about it, turning the cobbles into a river of scattered sovereigns. He looked up. The stars were falling so quick on the heels of one another that they could not be separated. The sky was a smelting pot of liquid light, picking out the ridges of the rooftops. And as the sky spat and hissed, William saw that the college he was set to guard had come alive. It was a creature with a bristled back. The bell tower was the neck of the beast, flame-snouted, snarling into the night. William shook his head, as if to shake the fancy from his mind. The college was a thing of brick and stone and well he knew it. A porter got his position for his watchfulness, not for his dreaming.

He set his shoulder to the door and walked across the threshold.

After her husband left for his night watch, Eleanor Jones sat restless by the fire. The quietness of her life was all so very new to her that often she found herself at a loss about what to do with it. As the daughter of a innkeeper, she had known every evening to be measured out by the beating of fists upon the table and the clashing of glasses. The roaring noise of the tavern was something that she had spent her life waiting to run from, and yet now sometimes she would find herself walking through her house at night, pulling books from the shelves to hear the hammering of them upon the floor, or racing up and down the stairs, for the echo of footsteps.

As a young girl she would kneel upon the window seat at the front of the tavern and watch the passage of the gentlemen striding down Broad Street, willing them to turn and notice her. These men that seemed to have a purpose out there, in the world beyond the beer barrels. So when William arrived she was ready for him. When he courted her with words of love stolen from poets, and flowers stolen from the college gardens, she was quickly won. He was a clever man, and kind and gentle with it. He would take her down to where the parkland roamed wild at the edge of the city. They would embrace in the shadow of the beech trees and he would tell her that together they would have a happy life and he would love her till the end of his days – how could he do otherwise?

She spent the few months of their courtship dreaming of the transformation that awaited her. No longer would she stand at the pumps, watching the beer froth about the tap like the foaming spittle around the mouth of a madman. No longer would she end every evening pitching her father up the stairs. She had found a better kind of man who loved her, and she would set her future alongside his. What matter if his hair was greying and there were lines gathering across his face? Better that than any of the young men who pulled at her across the bar night after night, calling out her name as if they were calling in cattle.

But as they embarked upon the great adventure of their marriage, Eleanor soon realised that what her husband meant by a better life did not quite match her own imaginings. When the college gifted them the cottage, William didn't see the mould on the walls or the tangled mass of briars and weeds that ranged across the garden. He didn't see that when they took their tea together, the china would slide slowly but surely across the parlour table, towards the western wall of the house. No, for William the cottage was a symbol of progress, and that was all that mattered. Eleanor loved William for his convictions, but privately, as she passed so quickly from the tavern to the altar, to the marriage bed, to her seat by the fireside with the unborn child turning somersaults against her skin, she suspected that there were things in this world that could neither be foreseen nor forewarned against. As her belly swelled and she could feel the pressure of fists and feet inside her, Eleanor thought about how life had an urgency all of its own, and no fact, theory or plan of advancement could contain it.

When they had first arrived at the cottage there was talk of hanging new wallpaper, fresh paint upon the window frames, the tiny kitchen and scullery being scrubbed from top to tail, even talk of the wilderness of the garden being razed to the ground and replanted by William. But, in truth, the only aspect that changed at all was the front parlour. The shelves became filled with William's books. He copied out scriptures and set them in picture frames to cover the peeling wallpaper. *The Lord bless Thee and keep Thee.* Beside them, he placed a map of the Empire and a map of the heavens. William's telescope was put upon the mantelpiece and, when not at his night watch, he would often be found kneeling up by the window with the brass barrel to his eye, sweeping the curve of the heavens. William, always half in another world.

But still Eleanor knew that having only half of William was a much better arrangement than the whole of her old life. It was worth the damp, the sideways slant of her house, William's absence at night and his long days of sleeping, for the trade of the beer barrels with the books. All for the lazy embrace of William's arm across her back when he came to bed at dawn. All for the promise of a daughter.

The child would be a girl, Eleanor was certain. And the midwife had confirmed it: the way the child was changing the shape of her, making her rounded but small-bellied. Boys push away, she was told, setting themselves staring out at the world before they are even in it. Whereas the girls sit close to the spine, embracing their mother.

And when the girl arrived she would want for nothing. In the long nights without William, Eleanor sat in the second parlour, a cupboard of a room set at the back of the house, stitching together dresses for their little girl. Eleanor loved making as much as William loved reading. As a child she would scout the corners of the tavern for scattered shillings, and save them up for a bit of ribbon or lace. For the beauty of the colour and the feel of it against her skin. Her daughter would not have to scrabble around in the dust for such pleasures; she would have them from the very start.

Eleanor was pulling a thread of gold across the cloth of a smock, a tiny thing no wider than the span of her hand, when the sky began to crack. She saw specks of light tumbling past the window and plummeting down into the wilderness. She stood up to get a better sense of it and a pain shot through her belly. There was a mass of water seeping through her skirts. She felt the child tumble inside her. It was too soon. When the pains come you must walk them out, the midwife had told her. Count your hours and send word accordingly. Eleanor braced herself against the doorframe and pushed her way into the front parlour. She began to walk, back and forth, forth and back across the hearthrug.

The grandfather clock loomed above her, the tick tick tick of the pendulum beating out the pain. The painted face of time spun round, a pale moon peeping out from the edge of a sea of stars. On the walls far above, the scriptures ranged. *As are the arrows in the hand of a mighty man, so are the children to the LORD.*

There was something very wrong in all of this, thought Eleanor.

She hauled herself out on to the doorstep. The sky spat, flamed and tilted. The fire in the heavens was the fire in her belly. Then all was darkness.

In all his twenty-five years at the gates William had never seen a sky like this. The firefall was gathering to a frenzy, streaming down in burning lines of light, arrows aiming straight for their target. Behind the curve of the city wall, behind the bristle back of the chapel, the heavens were emptying themselves into the cloister gardens. There is more to the guardianship of the college than watchfulness at the gate, William told himself, as he pulled his coat around his shoulders, turned the key to the door and set out across the lawns.

When Eleanor came to she was in the front parlour, her back braced by a pile of cloth. Her skirts were pushed up to her waist and there was a grey-haired woman fumbling about her belly.

'There, there,' said the woman, smiling a gap-toothed smile. 'Just lie still and let Nature take her course.'

'The midwife—'

'Has been sent for. But this one's an urgent little thing! It just needs turning.'

Eleanor watched as the woman's hands pummelled at her waist. The rings upon her fingers danced with light. The sky outside the window twisted and tumbled to the rhythm of the pounding.

Time slipped. Above her, on the painted face of the grandfather clock, the wide white moon smiled down.

Then there was the midwife at her knees. The woman with the grey hair and the sparkling fingers was nowhere.

'Now!' cried the midwife.

Eleanor pushed and cried and pushed again, and the child came out, head first, diving into the nest of cloth gathered beneath her. It came rushing out with such an urgency that if the midwife had not been so fast to cut the cord it would have ripped itself away.

'A boy!'

'A boy?' echoed Eleanor, no more than a whisper.

'A boy,' repeated the midwife, but she did not sound so certain.

The midwife had spent her life ushering in the lives of others. For over forty years she had, unwittingly, assisted into the world artists, arsonists, cowards, clowns, craftsmen, drunkards, dullards, magicians, murderers, scholars, showmen and men who believed they were God. If not for the spryness of her hands, Oxford would be half the city it was. If anyone had cared to ask her, she could have drawn up a fresh map of the land, marking out its peculiar districts of birth.

In the tiny cottages that carve up the roads to the east of the city, there were the artisans' children who came into the world running, drumming their heels on their mothers' bellies, as if eager to take the road to fortune. Then there was the mystery of the tribes who lived along the edge of the canal, the lock-keepers and the boatmen. Within every family there was at least one who was web-footed, or born with grey and slippery skin, as if the mists of the riverbank had crept into the womb and seeded the child. Then on the other side of Oxford, where there lived men who got rich by their thinking, the justices, the clerks and the bookbinders, there in the opulent bedrooms, frowned down upon by oil-painted ancestors, the pale wives over and over again gave birth to the same child: waxen and perfect, but reluctant to uncurl and face the world.

The midwife had pulled children from the womb every which way imaginable, of every shape and size, but never a child like this one.

He was a miniature model of what a child should be and all scrunched up in on himself like a fist. The midwife wiped the blood from his skin. He howled and pawed the air. She sponged down his back. And there, underneath the muck that comes with any child, was a thick line of hair snaking down his spine in a feathered crest. And stranger still, his skin was not that of a premature boy, not the parchment-thin veneer mottled by a blue fretwork of veins. His skin was sallow and dark, like the sunworn skin of a labourer. The skin of a man who had already lived his life, with every year etched upon his flesh by the elements.

Eleanor held out her arms. 'Let me see him.'

'In a moment, Mrs Jones.'

The midwife took a length of cotton and bound the boy up tight. Placed in his mother's arms, he stopped his howling.

'So small,' said Eleanor. 'Can you be sure that he will live?'

'He's a fighter,' said the midwife. 'He's got a determination about him.'

'A boy and a fighter.'

Eleanor gazed into the boy's dark and wrinkled face and saw nothing she recognised.

William scuttled around the edges of the quad and took the shadowed turning to the cloisters. The vaulted ceiling stretched above his head, the wooden lattice of the rafters sparked with reflected light, carving a great gold net out of the darkness. But this was nothing compared to the fire burning at the heart of the place.

The walls of the cloisters embraced a square of lawn, with a huge tree at the centre, and the tree was aflame. The ancient oak, older than the bricks and stone, older even than the idea of learning, was bursting with light. The branches caught the reflection of the star shower, and the tree was flame-leaved and beautiful. The tower reared above, and the streaming stars picked out the gargoyles cresting the battlements: one open-eyed and laughing, peering down from the eaves as if balancing himself on the edge of the stone to gain a better view; another, turning his back to the spectacle, shoulders hunched, face buried in his hands, as if bearing witness to the end of everything. And rampant above these creatures, stood the dragons, roaring out into the night.

By the foot of the tree was a great thundering hole. William peered down into it. Stuck a foot below the earth was a nugget of rock. He scooped it out and rolled it in his palm. It was still warm. It seemed impossible that something so small could cause such walloping damage. Even more impossible to think that, only moments before, this dull bit of stuff was flaming across the sky.

William placed the meteorite in his pocket. He felt the greatness of creation stretching all about him, the infinity of it crackling through the darkness. The flaming fretwork of the heavens seemed to him the wings of a great angel, beating across the firmament. No sooner had he thought this than the wings folded in upon themselves, sparked once more and were gone. The gap in the sky closed as swiftly as it had opened.

William was left stranded in the night, starblind.

He groped his way around the college walls and returned to his watch. Above him the sky seemed fragile, a curve of black glass that might fall and shatter in a moment.

His reverie was broken by a rap at the door. A boy came tumbling into the quad. A young boy, hatless, gownless, out of breath.

'Porter Jones?' he gasped.

'The very same.'

The boy handed over a scrap of paper.

The words were scrawled at an angle, as if trying to escape the page: 'A BOY'.

When the day porter arrived to assume the post, William could not run from the college quickly enough.

The crossroads at the top of Broad Street was already a scramble of activity: traders were bringing their wares to set up their stalls along Cornmarket. William dodged between the wheels of the carts and the hoofs of the horses. Men sneered down from their perches, souring the air with their curses.

William cried back, raising his hat in his hand, 'I have a son! A boy!' but his declarations were lost in the cracking of whips and the thrumming of wheels.

Once the words were out in the air William could not contain them. He went striding down St Giles, hollering up at the college walls as if he were a boy himself: 'I have a child! A boy, a boy! A son and heir!'

And as he ran, there was a voice at his back. It caught him just by the door of St John's College.

'Are you sure?' A laughing voice, as sharp as steel. 'Are you quite, quite sure?'

William turned. There was no one, just the wide empty street on either side of him, with the Martyrs' Memorial anchored into the ground like a great spike. He squinted up into the cloud line, but there was nothing but the scree of the college roof, studded with the bulge-eyed gargoyles, peering out from corner and crevice.

William shrugged the voice aside. It was a trick of the wind, or of the mind or both. In either event, not a thing to be listened to. He picked up his step again, broke into a brisk trot, down into the lanes of Jericho. He passed the townhouses, with their curtains still closed against the day. He turned the corner by the bridge and there, on a spur of land just before the canal separated the streets from the wide open meadow, sat the cottage. And inside the cottage, the bedroom, with his wife under the blankets and a cradle sitting in the bow of the window.

William kneeled down by the cot and plucked the boy out. He could not comprehend the smallness of him, the way the head of the child was dwarfed by the span of his hand, the way the bound-up body was less than the length of his forearm. It gave him a dizzying feeling, a sense that the world had suddenly become unfathomably large. The walls of the room retracted, the ceiling lifted, and he felt stranded in the centre of an echoing chamber. Looking down at the child, it was unimaginable to him that this was how all men began; that poets, priests and thinkers all came into the world as sour-smelling babes.

William pushed back the swaddling bands. The cloth fell

away, and there was the scrunched-up parchment face, and the high forehead crowned by the crest of black hair.

'Welcome to the world, my son,' he whispered.

The boy opened his eyes and stared straight back at his father.

William looked into those deep dark eyes and saw an undeniable attitude of wisdom. This was no ordinary child, that much was clear. This was a boy who had come into the world before his time, as if he had business to be getting on with that simply could not wait. This boy, made by Eleanor and himself, and yet, also, so utterly otherworldly, was a gift from God. The child came from a place of truth and light. No wonder the sky had flamed at his arrival.

'Where have you seen, little man,' William whispered, 'on your journey?'

The boy blinked but did not answer.

Banked up on the pillows in the bed, Eleanor began to stir.

She opened her eyes and saw William, with their tiny son held in his hand, pulling at the bands that contained him, as if he was unknotting a parcel. And with each unravelling, hair, and leathery skin.

William pulled at the binding cloth until the boy was gloriously naked. He held him up into the sunlight, turning him about. The more William looked, the more he saw that he was holding his own body in miniature. It was all apparent in the detail: the high forehead, the long thighs, the way that one ear was a fraction higher than the other. It gave William an overwhelming sense of pride to think that his son, like himself, was destined to make his way in the world wearing his hat at a slant.

'We have a boy, Mrs Jones,' he said softly, 'and a handsome one at that.'

William took the child to the bed. Eleanor watched impassive as the boy settled at her breast.

'A strong child is worthy of a strong name,' said William. 'We shall call him Edgar.'

Eleanor looked down at Edgar, suckling greedily at her. She found it difficult to hold him.

In the time before Edgar, William would return from his night watch and settle himself down to sleep. But not on this day. Now he sat by the fire and turned the meteorite over and over in his hand. Upon the mantelpiece crouched his telescope. William looked up at it impassively. There was no need to magnify the mysteries of the sky now that the greatest wonder of all had fallen into his house, bound up in skin and hair, and lay in the room above, sleeping.

William took the Bible from the shelf. On the front page there was his name, the dark ink turned rust red through the passing of the years. 'William Jones, b. 1800?' Underneath, 'Eleanor Jones, m. 1845'. He took out his pen and wrote: 'Edgar Jones, b. 28th February 1847'. William. Eleanor. Edgar. Names that followed each other well.

It was quite a thing for William to look down upon a page and see his name nestled in amongst the company of others, to have a family written out so straight and sure. William was a foundling child, gifted to the college in the dead of night, left shivering and silent by the back gate. He gave the porter who found him no name, and no explanation. But he was a meek and obedient boy, whilst too young to harbour much memory of his origins, quite old enough to be of service.

As he worked his way up the ranks of the college, scrubbing at the cooking pots or bringing a shine to the mirrors in the scholars' rooms, he was haunted by his own features. His profile was a map of questions. Did he gain his high forehead from his father or his mother? And his fair hair? And his blue eyes?

His questions seeped into his dreams. William would find himself a small child again, walking a maze of unknown streets with a mother or father, or both, holding his hand, pulling at his arm, urging him onwards, faster, faster. And William would be racing at their heels, desperate. But no matter how much he strained to see, their faces were always turned away from him.

William took his dreams and his questions to the college chaplain, the man who had given William his name – William, after free will, Jones as the universal adjunct of the common man.

'You must ask yourself which matters most in a man's life, my boy,' the chaplain said firmly. 'Is it where one has come from, or where one is destined? Has the college not been good to you?'

'Yes, sir, but I would still know my own family.'

'The college is your family now, Master Jones. I suggest that you apply your attention to your future, rather than chasing the ghosts of your past.'

And so William did. Under the tutelage of the chaplain he pursued his learning through his letters and his Scriptures; he chased his ambitions through the mechanisms of the college, up, up and up until he emerged at the gate. And then, in his recent years, he chased the possibility of happiness in his pursuit of Eleanor. Still, in truth, all the while there was still a part of him that was rootless. Even when he said his vows at the altar, in the sight of God and the College, he still felt adrift in his own history.

But now all that was corrected. William was no longer anchorless. He was a link in a chain; his blood flowed through the veins of another. He had a boy: a son who had hidden in his wife's belly under the guise of a girl. And this, William, was sure, would just be the start of his cleverness.

Edgar. The good son. And accordingly, he would have a good life. He would never be abandoned in the dark night. William would love his son and watch over him. Edgar Jones would know himself and his way through the world, and his life would be full of possibilities.

Despite the thrill in his blood and the joy of the new arrival, sleep reached out to claim William. His eyes closed, his pen sagged sickly in his hand and the soft spitting of the flames was a lullaby.

In his dream William was as he was: sitting in his parlour, the Bible balanced upon his lap and Edgar's name upon the page. The fire roared and the wood rattled against the grate. The fire roared and the fire laughed. William turned and saw his son, sitting there atop the logs. Edgar, naked, bristle-haired, laughing, with the flames licking up the range of the chimney – gold wings sparking from his back. William grabbed at him, but the fire flared, and he clutched only ashes. Edgar laughed and laughed, ran up the curve of the flames and was gone.

William woke with a start. The ink from his pen had run, staining his fingers soot black. He snapped the Bible shut and posted it back upon the shelf.

After the shock of Edgar's arrival, the household soon settled back around him. Days passed, with William shored up in bed dreaming his dreams of his son's future. In the parlour beneath, Eleanor sat by the fire and nursed Edgar. She became accustomed to the pull of him against her, but she still found it hard to look at him, at his sallow skin; at his dark eyes that seemed to stare into the very heart of her and read all her ungenerous thoughts.

Nights passed. William watched at the college gates and Eleanor watched over the edge of the cradle. Edgar kicked in his sleep, as if the bed was a wooden womb that he was eager to break free of. Eleanor's belly ached with the memory of his passage into the world. And her heart ached for the girl he was not.

Then one morning Eleanor was woken as she always was by the creak of the bedroom door, and the change in the light as her husband filled the frame. She watched as William knelt by the cradle. He babbled wordless nonsense and Edgar chirruped back in kind.

Eleanor went to stand beside them. Edgar had William's finger caught in his fist and William was grinning down at him as if this was the most astonishing thing he had ever witnessed.

'He's got a good grip on him,' he said. 'It shows determination.'

'He's a child a month old,' snapped Eleanor. 'He can't see

further than his own nose. Of course he's going to hang on to whatever is thrust before him.' *F162409*

Eleanor went downstairs and set the fire. She put tinder to it and it sparked, spitting her frustration back at her. She drew her chair close and began to pin up her hair, coiling, plaiting and stabbing all into place.

Above her there was the familiar thud of William kicking off his boots. Eleanor shook her head. It was no good throwing her dissatisfaction back at William, as if his love of his son was a thing to be punished. As if he had wilfully cheated her out of a daughter.

She rose from her chair and unlocked the door of the second parlour. The room had been left untouched for a month, and dust was gathering over the silks.

She looked down at the tiny dresses. A rainbow set across the table top: pink, green, blue, purple. All embroidered with flowers and fringed with lace. All useless.

There was a hammering at the front door. Insistent. Fit to shake the walls, fit to wake Edgar.

Eleanor ran through and hauled back the latch. And there, standing on the step, was the woman with the grey hair and the gap-toothed smile. She was wrapped in a velvet cloak and had a bunch of lilies cradled in the crook of her arm.

'I wonder,' she said, 'do you remember me at all?'

She thrust out her hand. The jewels sparkled.

'We never quite had the chance to introduce ourselves. I am Mrs Simm.'

The old woman had a strong grip. Eleanor thought of herself with her skirts pushed up around her waist and the hands pummelling at her belly, and she blushed.

'Eleanor Jones,' she said. 'And I do remember you, and the great kindness you did to me.'

'My dear girl, you were screaming fit to shake the street. I would have been a heartless women indeed if I had not come to your rescue.' Mrs Simm gestured behind her. 'We have been neighbours for the past year. I have seen you and your husband many times, walking the rounds of your garden and getting yourselves ready for the child.'

Eleanor did not like the thought of this woman peering into her life as if it was some kind of cheap amusement. And she could not help but wonder what else Mrs Simm had seen. Had she been there from the start, when William struggled to lift her across the threshold, his back sticking, almost pitching her into the brambles. And then what? She and William embracing by the window, and the beginnings of Edgar?

'So,' said Mrs Simm, 'shall we go in? Or would you prefer that we discuss our business on the street for the whole world to hear?'

'Business?'

'Women's business.'

Mrs Simm bustled into the parlour. She shrugged off her cloak and smoothed down her skirts. Wide skirts of green silk, and a tailored bodice to match. Eleanor was put in mind of the armies of ducks that paraded the meadow, slipping in and out of the canal, shaking their sheen and honking out their greetings.

Mrs Simm thrust the flowers into the water pitcher.

Eleanor put her hand under the ledge of the parlour table and lifted it an imperceptible inch. The pitcher stayed put.

'I know it is a little early for you to be receiving visitors,' Mrs Simm chuckled, 'but I confess my curiosity got the better of me. I am most eager to see the child.'

'The child is sleeping,' said Eleanor curtly.

'Then you are blessed indeed. And we shall be most careful and quiet in our conversation.'

Eleanor stood stranded in the centre of her parlour as Mrs Simm circled around the room. The tavern had taught her the ways of unwanted guests. She knew how to unwrap the hand of a drunkard from about her waist, how to herd crowds of men out of the door through the ringing of a bell and the flicking of her skirts. But with this woman, who strode up and down before William's books, peering at the spines, who tipped the telescope and chuckled at the sway of its brass belly, who seemed amused by everything she saw, well, she was like nothing Eleanor had ever encountered and she did not know how to begin to shift her from her moorings.

Once she had done her rounds of the front parlour, Mrs Simm strode straight through to the back, marched over to the table of dresses and began turning them this way and that.

'What a lucky little thing she is, your daughter, to have such a clever mother.'

Eleanor turned her face to the window, the dead world of the garden clouded with her tears.

Mrs Simm stopped. 'Forgive me. She came out before her time, did she not?'

Eleanor nodded.

'There was a deformity, I take it? You must not despair, the doctors are getting cleverer by the day.'

'Not a deformity as such.'

'Then what, my dear?'

'She came out a boy.'

'A boy!' Mrs Simm hooted with laughter.

Eleanor did not echo it.

'I do not mean to mock, child, but that is simply the most absurd thing in the world.'

'Is it?'

'Only think of the way the world is set! A woman is a daughter, a wife and a mother, and that is her lot in life. But a boy can be anything that he sets his heart upon.'

Mrs Simm dabbed at Eleanor's tears with the edge of a gown. Soft blue silk.

'You are tired, my dear,' said Mrs Simm. 'It is only to be expected. But, in truth, the only sadness I can see in your predicament is that all these lovely bits of stuff will never see the light of day.'

Mrs Simm swept out of Eleanor's workshop and made for the front door. Eleanor followed, pulled along in the wake of her rustling skirts.

Hovering at the doorway, Mrs Simm grabbed Eleanor's hand again.

'You are young, Mrs Jones,' she said softly. 'You should take pleasure in the surprises of this world rather than grieve over the disappointments.'

And before Eleanor could reply, the door was hauled open and slammed shut behind the visitor. The floorboards jumped with the force of it; the water pitcher went down the slope of the table and crashed upon the floor.

Eleanor squinted through the curtain, watching as Mrs

Simm bustled down the curve of the street and entered a house with a manicured garden, and all the curtains closed.

After the floor was mopped, the pitcher cleaned, the dresses stored away, and the flowers set in a vase, Eleanor went back upstairs. She inched open the bedroom door. William was spread across the bed, flat upon his back, mouth open, beached up on the shores of his dreams. Eleanor went across to the cradle. There was Edgar, sleeping with the same aspect as his father, mouth agape, sheets kicked aside, echoing the rise and fall of his breath.

The more she looked, the more she saw. Beyond the surface strangeness of Edgar, there was William rendered tiny and dark – his long limbs, his shock of hair, the way he pawed the air as he slept. And was not William the best man she had ever known?

Eleanor pulled Edgar's sheets over him and smoothed down his hair. *Seek Peace and Pursue It*, said the scripture hanging above the bed.

There would be time enough for her and William to set about making a daughter. Eleanor was resolved. Edgar was as Edgar was, and she would learn to love him for it, as she loved William.

But despite all her good intentions, Eleanor struggled with her resolution. Edgar was a slippery child, who fought against her at every turn. When she tried to dress him he would wriggle out of her grasp and burrow down into the blankets, chirruping and barking as he did so, the calls of an animal rather than the cries of a child.

As it was at home, so it was at his christening. Eleanor buttoned him into the robes made for the girl that he was not: a dress of ivory silk, patterned with lace and embroidered with doves, caught at the back by buttons of mother-of-pearl. But when the chaplain poured the blessing down on Edgar's head, he squirmed as if the holy water burnt him, thrashing about until, Pop! Pop! Pop! The buttons flew off and fell into the font. And there was Edgar in all his glory, with his hair-crested spine, sallow skin and arse tilted to the sky.

By the time he was six months old Edgar had learnt the trick of pilling up his sheets into a mound and scrabbling up to the top of it. Eleanor would wake in the night to Edgar howling into the darkness, and find him standing, hands gripped on the edge of the cradle, chin upon the lip of wood, his shock of hair frosted by the moonlight. She would lay him back and weigh him down with blankets.

But after such awakenings, Eleanor found it impossible to sleep. She would watch the sky turn pale and listen to the birdsong heralding in another day of motherhood. And as she lay there alone, the same question repeated with every rustle of the covers in the cradle: what kind of child have William and I brought into the world?

After eight months Eleanor had had her fill of fractured nights. As the dawn came, she took Edgar and bound him up in her bedsheets. Then she took the cradle and dragged it across the landing, into the room opposite: an upstairs echo of the back parlour. She hugged the belly of it to her and rocked the runners across the floorboards. The striking of wood against wood reminded her of her father, walking the beer barrels across the cellar floor. Her father who, once she left the tavern, had slipped his way to a liquid death within a month.

It was no easy task, she knew, to protect a family against the difficult parts of itself.

The room had been unopened since their arrival and was rimed with dirt. Eleanor fetched a brush and a bucket of hot water from the scullery. The rhythm of the bristles against the floorboards soothed her. As the muck was washed away, everything came up gleaming.

William, returning home, went to his bed, only to find Edgar wrapped up in the centre of it, smiling up at him.

'Hello there, little man,' he laughed. 'You set to take your pa's station already?'

William untangled Edgar, and Edgar was off in an instant, tumbling down the side of the bed, pitching himself on to his hands and knees, racing out the open door, across the landing, into the other room, and hauling himself up against the side of the bucket, set to plunge his fist into the water if Eleanor hadn't tugged him away.

William stood in the doorway, neither in the room nor outside it.

'This is all very industrious, my love,' he said. 'But surely it's a little too soon to be best for Edgar.'

Eleanor turned her face to the floorboards and scrubbed harder. The heads of the nails caught against her brush and twisted.

'And how can you tell what's best, Will, when you spend hardly a waking hour in his company?'

William looked at his wife. He was a man who prided himself in his observant nature and the change in Eleanor had not gone unnoticed. It seemed to him that for every month of Edgar's existence Eleanor had aged a year.

William leant down and took Edgar from her, nestling his son to his chest.

'What do you think, Edgar?' he said. 'Shall we set you up with a room of your own and give your mama a little peace? Would that please you?'

Edgar chirruped and smiled and grabbed at William's watch chain.

'Edgar is in agreement,' he said. 'As am I. It's never too early for a man to gain his independence, after all. Most likely it will bring him on for the better.'

'It might.'

William smiled and went thundering down the stairs, with Edgar set upon his shoulder.

Whilst Eleanor scrubbed she could hear them, father and son, babbling away in the rooms beneath her. When she put her cloth to the windowpane, she saw, careering through the brambled wilderness, William, with Edgar swinging from his arms, crying, again and again, 'Edgar HO!' And with each great 'HO!' he pitched Edgar up into the sky. Edgar flailed out with his fists and laughed his birdlike laugh, stretching up to the apple tree and ripping the golden leaves from the branches.

So things continued, with Eleanor's concerns and William's dreams wrapping themselves around their son, and Edgar, tumbling his way through the beginning of his life, unaware of the hopes and fears set upon his shoulders.

Then came the turn of the year. Edgar was ten months old. And as the old year passed and the new one came in, the sky opened up again.

It began with the applause of the evergreens. As William

walked the windswept road to the college, the trees whose branches had not been wasted by the winter bent their backs and bowed as he passed beneath them, and the branches came clattering together, leaves playing in the sway of the great wind, giving William an ovation. A polite kind of applause such as might be heard around a dinner table after an apposite observation.

In Jericho the wind whipped through the wilderness to very different effect: brambles struck against each other, and the branches of the apple tree beat upon the windowpane. It sounded as if an army was gathering outside the house. Eleanor sat by Edgar's cradle, rocking him to sleep. Then the heavens roared and the sky broke across the meadows. The night was shot through with a web of light, a many-fingered claw. The rain followed, falling so hard it sounded like the roof was being hammered apart.

Edgar kicked his feet against the cradle in an echo of the elements.

As William whiled away the night watch, the bells of Oxford competed with the rain, pealing in the new year. At the beat of the final bell, the downpour ceased, as if a valve in the sky had been turned. Then came a bitter cold wind. It licked along the grass, and all that had been fluid was suddenly fixed. William sat there, caged in ice until dawn. When he walked out on to the snow-strewn lawns, the college was a fragile place. It seemed the frost had seeped into the very bricks and turned the stone brittle. The walls shimmered as if they were half glass, half mirage. The dragons on the tower were bearded with stalactites of ice, and looked all the fiercer for it.

In Jericho, Eleanor woke to a street full of cries and hollers. From her window she could see a great crowd of people racing down the road, as if they were fleeing the city.

She went across to the nursery. Edgar was hauling himself up against the side of the cradle and pounding the wood with his fists.

'That's right, Edgar,' she said. 'There's something out there and no mistake. It seems like half the world is running to it.'

She pulled back the curtains and there it was: beyond the black stick silhouettes of the wilderness the meadow was gleaming liquid silver. The river had burst its banks and the land was charmed into an icy mirror, which spread out to the mist-shrouded horizon. It was as if the house had upped in the middle of the night and replanted itself at the edge of the world.

William joined them at the window.

'A new year!' he cried, kissing his wife and hauling his son into his arms. 'And what a start to it! We must investigate. Would you like that, Edgar?'

Edgar chirruped on his shoulder.

'Quite right, you would!' said William. 'Put on your warmest stuff, Mrs Jones, and let us set out to the ice.'

William wrapped Edgar up until there was nothing to see of him but his dark eyes peering out of a bundle of blankets. He stuffed the boy inside his coat, strode out of the door, across the bridge and into the meadows, cutting an absurdly pregnant figure as he pushed through the crowds, with Eleanor trailing in his wake.

It was as if the ice had drawn all of Oxford to it – all the tribes of the city, floating across the surface of the frozen world. A few dons clustered under the bridge, conducting cautious expeditions out along the line of the river and back again, their gowns folded behind them. They moved with slow determination, cutting through the sea of people like the great ships of the empire chartering the ocean. Roaring boys darted about like wheeling sparrows, their shouts and hurrahs snapping through the air. They were gathering snow up in their fists and letting it fly across the ice. Couples teetered across the expanse together, some matching each other stride for stride, others falling against one another as if their love had made them drunk. And there, skidding underfoot of all, was a congregation of fat-bellied ducks. Their paddle-feet were unable to find a purchase on the ice as they swayed this way and that, honking out their distress.

The spectacle was matched by a fierce sound that sliced through the air. It was as if the frozen water still held a memory of its fluid form: the turn and tumble of the roaring river rendered sharp and brittle by the swish and sway of the iron against the ice.

William braced his arms around his son. 'See how slippery the world is, Edgar,' he whispered. 'See how most folks spin their way across it without thought or direction. But find a straight line through it and there's nothing you can't achieve.'

'Perhaps the ice is just ice, Will,' said Eleanor with a smile, 'and there is nothing more to it than that.'

William shook his head impatiently. 'There is a lesson in most parts of life, my love, if you have the wits to apprehend it.'

Eleanor looked out into the shifting crowd and saw there at the centre of it was a man spinning free from the masses, turning in circles, dancing across the ice as if it were solid ground. His chest was shielded with armour. A shifting breastplate of sparkling silver. He looked to Eleanor's eyes like a great coin set spinning across the meadow. It reminded her of the games she played as a child, setting shillings tipping across the bar, taking bets on which way they would fall. Head or tails.

As he spun closer Eleanor saw he was not wearing armour at all, but stacks of ice skates slung about his neck. He came to a halt before them and bowed, and the iron applauded with the movement.

'Only tuppence for hire, sir!' he cried.

William shook his head. 'Still too high a price to pay for breaking my back.'

From the inside of William's coat Edgar laughed.

The hawker thrust his hand to William's belly and patted it.

'Well, aren't you a funny-looking fella? I bet you ain't as lily-livered as your pa, are you?'

The hawker swung a pair of skates from their laces. They spun like a weathervane, twisting the light around the metal.

Edgar reached out towards it.

'If not for your own pleasure, then for the boy's, sir . . . ?'

William sat down on the snowy verge and exchanged his boots for the skates. As he took to the ice the land beneath twisted against him. The metal teetered one way and then another, and William could not believe that such a thin blade could ever hold him. He curved one arm around Edgar to shield him from the inevitable fall. The other arm flailed in circles like a broken wing.

'Courage!' cried the hawker, and he shoved William forwards.

All around there was slicing iron. The trees at the edge of the meadows ran in a black line, turned liquid by his movement. William spun and he twisted until he could not separate the sky from the land. The light on the ice dazzled him. All the elements were rushing into each other and nothing was safe.

Edgar watched from his father's coat as the sky and the land and the sunlight danced together. The iron shoes of the crowds sparked silver fire and spat up clouds of crystal. The black trees tipped sideways, the blue sky was at his shoulder. Edgar was flying over the skin of the world. The mists opened up in front of him, he was sailing through the clouds.

Eleanor watched from the bank as William and Edgar skated away. She thought how a good mother would never let her child out into such danger. But she was not made of the stuff of good mothers, not completely.

She observed the spinning crowds. Near the tree line girls circled about each other, arm in arm. Girls with all their lives still ahead of them, their futures as wide open as the glistening meadow.

Eleanor placed one foot upon the ice. It would not take much, she thought, just a little push and I could slip away into the mists and be gone.

Her other foot left the snow bank, and then there was a tug at her back and she was pulled back to land.

She turned and there was Mrs Simm, with the edge of Eleanor's cloak gathered up in her fist.

'It seems my lot in life, Mrs Jones, to rescue you from disaster,' she said. 'The ice is as treacherous as it is beautiful, like so many things in this world.' She patted Eleanor's hand and smiled. 'But it is a pretty picture, none the less, is it not, to see all of Oxford cavorting about?'

'My husband is out there in the thick of it. I rather fear for him.' She pointed to where William skirted along the tree line, teetering.

Mrs Simm followed her gaze and chuckled. 'Tell me, how is the child?'

'Edgar? He remains a boy.'

Mrs Simm let out a hoot of laughter. 'He remains a boy!' she cried. 'I do declare, Mrs Jones, you have a sharp wit when you choose to use it. He remains a boy, indeed.'

Eleanor smiled.

'And yourself, Mrs Jones, are you content?'

The question froze in the air before Eleanor. It hung there like a block of sparkling ice that burnt the skin when it was touched.

What was it to be content? Was it to be set on a better path than she could have hoped for her life, and to have a clever husband who loved her despite her origins? To have her lap weighed down by a child? It was, in part.

But then there was also another kind of contentment, which Eleanor had known once, in a different time, it seemed, when her days were full of promise, and nothing was decided. The pure joy that came with the swelling of the belly and the unknown child it contained. And alongside it, a love for the beautiful things in life, the sensation of the push and pull of a thread across a piece of cloth.

'I am blessed with a healthy child and a good husband,' said Eleanor quietly.

Out on the meadow, William turned in circles amongst the ducks.

'For some women that is all they need in life to keep them happy,' replied Mrs Simm. She flicked the edge of her cloak and a cloud of snow went sparkling through the air like scattered diamonds. 'And for others it is not. There is no crime in it either way.'

Eleanor blushed. It was remarkable that Mrs Simm spoke to her as if they had known each other a lifetime.

'And with regard to your situation, Mrs Jones, I do believe that you have a great talent, and if you let it go unpractised you will never be satisfied.'

Eleanor frowned down at the ice. Beneath the sheen of the frost she could see pockets of black water stewing under the surface.

'I am not sure I understand you, Mrs Simm.'

'Oh, I think you do, my dear,' the old lady chuckled. 'You are a born seamstress and no mistake.'

Eleanor did not shift her gaze. It was even more remarkable the way that this woman could pull out Eleanor's innermost thoughts without even stopping for breath.

'And I do confesses that I am in dire need of one.'

'Of what?'

'A seamstress, my dear, a seamstress,' smiled Mrs Simm. 'I have some bits and pieces requiring attention.'

'I am indebted to you, Mrs Simm, but I do not think—'

'It is what you can do that matters, Mrs Jones, rather than what you think. I shall call on you in the evening, when your husband is at the college and your son is sleeping, and we may go about our business undisturbed.'

She patted Eleanor upon the arm, turned upon her heel and went tramping back over the bridge and away. As Mrs Simm retreated, Eleanor tried to shrug away the unsettling sensation that crept across her skin. Again, she felt that her life was nothing but a sideshow amusement, a world in a box that could be squinted into for tuppence. And yet, and yet, she could already feel the cloth gathered in her hand. The softness of it.

A cry came from across the ice.

'Hold fast! Hold fast!'

Eleanor turned and there was William, flying straight for her. His skates spiked the bank and he pitched forward, falling into her arms, with Edgar pressed between them, chirruping with laughter and William echoing it.

That night, whilst William knelt by Edgar's bed and chanted his prayers, Eleanor went through to the back parlour. There were the shelves stacked with silk. There was her pincushion, with its spiked back of needles and pins. There were the rolls of ribbons, peppered with dust. She looked out at the wilderness. The snow had gathered across the bracken, and the thorns were lost in the darkness, and all that could be seen was the cobweb carpet of whiteness laid out across the land: a blanket of lace, every loop and curl and curve of it a fragile, shimmering beauty.

That frozen New Year marked a change for the Jones family. As the ice slipped its hold on the world, something inside Eleanor also began to thaw.

Within a week Mrs Simm bustled into the parlour with a sack of stuff cradled in her arms. There were petticoats, gowns, bodices, all tangled up together, torn along seam and hem. It was unthinkable to Eleanor that such beautiful things could be treated with such disregard. But over the following weeks, when Eleanor set her hand to the work, whilst Edgar slept and William watched, something inside her settled. There was a simple pleasure in putting back together the puzzle of the cloth, turning the tears in upon themselves and making the damage invisible.

When Mrs Simm returned to collect her wares, she ran her fingers over the seams, cooed out her approval and placed a stack of coins upon the table.

Eleanor shook her head. 'There is no need, Mrs Simm. I could sew back together all the dresses in Oxford and that still would not be payment enough for your kindness to me and Edgar.'

'Nonsense! No man would give away his skills for free, and no woman should either.' Mrs Simm pressed the coins into Eleanor's palm, bunching her fingers into a fist around them. 'And this is just the start of it. We shall form a great alliance, you and I.'

After Mrs Simm left, Eleanor found herself spinning the coins across the table top, a child again, laughing at the tumble.

When Eleanor told the tale to William she kept the alliance simple. Mrs Simm was nothing more than a chance meeting upon the ice. A skirt ripped by a stray blade, and Eleanor offering to help her. Good work begetting good work. She dropped the coins into his hand and a great grin spread across his face.

'I do declare,' he said, 'I am the luckiest man in Oxford.'

'Truly, Will? Many folk would think it a common thing to have a wife at work.'

William laughed and embraced Eleanor. 'Many folk are misguided, Mrs Jones. You continue on this road, my love, and you and I shall live like king and queen, and Edgar will want for nothing. And where's the shame in that?'

So it was that the back parlour became Eleanor's workroom, a room of colour and softness and pleasure. A room where she was neither wife nor mother, but just Eleanor, who loved a bit of finery, who loved the beautiful things in life.

Things were different for William, too, after that day on the ice. When he returned home, red-cheeked, breathless, with Edgar shaking the sides of his coat with his laughter, William was invigorated. Edgar was an adventurous child. And who had made the greatest mark upon the Empire but the adventurers? William was decided. He and Edgar would walk hand in hand through God's great landscape, they would investigate and experiment together, and William would give him a proper way of looking at the world. He would develop Edgar's rational mind, his ability to observe and assess, qualities that would prove invaluable when he set out into the world. It was just a matter of waiting for him to be a little older.

Meanwhile, every night before he departed for his watch, William would rock Edgar to sleep in front of the map of the Empire. It was studded with pins to mark the places that had been conquered. William would recite the names of these foreign lands and mix them with half-remembered tales from his own childhood. Tales told by the cook in the depths of the kitchens, tales of battles, and heroes. Tales of men who built machines of war and ransacked cities. Tales of sailors lost at sea, who tricked ogres and witches and spirits of the wind, and made their way back home with the bows of their boats weighed down with treasure. Edgar would stare at the light dancing off the pinheads, like jewels set into the wall, and open and close his little fists as if he could pluck them out of their fixtures.

The investigations proper began when Edgar was two years old and William introduced him to the wonders of magnification.

He would put Edgar upon the parlour table, place the telescope in his son's fist, align the eyepiece and show him how the sweep of the heavens could be brought to just the other side of the window.

But Edgar preferred another trick of the machine. Whilst his father was flicking through his sky maps, Edgar would turn the instrument round. He laughed to see all the things that towered above him about the house reduced to nothing, just pinpricks of colour set within a curved world.

Every New Year would herald in the arrival of a new invention. The parcel would be placed upon the parlour table and Edgar would be given the privilege of ripping away the paper. The first unwrapping revealed a brass barrel with a tipped end, encasing a red liquid: a thermometer. Edgar was shown the miracles of measurement when snow from the garden was gathered in a cup and the thermometer thrust inside. Down the line shrunk, to nothing, just a rolling red eye settled in the bulb tip of the brass. Then it was placed against a piece of coal hauled from the fire and the red stuff raced upwards like the streaming of blood from a cut. For weeks to follow, the thermometer was William's constant companion, plunged into the teapot in the morning, into Edgar's bathwater at night. It was even taken down to the meadows, tied to a piece of string, and Edgar was given the task of casting it out into the depths of the canal. Again and again the brass flashed through the sky and went plummeting down into the swirling waters and again and again it was pulled back out and the run of the line noted. Again and again William applauded Edgar's strong and certain throws.

The next year the parcel's paper was ripped away to reveal a glass box containing a stack of paper coiled upon a spring, with a needle set above. The spring turned, the needle scratched and the machine spat out its measurements in a rolling white tongue that peeped through the mouth of the box. Edgar grabbed at it, and set the spindle trembling.

'What do you think, Edgar, of your father's invention?' asked Eleanor, 'His barograph – can you say it?'

Edgar smiled and waved the paper tangled up in his fist.

Edgar's fifth year was heralded in by the arrival of an orrery: a miniature model of the universe set upon wires in a box. The planets could be made to dance simply by the turn of a handle.

'See how balanced and beautiful God has made his universe,' said William, placing Edgar's fist around the handle. Edgar tugged and turned, tugged and turned until the planets were spinning whorls of colour.

Eleanor laughed. 'He thinks it's a kind of fairground invention,' she said, 'as if it should be playing us a tune for its troubles.'

But it was not just William's inventions that Edgar was eager to get into.

As the months turned to seasons turned to years, Eleanor spent her daytimes running after Edgar, catching him as he crawled from room to room, as he clambered up his father's bookshelves to get to the telescope, as he ran through the scullery beating out tunes upon the saucepans. But at night, as the house stood silent, Eleanor retreated into her world of stitches. Mrs Simm kept her word, and the alliance between them went from strength to strength. In the summer nights Eleanor would often find herself stitching until the light turned. The early dawn, with its pink feather clouds and sea-blue sky seemed an echo of the dresses laid out across the table. A great net of silk stretched over the land, lace-fringed, beautiful.

It was after one such night of Edgar's fourth year that Eleanor forgot to lock the workshop door. She was in the scullery, washing out the breakfast things, when she heard a great thud and sound of something tearing.

She ran through to the parlour and her workshop door was wide open. The floor was a sea of silk. And the sea was rolling and laughing. Edgar.

Edgar wrapped the rainbow around himself, and crawled through the heart of it. There was gold and there was blue and there was green and red and pink, and all was soft and all was light and all held the smell of roses. The smell of his mama. He laughed and laughed, twisting about in the world of colour. The cloth bound tighter and tighter around him. He pushed and pulled, pulled and pushed, and there was a great rip and the rainbow split, and there was the room, and there was the table, and there was his mama, reaching into the softness and yanking him out.

Eleanor pulled Edgar out of the skirts and a night's work

was torn to shreds around him. She dragged him through the parlour and out on to the doorstep.

'If you will run wild, Edgar, then you will be put out of the house until you learn better.'

The door slammed shut behind Edgar. Before him, the wilderness ranged. A tangle of brambles, wild weeds, flowers and grasses.

In the workshop Eleanor knelt by the wrecked silk. She shook out the fabric, wide wings of colour set upon the air. And for a moment, playing hide and seek between the folds, there was the girl that Edgar should have been, fair-haired, blue-eyed, bunching up the cloth in her fat little fists. Helping her mama roll up the running ribbons and the dirtied lace, smiling. Then she was gone. And there was only Eleanor and the ripped skirts, and the knowledge that Mrs Simm would come to her door that very evening expecting everything to be fixed.

Eleanor sat upon her chair and began to make good.

Lost in the play of the needle, it was late in the day before Eleanor's hunger pulled her away from the work. The grandfather clock declared four o'clock, the cherub-faced sun smiled out of the frame.

She went to the doorstep and called out: 'Edgar! Edgar Jones!'

But there was no reply.

She walked the rounds of the garden. But there was no sound or sign of him, just the wide-ranging wilderness.

Eleanor ran up the stairs and pulled William out of bed. Nightshirt flapping at his ankles, he ran into the garden.

'Edgar!' he called. 'Edgar HO!' He pushed his way into the brambles. 'Edgar!'

And somewhere deep in the heart of the tangle, the wilderness laughed.

William dropped down on to his hands and knees and peered into the bracken. There, at the very edge, was a hole in the thicket, no wider than his head. He thrust forward, and the wilderness opened up before him. The brambles had been pulled apart from each other and bound up into a bower, thorns and flowers tied up together like the open arch of the college gate: vaulted, beautiful. The weeds were trampled flat and the tunnels snaked away into shadow. But the shadow was laughing and there, crawling down the curve of it, came Edgar. He burrowed out of the bushes and tumbled into his father's arms.

'Well, well, little man,' said William, 'aren't you quite the architect, Edgar Jones?'

Eleanor hovered by the doorway. She looked at William, with his nightshirt torn, his hair sticking up every which way. She looked at Edgar riding high upon his back, grubby-faced, with not a scratch on him.

Once Edgar had been given the run of the wilderness, it was impossible to keep him from it. He would sit by the door, howling fit to shake the walls until Emily put him out to play. He took the poker and shovel from the fireplace and they proved excellent as a rapier and a spade for cutting through the undergrowth. Edgar played out his father's stories: he was the brave hero, fighting his way through the forest, slaying bramble dragons.

But most of all, Edgar loved to climb. The marbled skin of the apple tree was a face of furrows and handholds. It was easy to dig his nails in the bark, set his knees to the trunk and shin his way upwards.

In that fifth year, Edgar advanced further and further, outlaughing the birds. By autumn he made it to the level of the rooftop. He would walk along the branches and bounce the apples free, sending them hurtling like cannonballs into the thorn bushes.

As Edgar explored the tangled world, shredding shirts and trousers in his wake, Eleanor found she was patching the same garments in the summer that she had in the spring.

She took to measuring Edgar every month. Before he was allowed out she would hold him against the wall with one hand, balance the Bible upon his head and score a line across the top of it. As summer pushed through to autumn, a mark grew on the parlour wall. It leached across the paper, tipping sideways, but was imperceptible in its upwards growth.

And that was not her only concern. When Edgar was shuttered up inside the house, there was not a moment's peace. There would be the thump and wallop as he slid his way down the stairs. The bang bang banging of him jumping on his bed, hammering the ceiling of the workshop fit to break it. And the great cascades of laughter as he ran to meet his father at the gate and was hauled up into the sky and down again, the roaring symphony of Edgar's high squeals and William's great bellowing 'HO!' But as time ticked on, from four years towards five, Edgar spoke not a word.

It was just before Christmas that Eleanor gave voice to her fears.

William and Eleanor were sitting by the fire. William was rubbing the cloth over his boots, readying himself for the watch. Every part of his preparation gave him a deep satisfaction. The swapping of the nightshirt for the dress shirt, the crisp crease of his trousers, the buttoning-up of his waistcoat. He could feel the authority gathering around him with the placing of every article. The polishing cloth snapped and cracked across the silence between husband and wife.

Eleanor, bowed over the embroidery of a corset panel, waited until William was lacing up his boots, fumbling over knots and eyeholes.

'It's time we looked at the facts,' she said softly.

William blinked up at her from the fireside. 'Facts? What facts might those be?'

'About Edgar. About the way he's turning out.'

'And how's that?'

'You know how it is, Will,' she sighed. 'There's an oddness about him. Running riot in the garden all day, not able to sit still for a moment.'

'He's a curious boy. It's a sign of intelligence.'

'I would have thought speaking might be a clearer one.'

William frowned. Of course Edgar's lack of speech was a slight concern. But he was rather hoping that the boy was biding his time until he had something worthwhile to say.

William took the dilemma with him to the night watch. He scanned the names ranging up the ranks of the pigeonholes. His wife's analysis was misguided, he was sure of it. No two men in this world were alike – why should any two boys be? But even so, there was nothing to be lost by consulting someone who understood how children were put together.

There was only one viable candidate: Professor Carter, the Master of Physiognomy. In all his time at the lodge, William had never once seen the man pass by his station. But often, as he watched through the night, as one by one the scholars' lamps were put out, there would be one light left, anchored in the corner of the quad like a guiding star, burning through till dawn: the lamp of Professor Carter. He was a man who had set his mind on a life of learning, and no mistake.

William began to write: 'Dear Sir, I come to you as a respectful observer of your studies and wish for some illumination upon the curious subject of my only son . . .'

So it was that the following week Edgar was dressed in his Sunday best and taken into Oxford for examination. William had the same attitude to the University streets that he had to the map in the parlour.

There was a lesson to be learnt on every corner. They stood by the Martyrs' Memorial and William pointed up at the men carved into the stone. Saintly men, who loved God so much that they would die rather than denounce him.

'True heroes, son,' he said. 'An example to us all.'

Edgar frowned up at the men, clutching their stone books, and the men frowned straight back at him.

Every college gate was stopped at, and the name announced. St John's. Balliol. Trinity. 'This is the empire of learning, Edgar,' declared William. 'It is behind these walls that the great minds of the future are forming, becoming the best kind of men possible.' Edgar looked up at the golden walls ranging above him. There were turrets and spires and battlements: a land of adventure set in the clouds. There were creatures up there: animals with the faces of men, grinning down at him. Edgar strained against his father's grip.

William pulled him onwards.

Under the arch of the college they went, round the edge of the lawn and into the mouth of a staircase, up to the top of the spiralling steps to a door embellished with a brass plaque: 'Professor Carter's Rooms'.

William pushed open the door and saw a room stuffed full of learning. Three windows stretched from floor to ceiling, framing a view of the quad. The wall opposite was lined with shelf upon shelf of leather-bound books with embossed spines. Perched in amongst them were the instruments of Carter's craft: a set of scales, measuring sticks, instruments with hooked ends, things made of levers and lenses. Opposite the door was a broad desk piled high with papers that were weighted down with more curiosities: bowls, lumps of rock, a decanter filled with a shimmering green liquid.

The physiognomist sat behind the desk, the sleeves of his gown rolled back to reveal thin, pale arms the colour of parchment, his hands plunged deep into the papers. His head was hairless, a white globe floating above the sea of knowledge, nodding this way and that as he scanned the texts. On the table beside him sat a bust of white porcelain with the cap of a scholar set upon its head.

Above the desk two plinths stuck out from the wall. On one the head of a tiger snarled from its fixture. On the other an eagle soared, wings spread out, talons splayed as if at any moment it might swoop down and grab the papers from its master's hand.

If there was a place where questions might be answered then this was surely it, thought William.

His father pushed open the door and Edgar followed. Edgar saw a man with two heads bent over a desk. He saw creatures trapped in the wall, fighting their way out with teeth and claws. He saw a wall of leather bricks wriggling with golden worms and spiked with bits of iron.

One of the heads looked up.

'Ah!' said Professor Carter, 'Porter Jones and his anomalous son. Edmund, is it?'

'Edgar,' said William, holding out his hand. The professor did not shake it.

'What's in a name, eh?' Carter chuckled. 'Now, I must remind you, Porter Jones, that this is a most irregular privilege, most irregular indeed. But I must say, I was intrigued by your letter. An exceptional case warrants exceptional attention.'

'And I am most grateful, sir,' said William, rolling his hat in one hand and holding Edgar's shoulder with the other.

'And you are welcome to it, but not a word to your fellows. Otherwise I will be beset by all the ills of the underlings, from the cook's bunions to the scouts' distemper. And that will not do.'

Carter crouched down so that he was level with Edgar. He placed his hands upon Edgar's skull. The long fingers wrapped around the circumference, burrowing this way and that, Edgar's hair sprouting between the digits.

Edgar could feel a hand clamped upon his head. He looked at the big bird flying out of the wall at him, claws sharp. He squirmed and he cried, but he was held tight.

'Be still, boy,' barked Carter. 'This is for your benefit.'

Carter pulled the second head across the desk. It was a ghostly ornament. The sockets held lidless eyes, nothing but blind bulges of porcelain. Its lips were puckered together into something like a smile. Carter pulled the cap off to reveal a skull segmented and scrawled upon. The cranium was cut up into continents of character: emotion, thought, imagination declared the territories of the front dome. Deceit and watchfulness crept around the back.

William frowned. 'Do you mean to tell me you hope to diagnose Edgar's condition from the shaping of his skull?'

'Precisely,' said Carter, with one hand upon Edgar, the other scribbling on paper. 'The evidence is overwhelming. Studies have been undertaken across the Empire. From the savages of the islands to the criminals in the Oxford gaol, the patterning of the skull is proved to be a portrait of the soul.'

Carter plucked out an instrument from the shelf: a curved band of iron with pointed tips, held together by screws and springs.

'Sir, please,' cried William, 'that cannot be a thing to be placed upon a child.' He stood between the professor and his son, wrapping his arm around Edgar.

'It is merely a measuring device,' replied Carter briskly. 'A craniometer. Its form is deceptive. It will cause little discomfort.'

Edgar saw the silver claw coming down down down towards him. It would spike him, it would hurt him, it would catch him and never let him go. He jumped up, grabbed it, twisted it, and it came apart in his fist. He dropped the pieces on the floor and clung on to his father.

Carter smacked his hands together and laughed. 'The action supports the analysis!'

He held his paper out to William. An exaggerated Edgar

stared back from the page. His profile was bulbous and irregular. The right side of his head was swollen and his ear protruded at an extreme angle.

'Your son is a most volatile mixture,' said Carter with a smile. His finger navigated the page as if it were a map of the land, and he announced every corrupt curvature. 'Strong Secretiveness! Acquisitiveness! Individuality! Negative Affection! Destructiveness! Conscientiousness!'

William looked from the paper to Edgar and back again. It was the same as when he looked down on Edgar in the cradle: he was staring at himself in miniature. If these elements ran through Edgar's character then surely they should run through his own. And he a watchman, the man with the key to the college. It was an absurd argument.

'These are strong words, sir.'

'Such tendencies do not stand alone, Porter Jones. The key to the character lies in the combination. The bulge above the ear, you see – that points to a destructive nature. This may lead to vengeance and violence, a primal cruelty. But it is also a potent energy and, if tempered by clear moral faculties, it might combine with his conscientiousness, apparent here . . .' Carter tapped Edgar's head with the tip of his pen. 'This irregularity of the forehead gives us hope. It shows a strong attachment to moral value. A clear desire for justice. An integrity of the self. And if this can be encouraged as the predominant trait then even the most extreme tendencies, the ruthlessness of negative affection, and the hoarding greed of his acquisitiveness might be contained within a life lived with a proper moral purpose.'

Vengeance. Violence. Greed. The words rang hollow in

William's ears. This was not the Edgar that he knew. Not his bonny boy, who loved to be swung up to the sky and back again.

'It seems your son is destined to make a mark on the world, Porter Jones. What kind of impression that might be is another matter entirely. I would like to examine further, if I may.'

And before William could answer, Carter was crouching behind Edgar and wrestling with his collar. William watched as the professor poked and prodded, as if he were trying to push something out of the skin.

'But what have we here?' exclaimed Carter. 'I do declare, I have never seen anything the like!'

Edgar squirmed, but Carter held fast, stripping Edgar of his jacket and shirt, and tossing them upon the floor so that Edgar stood in all his glory. The hair upon his spine stuck up on a thick line of bristle, like the hair on the back of a cat when it is cornered.

'Fascinating,' said Carter, stroking Edgar's spine. 'Truly fascinating.'

William took off his coat, draped it over Edgar and pulled him close.

'I did not bring the boy here for your amusement,' he told Carter firmly. 'It is as I set out in the letter. I am in search of a cure.'

'A cure?' smirked Carter. 'Well, that is an ambitious demand, if ever I heard one.'

'A hypothesis, at least. Anything that I might take back to my wife for her comfort.'

'Of course no one knows why some men come into the

world in such ill-fitting forms. I personally favour the theory of bad blood.'

Bad blood. The words stirred up an anger deep in the heart of William. These were the words of superstition and nothing more. He felt his blood roaring in his ears. The blood that he had inherited from the man who left him stranded upon the college steps. The blood that he had passed on to Edgar. He looked down upon his son, wrapped up in the long robe of his coat. His son, who echoed him in form and feature. His son, who would not be subjected to any further indignity.

William gathered the scattered garments and wrestled them on to Edgar's back.

Carter smiled. 'Do not be disheartened, Porter Jones. Your son's character is still forming. Nothing is altogether decided.'

Carter pointed to the chart on his wall. On one axis was written 'Influence', the other, 'Nature'. A crooked red line rose and fell between. A twisted seam.

'Whilst the skull is still setting, and Edgar is shaping himself within and without, you must be sure of the influences you place him under. Tell me, does he have any playmates?'

William shook his head. 'He spends most of his days in his own company, ranging around in the garden.'

'And you wonder why he has not learnt the discipline of speech? A child is a vessel, Porter Jones. He will absorb whatever influence is poured into his soul and his mind. You must pay closer attention to him, if you wish his tendencies to turn out for the best.'

'And this is all the guidance you can offer?'

'Unless . . .' Carter tapped his fingers upon the porcelain

skull. 'Unless you would be willing to give the boy to my specific care. As an ongoing study. There are men I meet with in London, forward-thinking men, who would doubtless have opinions on his condition.'

William looked at the spikes of the craniometer scattered on the floor. They looked like the severed limbs of an iron crab. He imagined this instrument and others beside it snapping away at his son's skin. All in the pursuit of some theory. All in the pursuit of Carter's reputation.

'I am grateful for your attention, sir, but I do believe Edgar would be better cared for by his parents, who love him for who he is rather than for what anomalies he may manifest.'

William slammed Carter's door, led Edgar briskly down the stairs and out on to the sunlit lawn.

Edgar looked up at the line of the city wall, cutting up the clouds. He looked up at the college gate, the great carved arch of it, a forest of stone, with creatures grinning down at him from the branches.

'Edgar,' snapped William, 'this is not a place to loiter.'

'Papa,' said Edgar softly.

The world around William stopped. There was no college, no lawns, no gate, no street beyond. Just him and Edgar, standing side by side. Edgar's mouth open, pulling at his sleeve. Edgar speaking. Edgar saying his name again and again.

'Papa. Papa.'

William crouched down so he was face to face with his son and put his hand upon his cheek.

'Edgar?'

Edgar opened his mouth and the words came out, dropping one by one like pebbles into a stream. A high, clear voice, part birdsong almost. A voice that had been stoppered up.

'Papa, am I a bad boy?'

William laughed, and pulled Edgar to him.

'No, no, Edgar. You are my perfect and precious son, and let no man tell you otherwise.'

He took Edgar by the shoulder and steered him away from the gate. But as he did so another voice came calling down the wind. A voice like the scraping of steel against stone.

'Place yer bets! Place yer bets!'

He turned, looked back at the college. The lawns beyond the gate stretched wide and empty.

William steered Edgar down to the crossroads. The streets were thronging with the passage of people: the students in their gowns, jostling alongside the men of trades; the carriages, with their shuttered windows, rolling down Broad Street; men and women walking side by side, peeping in through the shop windows. The rusted sign of the White Horse pub beckoned in the drinkers. There was all the world going about its business. Life, in all its roaring varied glory. William looked at the crowds. What quirks of the body, he wondered, might lie hidden beneath their garments? And how could Professor Carter, locked away in his room, ever know about it – this man who had stripped Edgar of his dignity as surely as he had stripped him of his Sunday best?

And yet Edgar had spoken. And not just the parroted speech of a newborn, but a question. A question phrased with consideration and attention to the matter in hand.

By the time William reached the cottage, all unpleasantness

was forgotten and there was only the thrill of Edgar's first words.

He burst into the parlour, calling: 'A success! A veritable success!'

He strode over to Eleanor and kissed her. Edgar hovered at the doorway, watching, listening.

'A success? The professor knows of Edgar's condition and can find a way to cure it?'

'Ha! That charlatan! He would find anything in Edgar that might serve to fit his wild theories. But it seems that the process of examination itself has been cure enough.'

Eleanor looked across at Edgar. He was standing in the doorway, wide-eyed, with his hair sticking out in all directions. His shirt was pulled out of his trousers and the buttons of his jacket were done up skewed. For a moment she was back in the tavern, watching as the old street lunatics peered through the glass, tongues lolling fit to lick the panes.

'He does not look cured, Will.'

'You and Carter are one and the same. Too easily taken in by the appearance of things.'

Eleanor knelt by Edgar and smoothed down his hair.

'Is this true, Edgar? Did you speak to the professor?'

Edgar shook his head slowly.

'Not to the professor, but to me!' crowed William. 'He asked me directly!'

'And what did you say, Edgar?' asked Eleanor softly. 'What was the question you put to your papa?'

Edgar opened his mouth. His lips moved and the words came out high-whistling and slow.

'Am I a bad boy?'

Eleanor pulled her son to her and buried his face in her skirts. She looked over his shoulder, down the garden path, down to the barred gate at the bottom of it.

Above them, Edgar's first question still hovered in the air, unanswered.

That night, as his parents sat by the fire, discussing what could be done with Edgar's question, Edgar sat upon the floor of his room, rolling a nut, a bolt and a silver spring along the boards before him.

PART TWO

PART TWO

Once Edgar began to speak there was no stopping him. The air across the parlour table grew thick with his questions: how does a tree grow? Where does the rain come from? How do birds fly?

William's answer was always the same: the world is as it is because God made it so.

'But why did He?'

'It is not our place to question,' William would reply sternly. 'God made the world as He did for the good of mankind.'

Edgar would stare back at his father with those deep dark eyes and smile, as if he knew a secret that his father did not.

Then the questions continued: Why was he not allowed beyond the garden gate? Why did his papa sleep through the days? Why did his mama lock the door to her room? Why, why, why, why, until William's mind was tumbled into a great whirlwind.

And then, beyond all the whys and the wherefores, Edgar's first question still lingered.

William was adamant, there was nothing bad about his son.

The line of Edgar's growth crept slowly up the parlour wall. As the seasons turned the paper peeled and Edgar's history crumbled. Edgar continued to be Edgar, the lord of the briars and the brambles. When he was not slicing through the wilderness he was collecting creatures. He would carry them to the supper table, wriggling worms, and bright-winged beetles that scaled the walls of his father's newspaper or climbed up the curve of the teacups and tumbled to a watery death. And as Eleanor picked Edgar's specimens out of the parlour rug, from between William's books, off her silks, William just smiled and spoke of Edgar's wonderful curiosity about the world.

But at night, when William was alone at the lodge with only his thoughts and the dark skies for company, his certainty about Edgar's nature seemed to shift and slide away into the shadows.

He would stare out at the wall of the quad opposite and watch as the scholars' lamps were lit and then extinguished, marking out the passage of the night watch, a shifting scree of constellations. And as the lights died one by one, William found himself slipping back into his own history.

He was Edgar's age again, sitting in the chaplain's rooms, with the Bible open on the desk, a notebook set beside it and William was copying out the Commandments. Thou shalt. Thou shalt not. And with every stroke of the pencil on the page an understanding: there was a right way of living and a wrong one. A path to heaven and a path away from it.

Honour thy father and thy mother.

William's pencil hesitated.

The chaplain guided his hand across the page.

'It is quite proper that you should honour them, William,' he said. 'For in their abandonment of you they have afforded you a better life.'

In the lodge William watched until the only light left burning was that Pole Star in the corner of the quad: Carter's rooms. William imagined the porcelain head and the iron claw glowing gold in the lamplight. The majority of the physiognomist's argument was fraudulent, William knew that for certain. But there was something to be made of this theory of influence. William's character had been formed by a grasp of the letters and the kindness of a holy man. Edgar was his miniature; it stood to reason that if he was given the same education he would become another William.

It was a warm spring day in Edgar's seventh year that William announced his intention across the breakfast table.

'Today is the beginning of a great adventure, Edgar,' he said.

Edgar leapt from his chair and was running to the coat stand, jumping to pull his jacket from the peg.

'Not so quick, little man,' laughed William. 'This is an altogether different adventure that we are embarking on together. An adventure of a lifetime, and no mistake.'

But Edgar knew what adventuring was all about – his father had told him often enough. The Empire map was where adventures happened. There were brave sailors in strong ships, there were wild seas to be chartered and treasure to be found.

William fetched the Bible from the bookshelf, took Edgar by the hand and led him up to his room. He pulled out a notebook, laid it on the table and copied out the scripture.

'Honour thy father and thy mother,' he said.

Edgar frowned down at the page. His father's letters were crawling across the paper, weaving in and out of each other, like the tangling wilderness.

'How, Pa?'

William smiled. He took Edgar's hand and wrapped his fist around the pencil. 'How else but by setting your mind to the task before you?'

Edgar looked at the Bible. The small black script scampered across the page like beetles. His father walked away from him, shut the door and the lock tumbled. Edgar slammed his hand down upon the paper. The words wriggled free, out between his fingers, and went running down onto the desk, burrowing their way into the knots and whorls of the wood.

Day after day after day, week after week, Edgar tried to honour his Papa but he could not work out the trick of it. He stabbed his pencil at the twisting words until he ripped clean through the page. He scrawled out his frustrations across the expanse of his schoolbook. He missed his empire of the wilderness, the feel of the brambles bucking under the weight of the poker, the play of the wind lifting up his jacket, spreading it sail-like behind him as he climbed up the arms of the appletree. But most of all, he missed his Papa. He missed riding around the garden on his Papa's back; he missed sitting at his feet in front of the fire, listening to the tales of heroes, and picking out the shapes of the dragons hidden at the heart of the shifting flames.

Now the only stories he had were the ones he could piece together from the pictures of the Bible. There was God, fierce-eyed, cloud-haired and bristle-bearded, glaring down upon his people as he banished them from gardens, flooded the earth or trapped them in the belly of a great fish. It gave Edgar a chill in his blood to think that this wild old man was the God that his father talked of, the God who saw all and knew all and had every part of Edgar's life mapped out. Edgar took to flicking past the pictures of this angry old father and seeking out the angels. They were young men with curls of flaming hair, and feathered wings spanning the page. In their hands they held bright swords and spears.

They were warriors, adventurers of the skies. Edgar filled his notebook accordingly, so that when William came to release Edgar at the end of the day, he would be presented with knots of scrawl, arched about with great curved strokes of the pencil. William did not see wings. He could only see what Edgar's etchings were not: they were not the neatly ranked up alphabet that William had achieved when he was Edgar's age. They were not evidence of an advancing mind.

And as Edgar stared up at his frowning father he could only see what his Papa was not: he was not pleased. He was not proud. Edgar would follow him down the stairs, hovering beside him as he polished his boots, pulled down his hat and went marching out of the door without a word.

Eleanor watched on, standing side by side with her son on the doorstep, his tiny hand in hers, feeling him pull against her as he yearned after William.

'Do not fret, Edgar,' she said softly. 'Your father must keep his responsibilities to the University, it does not mean that he loves you any the less.'

But as the months passed, with William flinging page after

page of scrawl upon the fire, Eleanor could not be so sure she was telling her son the truth.

And when Mrs Simm came calling, Eleanor could not help herself: her anxieties came spilling out across the table, tears patterning the silk. This whole idea of education was a farce. William insisted on being William, dwelling on the son he wished he had rather than the one he had been given. And Edgar, being Edgar, was not about to set his hand to anything he did not want to, but still his father's boy, was desperate for his father's favour. And she was stuck between them, unable to see a way to make it right.

'And Edgar is not taking to the work at all?'

'If you were to see his schoolbook you might well think he is inventing his own language entirely.'

'His own language? Well, that shows a cleverness, does it not?'

But behind the laughter Eleanor's old fears hovered. The question that had been there for as long as Edgar tumbled through her mind, over and over: what manner of child had she and William brought into the world? A wild kind of boy, and no mistake. A boy who would not stay locked away with his lessons for ever.

Eleanor was right. As she worked through her days, Edgar sat in the room above his mother, setting his mind to the art of escaping.

The hardest part of Edgar's imprisonment was the nearness of the world that he hankered after. There was only a pane of glass set between himself and his freedom. But the latch of the window was rusted shut.

Edgar spent months staring at that stuck latch. It was iron

anchored against iron, and iron was strong. He knew that from the slicing of the poker through the brambles. It would need iron to shift iron, and he had none. But then, one morning, the sun came streaming into the room, setting sparks dancing across the floor. Picking out the run of nails across the wood. Edgar crawled across the boards, pulling at them. They were struck firm in the centre of the room but at the edges, beneath his bed, the wood danced under his weight and the nails leapt from their fittings. He eked one free and clambered up on his desk. Edgar twisted it in and out, the latch leapt, the window swung outwards, and his room was full of air and light and birdsong and scattering blossom.

Edgar pitched himself over the ledge and landed in the embrace of the apple tree. Up, up and up he climbed, away from books, away from lessons, up, up and up into the freedom of the winds. He anchored himself on a fork at the middle, where the tree opened up its arms like a signpost set at a crossroads. Edgar looked down at the world below. The wilderness was just a square of tangled bush land; the cottage, a pebble cast upon the ground. Edgar braced his back against the branches, undid his breeches and let flow a great stream of piss waving this way and that, raining down upon the roof of his enclosure.

Day after day Edgar would climb right up to the top of the whipping wood. Up in the treetops there was nothing but sky and air and Edgar Jones. Looking one way, out across the open meadow, there were the green, green fields and the cattle ploughing their way across it. Turning his face to the other side, there were streets ranked up with houses, with slanted roofs and turrets, and tall chimneys roping the sky with trails of smoke. And then sometimes, beyond, the clouds would open up to reveal a secret. On a clear day, the sun picked out a line of gold, bunched and bundled like a ribbon from his mother's sewing basket, separating the earth from the air.

A week after slipping the latch with one nail, Edgar tumbled the lock of his bedroom door with two, bunched together in his fist to form a spike. He took the staircase on tiptoe and, in the parlour, pulled his father's fattest volumes from the bookshelves. Edgar built up a staircase of poetry and argument, up to the mantelpiece until he was eye to eye with the telescope. He grabbed it. Thou shalt not steal but thou can borrow.

Then Edgar was up the apple tree in an instant and setting his eye to the instrument. He sought out the golden ribbon, twisted the telescope and brought everything into focus.

The ribbon unravelled to reveal it was not a ribbon at all, but a spiked line of stone. Spires and domes and battlements ranged, and there, at the top of them, there were stone men standing: men with spears in their hands and their faces tipped to the heavens. Angels. There were angels set upon the rooftops beyond the wilderness and this was the world that his father went into. It was the place of his father's stories, it had to be: the castles where the brave knights dwelt.

Edgar drew the shape of it out for his father: towers and turrets set in the sky.

William ripped the pages away and threw them upon the desk.

'No kind of cleverness was ever gained through daydreaming, Edgar. You must set your mind to higher things and be determined.'

'I am determined, Papa,' Edgar countered, kicking at the table leg.

'Well, then you must be more so, son,' replied William sharply. 'It takes time and application to achieve anything worthy in life. A man who abandons a task at the first sign of difficulty is not a man at all.'

After his father left for work, Edgar smoothed out the pages and posted them down in the spaces between the floorboards.

Time and application. Edgar turned his father's words over and over in his mind. Early one morning he crept down to the parlour. In the dappled dawn the grandfather clock stood like an upended tomb set against the wall. The stars still danced across the upper face; there was just the eye of the sun peeping round the edge of the frame. The cabinet was studded with two keys: one at the clock face and the other by the edge of the pendulum.

Edgar unlocked the pendulum door and put his hand upon the ball of brass. It tugged against his grasp. There was nothing behind it but empty space. On the dial above, the little hand trembled. Edgar climbed upon a chair so that his face was level with the face of the clock. He turned the key and the door sprung. The tick ticking of the clock echoed through the shadowed room. The hands of time were held on to the plate by a brass screw. He teased it in his fingers, the metal gave. The hands tumbled into his palm. Now there was no time, just the circle of the day, marked out by numbers.

The tick of the clock mechanism was drowned out by the thrumming of the blood in his ears. He could feel his heart beating fast, fast and faster. Soon there would be no measure by which his father could set him to his lessons. The screws twisted and the casing gave. Edgar held in his hand the wide face of the clock. Nothing but a painted piece of tin. But revealed underneath it was the most wonderful thing.

Wheels with teeth bit into other wheels. They tipped and turned on rods of iron, and beneath them a line of wire, a coiled spring, running down to a thread that burrowed through the wood and led to the pendulum. This was how the day and the nights were put together. Edgar thrust his hand into the mass of metal and began to pull at it. And as he worked away he saw that time had layers. The loosening of a cog revealed a smaller one running inside, and inside that, the tiniest ticking turn of a screw. Time was a thing that glinted in the sunlight, and that could be slipped piece by piece into his pocket.

Then there was a hand around his waist and he was being hauled from his chair. And there was his mother, holding him by the shoulder and shaking him.

'Edgar Jones! Is there no end to your mischief?'

She peered into the place that had once been the clock face and tapped against the wood. 'This is badly done, badly done indeed.'

Edgar just looked up at his mother and grinned. He had done very well indeed, and he knew it.

'This may seem to be a great joke to you, but I do not think your father will find it at all amusing.'

Edgar pulled out a fistful of cogs and held them up.

'That's of no use to me, Edgar,' she said sternly. 'It is you who has taken the thing apart, you must correct it.'

But Edgar had stopped time, and now there was not even time to reverse the action as the door swung open and there was his father, dressed all in black, filling up the space of the doorway.

William strode over to the clock and looked inside. There was nothing but twisted screws, and trembling wire and a great gap of space where there should be hands and numbers and everything that gave order to his day. On the floor the sun smiled up at him, the moon and the stars beside it. This was a piece of wanton wilful destruction, and no mistake.

'Is this your doing, Edgar?'

Edgar nodded.

'I can put it back, Pa.'

'Oh, is that so? You cannot put letters on a page but you can fix a clock?'

Edgar looked up at his father. The man dressed in black, towering above him, was and was not his papa. He was scowling down at him, and tugging at his arm. He was fierce and Edgar was afraid.

Edgar took the smallest cog from his pocket and held it up to the spool. But his hands trembled. The cog jumped from his fingers and struck upon the wood.

'Enough, Edgar.'

William hauled his son up the stairs, into his room and locked the door. Edgar took nails in his fist and sprung the lock, and sat with his cheek pillowed against the wood, listening.

In the parlour William stood trembling as if every muscle in his body was a piece of wire spun out to pure tension. Eleanor knew what this was.

'Will,' she said softly, 'do not let your anger turn you savage.'

'A beating might be just the thing to get some sense into him.'

Eleanor shook her head. Part of her was back in the tavern, six years old, with her father standing above her, the floor by her feet peppered with shattered glass, the handle of a tankard held useless in her hand, cupping nothing but air.

'It will not, and well you know it,' said Eleanor.

She put her hand on William's. He slumped down into his chair, with the wall of books ranging at his back.

'Edgar has always been getting into things,' she said. 'This business with the clock is nothing new.'

'What kind of man will Edgar become if he is not held responsible for his actions?'

'You can hold him responsible, Will, but you should not punish him for not being as bookish clever as you are.'

Above, Edgar heard everything.

He might not be able to place words upon the page or put back time, but he could be clever in other ways – his mother said so. His father wished him to be responsible, and he would be. Responsibility was a thing that was found out in the world, he knew that much. Out beyond the garden gate, down the street that his father travelled, out in the place of spires and steeples, where the angels stood upon the rooftops.

Edgar remained locked away all day long. He waited, sleepless through the night. The moon hanging over the wilderness was fat and watchful. It peered down at Edgar from above the apple tree, open-eyed, pucker-mouthed, as if it understood Edgar's intention and was trying to whistle out a warning.

Dawn came, the moon faded, the sky turned red gold, and Edgar was out of the window, vaulting the gate, and, at last, getting out beyond the wilderness. Out to the place of adventuring.

Edgar chased the dawn into Oxford. He ran down the curve of the backstreets and came tipping out at the crossroads of St Giles. All around him was noise and movement as the trades-men wheeled their wares into the city. Above him, striking through the clouds, stood the angels, pointing this way and that with their swords and their spears. Urging Edgar on in a multitude of directions.

The shops lining the street opened up their shutters, each one a spectacle. Cakes and sweet things piled up against one; in another stood row upon row of shoes, as if an invisible army of gentlemen were gathering. By another, a rack of petticoats was wheeled out upon the street, billowing in the breeze like a brace of clouds. Edgar went on. He was after something better, brighter, stronger.

The tradesmen's carts were rolling down the turn to Corn-market. Edgar chased the flashing of the bridles and the spin of the wheels. Each cart carried a different treasure: fruit, vegetables, grain, carcasses of animals split from neck to navel and their ribs open to the world.

And then, in the centre of it all, came a thundering of hoofs and a ringing of steel. A man sat atop a cart with two huge horses, one grey and one red, shackled to the front of it. And rearing up behind them were spikes and spines of metal, stacked on top of each: a great net of sparkling silver, chiming with the roll of the wheels, singing out to Edgar: 'For-tune, for-tune, for-tune . . .'

Edgar ran straight for the cart. All around him the world swerved. He could see the wild flashing of the horses' eyes, the hair cresting their hoofs, the cut of the leather upon their flanks as the man pulled tight the reins.

'What in the devil's name . . . !' cried the man.

Edgar took his hat from his head, holding it before him just as his father had taught him.

'Please, sir,' he called.

'What is wrong with you, boy? Out of the road before you are trampled.'

The red horse sniffed at Edgar's head, as if to munch the hair from his scalp. Beyond, the mass of metal sparkled in the light.

'Please sir, where does the iron come from?'

'More's the question, where do you come from, child?'

'From my father's house in Jericho.'

'Your father's house, indeed. And what kind of a father sends his son scuttling about the streets at this time, asking for the whereabouts of the blacksmith?'

'He has sent me out for work.'

'Work?' laughed the man. 'You are barely out of the cradle, boy.'

'I am seven years of age and I would be a good blacksmith.'

The man laughed again. 'Would you indeed? Well then, you should follow the smoke clouds. And when you get to the forge, ask for Master Salt.'

The man pointed to the sky with his whip. And there, hovering above the rooftops, leaching out into the new day, was a dark cloud.

The cloud beckoned to Edgar. He followed it. It led him down the winding backstreets behind the market. The walls of the colleges reared up on all sides, with their tall windows and their crested battlements, a maze of stone. Edgar turned corner after corner, and each street was the same. Creatures grinned down at him from the gutterings, laughing at him, their claws scrabbling out of the rock. The man on the horse had tricked him. Edgar would never get to the iron; he would be stuck in these winding lanes for ever, never making it back home.

The black cloud above spread across the sky like a stain. Still, Edgar followed it, turned down an alley, and the narrow street opened into a courtyard, and there it was: the forge. Dark and shrunken, it looked like a growth upon the skin of the city. The windows were shuttered up with sheets of steel. The iron door was hard to pick out from its fitting of blackened bricks. The dark-tiled roof was broken up by chimneypots, all belching out the smoke that spun together above Edgar's head. He walked towards it.

In the centre of the door hung a heavy ring made of strands of iron wrapped over and over each other, like the coils of his mother's hair. Edgar grabbed the knocker and struck. The walls of the forge rang like a great bell. The shutter dragged back and a pair of eyes stared down at Edgar.

'Master Salt?'

'Who is asking?'

'Edgar Jones. Come for work.'

The door swung open.

The darkness on the outside of the place was matched by the darkness inside. The forge was one long room, low-beamed and curve-walled. The first thing that Edgar saw was the fire set in the middle, a roaring mountain of coals. The second thing was the huge black pot swinging above it. It was tethered to the roof by a chain. The passage of air from the open door made the fire spit and the cauldron swing. The rafters chimed with the breeze. Edgar looked up, and through the smoke he could see hanging from the wood ladles, tongs and axes, and many objects he could not name.

Edgar felt he was caught at the heart of a huge mechanism, with all its cogs and levers clustering around the pendulum of the pot. Jacob Salt was standing with the fire behind him. It seemed to Edgar that he filled half the room. He stood the height of the rafters. He was clad in a suit of leather, which reflected the light so that he was sparking flame from his thighs and forearms. An ogre. A creature from his father's stories, who would eat a boy and cast his bones into the pot. And there was a sickening smell that filled every bit of the air. A smell of rottenness, and burning.

Edgar hesitated by the door. He could run back out into the light and the air, run, run and run through those winding streets until he was safe back home, and all he had to fear was a locked room and lessons. But then his life would be the same as it was before. He would have proved nothing. He would be bold and brave, still.

Jacob walked towards Edgar. The things hanging from the beams struck against his head and the room sang with the chime of metal against metal. Peering up through the smoke Edgar saw that Jacob was crowned by a mask of iron, like a tin pot upended on his face, with a slit cut through for the eyes, and the nose and mouth peeping out from beneath the lip of it.

Jacob Salt pushed back the mask. His skin was furrowed with soot. The whites of his eyes glowed wild in the darkness.

Edgar stood his ground.

'So tell me, boy, what makes you fit for the smithy?'

Edgar looked up at the things hanging from the rafters. Things made for poking and prodding and cutting. Things that would slice through the wilderness in an instant.

'I can work, sir. I can turn my hand to anything apart from lessons.'

Jacob's face broke into a grin for a moment and then it was gone.

'You are a bold little lad, are you not?'

'Yes, sir.'

'But are you honest?'

'Yes, sir.'

'Not the kind of lad who would spring his master's purse and run away with his earnings?'

'No, sir.'

'So said my last lad, and now here I am over-run with commissions and with no one to tip the bellows.'

Jacob pulled out a leather apron. He thrust Edgar into it, pulling at straps to bind every bit of him in.

'A smithy's work is hard,' said Jacob. 'It takes determination to stick at it.'

'I am determined, sir.'

'Do not get ahead of yourself, boy. You are not apprenticed yet.'

Jacob led Edgar round the cauldron and showed him all the things that worked together for the making of metal: the piles of ingots, the moulding blocks, the long trough of the cooler. Round the curve of the cauldron, and right up to the roaring heat of the fire. There, anchored on to a pile of bricks, with its snout pointed into the flames sat a great sack of leather: the bellows from his father's fireside, rendered huge.

'The bellows are the heart of the forge,' said Jacob. 'You must keep the rhythm even and the air set to the centre of the fire. If you do not, the metal will separate from itself and the work will not hold. Do you understand?'

Edgar nodded. He crouched down in the dust with the fire burning at his back, set both hands upon the handle and began to pump.

The bellows creaked at Edgar's touch, and the belly folded in upon itself. The fire leapt. Edgar released the pressure, and the handle sprung upwards, almost pulling him off his feet.

'Steady,' barked Jacob.

Edgar pushed down again, and his body sank. Up down, up down went Edgar, to the rhythm of the breath of the machine. Above him Jacob swung the pot about on its chain. Then he pulled a dark block up aside it and tipped the pot towards it. Out of the cauldron came streaming a river of white molten metal. The liquid light dropped down into the waiting moulds. And there, for a moment, running red gold across the floor of the forge, was a rack of sharp-tipped spears. Fit for an army of angels. Edgar's heart hammered in his chest. This is what it was to be a blacksmith, then – to cast things out of a fire and to fix them.

When the blocks were filled they were upended, and with a firm strike of the hammer Jacob knocked the spears from their fittings, picked them up in his tongs and threw them into the cooling trough. The water hissed and the room became clouded with steam. It wreathed around Edgar, stinging his eyes, filling his lungs. He felt as if he was drowning in it. He held on tight to the bellows handle.

Edgar pushed and pulled, pushed and pulled. The wrench of the mechanism echoed down his arm, through his shoulder, into his chest. He felt as if his bones were being pulled apart from each other. It was as if he was grappling with some huge creature that had crawled out of the fire, and if he did not keep beating at its back then it would drag him into the heart of the flames.

Then suddenly Jacob's foot came down on top of the back of the beast, stamping it flat.

'Enough,' he said gruffly.

Edgar crawled away from the flame.

'You are a determined little devil, I will give you that,' said Jacob.

'I would be a good blacksmith, sir, I know it.'

'Today you might; tomorrow you might desire to be a barrow boy.'

'No, sir, only a blacksmith, sir.'

Edgar heard his name being shouted down the street before he reached the cottage. 'Edgar! Edgar Jones!' echoed down the alley, as if the world had already heard of his achievement and was singing out his praises.

He turned the corner and there was his father, standing in the centre of the wilderness, smashing it about with the poker. His mother came running from the doorway, down the street, hauled him into her arms and took him back through the garden gate. As if he was an infant, a child to be carried through the world rather than a boy who could go out and find his own fortune. Edgar wriggled against her grasp. The front of her dress was patterned with soot.

'Wherever have you been, Edgar?' she said. 'Your father and I have been desperate.'

'Out in the world, Mama,' replied Edgar with a grin.

His father pulled him out of his mother's embrace and held him at arm's length. His grip was hard upon Edgar's shoulder.

'Out in the world without permission, and you come back to us looking like a savage. It seems your punishment was too lenient by far.'

'No, Pa,' cried Edgar. 'I have been out at work.'

Edgar pulled papers from his pocket and thrust them into his father's hands. They were soot-stained, crumpled up into a ball. This was not William's idea of a contract.

Whilst Edgar splashed about in the scullery bathtub, turning the water slick black, his mother and father sat in the parlour with the apprentice papers set on the table between them.

'I should have paid more attention to your analysis,' said William. He was smoothing the pages over and over with his hand as if he could rub the text clean away.

'Analysis?'

'You saw it from the start. There has always been a wildness about Edgar, and now I think it will take drastic measures indeed to correct it.'

'Correct it?'

Eleanor frowned. She had a sudden vision of Edgar, cuffed, chained, set behind bars, with William dictating his lessons from the other side of the enclosure. Then it was gone, and there was only William, gentle William, peering down at the papers as if they were written in a foreign script.

'I have been patient,' said William, 'and what good has it done? A blacksmith, indeed. It is shameful.'

'Shameful for you, Will, but perhaps not for Edgar.'

William turned his face to the fire. He imagined how it would be for Edgar, working away amongst the ashes. And as he stared at those licking flames, a part of him was Edgar's age once more, shut away in the college kitchens, scrubbing his way through his hours, with the muck of the scholars' suppers seeping into his skin.

'Any apprenticeship is savage labour. It is not a thing I would wish for my son.'

'And I would not wish him to spend the months running wild. I think a spell in the smithy might correct him better than anything,' Eleanor replied.

The fire spat and tumbled in agreement.

'Besides, have you not said yourself that Edgar is lucky to have been born into the age of invention? And are not the best inventions made of iron?'

'That is quite a leap of rhetoric, my love.'

William took the dilemma with him to the lodge. He watched the lights of the scholars' rooms ripple across the darkness. As they were extinguished one by one, until the college was nothing but a shadow set against the sky, William felt a heaviness in his heart. It was as if he was watching Edgar's opportunities fade away until there was nothing left for him but soot and darkness. And yet, and yet . . . William was tired. All day when he should have been sleeping, he had been running around the wilderness, up and down the street, hollering out for his son. He was tired in his bones and he was tired in his heart. For month upon month now he had been tearing the scrawl from Edgar's schoolbooks. It was a harder thing than he could have imagined, this fashioning of his son's mind. Perhaps Eleanor was right, perhaps giving Edgar a spell of hard labour would be enough to show him the error of his nature and bring him running back to the books.

'A blacksmith?' said Mrs Simm as she unfurled a dress the colour of flame. 'Well, my dear, you know what they say about blacksmiths.'

Eleanor, her mouth stuffed full of pins, shook her head.

'A blacksmith will bring the luck of the devil into your house, and that's a hard thing to shift.'

William returned home at dawn to find Edgar sitting upon the front step, as still as a statue, arms wrapped around his knees, staring out at the wilderness. The overgrown path from the gate to the cottage seemed impossibly long as William walked up it. He remembered how it had been, less than two years ago, that he would be striding down the curve of the street, and see the front door fly open, Edgar racing up to the gate, fists around the bars, and William would open it, swinging his son from the hinges and gathering him up in his arms, hoisting him up into the air and down. Edgar with his birdlike laugh. Edgar with his cries of, Papa, Papa, Papa, as if it was the only word in the world. A time before any disappointments. A time before any lessons.

'Papa,' said Edgar.

William sat down beside him. The wilderness before them was thriving with green new growth. The tangled grasses held echoes of the tunnels that Edgar had forged in the heart of it.

'You are taking after your old pa, I see,' said William.

'Sitting here guarding the gate as if you were the man of the house.'

Edgar shook his head. 'I was waiting for you, Papa.'

'Waiting for my answer, more like.'

Above them the birds were singing their choruses up in the apple tree, as if this was a day to be celebrated.

'A man's character is formed by his choices and the consequences of those choices,' said William slowly. 'God gave us free will as both a test and an act of trust.'

Edgar kicked at the pebbles scattered on the steps.

'It has been your nature from the start, Edgar, to be exploring the way that the world is put together. I only wish you had paid similar attention to your books and set your sights upon the University. But there is a kind of blasphemy in wishing that you were other than you are.'

Edgar stared up at his father. These were Bible words: blasphemy, will, God. There were the words of stories, not anything to do with the forge. But now his papa was pulling the papers from his pocket and smoothing them out. In the midst of the wriggling words, his papa was drawing his pen across the page.

'I will sign but I cannot sanction, Edgar,' said William quietly.

Edgar put his arm around his father's back. There was no great 'HO!' and a pitch up to the sky, just father and son sitting side by side with the wilderness blossoming in the dawn around them. Edgar looked beyond it, to the gate, to the curve of the street. His papa was letting him out into the world. Out to a place of iron and adventure. He would go into that shed of smoke and fire and he would swing from the lip of that great pot and he would pour down the white light and he would bring something back for his father. Something better than any book. Something better than the telescope, the thermometer, better even than the universe in the box. Something that showed his cleverness and would make his father proud.

So it was that Eleanor, not William, walked Edgar down the streets of Oxford, round the back of the market and up to the forge courtyard. She looked at the squat black building with the smoke pouring out of the top of it, and she shivered. When she had fought for Edgar's cause she had visions of a somehow grander place, not this cramped carbuncle that set such a stench out into the air.

'It is not too late, Edgar,' she said, 'to decide against this. Neither your father nor I would blame you for it.'

Edgar shook his head. 'I would be blacksmith, Mama.'

'Well, go then. It will do you no favours for your master to catch you clinging to your mother's skirts.'

Edgar ran to the door and hammered at it.

'Master Salt!' he cried. 'Master Salt, your apprentice is arrived!'

The door opened before him, and Edgar ran inside, handed over his papers and grabbed his apron. He clambered into it, twisting about to fix the straps. He was a blacksmith. The fire sparked beside him and the cauldron bubbled. He crouched down beside the bellows and pushed out a great gust of air. The flames leapt and tickled the base of the pot.

Jacob pulled him out of the ashes and turned him round to face him.

'Not so quick,' he said. 'There are laws to the forge. First, you must always respect the metal or it will turn against you.'

'Yes, sir.'

'Second, never turn your hand to a task that is not permitted by your master.'

'Yes, sir.'

'And thirdly, never question the ruling of your master.'

'Yes, sir.'

'It is one thing to parrot back replies, boy. It is quite another to act upon them.'

'Yes, sir.'

'Yes sir, no sir. Set yourself to work and let us see how we get on.'

Edgar hunkered down by the fire and pushed and pulled his way through the hours. The smoke gathered, the heat gathered, and the great pot swung to and fro above his head. The iron could turn, said his master. The pot could tip and Edgar would be swallowed in a river of liquid light. Edgar tuned his back to it; he would not be afraid. He set his eye upon the bellows beast and grappled with its leather belly.

At the close of the day everything about Edgar ached. He shut the iron door behind him and stepped out into the court-yard. He rubbed his soot-streaming eyes, and the twilight air before him danced with sparks as he took the roads home. But these were different roads from the ones he had walked by his mother's side that morning. Now iron ran through everything.

There was the clatter of the carriages streaming down Broad Street, the wheels and the horseshoes chiming out against the cobbles. There were the hinges on the windows of the shuttered-up shop fronts. There were the glinting gold crosses set on top of the college chapels, winking down at Edgar from the cloud line. The more Edgar looked the more he saw that there was a second Oxford hovering on top of the ancient stonework, an Oxford of fixtures and fittings. The city was held together by metal, and Edgar would learn the trick of it.

Edgar was correct. As he sat in the soot and the muck by the bellows for six months, he watched Jacob tip a whole world of iron out of the pot. There were wheels and chains and bridles, and great brass hinges and bolts and hoops and many things that Edgar could not name. But the shape that was forged over and over was that long line of metal ending in a sharp point. Edgar watched as his master laid these out in racks across the courtyard. Jacob connected the spears with other iron pieces, and Edgar worked at the rivets, tightening, fixing, until there, laid out before him was the very thing that had struck together and called to Edgar as he had made his way down Cornmarket in search of his fortune: fence posts.

Edgar took to walking the rounds of Oxford, spying out the fences roped around the backs of the colleges. He peered through the railings and saw men in black gowns walking through gardens. And these gardens were not like the tangles of his own home – these places were full of flowers and bushes and high-reaching trees. He looked at the run of the metal stretching above him, up and up into the air, the spike tips an echo of the spires set on the other side of them. Forbidden lands.

Edgar took his curiosity back to the cottage.

'Pa,' he said, 'why is Oxford so full of fences?'

'To keep common folk like yourself out of the places made for better men.'

'Will,' said Eleanor sharply, 'you should not speak to your own son so.'

'It was meant in jest,' snapped William. 'Allow me to find some amusement in Edgar's situation at least.'

Eleanor frowned and stilled the slow slide of the teapot. She loved her husband for many things, but his humour was not one of them. He was not a man who tended to jest about anything.

Edgar clasped his fist around his knife and sawed through his bread in silence. His apprenticeship was not a thing to be laughed at. He would become the greatest blacksmith of all. Then there would be no men in the whole of Oxford who were better than he.

But as the months piled up into a passing year, Edgar found that there was a great gap between his ambition and his station in the forge.

After serving his time at the bellows, Edgar was trusted to pick the pieces out of the water trough. For a while there was pleasure in the sport of it, fishing this way and that with the arms of the tongs until the object was caught, but the pleasure did not last.

Then Edgar was given the job of sorting the ingots of various metals, but this was only piling up rocks against each other. The chipping out of the moulds was a similarly tedious task. Even when he was allowed the task of bringing up articles to a good shine – and this was presented as a great privilege – Edgar had little time for it. The things he polished were already finished. A blacksmith who did not make anything, who did not beat a hammer on iron and did not pull the rivers of light out of the pot, was not a blacksmith at all.

But whenever Edgar shared his desire with his master to fashion something himself, the response was the same: 'You will stand at the pot when you have the stature for it, and not before.'

At the beginning of every week Edgar would stand beside the pot, measuring himself against the line of rivets that ran up the seam of it. In three years he grew the space of five bolts. The lip of the pot was still a good foot above him. This was a great joke for Jacob. Whilst Edgar went about his work, his master would shout to him from the side of the pot to fetch the scoop shovel, the hand axe, the hammer.

'From where?'

And the answer would always be the same. Jacob would point up to the iron-clad rafters above his head and laugh.

The more time Edgar spent shuttered in the forge, the more he missed his life outside it. His apprenticeship kept him in darkness. The world of soot and fire and metal took no heed of the seasons. The forge was the forge and it never changed.

But as Edgar's apprenticeship passed, it was as if every day he was bringing more of the forge back home with him. The passage of Edgar about the house could be tracked by the tidemarks upon seats, handprints on the walls and a fine dust that floated through the air in his wake. Soot seeped into everything. Eleanor would set the table for breakfast only to find the bread turning black at the edges, and the butter ash-speckled. She would strip back her son's bed to find a shadow Edgar etched upon the linen: curled up in the centre of the cloth, the outline of the body and the shock of hair. Not so very different from how he was when he came into the world.

Most insidious were the invisible pockets of blackness that followed him about. Deep dark seams of silence built up between father and son, invisible to the eye, but palpable to the heart.

William found it hard to look at his son, dirtied and dressed in the clothes of trade. Sitting at the parlour table, he would shield himself from the sight with the newspaper. Edgar would look at the wall of wriggling words set between himself and his papa, and at the pictures of men staring out of the page: men in caps and gowns and robes. The same kind of men that he had seen on the other side of his fences.

Throughout these years, William found himself beset by the same dream again and again. He was with Edgar at the riverbank and he was pulling away Edgar's forge clothes. He stripped back his son to his soot-stained skin. William took Edgar by the ankle and upended him into the water. But the minute that Edgar touched the river, the crystal water grew wild and boiled black. And no matter how often William plunged his son into the raging rapids, no matter how much he held him squirming in the stew of it, Edgar would not wash clean.

Only Eleanor's workshop was immune to the slick slow creep of the darkness. Eleanor placed hooks upon the walls and hung the articles she had repaired upon them. Even on the dullest days, when the wind shook about the windowpanes and the rain hammered down upon the roof, the walls blossomed with colour.

So Edgar sat in the ashes and he waited. He now had the same feeling that had beset him when he'd sat at his lessons in his locked room. There was a way for him to spring this trap, he was sure of it. It was simply a matter of finding the key.

It was in the spring of his eleventh year that an opportunity presented itself. Master Salt had left to pick a quarrel with a man about an unpaid contract. Edgar was left with the instruction to keep the fire burning.

He sat pushing and pulling, pushing and pulling, watching the shadows range up around him. There were fences upon fences piled up along the sides of the room. The firelight caught them and cast them huge. As Edgar looked, he saw that the shadow fences were not fences at all, but ladders. Huge ladders of iron that were there for the climbing. Edgar left the bellows and dragged a moulding block to the foot of the cauldron. He took a fence panel, turned it on its side and anchored a post into the mouldings from which it had been poured. It held, with the top spur anchored against the edge of the swaying pot. Edgar set his foot upon it and began to climb.

The iron set against the cauldron gathered heat into itself, but still Edgar climbed on, up, up, past the rivets, up, up and up to the lip of the pot. He gazed down into the depths of it. And the pot stared straight back at him.

At the heart of the pot was a huge white eye of liquid light fringed with an iris of flame. The molten metal licked up the sides and fell back into the burning centre. Refolding and reforming. Making and unmaking in the same moment of motion.

Each fold revealed a miracle. Droplets clung to the sides, golden beads, scattered sovereigns, hidden treasure. They slid slowly into one another, forming a delicate chain before they were pulled down into the great glowing eye. There were barrel hoops, spinning around one another, and scattered in amongst them things that Edgar could not put a name to: half-formed shapes, shifting.

The heat flared up against Edgar. He could feel the rim of the cauldron searing against his apron, but he could not pull away. His weight caused the pot to swing back and forth, back and forth, tumbling the molten iron, and it seemed to Edgar that there was a whole other world lurking underneath the skin of the stewing metal. The more he looked, the clearer he could see it: the cliff sides of fire, the verdant valleys of white light, the hidden land stretched out its borders, the sea spun at the edges, and on the sea, a single fleck of ore, a black raft upon a golden ocean, a bold vessel, scaling the fiery waters. Edgar would give his whole life to be a sailor upon such a ship.

This was a place of adventure, and no mistake. His master was wrong to keep him from it. This was a place where fame and fortune could be found, if a man was brave and bold and clever enough. And Edgar would be.

It was but a month later that Edgar's adventure began. He was sitting where he always was, pumping at the bellows, but it was as if his dissatisfaction was pouring itself into the fire. The flame would not take, but instead the coals gave out great rolls of smoke, enveloping Jacob and sending him into fits of coughing.

'More care, boy!' barked Jacob, but Edgar just grinned and pushed harder.

Then there was a rap upon the door, forceful, insistent, making the walls of the forge ring.

Jacob stumbled to the door, there was a gust of wind, and standing upon the threshold was a man. A tall, lean man, with a black cape drawn around his shoulders. He was hook-nosed, and his head was fringed with a crest of grey hair. The smoke feathered the edges of his gown, giving the impression that the man was sprouting wings. He had a bunch of papers anchored under one arm. In his hand he held a cane, which he used to cut a path through the billowing clouds.

Edgar shrunk away from the bellows and crept towards the wall. He had seen such a man before, he was certain of it. His skin shivered with the memory of a hand clamped upon his skull. He burrowed into a tangle of fence posts and sat listening.

'So this is what it is,' said the man, 'to be next to the heartbeat of industry.'

Jacob grunted and tipped back his mask. 'Only a man who has never worked with metal would be so poetical about it.'

'Quite so, quite so,' smiled the man. 'I have been discovered. I am a mere Professor of Anatomy. Nothing more.'

'It is not usual for the forge to deal so directly with the men of the University.'

'Well, we live in unusual times, Master Salt. I have come to you with a riddle of creation. I do believe that you are the only man to solve it.'

The Professor unfurled his paper. It stretched the span of his arms, a white sail set across the sea of smoke.

Edgar watched as his master scanned the page.

'It is an impossible task.'

'I agree, it is quite a conundrum,' smiled the Professor. 'But riddles are there to challenge our craft.'

'You come for the advice of a blacksmith, and I say again, sir, my advice is that what you have set upon the page is impossible.'

Edgar's curiosity overcame his caution. He pushed out of his hiding place, and the fence-posts clattered to the floor. The Professor started at the sound, and peered down at him through the smoke.

'Aha!' he cried. 'We are not alone.'

'This is Edgar Jones, my apprentice,' said Jacob gruffly.

'An apprentice indeed.' The Professor crouched upon his haunches, held his hand out to Edgar and smiled. 'I am delighted to make your acquaintance, Edgar Jones, and I would be most grateful if you could cast your eye over my plans.'

'He is but three years in the craft!' snapped Jacob.

But the Professor was already spreading his paper out across the floor, weighting down the corners with lumps of rubble. 'Forgive me if I seem presumptuous,' he said, 'but it is my experience at the University that the untrained minds are often more agile than those who have spent their lives at study.'

Jacob shrugged. 'That maybe so at the University, sir, but I think you will find it goes very differently in the forge.'

Edgar looked at the paper laid out before him. There was a great globe of a pot, set upon a scaffold of wood, tied with ropes. And a man stood beside it, no taller than the stack of firewood set under the pot. Edgar looked from the man on the page to the man standing over him. Each wore the long black gown of the University. This was a man from his father's world, come to ask him for help. He wished it was his father, not his master, who was standing beside him.

'Do you understand the challenge, child?'

Edgar thought of how the pieces of fencework were poured out spur by spur and bracketed together. He thought of how, if all that iron was rolled up into a ball the pot in the forge would not hold it. He thought of how his mother sat at the fireside and tugged sheets of silk together with her needle.

'It might be done in pieces,' he said.

'In pieces?' echoed the Professor. 'Explain.'

'Like the making of the fences, it could be done in pieces and fitted together in the courtyard.'

'Indeed?'

'The pot of the forge was made like this.' Edgar pointed to the thick lines running down the side of the cauldron, cutting it into quarters, and the rivets joining them. His measuring stick.

'Is this true, Master Salt? Is such large piece-work possible?'

'It might be so,' replied Jacob gruffly, 'but it would be an expensive and uncertain process.'

'But what is life without uncertainty?' replied the Professor with a smile. 'A dull road to travel, I warrant you. And as to the expense, the University will provide.'

Jacob scowled down the smoke at Edgar but the Professor smiled still.

'Good work, Edgar Jones! You continue paying such keen attention to the world and you will be destined for great things.' The Professor took Edgar's soot-soiled hand in his and shook it. Then he stretched himself back up to his full height and all the conversation above Edgar's head was about weights and measures and ratios and payments and designs.

Finally there was the sway of the forge door, a clang of the metal bolt, and the Professor was gone.

Down in the ashes, Edgar smiled. He had solved the

Professor's riddle. He was a better blacksmith than his master.

Edgar was nearly pitched into the railings with the force of the blow around his head.

'What is the second law of the forge?' barked Jacob.

'Never turn your hand to a task not permitted by your master.'

'That includes talk, boy.'

'But we have the work.'

Jacob cuffed him again. 'And the third law?'

'Never question the ruling of your master.'

'Do I have to beat the words into you to make them stick?'

'No, sir. But we have the work.'

Jacob hit out again. Edgar dodged his fist and he swiped only smoke.

'And what makes you think the work is welcome? It is easier with these university men to tell them that a thing is impossible than it is unwanted. Now we will have this Professor poking about our business as if he was the master of the forge.'

His ear smarted with the blow, but Edgar smiled still. He was set to have a new master, and he was destined for great things.

When Edgar returned to the cottage everything was just the same as it always was: his mother laying out the supper things for herself and Edgar, his father sitting by the fire, polishing his boots, all his books stacked up behind him.

Edgar stared at the lettering slithering across the spines.

'Pa,' he said, 'what does it mean to study anatomy?'

William looked up, his cloth suspended in the air.

'Anatomy?' he said curtly. 'It involves the slicing up of dead creatures and examining how they were put together.'

'What kinds of creatures?'

'Anything that these so-called men of science can gain possession of.'

'Why, Pa?'

'It is entirely beyond me. If God had meant us to see our inner mechanisms then why would He have clad our bodies in flesh?'

Eleanor did not cease from setting the places for supper. The knives and forks knocked upon the wood.

'Anatomy!' huffed William. 'Is this what you will set your mind upon now, Edgar? Not content with a life in the furnace you must turn your hand to butchering?'

He thrust his hat down upon his head, kissed his wife, and strode out of the door.

Eleanor pulled Edgar to her and ruffled his hair.

'Oh, Edgar,' she said. 'You and your father are too alike. Why can't you just let the world be as it is and be done with it?'

Anatomy. Edgar turned the word over in his mind. He thought of the pot stretched across the page, and the tiny man set beside it. He thought of how the pots in the scullery bubbled with his mother's soups of boiled-away meat, and the bones that rattled against the sides of them.

So it was that Edgar's life in the forge changed within a week. His work became large and magnificent.

Moulds were cut, huge curved moulds that took the length of the workspace. When the brass was poured into them, the whole room was aflame. All the other contraptions of iron flared out of the shadows. Bridles shone bright from the rafters, pokers, pots, posts, shovels and irons were all turned burning gold as if all that had ever been made was taken back to its liquid origins.

Splints were set up out in the courtyard and, one by one, the pieces of the pot were slipped into the frame. Jacob soldered the joints and Edgar fastened the rivets from tip to toe. The weeks were charted in the completing of the circle. And then it was done. The pot stood the height of a man and a half, and the width of two horses. All that was left was the polishing.

Hessian bags were brought out, weighty things, the length of Edgar's arm, with grit and sand stuffed inside them. Edgar ran round and round the cauldron, until the courtyard spun and the golden pot was like the sun at the centre of his father's orrery, drawing all things into its orbit. The walls of the courtyard circled, the stones slipped round in elliptical circles. But Edgar was not done with his pot yet. He tied grit-bags to his back, anchored a rope, hauled his way up to the lip of the cauldron and launched himself over the edge.

He flew down the sides, riding the wave of the belly of the brass, and came to rest laughing at the bottom.

He spun inside the cauldron until all was shining. He lay on his back and stretched out his limbs. He did not touch the sides. His body lengthened and ran up the polished curves. He was the pot and the pot was him, and in the pot he had the stature of a man, multiplied.

And then the pot began to sing, a long drawn-out low note, which echoed all around.

'Ho, ho, and what have we here?'

The Professor grinned down at him, tapping the side with his cane.

Then Jacob was there, scowling over the lip. 'Get out of there, Edgar. The Professor's pot is not a plaything.'

'In truth, Master Salt,' smiled the Professor, 'it is.'

Edgar scrabbled up the sides but his feet could not find a grip. Jacob laughed as he fell on his back, on his arse, and went sliding back in to the heart of it.

'Looks like you will be taking Edgar along with you in your great pot, Professor!'

'I am sure I could make use of such a quick lad as Edgar. However, it would be a great disservice to the forge.'

The Professor leant over the side and held out his cane. Edgar saw that the top of it was set into the shape of a silver fist. Edgar grabbed it, the Professor gripped Edgar's wrist, and pulled him out.

Back on the land, Edgar braced his back against the pot and stared up at the Professor.

'Sir, what is it for?'

'You made the thing, young master. What do you suppose its purpose might be?'

Edgar thought of how the brass had cradled him.

'I think it must be a boiling pot.'

'Quite so.'

'And my pa tells me that anatomy is the study of bones, so I think you must be boiling up a monster.'

The Professor laughed. 'Not a monster as such, child. But if you come to my college this Sunday, all shall be revealed.'

The Professor swept through the dust of the courtyard with the tip of his cane, drawing in the dirt the line of Cornmarket with the forge marked upon it; he sketched out the crossroads at the top, and the road that sloped down from it.

'Give me your hand, my boy,' he said.

Edgar did. The Professor grabbed it – that strong grip again – pulled at Edgar's thumb and pressed it down into the dirt, marking the map.

'There!' he said. 'My college has a tower at the entrance of exactly that dimension. My rooms face the meadows. You must go to the back gate and ask for me by name.'

'You should not favour Edgar so,' grunted Jacob. 'He has enough ideas above his station as it is.'

'It is my belief that a curious mind should be encouraged, Master Salt, especially in a child.'

Edgar watched as men came and hauled the cauldron on to the back of a cart. The brass sang as it hit cobbles and wood, and each strike of the metal rang out with promise: 'Sun-day. Sun-day. Sun-day . . .'

When Sunday morning came, Edgar dressed for church as he always did. As he buttoned up his collar he could hear the murmur of his parents' voices echoing up the stairwell. Edgar knew well enough that any talk of pots and bones would come to no good. So he made his escape in the old way of his childhood: slipping the latch, descending the apple tree and vaulting the garden fence to freedom.

He followed his memory of the dust map, striding down Cornmarket. The street seemed unnaturally wide without the carts thundering along it. The shuttered-up shops gave Edgar the sense that he had slipped into a different Oxford – a place where nothing was made and nothing was sold. The only sound was the ringing of the bells as all the towers of all the chapels called in their faithful.

He came to the crossroads. There, set upon the slope of St Aldates hill he could see a squat tower, a thumbprint indeed. He ran down the hill towards it.

Edgar meant to follow the Professor's instruction, to skirt the main gate and take the turn to the meadows. But as he passed under the shadow of the tower he was caught by the vision framed in the gateway: the college opened up into a great courtyard and there, sitting proud at the heart of it, was Edgar's golden pot. It was suspended upon a scaffold, just as the Professor had set out on his papers. There was a fire roaring beneath it and spewing out from the lip, a streaming cloud of black smoke. It feathered the sky, outreaching the walls of the quadrangle, rolling up the sides of the cathedral. There were men dressed in working clothes, hovering at the side of it, staring up at the gathering darkness. Edgar knew well enough from the forge that such a cloud meant there was a great mass of stuff inside there. Whatever it was that the Professor was stewing up, he would see it.

Edgar felt a hand upon his shoulder. There was a man dressed in a dark suit and hat. A man in his father's clothes.

'This is University property,' the man said, 'and no place for vagabond boys.'

'I am a friend of the Professor of Anatomy.'

'A friend, are you? And do you have a paper, signed with the Professor's authority?'

Edgar shook his head.

'I thought not. You must peddle your lies elsewhere, child.'

The man hauled Edgar out on to the street. Edgar turned his back on the main gate and went round to the back of the college. This side of the building stretched along the edge of the meadows and was racked up with tall windows and balconies wreathed around with ivy. A big wooden door was flanked by two watchmen. The pot was boiling just the other side of the college walls. And no man dressed like his father would keep him from it.

Edgar followed his fenceposts, away from the watchmen, along the walkway and out of sight. Behind the bars stood a corner of the college banded with drainpipes, windows, lintels and roped around with ivy.

Edgar set his hand to a spur, his foot to a brace and vaulted the fence. He landed in the bushes at the edge of the lawn, roses spiking his back and daisies tickling at his nose. The smoke wreathed across the rooftops, beckoning, just as the forge smoke had called to him three years ago, on his first day of adventure. But this was an altogether better exploration. He was the other side of his own iron bars: he was in the University.

Edgar scampered across the lawn to the waiting wall of the college. He set his foot against the drainpipe and shinned his way up it as if it were a tree trunk. Up, up and up went Edgar, finding handholds in brackets and resting points in lintels. He would get up to the heights and he would peer down into his pot, and all would be revealed, just as the Professor had promised him.

He reached the level of the guttering. The lip of the roof was a ledge of lead, a tightrope walk set into the sky. Edgar crawled along it, with gargoyles crouched beneath him, faces turned towards each other, whispering beneath their claw-hands. He rounded the corner, creeping back towards the main quad, back towards the pot. Another rooftop rose up before him, spiked with cruciform spires: the cathedral. Smoke rolled over the ridge in banks of black fog. If he was going to see, he would have to climb right into the heart of it.

Edgar set himself against the scree of slate and pushed his way upwards. The black stuff closed around him. It was not like the soot smoke of the forge. It had a stickier nature and was a smell that Edgar knew: the smell of a ruined supper, blackened meat and burnt fat. Edgar could see nothing, not even the shape of his own hand before him. He felt his way along the line of tiles. Slowly, hand over hand, he crept on. The stewing matter had gathered upon the slates and given them an uncertain surface. The further up he climbed, the more the black cloud gathered, until it was hard for Edgar to make out the difference between the smoke and himself – as if he, like whatever it was in the pot, was being slowly boiled away in the stew of it. Up, up and up he crawled, clinging to the steep slate. And then he pitched his body forwards, but there was nothing to hold him. He tilted backwards, tumbled through the cloud, down, down. He could see the air opening up beneath him, the line of the gutter. He grabbed it, and held on tight.

Edgar looked at the darkness above, and the line of the drainpipe beneath him. He could be brave or he could go scampering back down to earth. Had not his own father once told him: a man who is not determined is not a man at all? And he would be a man.

Slowly, slowly, Edgar inched his way up the slippery slate, back into the blackness. Above him, a great gold crucifix emerged from the darkness. Edgar grabbed it the way a drowning man might clutch on to a bit of ballast. He hauled himself up so that he was sitting astride the spine of the roof.

No sooner had Edgar got on his perch than the wind changed and the dark cloud tumbled away. It ran down the side of the cathedral, back to where it had come from. Edgar could see his golden cauldron hanging in the centre of the quad, as small as a marble, a thing that he could flick aside with his finger and thumb. The smoke was unfurling across the quad like a pot of spilt ink, a huge hand made of shadow. The men standing beside the scaffold could not outrun the black-fisted grasp of it, and their shouts echoed up the air to Edgar.

'The devil! The devil's work!'

There was a creak, a groan of wood, a great thundering of metal, and there, rolling out of the stewing cloud came the cauldron. The men were pitching it across the quad, and out to the gates. Globules of stuff spilt out in slick black stains. Anger stewed through Edgar's blood. His perfect pot was being battered against the cobbles. His best bit of work was being stolen and spoilt, and he could do nothing to stop it.

He watched as the men heaved at the sides of it, the brass belly rocked and then upended, and the men gave out a great cheer as a flood of beast, bone, skin and death went coursing down St Aldates.

Edgar saw a great huge head, connected to a long neck, a ladder of bones, dragging behind it a rolling ribcage. The road echoed with the cracking of ivory. Impossibly long legs followed, scrabbling down the hill, as if the creature still had life within it and was attempting to stand. From the haunches a long tail swung back and forth. Edgar tipped himself out to the edge of the roof, to gain a better view. He looked down upon the sliding skeleton and laughed. The Professor had said it was not a monster that he was boiling up, but what else could this be? It was a thing from his father's stories: a fire-breathing beast from a foreign land that slept atop a mountain of gold. A creature that would be slain by a bold knight, its head severed from its neck and taken back as a trophy.

On the side of the street people stood frozen, mouths agape at the slippery miracle. And then a dog came running out from the crowd and went racing down the incline, barking out the joy of the hunt. He caught the tail of the beast between his teeth and tugged. It ripped from the haunches. The dog turned in its tracks and went scampering back towards the meadows, with the bone clamped tight in its jaws.

Edgar turned on his perch and followed.

Across the ridges, down the furrows of the gutters, down the brackets of the drainpipes, along the line of the fence, Edgar ran.

The dog squeezed through the railings at the meadow's edge. Edgar crouched on the other side and watched as the dog went about its doglike business. Because a dog must mark its spot and hide its treasure. The dog clawed through soil, buried the bone with a flick of its back legs and ran off.

Edgar waited as the shadows of the trees stretched longer and the dusk gathered. Behind him the streets echoed with cries and commotion, the Professor's voice amongst them. There was the sound of the skeleton striking the cobbles, an eerie kind of music. But Edgar stayed hidden.

The bone symphony faded, twilight came. Edgar jumped the fence and scrabbled at the soil. The tracks of the dog were shovelled away. Down and down Edgar dug, until his hands hit bone. And there was the tail: white ivory gleaming against the dark earth, coiled into a question mark curl. Edgar brushed the dirt from the digits and flexed it in his hand. He looked at the tapering knuckles. So this was anatomy. Underneath skin, underneath flesh and fur and all the slippery matter, the monster was held together by things he knew: the hinges of gates and the links of chains.

Edgar played with the tail, turning every joint in his hand. The larger bones were chipped; the slender tip was missing its end. How happy would the Professor be to have the lost part of his skeleton puzzle returned to him. But what good would that do Edgar? A pat on the head and a shilling in his pocket? And back to the bellows without a thought? It was not enough.

Edgar tucked the bone inside his jacket and walked through the darkening meadow. He took the backstreets to the forge. The door was locked, but the courtyard was scattered with bits of iron and it took Edgar only a moment to find a piece that fitted and could tumble the chambers.

He stoked the fire and pushed at the bellows until the flames roared. He rummaged amongst the ingots. The brass would be missed. The iron too. But common lead was plentiful. Edgar threw it into the pot, piece by piece arching through the air above him and making the metal sing. And with every strike, Edgar laughed. He was a blacksmith, but more than that, he held his fortune and his future in his hand.

By the light of the jumping flame, Edgar took a hand axe and cut the tail at the joints, separating knuckle from knuckle. He copied and cut out his moulds. He smoothed out the furrows of the chipped edges, and where the tip was broken he cut around the end of his little finger to a perfect match.

Edgar put together his fence-ladder once more, climbed it

and peered down into the pot. The rivers of lead roped around each other, a knotted tangle of tails. It was simply a matter of pulling out the one that would fit. Edgar aligned the moulds beneath the spout and tipped the pot. Knuckle by knuckle the metal fell into the waiting forms, and for a moment the tail was a lithe and liquid thing, running red gold. If his father's stories were true and God really had breathed life into all things then Edgar was sure this was how it would have appeared. But it was only a moment: then the air and the lead met and the flame died, leaving solid stuff behind.

He laid the leaden joints out along the floor, and set them side by side with the ivory. A perfect match, but better: the animal as it was before the damage. Edgar bored through the lead with a skewer, matching the hidden hollows of the bone. He broke the moulding blocks with his hammer, cracking their cases, then threw them into the rubble-cluttered corner. The true tail he cast into the fire and watched as the bone crumbled to ash – apart from the tiny tip, that fractured apostrophe of ivory. Edgar skewered it, threaded it with a strip of leather and tied it around his neck as a trophy from the hunt. The leaden joints he bundled into his pocket. As he walked home the forged pieces of tail jangled to the rhythm of his stride, and the ivory tapped against his heart.

When Edgar returned to the cottage his parents were waiting for him. His father stood by the fire, his arms folded, and a look of thunder upon his face. His mother got up from her chair and took Edgar by the shoulders. She turned him around and about. His skin was slick with the stuff of the boiling clouds, which came off upon her fingers in dark and oily stains.

'Edgar Jones,' she said, 'whatever in the world have you been at?'

'Adventuring,' said Edgar with a grin.

'That is not a thing to be done on the Sabbath,' replied Eleanor. 'And certainly not in your church clothes.'

'You are a savage, Edgar,' barked William. 'And you shame me.'

Edgar felt the lead weighing heavy in his pocket. Not for long would his father be ashamed, not once he had the favour of a University man.

'And yet you think this is a cause for amusement,' snapped William. 'But if you will not feed your soul then your body will also go wanting. Go to your room and think upon your transgressions.'

Edgar did. He levered up the loosened floorboards and piece by piece dropped the leaden tail down inside. He lay on his bed and rolled the ivory tip between his fingers.

For a week Edgar's invention lay hidden. Master and apprentice worked side by side in silence, the clang of the hammer and the creak of the bellows beating out the hours. The pot spat and sighed above Edgar's head – a liquid whisper of shared secrets. 'Soon, soon, soon' sighed the pot. Edgar smiled into the ashes. Soon, but not too soon. The more the Professor missed his tail, the more he would delight in Edgar's replacement.

On the Saturday, after the forge shut down its fires, Edgar walked the roads home with a purpose. Whilst his mother was busying herself in the scullery, Edgar slipped the lock of her workroom. For a moment he stood frozen in the centre of the room. The walls were blossoming with colour, clouds of silk set upon nails, billowing out from their fixtures. There were wire nets hanging from the rafters, the skeletons of bells. Reams and reams of lace were piled upon the table, white worms of the stuff – whiter still when set against Edgar's skin. A basket of beads sat beside jewels sparkling in the sunlight. Edgar smiled to look at it. It was not just he who had secrets. His Mama's forbidden room was a treasure trove. A cluster of corset wires were bunched together upon the table. He shoved one in his pocket, grabbed a scrap of silk and locked the door behind him.

As Eleanor stitched together the bones of a bodice, Edgar sat in the room above, threading beads of lead upon the wire. The weight of the metal twisted the wire into a curve, flexing at his touch. Edgar thought that if tails could wink then that's how they would go about it.

By the time Edgar slipped through the railings at the meadow's edge and came to the back of the college, to the place where the Professor had told him his rooms were, the night had gathered over Oxford. The drainpipes crested with ivy made a natural ladder, while the balconies ranging along the open face of the building gave him shadowed corners to hide in. Edgar clambered from perch to perch, searching. The college wall provided a picture album of specimen lives: room upon room, adorned with books, ranging forever up the walls, and desks spilling over with papers. Rooms full of solitary men, scribbling into notebooks or staring into fires. It was like peeping in on his father in the parlour, in duplicate upon duplicate, but every time younger. In other rooms the men gathered in groups, pointing, laughing, brandishing books and papers in their fists. Or in one case, they sat around a table, holding cards feathered out into fans. The thick glass rendered them dumb and ridiculous as they shouted and jeered and threw their hands upon the table. But the Professor was nowhere amongst them.

Edgar looked upwards and saw, at the top of the college, the hooded range of the attic windows, gaping mouths with wide-lipped ledges crowning the brickwork. All dark and lifeless apart from at the far end, where the last window let out a rope of light. He tugged upon the ivy and hauled himself up the guttering. He jumped from sill to sill and put his face to the glass.

On the other side of the window was a world of bones. Feet and claws crouched on the bookshelves. Racks of ribs were lined up along the table top. The floor was scattered with skeleton legs. On the wing-backed chair by the fireplace sat the head of something: an oval of ivory with a flat nose and huge hollow sockets, and a row of crooked teeth grinning at Edgar.

Books were piled up across the floor, balanced at angles against each other, fencing in the bones. On the top of one book stack stood jars clouded with liquid. The reflection of the fire in glass gave the impression of a collection of flames stoppered up. A desk was anchored in a corner and the walls above were feathered with scraps of paper, pinned on top of one another.

Kneeling on the floor, in the midst of it all, was the Professor, his shirtsleeves rolled up, and his back to the window. He reminded Edgar of his father at prayer, except that the Professor's prayer was of a more active kind. He was fishing out small bones from his collection and holding them up to the light.

Out on the ledge, Edgar shivered. Again, a memory of something. The feel of a hand upon his head, holding him down. A flash of bright metal. What had his father told him? That a man who studied anatomy would slice anything apart if it took his fancy. Edgar curled his fingers around the silk-wrapped tail, bunching it in his fist. He would be bold and brave. He knocked upon the glass.

The Professor started. He toppled a tower of books, and the bones danced with the fall. He grabbed his cane and strode to the window, pulling open the sash and thrusting the end of it out into the darkness, slicing through the night as if he was duelling with an invisible foe.

'Who's there?' he cried.

Edgar pushed himself into the corner of the guttering where he could not be tipped from his perch.

'A friend!'

'A strange friend who comes creeping across the rooftops in the cover of darkness. Show yourself!'

'I cannot until you put down your weapon.'

The Professor stilled the swipe of the cane on the sill but did not loosen his grip.

Edgar scuttled into the light and bowed.

'It is Edgar Jones, from the forge!'

'So it is,' said the Professor wryly. 'And under whose instruction do you come spying upon me?'

'I am no spy, sir. I have something for you.'

The Professor stood aside, but still kept his hand grasped tight around the cane.

Edgar clambered in through the window. The claws creeping along the shelves seemed about to pounce, the head on the chair ready to swallow.

'Well?' said the Professor.

Edgar opened up his fist. The Professor plucked the package from it and tugged at the silk. It came away piecemeal, revealing the tail knuckle by knuckle.

The Professor held it up, twisting it this way and that.

'The tail of the giraffe,' he said softly. 'It is a miracle.'

'It is not the real tail, sir. It is a lead copy.'

'I see that, my boy. But it is more than a copy. It is a perfect replica.'

The Professor grasped the top of the tail and the articulated joints fell down in their apostrophe curve.

'There is nothing made of metal that I cannot put together, sir.'

'It seems not,' laughed the Professor.

He kept the tail cradled to his chest as he strode to the fireside, where he shoved aside a tower of books to reveal a cupboard set in the wall. He tugged it open and a cascade of bones came tumbling out. Heads, ribs and legs scattered across the carpet like spillikins.

Edgar hovered by the books. He looked at the wall of paper. It showed a world of cut-open things: a cat, a rat, ropes of blood running red, pockets of flesh, yellow, violet, blue, bunched in between the bones. The mechanisms that his father told him no man was meant to look upon.

'Aha!' cried the Professor.

Edgar turned to see him cradling a bowl of bone. Two broad flanks of ivory stuck out from his stomach like wings set the wrong way round. It looked to Edgar like a kind of muzzle, a large piece of a bridle perhaps, a thing made to tame an animal. But he knew that it was not. It was a part of a creature and no mistake.

The Professor set the thing upon the edge of the table. He took the tail and held it in the gap of air between the bone.

'This is where the specimen was snatched from, do you see? But how to fix it?'

Edgar took a pen and balanced it along the back flanks of the beast. He took the tail and teased out the wire from the top. He looped it around his finger, hooked it over the pen and the tail fell down, just as tails should.

The Professor clapped his hands in delight. 'It fits! It fits to perfection!' He poked the tail. It swung back and forth like a pendulum. 'I don't think you understand what you have done, Edgar Jones,' said the Professor softly. 'This creature was sent upon a ship from Africa. It is the first specimen of its kind to be brought to our shores. Without a tail, it is useless. But with one, it is the crowning jewel of my collection. The first giraffe of England, and I have it!'

Edgar looked down at the haunches. He remembered all the other bits of the beast that had been connected to it. The rolling ribs, the ladder-neck, the skull. He imagined how such a creature would have looked, standing on the prow of a ship as the wild seas tumbled all around it.

'You must forgive my earlier abruptness, my boy,' continued the Professor. 'There are many men in Oxford who are jealous of my bonework and would steal my secrets. But I see now, you and I are of the same mind. We are both on the side of progress.'

'Yes, sir.'

Edgar smiled. He was on the side of the Professor. And there was more to the Professor's work than fetching and carrying and kicking at the bellows, he was sure of it.

'And now we must settle your payment. Although how to quantify such a wonderful piece of workmanship is entirely beyond me.'

'I want no payment,' said Edgar.

'No payment?'

'Not a wage but . . .' Edgar looked at the bones scattered across the room. Grinning, crouching. He would be brave, still.

'But what?' said the Professor gently. 'Do not let formality still your tongue, my boy. If there is something you desire then you must ask for it.'

'I wish . . .'

'What do you wish, Edgar Jones?'

'I wish that you take me as your apprentice.'

The Professor chuckled. 'An apprentice of anatomy? Believe me, if there was such a station it would be yours in an instant. However . . .' He gestured to the papers feathering the wall. 'A scientific life requires hours of study, and you do not strike me as a boy who is made for a life amongst books.'

Edgar looked at the pictures of cut-apart beasts. It seemed to him that some kinds of books were better than others.

'No, indeed, Edgar Jones. It strikes me that you are made for an altogether more adventurous kind of existence.'

As Edgar climbed back down the face of the college and ran home through the backstreets, his heart pounded and the blood roared through his veins. His thundering pulse beat the Professor's words back to him. He was made for adventure.

And in the meantime, he had seen the secrets of stripped-back bone. He had seen the workings of God's own inventions. He may not have broken free of the forge yet, but he would hold those skeleton pieces in his mind, and he would think of how to make them. The tail was just the beginning.

Meanwhile the Professor sat up comparing his diagrams to Edgar's creation. So enamoured was he that he never thought to question how Edgar, who had never appeared for his appointment, had come to know about the loss of the tail. All his attention was fixed upon the miracle of the metal. He pushed the tip of the tail and watched how it marked time with the precision of a metronome. He thought about the great variety of life, and how, even in his ageing years, a mere stripling of a boy might be such a source of great wonder.

It is one thing to be promised a fine future and quite another to sit and wait for it. The better life that the Professor told Edgar he was assured of seemed as dizzyingly distant as the lip of Jacob's pot. Harder still was the way that Edgar saw an echo of the Professor's room in every article at the forge. Whatever Edgar set his hand to took on a boneish aspect. A poker hammered out upon the anvil became the thin thigh of an unknown creature; the links and curves of the bridle a tiny ribcage in the making; the spike-tops of the fence posts the teeth of some huge beast.

It was just the same for Edgar at home. He would see the claw of a great crab in the snap of the fire tongs; his father's instruments, shuttered up in their glass cages, had an echo of the laboratory about them. Even the corsets his mother mended, left hanging upon the arm of a chair, were the skins of an exotic wire-veined creature.

Edgar decided: if the Professor would not give him an apprenticeship of the bones then he would make one himself. He addressed the wall of his father's newspaper.

'Pa,' he said, 'do you have a book of animals?'

The paper snapped back and the cups danced upon the parlour table.

'Animals? Whatever for?'

'I would like to look at them.'

'You are far beyond the age to be amusing yourself with a picture book.'

'Will,' snapped Eleanor, 'how can you expect Edgar to set himself to any kind of study at all when you speak to him as if he is a simpleton?'

William flung his paper upon the table, pushed back his chair and went thundering up the stairs.

In the parlour Eleanor pulled a book from the shelves and set it on the floor in front of her son.

'There was nothing I loved more at your age,' she said softly, 'than getting out into the meadows.'

She opened it, and flowers blossomed from the page. Beyond them, animals: rats, shrews, otters, birds of the air and the water.

Edgar grabbed it and flicked the pages: lop-eared hares, horses, stags of the forest. The paper bristled with fur and feathers, but all seemed unremarkable after the Professor's giraffe. And there were no views of the insides of any of them.

'You keep this as long as you have need,' said Eleanor. 'And never mind what your father says about it.'

Edgar placed the book upon his desk and spent nights drawing the shape of hoof, beak, claw and tusk, and thinking about how such things could be forged. He stowed his sketches beneath his floorboards. The next time the Professor had the need for a broken bit of animal he would be ready.

It never occurred to Edgar that the Professor might come back for him, and only him.

It was a crisp February morning. Edgar had been at the forge for less than an hour. The coals were black with just specks of red at the heart of them, their fiery eyes inching open with every push of the bellows.

There was a knock at the door and then there was the Professor, striding up to the furnace.

'Master Salt!' he declared, taking Jacob's hand and shaking it firmly. 'I come to you with a most urgent proposition.'

'What might that be, sir? A ladle as tall as the forge to fit your boiling pot?'

The Professor smiled. 'Alas, no. I fear my boiling days have been curtailed.'

'Then what, sir?'

'It is a sensitive request. I have come to borrow your apprentice.'

'Borrow!' barked Jacob. 'And will you send me one of your scholars to sit at the bellows in his place?'

'I do confess, I can think of a handful of gentlemen whose attentiveness might benefit from a day in the forge. But no, sir. All I can offer you in return is compensation.'

The Professor handed a purse across to Jacob. He pulled at the string and a cascade of coins fell into his hand.

Jacob stamped upon the bellows, sending up a feathered cloud of smoke.

'Take him, sir, and perhaps you can put some sense into him whilst you are about it.'

The world outside the forge was bright and full of noise. The carts were thundering down Cornmarket. The working boys pitched their goods across to their masters. Edgar smiled to see them. For this day he was different from all these boys, and their set apprenticeships. The Professor had come and taken him out of the forge. And for what? For the piecing together of some broken beast, he was sure of it. Claw, hoof, head, tusk – he could cut any one out of a mould. And then the Professor would invent a station for Edgar accordingly. Edgar would cast off his forge clothes. He would be given a gown and a cane, and no man would stop him at the door of the college. And his father would be as proud as proud could be.

The Professor cut through the crowds with sure-footed strides and Edgar had to run at his heels to keep pace with him. It took Edgar a moment to understand that they were not setting back to the Professor's college. They were turning down a side street, and all sound of trade folded away behind them.

'Please, sir, where are we off to?'

'Patience, Edgar Jones, patience.'

They emerged on to Broad Street. They walked past the ring of the Sheldonian statues, which looked down at Edgar from their plinths, wide-eyed, as if they were as surprised as he at this turn of events.

The Professor steered Edgar left at the crossroads. They passed the last of the colleges: castle-fronted Wadham. There was nothing ahead but the road and the parkland spreading out on either side, with Edgar's fences set along the boundary. Freedom, just the other side of the iron.

They rounded a curve in the street, and there was a gap in the fencing: a gateway. Beyond it stood a construction the like of which Edgar had never seen before. The yellow stone was clad in a second skin of wood: planks and poles roped around in a scaffold, as if the building was being kept in a cage.

As well it might be. The sandstone edifice sat in the centre of the University Parks, with row upon row of arched windows looking out across the land. It gave the impression of a crouching creature, many-eyed, watchful. In the middle of the wall was an arched wooden door, rearing up between the windows – a great mouth. The structure was skirted by a wasteland of rubble. It seemed to Edgar that this rock-beast had pushed itself up from under the earth, uprooting the parkland on its way into the world.

Edgar looked up to the rooftop. There, thrusting out from the slate, was the stump of a tower. This was unlike any tower that Edgar had seen in Oxford. It was a great wedge of a thing, topped by a lattice of joists, combing the clouds. The unfinished nature of it all set Edgar's blood racing. He had never thought that the buildings of Oxford were like the fences set around them: put together piece by piece.

The Professor was steering him across the mud, under the scaffold, towards the door.

'Please, sir,' said Edgar, breathless, 'what is this place?'

The Professor took a key from his pocket and tumbled the lock. The dark eyes of the unglazed windows stared down at Edgar.

'At present, it is neither one thing nor the other, Edgar Jones, as you will see for yourself.'

Behind the door there was a shallow set of steps, a second archway, and another door opening into the belly of the building. There was a vast courtyard, squared by a two-tier gallery, set with columns of polished marble. The courtyard floor was a churned-up field of mud. And sitting in the centre of it: a magnificent monster of metal.

It stood on legs as thick as tree trunks, legs upon legs, too many to count. Its back reared up to the height of the walls. Its belly was a knot of sparkling silver. And upon its back, a pair of vast iron wings, crosshatched like fences. It was as if all the crawling and flying things that Edgar had ever pulled out of the wilderness had been somehow stitched together, cast in iron, and rendered huge.

And then there was the sound of it. The courtyard rang with the beating of iron against iron, as if the creature was thrumming its wings, preparing for flight.

'So, Edgar Jones,' said the Professor. 'What do you make of this?'

'It is wonderful.'

The Professor laughed drily. 'Oh, it is wonderful, no doubt,' he replied. 'A wonderful expense for the University. And a wonderful asset for my enemies.'

'I don't understand, sir.'

'Come, come, child, do you think that this is what was intended?'

The Professor followed the shape of the beast with the tip of his cane. Edgar squinted along the line of it and saw, where the iron was set upon the ground, there were squat stone plinths, rising from the earth, like hoofs that were utterly cloven. The stone was blasted apart and in the heart of it, a cluster of split spurs, shattered ribs. Stuck under the bow legs were huge blocks of wood, anchoring them. The clatter of the iron was not the beating of the wings at all, but all the buckled pieces rolling against each other. The creature was a broken thing. It would take more than the casting of a tail, knuckle by knuckle, to fix it.

'It is split apart from itself, sir.'

'Yes, yes,' snapped the Professor. 'All that should be upwards has plummeted downwards, much to the delight of my enemies.'

Edgar looked at the iron and tried to turn it around in his mind, like he turned the curves of the bridles over and over upon the floor of the forge. Upwards. Downwards. The tangled legs stretching up and up. A ribcage. A net cast across the sky. A great arch. Like a thing he had seen before. Like the vaulted ceiling stretching above the college gates.

'It was a roof, sir?'

A roof of iron, pouring down in great rivers from the lip of a giant's pot. Set across the courtyard and pieced together, spur by spur. Poorly set.

'I did not bring you here to tell me things that are already known to me. I need to find the cause. My enemies are already claiming that the levelling of the roof is the will of God.'

Edgar squinted up at the sickly sagging iron. He thought about the God of his father's Bible, with His floods and His plagues and His punishments.

'Why would God do such a thing?'

The Professor chuckled. 'That is my argument entirely. This

place is intended to be a museum that glorifies all of His works. It is a nonsense of philosophy that He would smite it down.' The Professor pointed his cane up at the broken metal as if he could push the rolling spurs secure into the sky. 'I have had enough of the engineers, who are so fearful of the collapse that they cannot reach any fixed conclusion. Which is why I have come to you, my boy.'

'This is like nothing I have ever seen at the forge, sir.'

'And I doubt you ever saw a boiling pot or a tail before you wrought them. Use your wits, Edgar Jones.'

Edgar stepped towards the structure. It rocked and rattled at his approach. He passed by the wooden blocks. Beyond them, the iron was knitted together into a tight knot. Edgar put his hand upon a bar of it and pushed. The iron scraped and screamed and opened above him and he burrowed his way through into the tangled heart of it.

The Professor was gone. There was nothing but the bright shining metal arching over his head. Edgar saw the run of the rivets. He saw where struts had been ripped apart: dark mouths with jagged teeth. He saw, hanging above, iron flowers, ferns, grasses sprouting from the spurs, as if the creature had come galloping out of some great steely wilderness, with the remnants of the forest still caught upon its bones. But there, in the midst of all that was broken, a set of spurs stood whole. They had fallen in straight lines, like a fence set sideways. Like a ladder.

Edgar set his foot upon it and hauled himself up, up and up through the innards. Beyond, the broken bits stabbed the sky. He could see how metal had fallen upon metal, pushing it down, down, down. The wind played across the apertures, whistling around Edgar, an eerie kind of music. But the metal that Edgar set his foot to stayed sure and true. He clambered onwards, upwards, and laughed as he did so. This was freedom and no mistake. He was climbing out of the forge as surely as he climbed the arms of the apple tree to be rid of his lessons. Up, up and up he went, beyond the shadowed heart of the structure, up towards where the metal sparkled silver.

He felt a breeze playing upon his skin, and there, opening before him, was the clear blue sky, with birds wheeling across it. Three more struts, two, one, and Edgar poked his head through the gap. He set his hands upon the bracing bar and pulled himself out into the sunlight. Clouds raced before him. Edgar felt that if he just stretched out his hand he could plunge his fingers into the thick of them. There, spiking the clouds were the roofs of Oxford. And there stood the angels, their swords drawn and their spears sharpened.

Edgar looked down at the mass of metal beneath him. He was sitting upon the backbone of a huge and wonderful beast. Why, if it took his fancy, he could kick upon its ribs and set it thundering down the streets of Oxford. He could ride it up to his father's college and command it to knock upon the door with its steely great foot, and wouldn't that be a thing?

The iron was calling out his name. 'Edgar! Come down! Immediately! Edgar Jones!'

Edgar squinted down at the courtyard. There, at the foot of the creature, was the Professor, waving his cane, nothing more than a needle-thin stick slicing through the air. Those open mouths of torn spurs were carrying his cries. Edgar waved his cap to the Professor, and then to the angels, slipped himself off the backbone and began his descent.

As he climbed down it was as if the iron knew that he was its master. It opened up footholds and handholds. When he came to land upon the courtyard floor the iron jumped also, and the structure spat out a spur.

The Professor dragged him out from under the shadow of the skeleton.

'That was a dangerous bit of sport, and not at all what I intended.'

'I needed to get up close, sir, to see the metal. It is no higher than your rooms in college.'

'That's a different matter entirely.'

Edgar and the Professor stood looking at the swaying beast, listing from side to side as if it were trying to wrench itself free from the earth.

'I know why it is broken,' said Edgar, shouting above the screech of the metal.

'And am I to guess the cause, or will you deign to tell me?'

'The iron was wrought when it should have been cast, sir.'

'Explain.'

'The metal of the arches is hollow and weak. The wings crushed it.'

'Wings?'

'The larger panels at the top of it.'

The Professor sighed and beat his cane gently against his palm. 'My chief engineer confessed as much. This is the trouble with new invention. Grand plans often involve grand disaster. So what is to be done? Must it all be pulled apart?'

'Yes, sir, but it must be done from the top.'

'And why is that?'

Edgar pointed into the heart of the collapse. Iron was knotted in amongst iron, a stout trunk of metal.

'All the support is at the bottom. It would be like cutting one of your skeletons off at the legs, sir, and still expecting it to stand.'

The Professor shook his head and laughed. The iron echoed the laughter back to him.

'Tell me, Edgar Jones, would you have any interest in assisting me with the dismantling?'

'Oh, it would take more than you and me to shift it, sir.'

The Professor smiled. 'No doubt it would. My suggestion is that you join our company of ironworkers.'

Edgar looked up at the silver-bright spurs, shimmering across the sky. To be up there, alongside the angels. To be out in the light and the air, with the sun and the wind and the seasons. No more soot and smoke and burning coals. No more Master Salt laughing at him from the shadows.

'I would, sir, but my master—'

'I suspect that your master is ruled by the purse rather than the set terms of contract. Do not worry yourself, my boy. We will have you out of the forge and into the museum within the week.'

The Professor was correct. When he told Jacob of his intention, the blacksmith laughed until the forge walls rang.

'Take him,' he cried. 'And I wish you luck with him. Though I think you would be better boiling him up in that great pot of yours and be done with it.'

The Professor smiled as Jacob went rooting around for Edgar's papers. It was a source of constant surprise to him the way that men very rarely recognised the worth of what they gazed upon. But all the better for him. If every man had his keen perception then the world would be overcrowded with collectors.

Jacob handed over the apprentice papers.

'There is a payment due for the breaking of the contract,' he, said stabbing at the page, utterly obscuring the figure with the fatness of his thumb. 'And his father's signature is needed to secure it.'

'Neither of which should provide any obstacle.'

'What the University wants the University gets, isn't that so, sir? Although why you should set such store by Edgar is a mystery.'

The Professor's conversation with William at the lodge had a similar air of disbelief about it.

'Edgar Jones, my son – are you sure of it, sir?'

'As sure as you are that he is your son, so sure am I of his worthiness for the University's attention.'

William looked through the glass at this old man, in his professor's gown, who just a second before had come striding up to the lodge, thrust his hand through the window and given William the sort of handshake that a long-lost friend might give.

'Professor, I feel it is my duty to inform you, I do not know what skills my son has boasted of, but he has not yet grasped his letters.'

'Letters are of no concern,' said the Professor. 'It is my opinion that your son has a different kind of cleverness.'

'A different kind?' William thought of Edgar's high-whistling first words, and all the words that followed them.

'And if Edgar was any other way then I would not have such an urgent use for him.'

'Use?' echoed William. Books and instruments were things that were used. A boy was a boy.

'I do believe that it is not just the intellectual faculties that separates man from the beasts,' continued the Professor. 'I believe much of God's favour is manifested in the way that He has put us together.'

'Put us together?'

The Professor chuckled and spread his hand out, contorting it this way and that. William was not sure whether he was expected to shake it or to strike against it. He did neither.

'The versatility of the digits,' said the Professor with a grin. 'That is what makes a man a man. The ability to make monuments that are a fitting reflection of our higher nature.' The Professor traced out the skyline of the college with the tip of his cane as if he were etching out a theorem on a blackboard. 'What your son needs is to learn how to ally his mind to his making. And this is what the University proposes to teach him.'

'So Edgar will be given lessons?'

'Yes, Porter Jones, and in a manner that is altogether more suited to him than the study of books.'

William frowned. Books and learning were the selfsame thing – what else could the University sanction? And yet anything had to be better for Edgar than the forge. William could feel the argument drifting away from him in the twilight, fading at the edges and turning dark. He would not allow Edgar's opportunity to drift away with it.

'You said that there were papers?'

The Professor handed over the documents, and there it was: proof that prayers are answered. The University crest shone out of the page.

William signed his name across the bottom with great speed, as if he feared the Professor might rip the contract away.

'Excellent!' cried the Professor. 'This is a fortuitous day for the University and for Edgar Jones.'

Then he shoved the papers under his arm, bowed to William and was gone.

It was only as the tap tap tap of the cane upon the cobbles retreated under the archway that William realised that the air was thick with questions unsaid. The Professor had spoken of a museum and iron, and a cathedral for all creation. But the Professor had said nothing of his own station within the University, and nothing of the title that would be bestowed upon Edgar.

It was no matter. Had not William, quite literally, been plucked from the gutter by the University, and set upon a higher path? It would go the same way for his son.

And so it was that Edgar was released from the forge, dusted down, reclad and sent back out into Oxford on an entirely different trajectory. The apprentice papers were framed and set upon the parlour wall, the seal of the University outshining the fading scriptures.

Only Eleanor, as she starched Edgar's shirt and set about stitching together the apron of the ironworker, viewed the quick twist of fate with suspicion. A man of the University did not go seeking out working boys and showing them such favour without some plan in mind, she knew that for certain.

PART THREE

On the morning that Edgar was set to take his place at the Museum there was no wall of newspaper set between father and son. William reached across the slope of the table and took his son's hand.

'Such an opportunity as this is all I could wish for you, Edgar,' he said. 'It is a remarkable blessing.'

Edgar smiled. He smiled for the feel of his father's hand in his again. And he also smiled at all the things that his father did not know – the way that opportunity was a thing that could be forged: by the casting of a pot, by the mimicking of bone with lead, and by climbing brick, gutter and metal to get to his future.

'Yes, Pa.'

'You must set your mind to whatever course of study the Professor has prepared for you. No matter what, you must not shirk from it.'

Edgar smiled again. He thought of the great creature of iron, with its spine stretched up to the sky.

'Yes, Pa.'

'Well, then, let us set out for this Museum of yours.'

The March morning was spun with a fine mist that clouded the air. Eleanor watched from the window as Edgar and William strode through the wilderness, out of the gate, round the bend of the street and were swallowed by the fog. Edgar, hands in his pockets, matched his father stride for stride, so like his father in the way that he went marching down the street as if he owned it. A man in the making.

As they walked through the mists together, William thought of himself at Edgar's age, stuck in the catacombs of the college kitchen. He thought of how often he had dreamt of his father coming to rescue him. A man with his own features, appearing at the side of the cooking pots, peering down at him through the steam, taking his hand and leading him away from the muck and heat, out into the bright new day, out towards a better future.

As they walked through Oxford the fog was opening and closing curtains across the faces of the colleges. The angels came and went from the rooftops, smiling down at Edgar as though they knew of his new life and were granting him their blessing.

Father and son took the turn off St Giles, down towards the parkland. Edgar's fence spiked the fog. Edgar ran his hand along the bars; the metal was slippery to the touch.

'I made this, Pa,' he said.

William looked at the line of iron, then back at his son. 'Well, it is a blessing that now you can set your skills to a nobler cause.'

Edgar scowled. His father kept a gate. He should favour fences too.

They came to the gap in the railings, and the wide white expanse of fog behind it, and the Museum, somewhere beyond, in the thick of it.

'This is it, Pa.'

'I should hand you over to the Professor, Edgar.'

But Edgar shook his head and went running through the gateway before William could stop him. William stood by the fence, watching his son run and run until he was just a shadow, a shape in the mist, and then was gone.

In the heart of the parkland stood the Museum. But it was not as Edgar remembered. The fog rolled around it, revealing a window here, a buttress there. The tower was lost in the clouds, as if it had been snapped off in the night. The mist was loosening the stones, and the whole place was shifting and shimmering in the air. Nothing was settled. Nothing was safe.

Edgar thought of the steely creature caught behind the bricks. He imagined its stump feet dragging across the courtyard, kicking at the walls, shunting the structure across the land. The air was thick with chatter, and through the fog Edgar could see the shape of men. Then, with his black cloak and his cane, there was the Professor, moving amongst them. Edgar felt a pang in his heart. He was one of many, all of whom the Professor favoured.

He loitered at the edges of the crowd, clenching his fists in his pockets. But then the Professor turned on his heel and was striding towards him.

'Edgar Jones!' he hollered. 'Edgar Jones, indeed.' He put his hand upon Edgar's shoulder. 'This rogue weather belies the occasion,' he declared. 'This is a happy day for the Museum.

All that has gone awry will be set straight again, I am sure of it.'

The chatter silenced as the Professor led Edgar up to the entrance, and under the scaffold.

'Men!' the Professor cried. 'I salute your courage in your return to the Museum in these difficult times. I do not need to tell you that Master Thomas was an irreplaceable man. But I sincerely believe the best way to honour our friend's memory is to continue his work and hold him in our hearts at every rivet and every fixture.' He clapped his hands together.

A few of the men echoed the applause – a few, but not many.

'I also do not need to tell you that we require a full company of men to complete the work. Therefore, gentlemen, allow me to introduce to you the ingenious Edgar Jones.'

The Professor pushed Edgar forward. Edgar stumbled. The fog was wrapping itself around the men and he could not make out the shape of them. And there was a muttering coming out of the mist, a jeering.

And a shout: 'A child cannot do the work of a man!'

Somewhere behind Edgar the Professor laughed.

'Quite true, sir, quite true,' he chuckled. 'But a child may do the work of a child, which can be an inspiration to us all.'

In the courtyard, the metal creature was changed. It stood cloud-headed, a great dragon of a thing. The fog swallowed the sound of the rolling iron and the walls rang with long, low bellows – the cries of a wounded animal. The shifting air made it animate, as if it were pawing the ground.

Edgar shivered. The Professor may have taken him from the forge, but he had taken him to play the part of another man, a man who had been lost. Edgar was certain that this iron skeleton was the cause of it. And now the Professor was pushing him closer and closer to it.

A ladder was roped against the structure, stretching up to the clouds. Beside the ladder stood a squat man with a wide face crowned by a thick thatch of fair hair. He was squinting at the metal and scribbling furiously into a notebook.

'Edgar Jones, may I introduce Mr S, our chief engineer.'

The man glanced at Edgar. 'When you told me you were apprenticing a boy to the cause you did not tell me he was such an infant.'

'I am a good worker, sir,' said Edgar.

'This is more than a matter of work, boy. The iron is a dangerous thing. You need to have an understanding of it.'

'I know that I must respect the metal, sir. My old master taught me so.'

'Your master at the forge? An apprenticeship of barrel-hoops and fence posts is hardly the same craft.'

Beside them, the structure let out a great groan as if it were waking from a long sleep.

Beyond that sound, there were others: creaking and swaying and knocking, and men shouting. Edgar looked down the courtyard and saw the ironworkers marching through the doorway, two by two, with great lengths of wood set upon their shoulders. The planks were studded with bolts and spikes of iron. It reminded him of his hiding place, the floorboards under his bed, pulled apart and rendered huge.

Mr S marched across and began to kick at the bolts as if he were trying to split the parts away from each other. Other men came carrying huge rolls of rope. They tossed them upon the ground and the tongues of hemp snaked across the floor.

'You must not take Mr S's demeanour to heart,' said the Professor. 'He fears that his reputation has fallen along with the roof.'

Edgar looked up at the buckled iron. A roof could fall, a reputation could fall, a boy could fall also. Fall down, down and down, right into the heart of the beast, where the ribs were split and the metal stood like a line of spears. But his papa had told him: he must set himself to the work the Professor prepared for him, no matter what.

Edgar watched as the men ran the ropes through the bolts, tying the wood together. Not one of them so much as looked at him.

The men took the ropes in their fists and tugged. The wood lifted slowly, creaking and swaying, like a long-limbed animal struggling to stand, until the tapering top of it was swallowed by the mists. Hanging down from the centre came a thick length of rope. The machine set side by side with the structure looked like a second creature: a beast of wood with a great lolling tongue, set to feed upon the metal bones.

The men cheered, ringing the walls. Mr S emerged from the ranks with a brass speaking tube set to his mouth. To Edgar, it gave him the same aspect as the broad-bellied ducks that charted the canal at the bottom of the wilderness.

'Master Jones!' he quacked. 'Are you ready to prove that you are the kind of boy that the Professor declares you to be?'

'Yes, sir!' shouted Edgar. But his voice wavered, and when he set his foot upon the ladder, it trembled.

'Have courage,' said the Professor.

Edgar looked up the line of the ladder. Mist crowned the

top. He shivered. The Professor was urging him up into nothingness.

Behind him, the wood creaked and the men muttered.

'Master Jones!' quacked Mr S again.

Edgar gripped the bars of the ladder in his fists. It was either upwards into the fog, or out the door and back to the forge. He began to climb.

The ladder had the wide-spaced rungs of a man's stride and Edgar had to stretch to gain his footholds. Up and up he climbed, and the wood struck against the iron, beating out his progress. It was a different thing to be clambering up the outside of the tangle than through the innards. The metal rolled against the wood, twisting against the pressure.

Edgar felt the creature rearing up against him, ready to shrug him from its back. Courage, the Professor had said, and Edgar would be courageous. He had clambered through a great black cloud at the top of the Professor's college. He had climbed through the dark night, hauling himself up ropes of ivy, with a tail in his pocket. But this was different. The iron shifted, and the air shifted, and nothing was clear and nothing was fixed. This was a place where a man could get lost, swallowed up by the uncertain air. And a man had. Or was he here still, waiting?

The knock knock knocking of the ladder became the footsteps of this Master Thomas, clambering up behind him. And the cold breeze that tickled Edgar's skin became his breath. This man whose place Edgar had taken. This man who would pitch him from his perch if he caught him. Edgar's heart quickened and he was hauling himself hand over fist, hand over fist, faster, faster. From between the rungs of the ladder the iron lurched out towards him, jagged mouths, broken bones. He climbed up, up and up, outracing his own heartbeat until there was no more ladder, just the shadow-shape of a spur above.

Edgar inched himself on to it. The spur had a slippery surface and was so cold that it burnt like fire. Edgar could feel the great distance yawning open beneath him. He could feel it, but he could not see it. All the world had been erased. There was no Oxford, no angels, no sunlight, just thick-fogged emptiness. Then there was a creak of wood, and a sound of distant thunder and Edgar looked up to see the air above him shifting, and something coming burrowing out of the cloud. A thick black eel of a thing, whipping through the air, twisting, turning. It the struck upon the metal and the structure lurched. Edgar cried out. The iron called back.

'Edgar Jones!' The iron took the Professor's voice and turned it steely.

'Here!' cried Edgar.

He squinted into the mist. The tumbling worm lay still; the fat rope, set dangling before him.

He ran it in and out, around a spur, pulled again. There was a cry from beneath, the rope ran taut and the knot tightened. The iron trembled, like an animal pulling against its tether.

Back on the ground, Edgar watched as the men set themselves to the machine and hauled. The metal screamed as if it was a living thing. The spur came swinging out of the clouds, rocking this way and that, catching against twisted pillar and post as it came down. Metal sang against metal and the whole structure shuddered and reshaped itself.

Three times Edgar went up into the great wide white

nothing, and back again. Three spurs were lifted. Edgar's palms were cut open by the running of the rope across them. And, at the end of the day, as the mist was burnt away by the dying sun, the structure revealed itself again. It lurched to one side, a creature whose back had been broken.

The Professor came to stand at Edgar's side.

'I do declare, Edgar Jones, you are a champion of the iron and no mistake.' He patted Edgar on the head – more as if he was child than a champion.

On the other side of the courtyard Mr S quacked away to his men as they gathered their satchels and piled out of the Museum in a wave of chatter. Apart from one. A tall man with a mop of red hair loitered in the east gallery and called across.

'Boy!'

The iron rang with the sound of it, boy, boy, boy, echoing through the chamber. The man was standing with a hand braced about a polished pillar. He was thickset and his arms were roped around with muscles. He could push the very bricks from their settings if he had a mind to.

'You, boy.'

'My name is Edgar Jones,' called Edgar. Boy was the name that he had in the forge. Not here. Jones, Jones, Jones, called back the iron, pealing out his name, but not all of it. And now the man was striding across the courtyard and coming to stand beside him.

'My name is Master Fisher, and you would do well to remember it.'

'Why?'

'Why?' Fisher laughed. 'Because I am the only man who might speak the plain clear truth of your situation.' Fisher crouched down on his haunches and turned Edgar round to face him. 'And the truth is this, you should quit this work immediately. There is great danger in it.'

Edgar looked up at the beast with its broken back. The metal caught the sunset and the bones looked as if they were running with blood, or fire, or both.

'The Professor says that I am the champion of the iron.'

'Well, he would say that, boy, to flatter you. He has no more understanding of ironwork than you or I do of the savages of Timbuktu. The truth is, he is gambling with your life in setting you to such a task.'

Edgar thought of all the bones crouching in the Professor's attic. All the boiled-back split-apart things. All the things that once had life but now did not.

'He would not, sir.'

'He would, boy. He has done it before.'

Edgar thought of the Professor, standing on the Museum steps, and the men glaring out of the mist at him.

'Master Thomas . . .?'

'That's right, boy. Master Thomas knew the ways of iron like no other man in the company. As we set about the roof he was always peering up at it, saying look to the detail, the detail, men. And what do you think your precious Professor said to that?'

Edgar shrugged.

'He pulled Master Thomas up before us all and he shamed him. He called him a coward – and this to a man who had spent his life upon metal.'

'Why?'

'Why? Because all that your Professor cared for was getting

the roof up as quick as he could and damn the consequences. He is not a man to be trusted. He can change his favour in an instant if you do not fit with his schemes.'

Not a man to be trusted? Edgar frowned. The Professor was a University man, and had not his father told him that the University was a place where men became the best kind of men that they could be. And more than that, the Professor had plucked him out of the forge and told him he was made for better things. Was this a lie also?

'Are you listening to me, boy?' snapped Fisher.

'Yes, sir. So what became of Master Thomas, sir?'

'He did what any man would do. He set out to save his reputation. He returned to the Museum at night, set his ladder to the spurs, that very ladder that you were dancing up and down today, climbed up to the top of it, set out across the structure – and what do you think happened then?'

Edgar looked at the mass of metal, the torn-apart howling mouths at the heart of it.

'It fell.'

'It did indeed, taking Master Thomas with it. His bones were smashed to pieces and the floor ran thick with his blood.

Edgar stared out into the courtyard. For a moment the mud ran blood red, churned up, stewing.

'You have stepped into a dead man's shoes, boy, and as such you will never find favour with any of the men here. You should quit this place before the iron gobbles you up as it did Master Thomas.'

Edgar turned his back and he ran. He ran out of the door, under the scaffold, out into the parkland. Gobbled up, Master Fisher had said. As if he knew the iron as Edgar knew it: a tethered monster. The sunset sky spread above was the blood of Master Thomas, cast up on the canvas of the clouds. The pace of Edgar's footsteps beat out his fears. The Professor would sacrifice him. He would. He would not.

When Edgar pushed open the cottage door he found his father sitting in his chair, snapping the cloth across his boots, and his mother setting out the supper things. As if the world was the same place that it had been yesterday.

'The man of the Museum returns!' cried William. 'So, tell me, how went it?'

Edgar hesitated. A part of him wanted to tell his father the truth of it. That lonely and misted place at the top of the iron. The whipping line of rope.

'Well, Pa.'

'And the Professor was satisfied?'

Edgar frowned. He could feel the Professor's hand on his back, pushing him towards the metal. Pushing up towards the place where a man had fallen.

'He says that I am a champion of the iron.'

William grinned. 'Do you hear that, Eleanor? His first day at work amongst men of learning, our son is told he is a champion?'

'Is he indeed?' replied Eleanor, not ceasing from her placing of the china upon the tablecloth.

That night when Edgar lay down to sleep, every part of his body ached, as if it was his own skeleton that had been pulled apart, limb by limb. And his ears rang with the clank and the clatter of the iron, and the mist-muffled groan of it. Very like the cries of a man whose bones were smashed apart. But above it all, there was the Professor's voice, and his father's echo of it. He was a champion. And his father loved a champion much more than he loved a boy from the forge.

Edgar returned to the Museum resolved. He had not feared the iron beast the first time he set foot on it, when it was just him and the Professor, and the open courtyard and the metal sparkling in the sunlight. He had rode upon the back of it and laughed. He would not be frightened away from the work. He would take Master Fisher's story and he would use it. Look to the detail, Master Thomas had urged. And Edgar did. He listened to the iron and learnt the language of it: the way that the weaker parts moaned if he stepped upon them. No, no, no, they said, and Edgar would shift his weight away, and take a different path across the shifting bones.

As the metal was lifted, spur by spur, Edgar's fear was carried away with it. The more time Edgar spent up in the heights of the iron, the more he became like the thing he worked upon: steely and strong. The spring weather turned, and there was no more mist, no more ghostly footsteps, just the bright sunshine, picking out the silver pathways up in the clouds. Edgar grew to love his sky-perch, from where he could peer down at Fisher and his companions scuttling along the lines on the ropes, like flies caught in a web. He whistled out at the birds as he marched along the metal, he swung round spurs, skipped across rivets and waved his cap at the angels.

The parlour became a second Museum as Edgar built the tangle of the metal out of the supper things, using his mother's thread to demonstrate the methods of removal.

His father smiled and asked: 'And what of the Professor – is he satisfied with your progress?'

'He is, Pa.'

Whilst William applauded, Eleanor stood silent by his shoulder, looking down at Edgar's hands, gripped tight around the silver. They were red raw and patterned with blisters.

She poured out her misgivings in the only place she could: into the confidence of Mrs Simm.

'I would rather have Edgar back at the forge and set with a proper trade than this labour under the Professor, which is nothing but skivvy's work.'

'But father and son are reconciled?'

'Oh, now that Edgar has been taken up by the University he cannot set a foot wrong.'

'And Edgar is content with the work?'

'He is. Morning and night the talk is of the Museum and little else.'

'You should not fret so much, Mrs Jones. We both know that talent finds its true path. And in the meantime, it is better for a boy to have his father's favour than not.'

Eleanor shook her head, and frowned down at the tangle of corset wires piled up before her.

'There is father's favour and there is mother's intuition, Mrs Simm. There is more to this Museum than Edgar is letting on, I am sure of it.'

There was some truth in Eleanor's misgivings. Amongst all these lessons of courage and construction there were other things that Edgar was learning. Things that he would not reveal at the parlour table. He was learning that the hearts of men are not at all like iron. They do not bend with the pressure of time, but rather they harden and become utterly fixed. Every morning Edgar would greet his fellows, and every morning they would turn their backs to him. Often, at the close of the day, he would open his satchel to find some token of their affections: a piece of paper scrawled upon with text that he could not read; a padded pair of bloomers, the kind of thing that would be worn by a child who could not control his motions, and, once, a bird with its neck wrung.

Most of all, Edgar was learning something that his mother had learnt before him: that life was a thing to be weighed in a balance. And set against all the ironworkers' silence, there were countless more words of praise from the Professor. Edgar had a born agility, he was the epitome of courage, he was a paragon of virtue and an exemplary man amongst the metal. These were not the words of a man who did not care for him.

Edgar took these words home, and, when translated by his father, and matched by his smile and a rough embrace, Edgar had no doubt that the balance was weighed in his favour.

But it is the nature of a set of scales that they do not stay fixed. The structure shrunk, down, down, until it was just a few feet high. Edgar's ladder was abandoned, and he was back as he had started: hauling himself up the innards. There, at the heart was other iron than pillars and posts: there were flowers and grasses, cast out of metal. Edgar burrowed his way inside and undid them from the rivets, and took them out to the Professor: sharp, steely posies, set out across the Museum floor.

The Professor crouched down in the mud and ran his hands

across them, as if they were the most precious things in the world.

'See how beautiful metal can be, Edgar Jones,' he said, 'when it is used to echo the work of our Creator.'

But Edgar was not listening. He was looking over the Professor's shoulder at the pile of iron that was left, the wide expanse of the courtyard stretching all around it, and the men with their ropes, tugging at it from every angle. There was nothing creaturelike about it any more; it was just a stack of scrap metal.

Then one day it was done. There was nothing but the split pillars sprouting from the shattered stone. Two by two, the ironworkers hoisted the metal from its bearings. Edgar watched on from the edges as the pieces were hauled up on to the men's shoulders and carried out of the door. Edgar was left alone, landlocked, staring up at the great mass of sky far above him, impossible to get back into.

The Professor came to stand beside him.

'What now, sir?' asked Edgar quietly.

'Come, my boy, do you think this is my final intention?' The Professor swept across the empty expanse of air with his cane. 'No, Mr S has his instructions. The roof will be remade at his foundry, and it will return sure and sturdy by the New Year, he has assured me.'

'Not for the Museum, sir, for me.'

The Professor chuckled. 'Why, do you fear that I will cast you out, Edgar Jones?'

Cast out and cast back into the soot and heat of the forge, with nothing to set his hand to but the bellows.

'I would not do that to my best boy. This is more than a

place of apprenticeship, Edgar. The Museum is your home now.'

'My home?'

Edgar looked across the open courtyard. He thought of how he had gazed down at the cottage from the top of the apple tree. Nothing more than a dirty pebble. This was an altogether better place.

Edgar, however, soon discovered that whilst the Museum was still his home, with the iron gone his place within it was very different. The ironworkers were replaced by stonemasons, who set their ladders along the western side of the gallery and chipped away at the plinths that held the pillars. The Professor walked amongst them, pulling out plants from his pockets and hanging them upon the tops of their ladders. Edgar, scuttling along in the Professor's wake, listened to his declarations: their work was exemplary; it was the epitome of craftsmanship; they were rendering nature immortal. And with every word that rang down the gallery to Edgar, there were Fisher's words echoing behind it: the Professor could change his favour in an instant. It seemed there was truth in it: the Professor now had eyes only for the stones and the men who worked upon them.

To the stonemasons Edgar was just a boy, a child to be shouted at down the run of the gallery: fetch! He would sit at their feet, sweeping away their chippings and sharpening their tools. There was some kind of pleasure in the feel of the instrument in his hand, the sparking of fire from the iron and the whetstone. But this was small work, and there was no bravery or adventure about it. Above him, the stone leaves unfurled, set like spears against the rock. Sometimes, when the stonemasons had quit the gallery, Edgar ran from ladder to ladder, swapping the specimens about, just for something to set his hand to.

Back at the cottage, his father's questions continued.

'And what now, from this Professor of yours?'

Edgar frowned. The Professor was not *his* Professor – that was the whole trouble. Still, he would give his father an answer that would make him proud.

'He is giving me lessons, Pa.'

'Lessons, indeed?' grinned William. 'Of what kind?'

Edgar thought of the way the samples set upon the ladder tops became set in the rocks.

'Lessons about copying.'

'You never were much of a copier, Edgar, as I remember it. You must be most diligent in your work if you are to remain the Professor's champion.'

Edgar frowned down at his plate and did not answer. What would his father say if he knew the truth of the matter? That he was a fetcher and a carrier and a champion of nothing.

Once, in the height of summer, when Edgar had been at the Museum for more than a year the Professor showed something of his old favour to him. He took him down to the Botanical Gardens: a maze of lawns cut up into segments and sections, with flowers and grasses and bushes and trees ranging far and wide. The Professor strode through it, stopping every now and then and pulling at the top of his cane. Pulling at that silver fist to reveal, sheathed inside the ebony, a second stick with a razor-toothed claw set on the end of it. He thrust it into flowerbed and hedgerow, cutting out stem and stalk.

He smiled at Edgar as he snapped the metal around his quarry.

'A good collector carries his instruments with him at all times,' he said. 'In my youth I lost many a rare specimen for want of a knife or a trap.'

For the perfect piece of yew, Edgar was sent up the tree with a blade in his pocket. He climbed to the very top, and cut away at the saplings. Huge glasshouses stretched out above the walls of the gardens, with ferns tickling at their windows. The sunlight caught the run of the girders, streaming silver across the sky. The fronded branches of the yew tree swayed in the air and whispered to him: 'patience, patience, patience . . .'

As summer turned to autumn, the stonemason's samples withered upon their posts. But what was set in the rock remained, perfect and unblemished. In the courtyard, men came with fresh blocks of stone and anchored them into the places where the shattered plinths had stood. Edgar fetched earth for the filling of the post holes. But still the iron did not return. It seemed that everyone in the Museum was setting his hand to something apart from him.

One November day, he was walking the rounds of the upper gallery when he heard a knock knock knocking coming from behind the walls. The more he listened, the more it became a sound he knew. The sound of hammer blows. There was stuff being put together still, up in the sky, beyond. The sound led him to a door in the corner of the gallery. He pushed against it. There were steep stairs, set in a spiral. He climbed up them, up, up and up until he emerged at a second door. He was in the tower. There was a scaffold stretched out into open air and, at the edge of it, a great bowed rafter, a doorway to the clouds. Around this, there were men setting spurs and crossbeams of wood. Edgar inched towards them, the wind roaring around him.

'Boy!' A man was towering over him, a hammer in his hand. 'Get out of here. This is no place for a child.'

Edgar looked at the stripped-back bones of the tower, a ladder set against the sky. He looked at the scaffold boards scattered with bent nails. Dirt spiralled across the wood and went scattering down the winds.

'The Professor sent me. For collecting.'

'Collecting? Well, be quick about it.'

Edgar scuttled at the men's feet. The lattice of wood stretched above his head. Every part of Edgar yearned to be up there at the top of it. He gathered up fistfuls of nails. They jangled in his pocket as he ran down the stairs. And behind that sound, a memory: walking the streets of Oxford with a tail in his pocket, full of hope, and thoughts of fame and fortune. Up to the tower and back Edgar ran, day after day, building up a collection of discarded metal. He took it home and jumbled the nails together on his bedroom floor in a mimic of the collapse. Then he picked them apart spur by tiny spur and stowed them under his floorboards.

It was from this second sky-perch that Edgar saw the iron come back. It was a clear January day, and Edgar could see far and wide across Oxford.

Beyond the fence, beyond the line of winter-withered trees of the parkland, something winked out of the road at Edgar. A steely something. A great piece of metal, playing hide-and-seek between the black branches. Edgar crept on to the ledge, right out to the lip of it. Again, a semaphore flash, a light. Then nothing. Then, calling down the wind, no stronger than the strain from a music box, a delicate chiming. There, in the gap in the fence, a cart came rolling. And in the back of it, the steel glowed white silver. It slowed and took the turn through the gate. Behind it came another, and another, rolling across the frozen mud. The uneven ground set the iron striking into a symphony, Edgar's heartbeat a thundering accompaniment. As the carts drew closer, the mass separated into struts and girders. Nestled in amongst it all were men. Mr S sat by the driver of the first cart and there, bringing up the rear, letting out great whoops of laughter was James Fisher.

The carts came to a halt. The men leapt down from their seats, wooden rollers were hauled out, and two by two the men were laying them down, long-limbed stepping stones, leading straight to the Museum door.

Edgar scrambled up the back of a cart. The pieces were roped tight to the wood – huge ridges of arches and brackets. Edgar put his foot upon a brace and was shinning up the curve of it when there was an arm about his waist and he was tumbled down into the mud.

There was Mr S, glowering down at him.

'Master Jones,' said Mr S, 'what in the devil's name do you think you are up to?'

Edgar grinned. 'Testing the metal, sir.'

'And you think that this is your place, do you? To judge the work of your betters?'

'I am a champion of iron, sir. The Professor said so.'

'And where is your precious Professor?' snapped Mr S. 'Holed up with his books and his bones, no doubt. He understands that the iron can break a man's bones in an instant, and knows well enough not to meddle with it.'

By the Museum door, the men were pitching the spurs down on to the rollers.

'I am not afraid, sir.'

'Well, you should be, Master Jones. Go home, and return tomorrow in a humbler mind.'

Edgar turned his back on Mr S. In his months of fetching and carrying, sweeping and filling, he had learnt many other ways into the Museum than the front door. Go home, said Mr S. Well, had not the Professor told him that the Museum was his home? It was not Mr S's place to turn him out of it. He walked away from the unloading, went round to the back of the building, vaulted a window and took the stairs up to the gallery. He hid in the shadow and watched Mr S scuttle around the courtyard, quacking out commands down his tube of brass. Edgar splayed out his hand before him and flicked at Mr S with his finger and thumb, squashing him down into the dirt of the courtyard like a beetle. Two by two the men came with iron poles set upon their shoulders. They put them in rings around the plinths. It was as if the stones were sending out shoots of metal, bright new growth. Along the lines of the gallery, great curved pieces were waiting in ranks. Edgar was back in the Professor's study, peering in on that world of ribs and legs all jumbled up against each other. His creature was returned, strong and magnificent. And tomorrow Edgar would be putting it back together.

Back in the cottage, Edgar set the salt and pepper pots

on their sides and steered the cutlery across. And he was full of stories of how he was set to walk upon the girders, the only man trusted to test the strength of the roof before it was placed.

'It is quite a thing to have such trust placed in you by your fellow men,' said William sternly. 'You must prove yourself worthy of it.'

Emily frowned, catching the run of the silver as it slid down the incline. She did not see what was so worthy about clambering up and down great pieces of metal. It sounded dangerous and reckless. Not the kind of work that a child should be put to.

That night Edgar sat at his desk, sketching out the pieces of the roof as he remembered them: the poles, the brackets, the run of the arches. He fitted them together across the page: a forest of steel. Then Edgar was out of the window and up the apple tree. The sky was cloudless and the moon was fat and the wood had a skin of silver. Back and forth, back and forth, Edgar marched. Step after balanced step, out along the branches and back again. He was sure-footed and he was courageous. He was ready for the iron.

The next morning Edgar woke at dawn, and was racing out of the cottage in an instant, the birds singing his praises as he ran down the roads to the Museum door: 'Champion,' they called across the sky. 'Champion, champion . . .'

Edgar vaulted the window. The iron was already gaining its ascent. From the central line of pillars, columns were shackled together in clusters, like the start of new seedling growth. The larger pieces sat by the walls, waiting, dwarfing the run of the gallery. And there was Mr S, tapping along the lines of them with a claw-headed ratchet. The iron rang pure and true.

Edgar ran across and tugged at Mr S's coat.

'What are you doing here at this hour, Master Jones?' he snapped. 'Your fellow men are still in their beds.'

Edgar gazed up at the arches towering above him.

'I wanted to get to the work, sir.'

Mr S frowned down at Edgar for what seemed an eternity, tossing the ratchet from hand to hand.

'Tell me, in your time at the forge, were you taught the ways of riveting? Barrel hoops and such?'

Edgar nodded. 'And fences, sir.'

'Then let's put you to work, boy.'

Mr S led Edgar away from the arches and down to the stumps of iron set in the stone. He took his ratchet and wrenched it around the bolts that held the banded shackles.

'The men will undertake the first fixture and you will follow in their wake to secure it, thus.'

Edgar looked at the pieces pushing out of the stone. They barely reached the height of his shoulder. This was not what he had sat in the dust and the dirt waiting for.

'I should be at the bigger pieces.'

'Oh you should, should you?' scowled Mr S. 'I rather think you should not be in the Museum at all, Master Jones.'

So it was that, as the weeks passed, and the lower levels of the iron were placed, Edgar ran in rings around the Museum, pulling tight screws that were already fixed. Mr S smiled down at him from the gallery as if Edgar's apprenticeship was a joke arranged for his private amusement. And with every turn of every rivet, Edgar's anger twisted about in his gut. He was better than this little work. He knew it and the Professor knew it also. But the Professor went marching past his station without a word for him, shaking the hands of other men.

Once the pillars were set up to the level of the gallery, it became all the worse for Edgar. Scaffolds were placed around them, creating a walkway across the length of the courtyard. Under Mr S's instruction, Edgar was to squeeze himself between scaffold and pillar to work away at the upper joints. Edgar was stuck in a cage, with the men running back and forth across the boards above him, kicking dirt down into his enclosure.

The weeks passed and the iron grew, and the walls sang with the hammering of metal upon metal. The sound rang in Edgar's ears long after he crawled out of his cage and made his way home. When his father interrogated him over the parlour table, Edgar strained to make out his meaning from the shape of his mouth.

'What great plans has the Professor set you to, Edgar?'

Edgar sat silent. There were no more invented lessons that he could think of. And how could he tell his father the truth of his position, in the dust and the dirt? It was shameful, no better than sitting in the ashes of the forge. He would keep his work a secret. And he would set his mind to the springing of this scaffold trap.

After the pillars had been secured, the hauling machine returned: not just one, but half a dozen of the contraptions. The men gathered at the ropes. Spurs went swinging up into the clouds. And up there the very same men who had not the courage to stand in the shadow of the collapse were marching up and down the scaffold and pulling the iron together. Edgar found himself playing with the run of his wrench around the rivets. All it would take would be a few tugs in the wrong direction and the roof would fall. But he knew, well enough, this was not the way to go about getting the Professor's attention.

Instead, Edgar looked to the detail once more. He watched from his scaffold-cage as the Professor went to stand beside the cranes, peering up at the run of the wheel around the rope, and the metal swinging up into the place where Edgar should be. The more Edgar watched, the more he understood. No man would come and pull him from his enclosure and hoist him up to the heights. He would have to make his own way up.

At the end of his day at the rivets, Edgar stayed within the scaffold until the Museum emptied. The floor of the courtyard was littered with discarded bits. Slipped bolts jewelled the earth, cut-away pieces of rope snaked across the mud. Edgar took one such length and coiled it around his waist, hiding the run of it under his jacket. On his approach to the cottage, he threw it into the wilderness, a great grey worm burrowing into the bracken.

'And what have you learnt this day at the Museum, Edgar?' snapped William, as he buttoned himself into his jacket. 'Or are you still too proud to answer your father's questions?'

Edgar smiled. 'It's a secret, Pa.'

'A secret? The Professor has set you work that he has instructed you to keep from me?'

'No, it is my own secret, but you will know about it soon enough.'

'It seems to me that this Museum is encouraging a certain arrogance in you, Edgar,' said William. 'I am not sure that I like it.'

'And will you share this secret with your mama?' asked Eleanor, after William had set out for his watch.

Edgar grinned and shook his head.

After supper was done, Edgar sat in his room sketching his future upon the page. And once he was satisfied with the shape of it, he began his invention. He ripped the sheet from his bed, bundled it upon his back, went out of the window, down the apple tree, into the brambles and pulled out the rope. There in the sharp moonlight, he unfolded his sheet – a wide white wing set flying across the wilderness. He ripped off a length of it and started to put the rope and the cloth together.

The next morning Edgar woke at dawn again and went running down to the Museum. And again, he made his own way in. This time he vaulted into an empty courtyard. He plucked rubble from the floor and put it in his pocket. He wrapped sheet and rope around him, and hauled himself up the scaffold, hand over fist. The beginnings of the arches were sprouting from the frame above, with a great expanse of sky between them. At the top of the scaffold Edgar unfolded his invention. The sheet was gathered together into the shape of a teardrop, with the rope knotted about the tip of it. The other end of the rope held the ripped-away scrap. Edgar piled his rocks inside and flung it over the lip of the arch. The sheet rose up in response and Edgar jumped into the embrace of the linen. The rope twisted and Edgar was sent spinning, the wood and the metal and the sky all rushing into each other. He was out of his cage and soaring through the air. The angels were pitching themselves off the rooftops and joining him in flight. The harness at his back was a sail, catching the wind and carrying him across the aerial ocean. And the iron was calling out his name as he went soaring past. 'Master Jones! Master Jones!' urging him outwards and onwards.

Then there was a sharp pull at his back; Edgar went plummeting down the wind and Mr S was pitching him over the scaffold, bringing him down on to the boards with a great thump.

'What is the meaning of this?' barked Mr S. 'Do you think the Museum your playground, boy?'

Edgar thought of his perches around the Museum: the buckled back of the beast, the lip of the tower, and the windows that he vaulted. It was his playground more than any other man's.

'I am not playing, sir, I am experimenting. For the good of the Museum.'

Edgar explained: how he had seen the way the cranes had hauled the iron into the sky, and how a man could be hauled up there also, at least a boy could. With Edgar Jones swinging from the spur lines, there would be no need for so much scaffold work. The roof could be pulled together in half the time.

'And you think that this is what it is to be an apprentice, Master Jones, to act outside the orders of your master, and challenge the way the work is done?'

'The Professor is my master, and he is on the side of invention.'

'There is invention, and there is insurrection,' snapped Mr S. 'The two are very different, as I'm sure your Professor will agree.'

Edgar looked at the harness hanging at his shoulder. It twisted and fluttered in the breeze like a huge moth. An unusual specimen and no mistake.

Up in the Professor's attic the harness was spread across the floor. The Professor chuckled with the unfolding, and the bones grinned down from the tabletop.

'I do declare, Mr S,' he said, 'we have been undertaking an unnecessary expense. It shall be decreed from now that the men should bring their bed linen to the museum door and string themselves up accordingly.'

'This is a serious matter, sir. Master Jones put himself in grave danger.'

'I did not, sir!' protested Edgar. 'I tested it from my own apple tree.'

'You hear that, Mr S? Edgar Jones followed the principles of the Museum: observation and then experimentation. I rather think he should be applauded for it.'

Mr S kicked at the cloth and did not answer.

'Edgar, you will await us outside the door,' said the Professor.

Out in the hallway Edgar pressed his eye to the keyhole. On the other side of the wood he could see the Professor crouching over the contraption.

Alone with the engineer, the Professor pulled at the harness, and the cloth and rope stayed fixed.

'Is this not wonderful, Mr S?' he said. 'Edgar Jones has set his sights upon a problem that entirely escaped our notice and he has solved it in the most ingenious fashion.'

Mr S scowled. 'It seems to me, Professor, that you are more ruled by your apprentice than he is ruled by you.'

'Come, Mr S, do not let your pride stand in the way of the work. The sooner the roof is fixed, the better it will be for both of us. And if Edgar Jones has the wit to aid us in this task, well then, he should be praised, not punished for it.'

'Even if I was in agreement, there is an impossibility in the design. Master Jones's invention needs another man to steady it and I doubt you will find any willing.'

'Then we shall appeal to the base nature of your men, sir,' replied the Professor sharply, 'and offer twice the pay to he who will set himself as the steerer of Edgar Jones's flying machine.'

On the other side of the wood, Edgar smiled. The way the Professor was grasping his harness tight in his hand, white-knuckled, was a thing Edgar had seen before, when he had pulled a tail from his pocket. Mr S could kick away at his invention all he liked; if the Professor wanted a thing then he would take it. Edgar could feel the balance of his life tip up, up and up in his favour, up, up and right up to the sparkling skyline.

And so it was that Edgar claimed his place in the apex of the iron. The bed-sheet harness was copied and made into a more workmanlike thing. Five days after his first flight, Edgar returned to the Museum to find a wide wing of hessian strung from the rafters, and James Fisher standing beneath it, holding the rope.

'Well, well, Master Jones,' he said, 'it seems that I am to be hauling you about the rooftops. How does that suit you?'

'It suits me very well, sir,' grinned Edgar.

'I should think it does, sir, now that you have got your Professor to set you up above the rest of us once more. I should think that it suits you very well indeed.'

But Edgar was not listening. He was already scaling the steps of the scaffold, up towards his flying fortune.

And so it was that Fisher and Edgar formed an alliance in

the ironwork. Fisher let the rope run wide along the courtyard, letting Edgar fly from pillar to pillar. And Edgar laughed and laughed, until the whole roof was ringing. Up there, in the heights, swinging amongst the clouds, part of Edgar was a small boy again, in a time before the iron, before the forge, before lessons. Part of him was back to racing through the sky with his father's arm around him and the whole world echoing with 'Edgar, Edgar Ho!' Fisher would laugh back in kind, and turn the rope, twisting up the tension and then let it free, so that Edgar was set spinning around the rooftops, so that the metal ran streaming about him, as if he was caught in the centre of Jacob's great pot. Sometimes Fisher misjudged the run of the rope and sent Edgar walloping into a bracing point like a mace upon a chain, set to tumble the iron a second time. And then the roof would ring with Edgar's screams, a high-pitched, terrifying thing.

'Master Jones?' Fisher's cries would echo up the vaults.

And Edgar would chant back, 'Master Jones, no broken bones!'

Back at the cottage, Edgar's secret came spilling out across the parlour table: tales of how he was taken from the scaffold and hauled up into the sky. Tales of his friend Fisher, who tumbled him about the clouds. Tales of his wonderful flying machine.

William sat on the other side of the table, twisting his knife around and around in his hand.

'I am not a fool, Edgar. I know there is no such thing as a flying machine.'

'There wasn't, and now there is. I made it myself from bed linen.'

'Enough!' barked William. 'If you cannot speak the truth of your work then we shall not speak of it at all.'

Eleanor thought back to the morning, a week or two before, when she had gone up to Edgar's room to find the bed stripped back, the window open, and Edgar nowhere to be seen. It was becoming all the more apparent that neither she nor William really knew their son.

But back in the Museum there was nothing but praise for Edgar. The ironworkers clustered around Fisher's rope, staring up the line of it. It was quite a thing to see the boy working his way around the web of iron, nothing more than a speck of a shadow, one foot upon an arch, the other treading empty air. And watching led to talking. Could a man really call himself a roofworker when a boy was flying under spur and spandrel above him?

Within a month one harness, two, three, six, ten went flying up the run of the iron. It was as if the steely trunks of the roof were putting forth fruit: strange seed pods, with men stuck at the centre. Up there in the clouds, there were cries and hurrahs and whistles as the men swung out amongst the metal. And Edgar was in the thick of it. His fellow workers were no longer nameless adversaries. There was Master Pike, a tall skinny youth who wrapped his legs around the riveting posts and half stood out of the harness to pull down the spurs; there was Master O'Brian, who sang his way through the day, shaking the pillars with his great booming voice. There was Master Peach who, whenever the pieces were hauled into place, hammered back against the iron, so that the roof applauded itself. And there were many other Masters beside, all of whom raised their caps to Edgar as they passed him. There were many other Masters, but Edgar was still the champion. He had a quickness in his flight and a spryness in his fixing that no other man could match.

Far below, the Professor looked up at the men in the sky and he smiled and congratulated himself once more on the wise purchase of Edgar Jones. His initial suspicion had been proved correct: the men were shamed to action by this agile boy. But the fact that this had come about through an invention of Edgar's own making, well, that was a thing he could never have predicted.

As the arches were fixed, the second part of the roof returned. It came in large rectangular pieces, and piled out around the outer edges of the Museum like a chessboard set upon the lawn. The cranes swung the panels across the heavens, and the men flew beneath them, riveting. Nothing bent and nothing buckled.

Spring turned to summer and another cart came up to the door, singing its song of metal. This time no man stopped Edgar jumping upon the back of it. The iron was wrapped up in swathes of cloth. When Edgar pulled them away, there was a whole world of fruits, flowers and grasses spun out of metal. The trumpet-tulips, the wide-eyed daisies, the horse chestnut fronded out like a fan – all the plants that Edgar had eked out of the tumbled structure were returned to the Museum, hammered out and handsome. They twisted and turned in his hands, as if they were living things, seeking out the sunlight, altogether better than anything that the stonemasons had chipped out of the rock.

Edgar and his fellow men swung their harnesses down the

main arches and the roof blossomed around them like the wilderness of Edgar's childhood, but steely and strong. Flying up amongst it all, Edgar could see now that his father was right: his place in the world had been marked out from the very start. From the day that he had built a bower of bracken and all the days that followed – the slipping of the latch; the seeking out his fortune; the tipping of the tail, and all his climbing – all was leading to this forest in the sky, and the great iron bones that embraced it, the place that he had pulled apart and put together again. This utterly new piece of Oxford that he would, one day, walk through with his father. And when he did his father would see that he was not a liar at all. Instead he would see that his son was everything that he had ever told him to be: brave, bold, determined, clever. The ingenious Edgar Jones of the ironwork.

These thoughts and others besides were playing over in Edgar's mind the day that he was pulled out of the sky. He was up in the eaves, a couple of feet shy of the gallery wall. Fisher had anchored his rope around a pillar of green marble, and Edgar had his back to it. He was bolting down a great fan of chestnut that was set to spread between the main arches. A soft wind was rippling down the belly of the Museum. It caught upon the fronds of iron, and plucked a song out of the air, something between the thrumming strings of a harp and the rasp of knives being sharpened. Edgar was smoothing out the tips of the grasses when there was a tug at his rope and he went flying backwards. A hand caught his seat and he was tumbled over the gallery wall.

Edgar looked up and saw a man he had never set eyes on before staring down at him. A man of middle years with fair hair swept back, bristling sideburns and hooded eyes.

He was dressed in a dark suit, and in his hand he held a long walking stick. The hook of it caught around Edgar's rope.

'You are, I do believe, Edgar Jones?'

Edgar nodded.

'I have, for many months now, been most eager to make your acquaintance. My name is Mr Ruskin.'

He held out his hand. Edgar shook it. The skin was rough, the fingertips worn and stained with bits of dark stuff. The hand of a man who made things.

'I have heard many tales of you from the Professor. Tales of tails, no less,' Ruskin chuckled. 'And tales of how you were so eager for the work atop the iron that you made yourself a harness from a handkerchief.'

'It was a bed sheet, sir.'

'A bed sheet, a handkerchief, forgive me if I prefer the more poetic rendering. What age are you child?'

'Twelve years.'

'Twelve years,' Ruskin smiled. 'It is in my opinion the most noble age for any man. You are finding your own way of looking at the world, without being subject to any distractions of the blood. It is a privilege indeed to be twelve years old in times like these.'

Ruskin crouched and took hold of Edgar's shoulders, anchoring him down so that he had no choice but to meet Ruskin's gaze.

'And part of the privilege of your age is your innocence. You have no sense of what the world might hold for you or what you might hold for the world.'

Edgar smiled. He did know, full well. The Museum was just

the start of it. He would make a name for himself, building up iron bones across the land, flying from pillar to post in his great machine. The Oxford of spires and steeples would stand side by side with great steely structures, all put together by Edgar Jones.

'Therefore allow this man who has seen a little of the world to enlighten you upon the nature of the road ahead. Men like you, child, who have the wit of invention within them, are born closer to God than the rest of mankind. The part of you that must create a thing, that would tie a bed sheet to a rope and, in that moment of union, make both things utterly anew, that is the very breath of God at work within you.'

'The breath of God?'

'The breath of God indeed,' smiled Ruskin. 'And this my gift to you, Edgar Jones, in your thirteenth year. In your passage from child to man you will encounter many temptations: weak men, false riches and the flattery of women. But at all times have courage in your own self: you are an inventor, child, and the breath of God burns all the more brightly in you for it. You have an ability in your blood, and you must never betray it.'

Ruskin smiled and swept down the gallery, leaving Edgar staring back at the run of the flowering arches. They sparkled in the sunlight, their edges tipped with liquid light. Edgar knew, now, he had the answer to any question that his father might put to him. But he would not let his breath out until he was ready.

It was a couple of days later that Edgar brought his new understanding to the breakfast table.

'Pa, do you know what God used to make the world?' asked Edgar.

William froze, his knife suspended, slicing air. 'What kind of a question is that, Edgar? You know your Scriptures. First He separated the light and the darkness, then the land and the sea. Then on the sixth day He created the various beasts and mankind.'

'But what did he make it from? What materials?'

William went to his wall of knowledge and pulled out the Bible. '"In the beginning there was the Word, and the Word was with God."' This is a thing that you know by rote, Edgar.'

'You cannot construct a thing from a word alone, Pa,' said Edgar. He picked up his spoon and sliced across the top of his egg. 'Just because I say this is a spoon, or this is an egg does not make it so. One has to be smelted, the other laid.'

The Bible pages whipcracked the air as William turned them.

'In the texts, God is also known as the Word. This clearly tells us that God made the world from Himself.'

'But if He made it from Himself, then God must be made of mud and grass and water and all the other things, and then we would be able to see Him, wouldn't we, Pa?'

Eleanor could not help herself. The laughter that she had been swallowing came bursting out in one great yelp. William threw the Bible down upon the table. The china danced with the force of it.

'I am glad that it amuses you so much, Mrs Jones,' he snapped, 'to hear your son mock his faith.'

The family sat in silence, the only sound the picking apart

of eggshells. Edgar licked the yoke from the spoon and laid it upon his plate.

'I think that God made the world out of iron.'

'Iron?'

'Liquid iron burns bright in the darkness. And iron is dug out of the centre of the world.'

William frowned down at Edgar. This was heresy indeed, and a sophisticated heresy at that. Not the kind of thoughts to be expected from a boy who could not even copy out his Commandments.

'Edgar, is this from your lessons under the Professor?'

'No, Pa.'

William took Edgar by the shoulder and shook him.

'The truth, for once, Edgar.'

Edgar twisted under his father's grasp. Strong-muscled from the ironwork, Edgar kicked his way free, tipping the leg of the table and sending everything sliding down the incline. There was a smashing of china, and all the breakfast things spilt across the floor.

Edgar ran through it, out of the door and was gone.

Eleanor looked down at the ruined meal patterning the rug.

'This is no way to go about being a family, Will,' she said.

The following evening, Eleanor laid out her dilemma before Mrs Simm. It was the same old tale: William wanting to shape Edgar into a different kind of boy, and Edgar becoming more and more his own man. And Eleanor, trying to reconcile the two, with very little pleasure in it for herself.

'It feels like a mockery of a family. I sit alone, day in day out, whilst my husband shakes the house with his snores and my son is put to work that brings him home wounded and full of arguments. I do declare, if it weren't for your company, Mrs Simm, I would be turned mad by it.'

Mrs Simm chuckled as she shook out a bundle of stuff from her bag.

'Well, my dear, it is well within your means to change it.'

'I am not sure I understand you.'

'Do you not?' said Mrs Simm, grinning out of one side of her mouth. 'Well, let me say it plainly: if it's a family you want, you should wake your husband from his slumbers and get on with the business of making another child.'

'Impossible,' said Eleanor. She pulled out a loose thread from the cloth and bit it away with her teeth. 'William gives all his attention to his books and his College.'

'There is no love between you? None at all?'

Eleanor shook her head. 'Not ever since Edgar spoke his first words.'

Mrs Simm shook out a nightdress, cut low at the chest and gathered with ribbons at the waist. The underskirt was a shifting sea of gauze, embroidered with a tangle of roses. She pressed it into Eleanor's hands.

'Then why don't you set about using your talents for your own benefit, Mrs Jones?' she said.

Eleanor hung the nightdress on the back of her workshop door. For three days it stood there, the skirts rising and falling in the play of the breeze.

On the third day Eleanor found herself rummaging deep in the garment chest stowed under the table. It was an excavation of fourteen years of marriage, down, down and down through all her old bits of making. And there, at the bottom of the trunk, folded away, were those tiny dresses, no longer than the stretch of Eleanor's forearm: pink silk, threaded through with ribbon; buttercup yellow, with a bonnet to match that sat proud upon Eleanor's fist, the Christening gown, with the buttons ripped from its back. Eleanor laid them out before her on the table. She took off her grey gown and put on the nightdress. The roses climbed up the curves of her. She went up to the bedroom door and pushed it open.

William was beached upon the bed, dreaming his way through the daylight. Eleanor lay down beside him.

William dreamt on. He dreamt he was out in the wilderness of the garden. It was springtime, and all was in blossom. He was looking for something – something precious that had been lost. As the dream sharpened around him he understood: he was looking for Edgar. William hunkered down upon his hands and knees and squinted into the undergrowth. It opened up before him, the brambles parted, tangling together into arches, bedecked with blossom: the tunnels of Edgar's childhood. William crawled into the mouth of one, calling down the length of it: 'Edgar, Edgar HO!'

The wilderness echoed his voice back to him. There was nothing inside but shifting leaves and shadows. He burrowed further.

The bracken grew thicker before him. He put his hand upon it to swipe it aside. He put his hand upon it and a trap was sprung: the brambles came swooping down to claim him. But the bracken was not bracken. It clanked and clattered as it fell. It beat at his back, ripped apart his coat, his shirt, and clung on to his skin with its barbs. The world was made of iron and William was stuck in the heart of it. And behind all the scraping and the slicing and the chiming together of the weapons there was another sound: laughter.

William woke with a start, in a tangle of bed sheets and there, lying beside him, was Eleanor. She was laughing, a quiet kind of laughter. She had her hand upon his face, rubbing the sleep away from his skin.

'You were caught in a dream,' she said. 'Nothing but a dream.'

She put her hand around his waist and drew him closer to her. Eleanor was all softness and tumbling golden hair. She took his hand in hers and placed it upon her breast.

William could feel her heart beating just beneath his fingertips.

And then in a moment, the desire that had been dammed up for years came rushing back through his blood. Every part of him yearned towards his wife, but he would not be ruled by it. He twisted his body away from hers and tumbled off the bed.

Eleanor laughed down at him. 'There's no harm in it, Will, no harm at all.'

'You are not yourself,' he stuttered.

'I am every bit myself. There is more to being a wife than the laying of a breakfast table and the darning of a shirt.'

William stood stranded on the other side of the room. Eleanor's blue eyes glittering with the beginning of tears just made his blood beat faster. But behind the thrumming of his desire, there was fear, pure and simple: fear at his suddenly brazen wife. Fear that they might put together another Edgar.

'If this is you being a wife, Eleanor, then I do not want any part of it.'

She rose from the bed. The wide white expanse of the sheets was a sea of emptiness set between them. Unchartable.

'Very well,' said Eleanor, folding her arms around herself. 'But you should be mindful, Will. Do not set yourself so high above the world that you cannot see your own reflection.'

Eleanor slammed the door hard behind her.

The scriptures rattled upon their hooks. *Seek Peace and Pursue It.*

Downstairs, Eleanor bundled up her daughter's dresses and threw them upon the fire. They flared bright for a moment and were gone.

By the time Eleanor repeated the tale to Mrs Simm, it had become a thing to be laughed at. William, all fumble-fingered and flustered, pitching himself on to the floor in a flurry of bed sheets and protest.

Mrs Simm laughed until tears came.

'Oh, my poor dear,' she said, 'I do believe that your husband is afraid of his own flesh.'

'And mine, it seems.'

Mrs Simm pushed the nightdress back into her bag.

'Then for all his wise words and his bookish ways, your husband is nothing more than a fool, Mrs Jones.'

The afternoon of tangled sheets and lost opportunity was never mentioned again. But when Eleanor retired that evening she found a bank of pillows set down the centre of the bed. In the night-time Eleanor slept with the barricade pressed against her back. In the daytime, William curled his body up to the divide and embraced it as if it was flesh.

The parlour table became a place of utter silence. Edgar

kept his thoughts of iron to himself. William repositioned the wall of the newspaper between himself and his family. If Eleanor felt the weight of the wedding ring around her finger to be heavier than before then she did not speak of it to anyone. Instead, she retreated into her world of silks and stitches. She turned seams and hems, and as the dresses reformed themselves, low cut, full-skirted, Eleanor held them up against herself. Peacock blue. Bright scarlet. Verdant green. She imagined the kind of lives these dresses might have. They would dance beneath sparkling chandeliers in the richest houses of Oxford. They were the dresses of love and adventure. They were slender, small-waisted things. It would take three of them stitched together even to begin to hold the shape of Mrs Simm.

On one such night, Eleanor was interrupted from the push and pull of the needle by a knock upon her door.

There, standing upon the step, was Mrs Simm, her arms around the shoulders of a tall woman, dressed in a cloak, with a dark veil shrouding her face.

'Mrs Jones,' she said with a smile, 'let me introduce you to my friend Lady Arabella.'

Eleanor hovered at the doorway. It was one thing to let Mrs Simm into her home, quite another to allow a smartly dressed stranger across the threshold.

Eleanor held out her hand. 'How do you do?'

The woman did not move an inch.

'Oh, don't mind her,' said Mrs Simm. 'She's a quiet one, but she is a lady of substance.' Mrs Simm chuckled and pulled aside Arabella's cloak to reveal a hessian body, with a sturdy iron foot fixed below on wheels. A mannequin. 'Now, let's get her inside before she catches her death.'

Eleanor grabbed the thing by the neck, Mrs Simm hoisted it around the waist and together they went careering over the doorstep, across the parlour and into the workroom.

Arabella was placed by the door. Her cloak and veil were removed and there she stood: faceless, armless.

Eleanor passed her hands over the curve of her shoulder, the tapering of the waist. The hessian felt rough against her skin.

'She's a pretty piece of work, is she not?' said Mrs Simm. 'Quite the latest thing, brought up from London. She is set to the proper shape, everything in proportion.'

'I cannot accept it.'

'Why ever not?'

'The expense, Mrs Simm. It is too much.'

'Nonsense,' said Mrs Simm sharply. 'It occurred to me that we have been wasting your talents. A bit of embroidery and making good is all very well, but it is time you turned your hand to some proper work.' Mrs Simm pulled out a wad of paper from her bag. 'I have a sister in London—'

'A sister?'

Mrs Simm chuckled. 'A sister, indeed. We popped out like two peas in a pod, one after the other, can you imagine?'

Eleanor could not. The thought that there might be a second Mrs Simm in the world was altogether too remarkable.

'And this sister of mine knows all about the latest fashions.' Mrs Simm unfolded the papers. There were shapes of dresses, cut out in sheets. 'She provides the pattern, I provide the silk, you provide the stitching and we shall turn a handsome profit together.'

'It is generous of you but—'

'But what, Mrs Jones? Is it better for you to be sitting at home doing piecework and wishing for the way your life could have been? Nothing beats melancholy better than the weight of money in your pocket. See how Arabella agrees?' Mrs Simm put her hand upon the neck of the mannequin, and the head bobbed up and down in assent.

Eleanor smiled. 'Very well. If William approves then let us attempt it.'

'My poor sweet girl,' cooed Mrs Simm, 'your husband turns you out of the bed and you would still have him rule over you?'

Mrs Simm patted her hand. Eleanor felt the heaviness of the jewels set against her skin.

'This is an opportunity for you to make your life your own, my dear. And you will find that Arabella is most adept at keeping secrets.'

Mrs Simm pushed against the mannequin. It twisted upon the stand. There, at the base of the spine, was a cut in the cloth. Mrs Simm pulled a coin from her purse and posted it through the slot. Eleanor could hear the dull chime as it hit against the wire belly and settled.

At the same time, William found himself sitting at his night watch, frowning out at the buckled line of the city wall that stretched across the lawns, partitioning the college. It seemed to him an uneven echoing of the boundary banked up across his bed. As the stars jewelled the sky and then faded into the dawn, William found himself turning over the very same question that Eleanor and Mrs Simm had picked apart over the workroom table: what was it to be a husband? And right on the heels of that question came another: what was it to be a father? And, more to the point, what was it to be a father to a boy like Edgar?

William found himself thinking back to how it had been seven years ago – seven lifetimes, it seemed – when he had walked through the college gates in search of understanding. He remembered the feeling of Edgar's tiny hand in his. He thought of how he had wrapped himself around Edgar to keep away the swipe of Carter's iron claw.

Protection, throught William, that is what being a proper father is founded on. Protection and care. And the more he thought back to Edgar, standing shivering and hair-spined in the centre of Carter's room, the more he understood his own error. Had not Carter told him plain? Edgar could turn to the good or the bad, depending on his guiding influence. And what had William done? He had locked away Edgar alone with his lessons and measured his son's mind against his own; then, out of pure frustration, given him up to a base apprenticeship. But worst of all – and William was ashamed to put a name to it – he had allowed his ambition to blind his judgement. A mere mention of the University and William had signed Edgar away. He had sent Edgar off to this unknown Professor without his letters, without a clear understanding of the world. No wonder that his mind had been turned. No wonder that he was so full of lies, and boasts and wild theories. Well, it was time to correct the error. He would not risk another Edgar, but he would love the one that God had given him. He would seek out this Professor and hold him to account.

William finished his watch, and marched down to the Professor's college. He knocked upon the attic door and did not wait for an answer. He walked into the chaos of bones and bottles and books. It was all he needed to shore up his suspicions. The Professor was sitting in the midst of it, threading wire through a huge claw that crouched upon the table top.

'Porter Jones,' he said with a smile. 'Father of Edgar Jones, no less. This is an unexpected honour.'

William frowned. He would no more be caught by this man's flattery than he would be caught in the net of Eleanor's skirts.

'Yes, sir. And I am here because of Edgar.'

'Well, I did not think that you had come to debate the claw structure of *Panthera tigris*,' chuckled the Professor, waving the articulated bone at William.

William stood, hands thrust deep in his pockets, his back braced against the door.

'I am pleased to say that your son is an invaluable asset to the Museum.'

'But at what cost, sir? I have my suspicions that this apprenticeship of yours is placing him in great danger.'

'Well, this is a discussion more suited to my engineer than myself,' replied the Professor. 'I have a very limited understanding of the ironwork. But I do know that there are more measures of protection in the Museum for Edgar than there ever were at the forge, with its open fire and its molten metal.'

'It is not the physical work so much as the repercussions that your philosophies are having upon my son's soul.'

The Professor swallowed back a smile. For a moment he saw Edgar's soul as a solid thing: a sheet of metal being pounded upon by a great hammer. 'My philosophies?'

William paced back and forth across the room, telling the tale of the world of iron and the god made of mud and grasses. 'It is contrary to all scripture, and it will not stand.'

'Porter Jones,' said the Professor sternly, 'if you truly think that your son is the kind of boy who would spend his days discussing the finer points of creation when there is a rooftop to be run across then I think you do not know him at all.'

William clenched and unclenched his fists in his pockets. It was as he suspected. This man would not hold himself responsible for Edgar. Not one jot.

'I will not argue with you, sir. You have had your bit of fun with Edgar, and now it is time to let him go.'

The Professor looked sterner still. 'If you consult the terms of your son's contract I think you will find that there is a high price to pay for the breaking of it.'

William looked at the claw grasped in the Professor's fist, the razor-sharp tips tapping on the wood.

'My son is not a thing to be bartered over, sir.'

'Indeed not. He is a most valuable worker. The roof must be completed within a month. It will be an impossibility without him.'

'A month?'

'At most, two. So you must consider which is best for your son. Is it to curtail his apprenticeship and bankrupt your family? Or is it better to allow him to finish the work? Quite a dilemma, don't you think?'

William could feel all his intentions slipping away from him. He would grab hold of something.

'If you must keep Edgar then you will give me something in return.'

'But you said that your son is not a thing to be bartered over, Porter Jones.'

William scowled. He felt as he did when the Professor first came to him at the lodge. Every word he said turned back on itself. He would not be tricked again.

'You say that Edgar has been invaluable to you, and I am only asking that you honour his service. That you secure him an apprenticeship outside your Museum, in work that will give him a proper understanding of his place in the world.'

'And do you have any idea of what might provide such enlightenment?'

William stared down at the carpet. He thought back to the time when he and Edgar had investigated the wonders of the world together: through the eye of the telescope, and the run of the red heart of the thermometer.

'Yes sir. I do believe so.'

So it was that Edgar continued to fly from pillar to pillar, working at the rivets, oblivious to the fact that with each turn of the ratchet about the screw head he was pulling his own checkmate closer and closer.

Meanwhile Eleanor sat in her workroom, pinning paper to silk, and cutting out the shapes. As she sewed seam to seam she loved the moment when the cloth that had lain flat across the table suddenly gained dimension: the shape of an invisible woman pushing through the silk.

And as, beam by beam, the chequerboard roof was set upon the arches, in the belly of the mannequin the curve of the wires gently embraced a gathering fortune.

The final weeks about the iron had the feeling of a carnival.

The pounding of metal against metal and the creaking of the wood and rope, the striking of the hammers, and the wrenching of the ratchets around the rivets had the aspect of some absurd musical instruments that had been set out of tune.

Edgar was up there in the thick of it, shouting out along with his fellows: '"In all His words most wonderful, Most sure in all His ways!"'

And as he sung he smiled at the words. It was all true: his hammer struck sure upon the iron. The men flying through the air beside him were singing out his praises, and the iron was singing it back to him. And below them the Professor strode across the courtyard, swiping through the air with his cane, as if he were conducting an orchestra.

But when the Professor was not in attendance the choruses would change, and there would be songs about pegs, nails and holes which flew around Edgar. He could not grasp the sense of them, but from the men's laughter he knew that there was a meaning beyond a ballad of construction. He joined in the chorus, 'Bang, bang bang!' up at the apex, his high-whistling voice echoing down the iron, making the men laugh all the more.

It was in this spirit that Fisher approached Edgar.

'The men are proposing a race across the roof,' he said. 'We could give them a fine bit of sport, could we not, you and I?'

Edgar looked up at the great expanse of iron and grinned. 'I will need a long rope.'

'Then a long rope you will have, Master Jones. A long rope and a pocket full of gold, if we play this thing right.'

So it was two days later that the men gathered in the courtyard. It was sunrise, long before the working bell was to be struck. Edgar was hauled up to the eaves at the north side of the gallery. The roof blossomed red gold around him. Above him swung the last piece of the open air: a gap where the final panel of the roof was to be fixed. Below the men were huddled in groups, heads bent.

Fisher held the speaking tube to his mouth.

'The challenge is set,' he quacked. 'Master Jones will swing from the north to the south end of the Museum, touching upon each and every pillar. The touch will be witnessed by the striking of the iron, thus.'

Edgar hit against the bottom of the arch with his wrench. The roof rang like a bell.

'Master Jones assures me that this is a thing that can be completed in five minutes. And as his anchorman, I set my money to his claim. Am I correct in thinking that no other man will stand beside me?'

The courtyard below erupted in a chorus of jeers and whistles.

'Very well. I have your estimations registered.' Fisher waved a piece of paper in the air and the men cheered again. 'If Master Jones's boast is proven false, then the winnings will go to the man who is nearest to the resulting time.'

Fisher tilted his beak to the roof. 'Master Jones, strike upon the iron if you are ready!'

Edgar brought the wrench down and the rooftop rang. 'Then fly!'

Edgar pushed off and the roof rushed towards him. On the long sway of his rope he swung wide. He leant out of the harness, tipping into the air and swiped a tulip-clustered pillar. The ratchet caught the petals and the iron sounded. Edgar pitched himself around the post and his rope caught, thrumming through the air. His harness lurched and he flew on. The metal forest tipped and tilted around him, and Edgar's heart beat faster. It was as if the iron had life within it, and was trying to shake Edgar from his perch. Clang! Clang! Clang! Edgar beat at the bracing points as if he were hammering the roof into the sky. The iron was his iron and he would master it.

Unknown to all, there was another member of the audience. It was the Professor's predilection to come to the Museum at dawn. He would stand beneath the roof and watched as the great bones of it emerged out of the night, and were cast fiery by the rising sun. In these silent early hours the Professor could fancy that the Museum was every day being made anew by God's hand. Molten metal being poured down from the heaven in great golden ribs and finding its form upon the earth.

The Professor was watching from a window of the east gallery. It was quite a thing to come to see, Edgar Jones swinging up in the heights, like a dark little monkey thundering his way across the canopy of his kingdom, so lithe and fearless. So utterly unlike his father.

Four! Edgar was nearly at the south face where the wooden door swayed across the brickwork, to and fro, to and fro, as Edgar flew towards it. There were three pillars set between him and his victory. But the rope was stretched to pure tension and Edgar felt as if he was dragging the weight of the whole rooftop behind him as he flew. He stretched out to strike the iron and his harness pulled against him. Edgar fell forwards. The iron echoed with the cries of the men, Master Jones! Master Jones! Edgar caught the harness between his knees and pivoted: his feet were in the clouds and his face tipped to the floor, and the sea of men swung beneath him. All that had been upwards was now downwards, and for a moment Edgar saw the roof as he had first seen it: a bow-legged, tangle-hearted creature. But now the skeleton carried muscle and sinew: the lines of his rope threaded through it. Edgar pushed forward. Three, two, one, the pillars were struck, and Edgar was victorious.

The crowd erupted into a great cheer.

'Bravo! Master Jones, bravo!' cried the iron.

Fisher cracked the tail of the rope like a whip, and with the blood thrumming in his ears Edgar laughed and laughed. He the hero of the skies and the men loved him for it.

But at that moment the door swung open, and standing there was Mr S.

He walked across to Fisher and took the trumpet from his hand. He grabbed the rope, loosened the knot and Edgar came hurtling down, coming to a stop an inch above the floor, his hair dangling in the dust. He pulled at the harness and Edgar tumbled, rolled over the bracing and landed with his face in the dirt.

'What is the meaning of this, Master Jones?' barked Mr S.

Edgar spat the earth from his mouth. 'It was just sport,' he muttered. 'There was no harm in it.'

'No harm? Does this seem to you a thing without harm in it?'

Mr S held out the harness. There, beyond the first knot, the rope was worn thread thin. Mr S twisted it in his fist and snapped it.

'I'll warrant, from the great crowd gathered, that this was a thing that you were persuaded into, were you not?'

Edgar shook his head.

'It will be better for you if you speak the truth of the matter. Was it Master Fisher who created this spectacle?'

'No, sir, only me, sir.'

'Then you leave me no choice,' said Mr S. 'Edgar Jones, for unlawful use of the apparatus, you are dismissed.'

The Professor leant over the lintel of the window and tapped his cane upon the stone. 'I have born witness to the entirety,' he called. 'Send the boy across to me.'

The Professor took Edgar by the arm and led him away out into the centre of the lawn. Behind them the Museum crouched, expectant.

'Tell me, Edgar Jones, do you have any understanding of the science of Chemistry?'

'No, sir.'

'The principle theory is simple. The world is made from basic building blocks of elements. They combine to create the varied matter that we see around us.' The Professor swept his cane across the open space before them, the muddied lawn, the trees, the fences. 'And some of these combinations prove more volatile than others. They can prove most explosive when mixed. I fear it is thus with you and Mr S.'

'Am I to be dismissed sir?'

The Professor waved his hand as if to swipe away the question. 'Many great things are achieved through the calculated use of explosion. Why, to set the railways across the land vast mountains had to be blasted through. Such is the nature of Progress.'

'But am I dismissed?'

The Professor set his hand upon Edgar's shoulder. 'In a fashion, yes. But you must not take it to heart.'

'But you said, sir, that the Museum was my home. You said that I was your best boy.'

'Did I?' chuckled the Professor. 'Well, Edgar Jones, you must learn not to take things quite so literally otherwise the world will be full of disappointment.'

'And may I ever come back?'

The Professor smiled and shook his head. 'I think not. I have overruled Mr S many times in your favour. Now I must let him have his way.'

Edgar kicked at the ground, churning up the mud. This was not how it should be. Mr S, the man who had set the broken roof, was favoured over himself: he who had undone the mistake and put the thing back together again.

'It is unjust.'

'In truth, Edgar Jones, it is not. It is a punishment in appearance only. You were apprenticed for the completion of the ironwork and nothing more. Roof-swinging or no, you would have been out of the Museum within the month.'

Out of the Museum. Edgar looked over the Professor's shoulder, back at the broad walls and the tall door shut against him. And now it seemed there was only one place left for him.

'So you will send me back to the forge?'

It was unthinkable. Days upon days crouched upon the floor with the fire roaring at his back and the clang clang clang of Jacob's hammer marking out his hours.

The Professor chuckled. 'On the contrary, I have recommended that you are apprenticed to an altogether more adaptable man.'

'Another master?'

'Indeed. I have secured you a place with a manufacturer of scientific instruments. It is quite a leap of status from the forge.'

Edgar thought of his father's telescope in his father's parlour, and the way that it could bring the moon and the clouds and the angels of Oxford to a hair's-breadth away. It was not the same as flying up in the sky in a machine of his own invention.

'I am better suited to roofwork.'

'Do you think that Oxford is your empire? A place where you pick your station as you please?'

'No, sir.'

'Well, then, accept your new position with grace and thanks, and let us have no further argument about it.'

The Professor pulled out a sheaf of papers and thrust them into Edgar's hands. Illuminated letters crawled across the top of the page, red and black.

The Professor held out his hand, and Edgar shook it. That strong grip again. The hand that had hauled him out of the great golden boiling pot, back in another life.

Back inside the Museum, Edgar gathered his satchel from the gallery floor.

There, sitting inside it was a twist of paper. Edgar undid it and a stack of sovereigns tumbled into his lap. The bet was won, but at too great a cost.

Edgar turned his gaze to the roof. His rope had been cut away, his victory already forgotten. He watched as the men aligned themselves around the final panel, harness upon harness swinging from the spurs. It was more unjust than he could bear. Had he not proved, time and time again, that he was the champion of the iron? He should be up there, at the final rivets. He sneaked into the shadows at the back of the eastern gallery, and watched as the hole in the sky was shuttered up like a trap being sprung. The iron against the iron was a steely applause ringing through the gallery.

Then he heard his name being called out of the stone.

'Edgar Jones?' said the bricks. 'An instrument maker?' They laughed. 'Well, I pity the man foolish enough to take him on.' The bricks laughed again.

Edgar squinted down the corridor. At the far end stood the Professor and Mr S. The high walls were acting like the brass-beaked shouting tube, carrying everything back to Edgar.

'I doubt he will stick at it,' said the Professor. 'His own father confessed that our Master Jones did not even have the patience to learn his letters.'

'And yet you still recommended him for the work?'

'He was an amusing addition to our company, but Edgar Jones has served our purpose. It will do us no favours to have a boy like him loitering around the Museum. Let another man work out what to do with him.'

'That's your trouble, Professor. You are a collector of

oddities through and through, and one day it will be your undoing.'

Edgar's anger stewed through his blood. This was how it was then. He was a curiosity, a thing that had amused the Professor for a moment but now was to be cast out with never a backward glance. Cast out, with the door locked against him, so that he and his father could never walk through the court-yard, side by side, gazing up at the wonder of the ironwork. His father would never see and never understand, and Edgar would be a disappointment and a liar for ever.

Very well. If the Professor would banish Edgar then Edgar would have his revenge. Edgar went through the window, ran across the lawn and back into Oxford. He vaulted the fences of Christ Church Meadow, then walked along the line of the river, throwing great lumps of rock into the water, slicing through the undergrowth with a long stick. He sat himself down upon the riverbank and waited for the sky to grow dark.

At twilight Edgar returned to the Professor's bone loft the way he had entered, two years and a lifetime ago. A time before iron-walking, a time before flying. He scaled the balcony-ridged back of the college. The dusk gave him his disguise, and if he was seen at all he would have simply been mistaken for an irregularity of the stone, a shifting shadow, a trick of the light. Edgar scaled up the ivy, clambered on to the guttering and with a twist of metal in the lock was in through the attic window.

Edgar looked around him. The papers pinned to the wall rustled in the play of the wind. The bottles chimed against each other. He crept closer and peered in at the curve of the glass. A clouded, lidless eye stared straight back at him. Edgar picked up another: a cut-away part of a face, the lips and nose puckered against the side, as if expectant of a kiss. Beside it stood a bulbous-bellied flask, and floating inside was a child, a tiny thing, no bigger than Edgar's fist. He shook it and the child danced. So this is what it was, then, to be a collector: cutting out parts of people and stoppering them up.

The papers continued to rustle against each other and whisper out of the wall. Edgar looked closer and saw that the pictures of animals had been replaced by drawings of bones of iron. Pieces of the museum: spurs, spandrels and arches, repeated again and again from every angle.

It gave Edgar a savage anger to look upon it, so neatly drawn out across the page. As if the idea of the museum was all that mattered. As if the place could have come into being anyway, without the courage of Edgar Jones.

Edgar went to the cupboard and sprung the lock.

He was caught in an avalanche of ivory. Thighs thundered down from on high, claws clattered upon the carpet. Skulls and ribs and knuckles followed. Behind them sat a stack of specimen shrouds. He took one out and spread it out across the floor. He sifted through the pile of bones and tossed many parts of many animals into the cloth. Then he tied up the bones into a hump, which he set upon his shoulders. The remainder he scooped back into the cupboard and locked the door behind him.

He went to the wall, ripped the pictures from their pins and threw them out of the window. He climbed over the lintel and back down the face of the college. As Edgar made his passage down to the ground the pictures of the Museum followed him, spiralling through the air and flying out across the night, out into the meadow and beyond. And he could feel, on his back, claws spiking through the cloth, as if clinging on for safety.

Back home, Edgar upended his satchel upon his bed. The bones spilt out across his blanket – long thigh bones and shin bones, heads grinning with teeth as sharp as needles, ribs upon ribs, and a host of other connecting pieces that Edgar could not put names to. He prised up every floorboard beneath his bed and stuffed the stolen specimens down deep inside. He laid the bones out side by side, nestling amongst his school-book sketches. And as he placed the boards back, his blood calmed, as if part of his anger had been buried down there too, amongst the dust and cobwebs.

Once the Professor found he could not put his creatures back together he would have need of Edgar Jones again. And then it would be seen what kind of boy he really was.

PART FOUR

In the week that separated Edgar's time in the Museum from his time at the instruments, the cottage was full of industry. All the remnants of his tutelage under the Professor were removed. His threadbare trousers, his dust-worn shirt, his tattered apron were fed to the fire by his father's hand.

The University papers were taken down from the wall and the inventor's apprenticeship document hung up in their place.

'There,' said William, as he anchored the frame upon the hook. 'Now that's altogether better. This apprenticeship will give you a proper way of looking at the world rather than filling your head full of fancies.'

Edgar frowned up at it. The letters wriggled under the glass, as if desperate to break free.

The day before he took up his new position, Edgar was subject to more lectures about the way his future should go. This time it was his mother, turning him this way and that, pinning him into his new suit , turning up the cuffs and tidying the ends of the trousers.

'You are twelve years of age now, Edgar,' she said, 'on your way to becoming a man. And here we are setting you up for another apprenticeship. Your father may see it as progress, but it is not a good way of life, to go flitting from one thing to another.'

Edgar shrugged. He had a better plan for his life than any apprenticeship could set out for him: a plan of hidden bones, and justice. Let her think what she liked, the truth would become apparent soon enough. In the meantime, he would dress up in the clothes of an inventor and he would take his place in the shop, so that the Professor would know where to find him.

The following day Edgar walked the roads to his new employment. The winds were stripping the golden leaves from the trees. Edgar kicked through them. He thought of the other leaves, the specimens that he had bolted to the roof of the Museum. Strong, beautiful and never dying.

Edgar emerged on to St Giles. There was the Martyrs' Memorial, splitting the street in two. He loitered at the base of it, looking up at the men who frowned out of the stone at him, as if they knew of his banishment and were holding him in judgement. He walked on, down to the crossroads, left on to Broad Street, past the colleges, down to the end of the street to where Mr Stephens the instrument maker had his shop, sitting snugly side by side with the White Horse tavern.

The shop had a broad bay window, stacked high with metal, but a very different kind of metal from the iron that Edgar hankered after. Perched up against the glass were scales and the weights to fit them, thermometers and barometers, and long metal rulers. No wonder his father favoured such an apprenticeship. This collection was like all the instruments cluttered on the parlour shelf, multiplied.

Edgar pushed open the door. A chorus heralded his arrival, a singsong peal that echoed around the room. Edgar looked up and saw that the beams were clustered with spun wire and a miniature gallery of brass bells were swinging out a tune.

The front of the shop was no more than a low-slung table with a ledger set upon it, and thick green curtains hanging down behind, tenting off the room. Shelves were set on both walls, and stacked up with articles of invention. They were split between practicality and pleasure. On one side there were the instruments of science; on the other, toys and entertainments, things that Edgar had never seen before, the things that should be given to a child. There was a painted man set on top of a ladder made of brass. His head ballooned out of his body and was decorated with a wide-toothed grin. Edgar pushed at it and the man tumbled, head over heels, down the rungs, metal chiming against metal as he fell. There was a train set upon tracks, a bright brass engine with a funnel on top and painted carriages running behind it. There was a wheel of black card set upon a spindle, with eyeholes cut into the side, not unlike the windows of the Museum. When Edgar set his hand upon it, and peered through he could see a bird set flying off a branch, soaring up towards the heavens and coming down to land.

'Master Edgar Jones, I presume?' called a voice behind him.

Edgar turned and saw, standing behind the table, a man who could only be Mr Stephens. He was a tall man, slight, and with a crown of jet-black hair, and a beard to match. He wore a pair of spectacles cut into the shape of half-moons and set upon the end of his nose, and he was smiling.

Edgar leapt back from the shelf. He whipped his cap off his head and held it before him, the way that his father had taught him. Behind him the toys clicked and tumbled.

'I see that you are already acquainting yourself with the apparatus,' the instrument maker said.

'I am sorry, sir,' mumbled Edgar.

'No need for apology,' replied Stephens. 'These are things that are made to be tampered with.'

He came to stand beside Edgar and took the train off its tracks. Under its belly was a brass key. Stephens twisted it, laid it down again, and it went racing round and round the loop of the track, pulling the carriages behind.

'No doubt you have come from the Museum with a head full of rules and regulations.'

'Yes, sir.'

'Well, be assured, this is an altogether different place that you are now apprenticed to,' he said kindly. 'Nothing here is forbidden, Master Jones. There is no machine that you may not set your hand to, no book whose pages cannot be turned. It is my belief that true invention can only come from letting one's mind roam free across the world without fear of censure.'

'Nothing forbidden?' It was unthinkable. All his life had been charted out by rules and by his attempts to slip them.

'Nothing,' repeated Stephens. 'Now, let me show you to your station.'

He led Edgar round the table and parted the curtains like a man preparing the stage at the theatre. On the other side of the curtain the workshop was as disordered as the shop front was regimented. There was a bench set against the window at the back that stretched the width of the room, and every inch of it was piled up with pulled-apart machinery. Cogs and levers and nuts and bolts clustered in corners. All across the floor, the bigger specimens were scattered: blocks of wood spiked with backbones of brass screws. As if the hauling machines of the Museum had been cut apart and strewn across the floor. In an echo of the front room, the walls had deep shelves set on either side. But these shelves were all topsy-turvy. Books were stacked up at irregular intervals and in between them crouched wooden boxes, opened to reveal slim metal instruments with hooked bills and spike-toothed ends.

Just as in the Professor's room, the walls were feathered with drawings and diagrams, but instead of bones there were levers and cog catchments, and instead of muscle here were chains and straps of leather. Edgar looked at the workshop and he smiled. If he could not be up amongst the roofwork any more then this was not such a bad place to be. If nothing was forbidden then he could put all these bits of stuff together every which way he pleased.

'I do believe that the art of invention is the creation of order from chaos,' said Stephens. 'And so it is with the chaos that we must begin!'

With a sweep of an arm, Stephens cleared a space at the end of the desk. He pulled across a stool and patted it.

'Now, Master Jones, are you ready for the first challenge of your apprenticeship?'

'Yes, sir.'

'Very good, sir.'

Stephens pulled a box of instruments from the shelf. He

unfolded a piece of green baize across the bench and placed a pocket watch upon it. The hands told Edgar that it was quarter-past nine. The wood carried the tick tick tick of the mechanism, like beetles scratching along the underside.

'Now, what do you make of that?' said Stephens.

Edgar frowned down at it. So this is what his life would be now: working away at small and ordinary pieces of metal. Edgar took it in his hand, and felt its weight. He peered into the dial. Behind the glass the minute hand shifted.

'It is a working pocket watch, sir.'

'And what do you think I would have you do with this working pocket watch?'

Edgar looked at the box of instruments. They were things he knew: a wrench, a pick, a hammer, all tiny.

'I think you would have me take it apart, sir.'

'Take it apart?' Stephens cried. 'I am an instrument maker – why should I sanction a thing being taken apart?'

Edgar thought of the mass of the metal roof, the picking apart of it, and the reforming.

'Because the taking apart of a thing is putting it together backwards.'

Stephens chuckled. 'Quite so, quite so. The Professor did assure me that you were a boy of natural talent. And if your way of making is as sharp as your way of talking I think we shall get on famously.'

Edgar frowned again. Natural talent? That was not what he heard echoing down the gallery. The Professor had just wanted him gone and would have said anything to persuade a man to take him. But he would prove the prediction right.

So it was that on his first day under Stephens' employ,

Edgar was back at the clock face, picking apart time. And time was the very same as it had been when he was a child: a thing held together by cogs and levers, but now in miniature.

Edgar lined the pieces up across his baize. When the watch was nothing but an empty round of brass, like the tin in which his father sealed up his snuff, Stephens came to Edgar's side and applauded.

'Good and careful work, Master Jones,' he said. 'Now reverse it.'

So Edgar did, piece by tweezered piece, working back along the lines of his removal, fitting hammer, pick and wrench to the mechanisms. There was some pleasure in the puzzle of the piecing back together, but the more he worked, pinching the tiny tools between his thumb and forefinger, the more he saw what his work was not. He was not anchored at the crossroads of metal, tightening rivets the size of his fist. Edgar clenched the watch in his hand, snapping the glass back into the frame. He gave it to his new master. Stephens peered into the glass and chuckled.

'Look again, Master Jones.'

Edgar saw that the hands were set the wrong way, so that the minute hand inched around the face, but the hours raced. He stared down at the cloth, his cheeks burning with the shame of it. It was a stupid error. A child's mistake.

'Some might say that this is a truer reflection of time,' laughed Stephens. 'Once you get to my age you will find that this is how it is: you may get stuck in moments of minutes, but hours hurtle past, bringing with them an avalanche of years. However,' he handed the watch back and pressed it into Edgar's palm, 'most folk would rather their watches followed convention. And there is a lesson in this. There is little point in paying attention to the detail of a task if you are to race through the final moments and set all askew. The finish of a piece of work is everything.'

'Yes, sir.' Edgar blushed deeper and kicked against the desk. All the other bits of un-put-together machines jumped along the table top.

'So, we shall take our time,' said Mr Stephens. 'Yes, indeed, we shall take our time with the challenge of the pocket watch.'

When Edgar returned home his father was waiting for him.

'So tell me,' said William, 'how did it go with Mr Stephens?'

Edgar turned his face away, his cheeks still burning with the shame of his mistake.

'There will be no more sullenness in this house, Edgar. If a question is put to you, you will answer it.'

'Clockwork,' said Edgar quietly.

'Clockwork?'

'I took apart a pocket watch.'

William stared over Edgar's head, at the grandfather clock, and its pendulum, which always lurched a little to the left.

'And what possible use could that be?' snapped William. 'You are going to have to learn not to meddle with things if you are going to make anything of yourself at all, Edgar Jones.'

Edgar spent two months upon the watchwork, and spoke not a word about it to his father. Edgar would pick all the insides apart and Stephens would jumble them up together upon the cloth, until Edgar could take any piece out and put it back in the correct fitting. He learnt the trick of running a magnet along the underside of the bench, so that all the bits stood clustered around the pull of it. And he imagined how it would have been at the Museum if he could have placed such a thing against the collapse: a moon-sized magnet swinging from the rafters, the spurs jumping out of the tangle of their own accord and standing to attention. That would have been a thing to see.

After the watchwork, Edgar was taught how to put together microscopes and telescopes, and how to balance the sway of a set of scales. And as he worked away, the Museum came back to him in miniature. There were the same principles of hauling and balancing: the push and pull of pulleys and strings, and the point of pressure upon a lever.

This echo of Edgar's old life ran true through all instruments, not just those of investigation. When a collection of rusted handcuffs was brought in by a blustering constable, Edgar found, behind the iron casing, the pitch and tumble of the levers and springs. He pressed his pick into the keyhole and watched the shift of the mechanism, and thought back to the nails in his fist and the opening of his bedroom door.

Under his master's guidance Edgar also learnt the trick of thinking of a thing and setting it down upon paper so that the invention could not escape him. Edgar copied out the innards of the instruments placed before him. He also set down his memories of his own inventions: the wide wing of his harness; the articulated tail.

Stephens did not rip these from his notebook like his father would have done. Instead, he overscored them with his pencil, and showed Edgar the way to measure out a thing upon a page so that it was all to scale.

To encourage his apprentice, Stephens would pull down

books where Edgar's inventions were echoed in the work of masters. Again and again Stephens would return to the same tome: a leather-bound broad-backed book.

'This is the Bible of every instrument maker, of every inventor,' he would declare, slapping it down upon the bench before Edgar.

It was an altogether better kind of Bible than the one his father set in front of him. In this book, Edgar could look into the insides of anything and everything: cut-apart creatures sat side by side with the mechanisms of machinery, God's inventions and man's inventions marked out in equal measure. In this book, creation and destruction were also set side by side: machines made from cogs within cogs, which levered up their limbs and rained down pellets of fire; a city being ripped apart by a flood of water, which smothered the building in luxurious curls like the hair of some terrible maiden shaking out vengeance. A human leg, pared back to the bone, with muscles knotted about it like the cables upon the cranes. A human heart cut in two, powered by the same pistons and valves that powered the clockwork engine. Between the pictures there were pages of slanted writing, with tiny birds sweeping down the margin, as if the words were fruits and flowers that they were feasting upon.

Edgar, studying the detail, loved to flick the pages against each other. He watched bone become tree become bird become wind become flood become machine become bone again. He saw that the whole world was held together by supple shapes that repeated across all things. Inside and out, the same arch: the curve of the bone, the currents of water, the delicate branches of the shrunken forest that hides inside a man's heart.

Edgar stored up all this knowledge, of things made, of things set upon the page, like hoards of precious treasure hidden under the floorboards. And when the time was right he would put together such inventions, such wonderful things. And he would take them home to his father.

The mysteries of Stephens' shop held Edgar's attention for as long as he was sitting upon his stool, with his master beside him. But day after day, when taking the road home, he would find himself havering at the foot of the Martyrs' Memorial, skirting the side of it and running out to the parks, out to the fence line that separated the Museum from the rest of Oxford. Staring up at the high walls, his whole day's work suddenly seemed nothing but a disappointment. What was the pleasure in cogs and screws when, behind those golden bricks, his iron netted in the clouds? He watched as the final slates were set upon the tip of the tower, and he wished that turning time back upon itself was as simple as the winding of a pocket-watch. He yearned to be back up there, with the building still unfinished and the open arch of the rafters framing the clouds, staring out at the muddied lawn and watching the iron coming rolling across it towards him.

There would often be other observers: curious scholars, lovers walking arm in arm, men of the Church and of the colleges, hesitating upon the road. It was quite a thing to watch the men at work upon the scaffold, with instruments that sparked fire from their ends, smelting the glass into the windows. The more Edgar listened to the idle chatter of the crowds, with courage this and design that, and was the building a blight or a blessing upon the face of the city, the more he found himself clenching and unclenching his fists in his pockets.

When the workmen were gone the intrigue was the unpicking of the scaffolding from the structure, plank by plank and strut by strut, until all the bricks were uncaged and there stood the Museum. The many eyes of the vaulted windows staring straight across the land at Edgar. The Museum crouched in the centre of the park like a beast set free from its cage, wary of the wide world beyond. Waiting for something. Was it waiting for him, Edgar wondered.

Just as Edgar's sense of injustice could not turn back time, it also could not stop the ticking of the clocks and the passing of the seasons. Edgar's days were charted out by the little work of tweezer and pick, and the year rolled on to its end.

As Christmas approached the chime of the bells upon the beams never ceased. Edgar was set to polishing every article. He would hear, through the curtain, Mr Stephens' declarations as he pulled objects from the shelves.

'One of a kind!' he would declare. 'Be the envy of all Oxford with the latest of contraptions.'

So persuasive was Mr Stephens' sales talk that he and Edgar could not keep up with the demand. And there was no time to ship the things up from London.

'We must be resourceful, Master Jones!' said Stephens with a smile. 'Or rather, you must. I fear I do not have the stature for it.'

Stephens set his shoulder to the worktable and shunted it down the room. And there, in the corner, where the table had stood, was a low door. Behind the door, stairs, leading up into the darkness. Stephens handed Edgar a lamp.

'Go and have a good rummage about,' he said. 'And bring back whatever you think might prove useful.'

The stairs ran in a tight spiral up, up and up the side of the shop. A part of Edgar was back in the Museum, clambering up to the tip of the tower. But there was no sky-perch at the top. The stairs led up to a low-beamed attic in the eaves. Trunks were piled up against trunks, precariously stacked, like a city made from a set of child's building blocks. A tarnished mirror with a splintered frame leant against a wall, doubling the chaos. Edgar wormed his way into the heart of it, springing the catches of the stores. It was a treasure trove of broken invention. He found cogs and levers and hooks and springs all tumbled together. And nestled in amongst the boxes of bits were abandoned instruments and toys.

Up and down the stairs Edgar ran, filling his pockets. There was a set of scales left to rust for the want of a broken link in a chain. Edgar clamped the wire, persuaded the metal to meet itself again and everything balanced. A spinning top was given a new spur, repolished, and went whirling across the floor. A stringless marionette – a fierce-bearded man in a wizard's gown – was reanimated and hung in the window, casting spells upon every child who pressed his face to the glass.

By Christmas Eve, when Mr Stephens pulled down the shutter and turned the sign on the window, the shelves were all but bare. Just a few weights and a poorly cast candlestick cluttered a corner.

'Well, Master Jones,' said Mr Stephens, 'this has been a great success. Never before have I turned such a profit. And it is all thanks to you and your ingenuity.'

Edgar grinned. It was a long time since he had been given thanks for anything.

'And good work deserves a good reward,' continued Stephens.

Out of his pocket he pulled a bright brass key threaded on a piece of leather. He dangled it in the air before Edgar.

'Do you know what this is?'

'A key, of course.'

'*The* key, Master Jones, *the* key. To the shop. The tradition is that an apprentice earns his access over four years. But I do believe you are an exception.'

Mr Stephens hung the key around Edgar's neck. It shone like a medal.

That night as Edgar walked the streets home he felt the chime of the key and the stolen tip of the ivory beating out against his skin. He was an inventor. He had been given a key, a key, a key. And he would use it.

On New Year's Day, when the family sat down to breakfast, William offered up his prayers before the cracking of the eggs, as he always did.

'Dear Lord,' he said, 'we thank you for this new beginning. May you keep my family safe from harm and temptation, and may Edgar continue well upon his path to a better life.'

And Edgar, head bowed, hands clasped into a fist added a prayer of his own: and may I get my fame and fortune and make my papa proud.

Eleanor also prayed silently: and may William and I find our way back to a bit of happiness.

'Amen,' said all.

Then Edgar pulled out two packages wrapped up in brown paper. The larger one he placed before his father, the smaller by his mother.

'Oh, Edgar,' said Eleanor, 'this is no way for you to be using your earnings.'

'I wanted you and Pa to see a bit of my work,' Edgar said, smiling.

William ripped at the paper – so like Edgar, Eleanor thought, when he was an eager-fisted child.

A chunk of iron tumbled out on to the table. It had a hollow head and stubby spur spiked with teeth.

'What is it, Edgar?' said William, turning it over and over.

'It's a key, Pa. It will open all the smaller doors in Oxford.'

'And what makes you think that I might desire such a dishonest gift?'

'It's not dishonesty, Pa, it's freedom. Think of all those rooms of books you can get into.'

William scowled and pointed the key's hooked bill at Edgar. 'Such access is a thing that is earned by the privileged few, son, not gained by a criminal's trick.' William threw the key upon the table, pushed back his chair and went thundering up the stairs.

'Really, Edgar,' said Eleanor, 'you should know your father better than to present him with such a thing.'

Edgar stared down at the table top. He knew well enough what it was like to stand outside a door and have no way of entering. How could his father not feel it too?

Eleanor picked at the string of her parcel. 'And what is this, then?' she said with a smile. 'What kind of mischief would you encourage your old mother into?

She pulled away the paper to find a piece of blue velvet, and speared into the heart of it, a rack of needles. They sparked silver against the cloth.

Later that night, as Edgar slept and Eleanor cut the shapes of women out of silk, William sat restless at his watch. It was a watch in name only. The college was a wall of darkness, the scholars were absent, and even the old masters had deserted their books in favour of the New Year. William, unseen by Eleanor or Edgar, had slipped the criminal key into his pocket. It was not a thing to leave for Edgar to turn to his own purpose. He found himself rolling it over and over in his palm, feeling along the ridge of the teeth.

William had been at his post for thirty-eight years. He had grown from a youthful man to a man of middle age, his hair receding, his once-confident step beginning to falter. He had reversed the order of his days for the good of his college, spent his nights in the company of gargoyles rather than settled under the blankets with his wife; rather than guiding his son through the daylight hours of his life. And as every new year came around, he felt as if his family, and his understanding of his place within it, was ebbing further and further away from him. If only the guarding of his home was as simple as guarding a gate.

William turned the key in his hand, over and over. It might be a criminal instrument, but he need not use it for a criminal act. At times, a man might have to bend the rules of the world in order to comprehend it better.

For the second time in his life, William deserted his watch. He took the lamp from the lodge and cradled it to him so that the college revealed itself in piecemeal as he walked through it. There was the old city wall, there was the shadowed turning to the cloisters, there were the broad stone steps leading up to the library. He scaled them, softly, softly. He put the key to the lock, the chambers tumbled and the door swung open before him.

William stood at the edge of the room. His lamp gave him only spots of illumination. There was a wall of books set straight in front of him. It was endless, rearing up into the darkness above his head and stretching the width of the room. He crept along the face of it. Titles flashed out of the gloom, gold lettering caught by the lamplight, flaring out at him like a warning: *On Morality; On Faith and Revelation; Manifestations of the Spirit*. He skirted the edge of the wall and turned the corner. Another bookcase set at a right angle loomed out of the dark. *The Anatomy of Guilt* it declared; *On Justice and Practice*.

Round and round the racks of knowledge William ventured, turning book-bound corner after corner, through divinity, law, verse and numbers until he was dizzy and breathless. He stood in the dark cavern of the library and felt the force of all the wisdom gathered around him as a great weight pressing down upon his heart. He could stay within this room for the rest of his life and still what was known to him would be outweighed by the never-ending ranks of books unopened. What hope did he have of finding the tome that would give him guidance? There was no golden thread to lead him through the maze. His trespass had only served to show him his ignorance, and he had his son to thank for it.

Meanwhile back in the cottage, Eleanor picked out one of Edgar's needles. She took a thread, and held it up to the eye. The thread slipped through the needletop. She put the point of it to the blue silk of a skirt. The needle danced in her hand, sparkling silver as it went. It seemed to hover along the line of the cloth, push pulling of its own accord. The panel was set in an instant and when Eleanor twisted and turned it around before her lamplight, it appeared to her that the silk was flecked with specks of silver, pinpoints of stars at twilight.

The new year continued for Edgar in the same fashion as the one before. By day he busied himself with the little work, the assembling of the machinery, the placing of the displays, and the scouring out of solutions from that great book of inventions. But in the evening, he would go to study the Museum and the Museum would stare straight back at him.

Now that the building was done, the mottled mud sprouted grass in the springtime, undisturbed by the passage of working men. The Museum was slowly settling into residence, as if it had always been a part of Oxford, remarkable and yet just another marvel in this city of golden stone, spires and towers and angels.

Edgar watched as the wardens walked the rounds of the building, flitting between the lampposts like crows. He watched as carts rolled up to the Museum door, with the horses bulge-eyed and foam-mouthed with the weight of their loads. Men struggled to hold the boxes upon their shoulders, and walked with the stagger of seasickness as they took them up the steps. Edgar watched the door opening and swallowing the procession: men, crates and all.

He smiled. He knew full well what was inside those boxes: creatures, boiled down to their bones. It would only be a matter of time before the Professor would seek Edgar out, pleading for him to forge the missing pieces.

But the Professor never came.

Week after week, carts went to and fro from the Museum. Edgar had bold fantasies of shuttering himself up in one such crate. When the lid was cranked open he would jump out like one of Stephens' jack-in-the-boxes and race up to the gallery. He would grab a piece of rope and set himself swinging from a spur. But he knew well enough how that would play out. The wardens would catch him and pitch him out on to the lawn, and that would be that.

No, if Edgar Jones was going to return to the Museum then he would walk back through the door and the Professor would applaud him. He would ensure that he was recognised as the champion that he was.

In the meantime he fixed cogs to their treads, squeezed springs on to their fixings, planned and plotted a thousand inventions upon paper and became an expert in feigning contentment.

Then, one morning, everything changed. Edgar arrived at the workshop to find a wide sea of paper spread out across the floor, weighted down with bits of wood. There was a barrel lying on its side at the centre of the page, with something like a funnel sticking out of the end of it. And arching up on either side of it, the unmistakable shape of Edgar's iron.

'Ah, Master Jones!' cried Stephens. 'If only you had come a minute earlier you would have been reunited with your old master. He was most curious about the progress of your apprenticeship.'

'The Professor?'

'The Professor indeed. I told him that you were progressing admirably.'

'Did you, sir?'

'Indeed I did. And it was my impression that he was somewhat envious of our alliance.'

The Professor, the collector, always after something.

Edgar walked round the edges of the paper. The thing set on the page looked like nothing he had ever seen up in the Professor's attic. There was certainly nothing bonelike about it.

'And he is after an invention?'

'I think your Professor is out to test our skills to the limit, Master Jones. He has commissioned a magic lantern.'

'A magic lantern?' Edgar could not imagine what such a thing might be. He thought of the lamps they put together, the simple brass tubes of oil and glass. Where was the magic in that?

'It is a system of projection,' replied Stephens. 'A simple principle, sure enough. It is a trick of mirrors and lenses and the light, a contraption that is used in the music halls. The challenge lies in the scale of the piece.'

Stephens lifted the wood and turned over the paper. There was the barrel again, but cut open, with all its mechanisms exposed. Set inside were mirrors and tilting bits of glass. Stephens started scoring numbers along the sides of it.

'We will need to put together a beast of a thing if we are to meet his requirements.'

'The Professor is awfully fond of his beasts,' said Edgar.

'Very true,' chuckled Stephens, 'so let us set about making one that fits his purpose.'

It was a barrel indeed that was rolled through into the workshop – an old tar barrel, Edgar's height and half again. Stephens marked out fissures in the wood. The top and the bottom were cut away. It was set upon its side, and anchored on blocks. It was Edgar's job to crawl inside with a measuring stick and to call out numbers to his master. The wood amplified the sound and Edgar felt as if he was stuck in Mr S's speaking tube, with his voice shaking the rafters.

'This is what it is, Master Jones,' laughed Mr Stephens, 'to be right at the heart of invention.'

Then the glass and mirrors arrived at the workshop. The lenses came wrapped in reams of brown velvet. One was the width of the barrel base, the other smaller. Like a sun and moon of glass. The larger lens warped the edges of the room when Edgar looked through it, stretching the shelves and the table thin, rendering Stephens into a pinprick of flesh at the centre.

The larger lens was set in the heart of the barrel, the smaller set into a nose of lead and affixed to the front. A smooth sea of a mirror was placed between them. They were connected by fine wires that snaked out of the slats. Then an iron casement was slotted behind, and a clear chute cut through the wood. The back of the barrel had steps set into it, on which a lamp was fitted.

As Edgar placed the fixtures, his hands trembled at the touch. This was his key back to the Museum, he was sure of it. For wherever the barrel was placed, he would be beside it: who else knew its workings, and who else was small enough to get inside it?

It took three weeks to complete. The final touch was the wheels that Stephens bolted to the sides. The velvet coverings of the glass were thrown across the back of it. Looking at it from the outside, it seemed to be some kind of glass-snouted fat-bellied creature.

'This is a magnificent machine, if ever I saw one,' said Stephens. 'I would not be surprised if your professor sets it in pride of place in his Museum.'

Edgar smiled.

'But however splendid its appearance, it is for its function that it will be prized,' mused Stephens. 'We must test its capacity.'

The shutters were drawn across the shop front and the sign turned upon the door. A white sheet was pulled across the window. Edgar crawled into the back and lit the lamp. A rope of light went streaming out across the workshop. It grew as it travelled the length of the room, casting up a moon upon the wall. Stephens' hand came burrowing through the cloth, holding a plate of glass.

'In the slot, Master Jones!'

Edgar did so. And there, shining out of the darkness, with wings cast the width of the workshop and spear set to the sky, was a stone angel.

The next day, at dusk, a cart rolled up outside the door of the shop. Edgar and his invention were set upon the back of it. As they went careering round the corner, Edgar could hear the wire and the metal playing against each other inside the barrel. He set his body against it, anchoring the lantern under his arm.

The road curved and the wood knocked against Edgar's ribs as the cart rolled its way down to the parkland. Edgar watched the Museum emerge out of the gloom, playing hide-and-seek with him from behind the embrace of the trees.

The cart turned through the gap in the fence and there was the Museum, stuck fast in the centre of the open land. Across the sky, birds came wheeling, screeching, as if calling out caution to Edgar as they streamed this way and that, a black-feathered banner wrapping itself around the roof. The tower cut into the sky like a fat-bladed knife, with the sunset bleeding around the sides of it.

There, Edgar saw, leaning against the cornice of the door as if he was set into the stone, was the Professor. He had his cloak gathered around his shoulders, both his hands folded over the fist of his cane. He was nodding this way and that, scanning his lands. As the cart slowed, Edgar's heart beat loud against his ribs, a match for the knock knock knocking of the machine. This was the man who had cast him out. The man whose bones Edgar had stowed beneath his bed. The man who cared for his Museum more than anything. And now Edgar was bringing him this great invention of light and mirrors. Better than a tail, better than a harness, it was a thing that could conjure a specimen out of thin air, and render it silver, shimmering and wonderful. The Professor would fall in love with the magical lantern, Edgar was sure of it, and then Edgar would be welcomed back into his favour. Edgar saw how it would be: he and the Professor, standing side by side on the Museum steps, ushering his father through the door. They would walk beneath the roof together, and the Professor would sing his praises. He would tell how Edgar Jones was brave and bold and clever, a boy who would turn his hand to anything. A good son. His father would look up at the great iron bones, he would stare in wonder at the angel that shone out of the barrel-light and he would be proud.

'Edgar Jones!' cried the Professor, with a raise of his cane, 'Well met, indeed!'

He strode to the edge of the cart and held his hand out, but his gaze was fixed over Edgar's shoulder, upon the lantern.

'So tell me,' he said, his smile fixed, 'how goes your new apprenticeship?'

'Let me inside, and I will show you.'

Edgar jumped from the cart. The Professor put his hand upon his shoulder, as if he was still his boy, and led him to the door.

Edgar looked up at the windows. The glass reflected the dusk passage of the clouds. One lower ledge was sprouting flowers and leaves. From the window above, a face was grinning out of the cornice at Edgar. An animal face, a monkey. Or the beginning of a monkey. There was just the curve of the head, the pebble eyes, the snout-nose pushing out of the rock. The twilight shadows gave it a dappled fur. The rest of its body was still caught behind the stone. Except for one arm, which reached out of the lintel, as if the creature was trying to pick apart the bricks.

The Professor followed Edgar's gaze and chuckled. 'A curious-looking fellow, is he not?'

'Why a monkey, sir?'

'It was a bit of sport from the stonemasons. They were under instruction to carve whatever bit of creation they fancied upon the face of the Museum. However, it seems that the clergy took exception to the appearance of a primate. He will be corrected in due course.'

'Corrected?'

'Carved into something less contentious.'

Corrected. Banished. It seemed it went the same way for all of the Professor's difficult specimens.

The Professor set his shoulder to the door and pushed. There was the porch full of shadows, with the shallow steps leading to the second door. The walls were crawling with nature. Crawling, but dead: owls roosted in the eaves, their stone-feathered wings forever flightless. Snakes wound across the bricks beside them, tongues licking out across the rock. Edgar ran up the steps and pushed open the second door.

It swung wide and revealed a great mouth, ready to swallow.

There, upended against a pillar, was a huge jawbone, its aperture the height of a man, with teeth the size of bolts, grinning an untrustworthy welcome. Edgar gazed up the line of ivory and beyond it. There was his roof, rearing up into the twilight.

Except that it was not his roof. The iron was painted deep blue with gold flowers stencilled along the run of the curve. There were gaslamps hanging between the ribs at the level of the upper gallery, floating rings of fire. The painted iron gave the impression of a mass of stars, tumbling down into the courtyard. The pillars and the posts were swallowed by the dusk as if there was no metal there at all. As if all that Edgar had clambered up, bolted and swung from was nothing but a dream. As if there had been no courage, no invention, no skysailing. As if he had never even set foot in the Museum.

'So, Edgar Jones, what do you think of the Museum now?'

'The iron . . .' Edgar faltered.

'Is magnificent, is it not?'

Edgar clenched his fists in his pockets. He saw how it would have been done. Whilst Edgar was sat at his watchwork, another man, anchored in his harness, would have swung from the heights with a stencil in one hand, a brush in the other, and worked his way across the sky, turning the iron gaudy with every stroke.

'And there is more, much more, to be wondered at. Come.'

The Professor led Edgar up the stairs to the gallery. There the gaslamps played out a second illusion. Lit from below, the spandrels flared gold. There was a forest of fire set streaming down the body of the courtyard. Edgar's horse chestnut, the daisies, the tulips, and all the plants that Edgar could not name, blossomed out of the darkness, and they were also painted brash bright colours. They looked like women's work to Edgar, like the kind of thing his mother might embroider across a skirt. It was not for this that he had squeezed through the innards and eked out the flowering pieces.

The Professor was at his side, laughing

'We have turned the world upon its head, do you see? The stars upon the land, the flowers in the heavens.'

Edgar clenched his fists again. Who had done such a thing, precisely? Edgar and his fellows, swinging along the length of the place, anchoring iron to iron, had not done it just to create a cheap illusion; for the kind of trick that Stephens might piece together in a diorama box and put in the shop window. Edgar itched for a harness beneath him and a rope behind. He would let fly from the gallery wall and pull all the painted pieces apart.

The Professor steered Edgar back down to the courtyard, around to the far west corner and there, galloping out of the gloom, was the giraffe. It stood bow-bellied and knock-kneed, anchored on to a wooden plinth. Its bones were threaded through with steel. Its ladder neck stretched up above. The slender head was cast golden by the gaslight, tipped towards the flowering spandrels as if it had been caught by the trick of it and was yearning to feast from the painted iron. The tail dropped down from the haunches and disappeared into the dusk. It was as if the Professor was intent on turning invisible everything and anything that Edgar had ever made.

Edgar walked around the lower gallery. The pillars were polished to a fine shine now, and there were cabinets set between the arches. Edgar peered inside. Stuffed creatures stared back out at him: bead-eyed birds with wide-spanned wings and claws raised ready to strike. The corridor echoed with the memory of the Professor's words: Edgar Jones has served his purpose. And the anger came rushing back through Edgar's blood. He had a savage desire to plunge his fist into the glass, to rip apart the specimens, to spoil the Professor's work the same way that he had spoilt Edgar's iron. But there was a lamp to be lit, an invention to be shown, and favour to be won. Edgar walked on.

He emerged from the gallery, out into the courtyard, and stopped in his tracks. He and the Professor were not alone. There was a man, leaning against the wall, watching them. A pale ghostly man. Standing stock-still, and staring straight at Edgar. Master Thomas, returned?

The Professor chuckled. 'Come, Edgar Jones, let me introduce you to your ancestor.'

They walked across the courtyard. The man did not move a muscle. And as Edgar neared he saw that the man was not a man at all, but a stone statue. Another trick. Another instance of using a material to make it seem to be something it was not. The man stood with his gaze set upon a stone apple cast by his feet, as if the very act of observation had frozen him. The Professor tapped against the stone boots with his cane.

'This is Mr Newton. It is thanks to his discoveries that we had the wits to set the iron upon itself and the means to fly you from the heart of it.'

As Edgar recalled, he set himself in the harness of his own accord, without the help of anyone.

The Professor gestured down the run of the gallery wall. Edgar saw a line of statues, all standing with their backs to the wall.

'And these are all the great scientists, since time immemorial. All standing witness to the wonders of the Museum.'

Edgar squinted into the gloom. At the end of the row, a plinth jutted out into the courtyard. Empty.

'And this,' the Professor said, 'has been set for the future, for the great minds to come. The very minds that the Museum is made to nurture.'

Edgar glared at the empty space. If the Professor had any sense of justice at all, there would stand a statue of Edgar Jones, clutching a harness in one hand, and a tail in the other.

'So what is your impression of the place?' asked the Professor. 'Truthfully?'

Edgar looked up at the painted iron. Had not Master Stephens told him often enough that the finish of a piece of work was everything? This was not a place he would be proud to bring his father, and to call his own. It was shabbily done.

'Why, I do believe that Edgar Jones is struck dumb,' crowed the Professor. 'And well he might be. It is a wonder of the world, is it not?'

'It is . . .' Edgar faltered.

'It is what, precisely?'

'It is not as I would have finished it.'

The Professor's laughter rang hollow around the courtyard.

'I do declare, Edgar Jones, you have not changed one iota. Not as you would have finished it, indeed!'

Edgar glared at the floor and did not laugh at all.

'And yet there is some truth in your judgement, my boy. My enemies are waging a great war against the Museum. It stands incomplete and unvisited until the argument is resolved.'

'Why, sir?'

'Because, Edgar Jones, they fear that which they do not understand. They claim that the Museum has the power to break the minds of the men who look upon it.'

Edgar thought of the broken roof, all bowed down and tangled in upon itself, the jagged mouths of the torn-away pieces whistling in the wind. If a mind could break, would it break in the same fashion?

'And could it?'

'No, no, not at all. The Museum can only illuminate. And this is what I shall demonstrate, with the assistance of your magical lantern.'

As if in response, there was a clunk from the far end of the courtyard and there, rolling around the great grinning jaws, came Edgar's barrel-bellied projector.

'A most timely arrival!' cried the Professor.

'We need darkness,' said Edgar.

'Then darkness we will have!' The Professor went to the wall and pulled down upon a lever. There was a Pop! Pop! Pop! and the gaslamps were extinguished.

Edgar crept in and lit the lamp at the back of the barrel. The magic lantern cast its rope of light across the courtyard, a dancing moon, licking up the height of the lower court, right up to the line of the gallery. The light winkled its way into every crack and crevice, picking out the polish of a pillar, turning the faces of the cabinets into expanses of shimmering light. The Professor applauded and the roof rang with the echo.

'That will do, Edgar Jones,' crowed the Professor. 'That will do indeed.'

Edgar crawled out and there was the Professor, smiling down at him, just as he had when Edgar pulled a tail from his pocket.

'What is it for, sir?'

'To turn the mind of my enemies to my cause,' grinned the Professor. 'And I will undoubtedly need your assistance to achieve it.'

Edgar leant his weight upon the back of the barrel. It swayed upon its pivot, casting the beam up, up and up. And there, in the heights, flaring firecracker silver, lacing together the heavens, was the second roof, spreading its chequerboard wings across the width of the courtyard.

'Pa,' said Edgar, over the supper table, 'do you know what a magic lantern is?'

William frowned. 'No, Edgar, I do not. It sounds to me like another of your fantasies.'

'Not fancy, Pa, invention.'

Out it came, the story of the barrel and the lenses set inside it. Edgar took down the telescope, set his knife to the screws, and opened up the brass in an instant. He angled the glass against the lamp and set globes of light dancing across the walls.

'Clever enough, Edgar, but this seems like a cheap entertainment rather than the stuff of proper investigation.'

Edgar shook his head. 'No, Pa, the Professor says that the machine will change the history of Oxford.'

'The Professor?' barked William.

And Edgar told his father the whole of it: how the Professor was inviting all his enemies to the Museum for a great debate, and how Edgar and his invention would win the argument.

William stared at the barrel of his telescope, split open across the table, and the lenses spat out at either end.

'Have I not made it plain, Edgar? You are forbidden to go running about after this Professor.'

'The Professor has commissioned Mr Stephens,' replied Edgar curtly, 'and Mr Stephens has given me his orders.'

'This Professor seems to think that he can pick you up and put you down again according to his whims. But he is mistaken. You will not attend this debate of his.'

'Will,' said Eleanor sharply, 'you cannot decide how Edgar's apprenticeship goes. He must follow his instructions, unless you want him cast out on the street for a third time.'

Edgar picked up the screws and began to piece back together the telescope. His father would think differently after the event when his newspaper boasted pictures of the magical lantern, with Edgar at the helm of it and all the scholars of Oxford standing around him, applauding.

That night at the lodge William turned the argument about in his mind, over and over as the lights of learning faded. It seemed a cruel trick of fate that whatever road in life he set Edgar upon twisted against itself, and became a slippery slope to ruin, a stony path that led straight back to the Professor's door. Straight back to that room full of bones. And yet Eleanor was right: to forbid Edgar from following Mr Stephens' orders would not do. There must be a way to protect his son without damaging his prospects.

William thrust his hands into his pockets and his fist closed around the skeleton key. The teeth cut into his palm, iron pricking at his flesh.

Whilst the scholars slumbered, William deserted his post for the third and final time. He crept through the quad, around the wall, past the cloisters and round to the back of the college. There was the staircase that would take him to the dining hall. It yawned out of the darkness like a great stone mouth with a ripple-ridged tongue. William stepped inside and put his key to the door to the right-hand side of it. The chambers tumbled and William was standing in the vestibule of the Fellows' study. There, racked up on hooks like shed skins, like bats roosting on the rafters, were gowns upon gowns, some with their hoods lined with fur, others with tongues of silk peeping out of the back of them. What was it he had said to Edgar? Something about privilege needing to be earned. Well, in desperate times it had to be taken. William rummaged through the robes until he found one without adornment: the gown that a man of the Church might wear. He stowed it under his arm, locked the door behind him and returned to his watch, bundling the robe into a mail sack beneath his desk.

When dawn came, he folded the gown in upon itself, and drew his coat around it. He walked back to the cottage at a pace. The cloth against his chest carried an echo of Edgar about it. Edgar, wide-eyed, laughing, bound against his belly, set flying across the ice. William was beset by that same iron-bladed unsteadiness as he walked the streets home. The walls of the University seemed unfixed, shifting away from him in the waking dawn. The cobbles were turning and tumbling as he marched across them. The world he knew was splitting apart from itself and it was his duty to pull everything back into alignment.

The following morning, after a silent breakfast at the parlour table, William set his pen to paper and wrote out his first untruth. He claimed an uncommonly vicious head cold that was keeping him bound to his bed, sent the notice on to the college with a messenger boy and retired to sleep. But sleep did not come. William turned and tumbled, churning up the bed sheets, knocking aside the barricade of pillows. As his plan formed and reformed in his mind, question followed question until William was caught up in the dizzying circles of his own reasoning.

What kind of man was this Professor? And what kind of man could judge another man? And what kind of man was he, William Jones? Two days previously, he was sure of the answer: he was a loyal man, a man who knew his place in this world and the next. A man who trusted that God had a great scheme of life mapped out for him and who knew that if he followed a righteous path then all would play out in his favour. But now . . . Now the way before him was shadowed and uncertain.

Yesterday he was a thief, today he was a liar. He was in danger of becoming the very kind of man that he was set to guard the gates against.

And yet, and yet . . . a man is more than his station, more than a mere costume of authority. William had a duty to the University but he had a greater duty to his own blood. His son must be protected. And if William had to pretend to be something other than he was to achieve it, then so be it.

At six o'clock he came down the stairs, took his tea, polished his boots, kissed his wife and left home. He retrieved the stolen gown from the wilderness, turned his collar backwards, put on the robes of learning, and took the road to the Museum.

As William walked he became aware of the mass of men congregating ahead of him and behind. In their cloaks and gowns they seemed to be part made of twilight, emerging silent from side streets, from the doors of the colleges, flitting through shadows and gathering to a great wave, pouring down the road to the parks and up to the Museum door.

William looked up at the face of the Museum rearing above him and he did not trust it. The vaulted windows, the steadfast tower – even on the outside the Professor's deception was apparent: there was something churchlike about this place and, at the same instant, it had an open air of unholiness about it.

The men pushed through the porch and through the second door. William stood frozen on the threshold, with the crowd thronging around him. It was as if he had stepped straight into the stories of the Scriptures. As if, when he needed it most, God had laid out the lessons clearly before him.

His first impression was that he had stumbled into Noah's Ark, that God's favoured ship had struck against the hills of Oxford, and not all of its precious cargo had escaped the wreckage. The grand courtyard was the hull of it. In the corner stood a bone monster, stranded on a wooden island, running from its death. Around the edges of the room flew the birds, trapped in glass, smashing forever against the windows of the sinking ship.

No sooner had William seen this than the building shifted and changed its fable. He saw the jaws upended at the doorway and was suddenly terrified to pass through them. If he walked under that arch of bone he would become a second Jonah, trapped in darkness and crying out for mercy. The iron ribs of the roof shifted and were the ribs of the whale's belly. Beyond the gate of teeth he could see the men of Church and University walking their rounds of the cabinets. Already swallowed, and sadly ignorant of it. Spun rings of fire hovered over their heads. In the centre of the courtyard chairs were lined up, like ordered rows of tombstones.

A bell rang out, the iron catching the echo of it and magnifying it to a great hammering. The men moved to the seats. William took a place at the back of the ranks.

A wide white sheet hung down at the end of the gallery, and a makeshift stage was set in front of it, nothing but a few crates set side by side and lashed together by rope. This was an amateurish endeavour and no mistake. Then there was a Pop! Pop! Pop! and the gaslamps were extinguished. William and his companions were left in the half-light.

'Sensationalism,' mumbled a voice at William's shoulder.

William nodded to himself and smiled. The audience were

of his mind. It would not take very much to tip this Professor off his perch.

Then suddenly a rope of light came streaming down the courtyard, casting a great white globe upon the cloth. The room was silenced by the spectacle. William looked behind him. This was Edgar's invention, it must be. The light dwindled to a pinpoint under the sway of those huge jaws. That was where his son was trapped, William was sure of it. Everything in him yearned to run from his seat, pluck Edgar from between those bolt-tipped teeth, pull him out of the darkness and carry him home. But that would only create more argument between them. No, if William was going to do his duty by Edgar then he must stand firm. He must sit and listen to the bold claims of this Professor and, along with all the other holy men of Oxford, pick apart his philosophies. The Professor would be jeered off his pedestal and that would be the end of it.

The Professor stepped on to the stage. The boards boomed with his footsteps.

'Gentleman,' he declared, opening out his arms as if to embrace the entire room, 'you are most welcome here.' The Professor clapped his hands together. The iron echoed it back to him. 'I know that many of you perceive the Museum to be a place of heresy. This is an unjust misunderstanding. I am, like you, a true Christian, who believes God to be in all his works most wonderful.'

There was a muttering in the audience, like a distant echo of thunder before a storm.

The Professor raised his voice above it. 'Gentlemen, all that I ask of you is your patience!'

William looked at the profile of the Professor cast up in shadow, how like a crow he looked, with the hook of his nose and his cloak folded behind him. How like a carrion feeder. He spread his arms and up in the furrows of the sheet, his wings unfurled.

'It is not my intention to rip up your faith at the roots. Rather I wish to give you a proven foundation for such faith. It is my firm belief that God is a great inventor, and that the world he has created is full of wonderful riddles to be solved. It is through the apprehension of these puzzles that we inch nearer to a true understanding of our Creator.'

The world as a riddle indeed, thought William. A false argument if ever he heard one. The world was as the world was. There was heaven above and hell below, and the land mankind was placed upon was a world of trials and temptations set between the two. Understanding God was simple enough: He had set His will out clearly in His Commandments. Faith was purely a matter of following the letter of them.

The Professor swept off the stage, the white eye upon the sheet blinked and there, growing up the height of the gallery was a leaf caught in stone.

The eye blinked again, and there was another leaf. It was as if the shadow in the rock had grown a skin. It was a trick, a trick of the light. A trick of Edgar's. And now the Professor was asserting that the rock and the leaf plucked from the treetops were the selfsame thing. That rock was not rock forged by God's hand on the third day, but a thing that had settled over an unimaginable expanse of years. That the whole surface of the world had been a great stew of mud, water and chaos. That the layering up of the land could be read as a diary of all creation. Why else should God place one leaf inside a hillside, and the other upon the tree?

William folded his arms across his chest as if to shield himself from the argument. Why, why, why, said the Professor, hammering his cane upon the stage as if he was beating upon a drum. Why, why, why, like Edgar when he had first found his tongue. William knew why sure enough: the echo of the leaf in the rock was a test of faith, and nothing more. The world was full of such tests: the test of the sullen son; the test of the wanton wife.

But that was only the beginning of the argument. Click click click went the shutter eye and the images went galloping across the cloth. Bones stretched and grew and creature blended into creature. Shrew grew to cat to tiger. William saw it was all an underhand trick, like the flicking of a child's illusion book, where a lion is seen to run roaring across the page, just through the following of picture with picture and picture.

As the skeletons danced, the Professor continued his great tale. How the changes in bone showed the passage of time as clearly as the layering up of rock. How every creature was racing towards becoming another creature. It seemed to William that the Professor was simply ripping apart all creation and then putting it back together to suit his argument.

The skull of a sharp-toothed beast grinned out of the wall at William: fierce-spiked bone. The Professor was claiming that echoes of such animals had been dug out of the mountains. There it was, a piece of stuff that looked more like driftwood than ivory to William's eyes. And this was found just beyond the hills that embraced Oxford.

'This is blasphemy, sir!' cried a voice far ahead of William. 'You cannot create a story about the world and change the words of God to fit it. Either creation occurred as the Bible dictates or it did not.'

The room rang with steely applause. It would not be long now, William was certain of it. The Professor would be exposed for the charlatan that he was. A fantasist. A man with a corrupted mind, who did not deserve his robes of learning.

'There is blasphemy and there is misconception,' countered the Professor. 'Why, in past centuries, the world was believed to be flat. It is only through the courage of the explorers who sailed through their fear of falling off the edge of it that we discovered that we live upon a spherical earth.'

Now savage things from foreign lands galloped across the screen. Leather-faced, snout-jawed creatures stared out from the slime of rivers. Thundering creatures stood in the centre of vast deserts, tusks spiking the sky, fur cresting the ridge of their spines. There were cats with dappled coats and roaring mouths. There were huge monsters with rippled skin, and snouts that trailed down into pools of water. It seemed to William that there was a pretty picture to match every part of this argument.

The Professor stood beneath them all, telling how, an age upon an age ago, before a stone of Oxford had been placed, before Oxford was even dreamt of, the rock-calendar of the world declared that this land – this very land that the Museum was set upon – was a savage jungle of a place where giant beasts roamed. And after all the monsters had been slain, men built homes of wood and dung. And what did this prove? It proved, surely, that mankind was a race made to learn. The Professor was certain of it. God made us in a form that always strove to better itself, in body and mind and deed. The savages of the Empire, without God's guidance, were stuck in a primitive state. But not us, not the enlightened ones. The more we developed the godly part of ourselves – that part that must solve the riddles that nature sets before us – the more holy we would become.

'To look into the mysteries of nature is to look into the very essence of ourselves,' declared the Professor.

A click. The wide white eye. And then, stretching from floor to ceiling, a man stripped back to the bone, with a skull-wide grin.

'And what then awaits the Enlightened, Professor?' cried a voice from the crowd. 'Will we grow wings upon our backs and fly up to join the angels?'

Laughter rippled around the room, but it was not unkind, not the laughter of a hostile crowd.

'Perhaps,' said the Professor. 'To our ancestors it would be an impossible thought for us to set a net of iron out across the land and carry ourselves across it by the power of steam. And yet such a thing has come to pass. Who knows what great discoveries will be made by our children, and their children after them? But what I do know is this. There must be a place where such craft and enquiry is celebrated. Where a man can look upon all the wonders of the world and make his own connections and progress towards his higher nature. And the Museum, when completed, will be such a place. It will be a cathedral to Nature that celebrates the mystery and magnitude of God's work in all its glory.'

The picture shifted, and there were all the open-eyed

windows of the museum sketched out upon the screen, and every frame of every one was carved with the faces of creatures – bears, tigers, horses, stags. From some cornices the creatures came clambering – birds flitting from their nests, turtles swimming out into the air, and monkeys shinning along the line of the upper levels.

The room erupted with a mixture of jeers and applause.

'To have a cathedral crawling with creatures like a pagan thing simply will not stand!' shouted a voice at William's shoulder. 'Where men are wont to see angels, they are presented with monkeys. It will make them run mad in the streets.'

'Or stand in wonder at the great variety of creation,' cried the Professor. 'Through ornamentation the craftsman renders the works of God perfect and immortal. Through observation the scientists shall prove the wonder of the great design.'

A slow applause began at the front of the room, and grew to a wave of sound, echoed back by the iron. It drowned the mutterings of the dissenters gathered around William. It would swallow him, this great wave. He would be trapped under the force of it, flattened, pressed into a shadow of himself, just like the creatures caught in the rock.

He must fight it.

William knew, after all, what kind of a man this Professor was. He knew that he could turn any argument inside out if it suited his cause. He could gather up a room of men in his net of flattery, placing them alongside the angels. William had been caught once in this fashion, by the gold leaf of the University Crest winking out at him from the page. He would not be caught again.

William leapt from his chair and pushed his way through the applause. He vaulted the stage, and stood in the centre of that circle of light. The Museum and all its crawling creatures sat upon his shoulders. The rope of light blinded him, spotting his sight. The air before him danced with firecracker explosions, a world full of falling stars. He reached out into the darkness and closed his fist tight around the Professor's wrist. He could feel the bunched-together bones. He could feel the pulse of blood running under the flesh. And in that moment the room fell silent. William blinked. He could only see the shadowy shape of men, stretched out beyond the starfall.

'Clay and dust!' cried William. 'Was it not written so? It is the miracle of God's breath within us that gives us speech, that gives movement to our clay. It is blasphemy indeed to use this gift of speech to pick apart His holy words; to speak of this world as a shifting thing when the Bible tells us clearly that God made the world as He made it and He saw that it was good.'

The Professor pulled hard against William but William held fast. On the sheet above, their shadows twisted and turned and spread their big black wings.

'Sir!' said the Professor, tugging against him. 'Please, be seated. This is a debate, not a circus.'

'No, sir, it is a circus and no mistake. A circus of vanity and illusion. You are nothing but a false prophet, Professor.'

The Professor matched William's grip with his own: the grip of a man who has spent a lifetime hauling bones. He pulled William into the heart of the white light. The stars still danced at the edges of William's vision but he could see the Professor peering at him, his pinprick eyes two dark pebbles, staring straight at William as if he were trying to pick out the shape of his skull beneath the flesh.

'Porter Jones,' hissed the professor – a soft whisper, the voice of the serpent – 'you are here in false robes, and under false authority. You should be most careful.'

But William did not care. What was his reputation when set against his love for his son?

'You are false, sir!' cried William again. 'You would sacrifice the soul of a child as soon as you would strip the flesh from a creature if it might serve your cause.'

'Sacrifice?' smiled the Professor. 'I think not, sir. Did you not understand my argument? The rituals of the savages are proof of an undeveloped mind.'

The Professor released William and patted his arm, as if they were old acquaintances. As if they were allies.

'Of course, some men are still born more savage than others, as I am sure you know well.' A smile, a slight nod of the head. A shared joke, and all still at the expense of Edgar. Out in the audience, someone laughed. A quiet laugh, muffled behind a hand. But once released it crept through the crowd. The laughter licked up the arches and rang through the iron. Unbearable, echoing laughter, very like the chattering of monkeys.

William shouted above it, 'We were not made to question. To worship is to tremble. It is enough!'

But his words just fuelled the laughter. The Professor stood back from the light and there was William, and only William, set upon the stage, an example of superstition, an example of folly.

The argument echoed down the gallery to Edgar. He

crawled out of the barrel and looked on as the clergyman and the Professor fought upon the stage, with the creatures crawling out of the wall above them. Edgar laughed to see how his magic lantern cast the shadows of the men up into the air, so that the argument was turned into a comedy of shadows, a puppet show.

The men split apart. The man that was not the Professor shouted, jumped from the platform and then was forcing his way through the crowds, marching down the line of the barrel light as if he was harnessed to it, as if it was a rope that was reeling him in. The light cut the silhouette out of the darkness. A shock-haired, stoop-shouldered silhouette. It could not be, but it was – his father. His father dressed up as another man. Marching nearer and nearer. Edgar had spent months upon months dreaming of the day that his father would come to the Museum. Of how they would walk through the courtyard together, gaze up at the iron and how his father would be struck dumb by the beauty and the bravery of it. But instead his father had damned the Museum and everything in it. He had stood on the stage and shaken the Professor as if he was a schoolboy who would not take to his letters. If he could do that to the Professor, who had only thought of the place, what were his plans for Edgar, who had built it?

Edgar tried to squeeze himself back inside the barrel, but his father was too quick. He pulled Edgar out by the arm, yanking him up to his full height and embracing him. The black wings of the gown folded around Edgar. He took in great breaths of dust and the sour smell of an unknown man.

'We must quit this place, son,' William whispered. 'Immediately.'

Edgar pulled himself free, stumbling backwards, the teeth of the whale spiking his back.

'I cannot, Pa.'

'I came here for you, Edgar, and I will not leave without you.'

William grabbed at Edgar. He flailed wide, hitting the huge bolts of ivory teeth.

'No, Pa,' Edgar said firmly. 'I must stay with the machine.'

William lunged again. This time he caught Edgar by the shoulder and shook him.

'Do you not see? Or has this den of corruption turned your mind completely? There is a great deal of sin in this machine of yours. It has us peeking into the world in a way that God never intended.'

William kicked out at the barrel, once, twice, three times, and it shattered. Upon the hanging sheet, the museum split in two, a great webbed crack cutting down the centre of it.

Edgar felt the angry pulse of the blood in his veins. White-hot liquid metal. His father hated everything he set his hand to. His father, who acted as if he knew everything there was to know about the world. But he did not.

'And dressing up as clergyman when you are not one, Pa, is that not a sin also?'

He pushed his father away and William stumbled, tripping against the broken barrel. He twisted round to gain his footing and saw, behind him, the crowd of men was standing, splitting apart from itself. There was the Professor, marching nearer and nearer, with his cane raised as if he were ready to spike William upon the end of it.

'It is your choice, Edgar. Will you come with your father,

who loves you, or will you ally yourself with this pagan Professor of yours?'

Edgar stared down at the shattered lantern. If his father truly loved him he would not call him a liar and a sinner. He would not kick apart his best invention.

'I will stay,' he said.

'Stay?' echoed William. 'Then I am done with you, Edgar.'

William turned on his heel, raised his fist at the crowd, pointing over their heads to where the Museum crawled with creatures.

'The false temple is split from head to toe,' he cried. 'Let your great inventor God reach down from the heavens and fix it!'

Then he ducked around the curve of the jawbones and ran.

The world outside those bone-braced walls seemed impossibly vast. The twilight sky streched for ever above his head. The lawn before him was a shifting sea. William stumbled as if Edgar were still pushing against him. He fell on to the grass and put his hands upon it. He thought of all the rocks and stones lurking under the skin and the soil, and all the trapped creatures they might contain. For a moment he saw the world as the Professor had described it: the whole of Oxford consumed by a great flood, with all of life buried in the deep depths of it. Birds screamed across the sky above, the cry of drowning souls.

The vast walls of the false cathedral with their arched coving stared down at William in open-eyed surprise. As if the building itself was aware of the blasphemy it contained and was reeling with the shock of it.

Inside the Museum the gas halos flared bright and the iron flowered gold. The courtyard rang with chatter as the men walked the rounds of cabinets and carvings. The iron echoed the conversation back to Edgar. Proof, said the walls. Invention. Cunning.

Edgar knelt beside the barrel, gathering up the split sides. The Professor came to crouch beside him.

'It is a great shame,' said the Professor, 'that your father would treat your invention so.'

'My father?' said Edgar, his face tipped to the floor. 'My father is at the college.'

'Come, come, Edgar Jones. It was an amateurish disguise and we both know it.'

Edgar grasped the wood in his fist, the splinters spiking his skin. He could be done with his father, or he could not.

'Please, sir, my father loves the University as much as you love the Museum.'

The Professor smiled and stretched himself up to his full height. 'If I thought for a moment that his actions had damaged my cause then I would denounce him in an instant. However . . .' the Professor gestured behind him at the crowds thronging around the bones and rocks, 'I rather think this spectacle might work in my favour. Even my enemies seem reluctant to set themselves on the side of such theatrical ignorance.'

'So the Museum is saved?'

'It will take more than the rantings of an uneducated man to save my cause. It will take a miracle to utterly alter the minds of men.'

'A miracle, sir?'

Edgar remembered the miracles from the Bible stories that his father told him. A miracle was the changing of one thing into another, or giving life to dead things. It seemed a bold task, for even the Professor to attempt.

'And in the meanwhile, Edgar Jones, you must return to your master immediately. It will do me no favours for a working boy like yourself to be found here.'

The Professor touched Edgar on his shoulder for a moment, as if, despite everything, he was still his boy.

'Let us only hope, Edgar Jones, that you have the wits to rise above your origins and that you do not grow to inherit your father's ignorance.'

Edgar gathered up the pieces of the broken barrel. He bit his lip, biting back the tears. He had served his purpose and he was cast out again. And cast out to where? He must return to his master with his invention ruined, a cause to end an apprenticeship if ever there was one. And then where could he go? Back to his father, who could only see the bad in him. Who no longer even wished to be his father.

William bundled the stolen gown beneath his coat and walked the roads home.

He came to the garden gate. The cottage was a lump of rock overrun by the tangling wilderness. The only sign of life was the golden thread of lamplight fringing the curtains of his wife's window. He looked up at the starless sky stretching above him. The air was thick with emptiness.

For all his life he had trusted the path that God had set him upon – the path that had led from the college steps, down to the kitchens, up to the lodge and then in later years out beyond the walls of the University, out to the meadows, to this house.

But now it seemed that the path was as dark and tangled as the land before him.

What kind of father could he be when his son had more duty to a machine than he did to his own blood? And what kind of God would allow him to be laughed out of a false cathedral by men of learning? It was a test of faith and no mistake. Unless . . .

William stared deep into the darkness that stretched all around him. Unless both himself and the Professor were caught in the sway of a grand illusion. Unless the blackness was the truth, and the depth of life and all else just a trick of glass and mirrors, a projection of the mind?

The following morning Edgar and his mother sat alone at the breakfast table. The unfolded paper set at his father's place inched its way down the slope, worms wriggling.

'How went your debate, Edgar?' asked Eleanor. 'Was your invention a success?'

'No, Mama, it was broken.'

'Well,' smiled Eleanor, 'do not take it too much to heart, Edgar. You have years of your apprenticeship ahead of you. You can set your mind to making something better.'

Edgar frowned down at his plate and did not answer. How could he tell his mama the truth? It was likely he would be sent away from this apprenticeship also, and there would be no more inventions, and he would be back on the streets just as she said he would. And if he was, would she have the patience for it? Or would she be done with him also?

Edgar arrived at the workshop to find Stephens crouching beside the projector, unshackling the iron from the wood, picking apart the cracked lens and letting it fall in fragments upon the floor.

'I hear the great debate was a great débâcle,' he said with a chuckle.

Edgar looked at the scattered pieces of the lantern. There was anger, still, stewing through his blood. His father had spoilt his best piece of work, and now Edgar stood to be punished for it.

'I am sorry, sir,' said Edgar quietly. 'It was an accident.'

Stephens looked up at Edgar and smiled. 'Do not look so serious, Master Jones,' he said. 'It is the end of the project of the projector, but it is not the end of the world. If I despaired of my work every time an instrument was returned to me destroyed then I would have shut up shop years ago.'

Edgar smiled back. Not the end of the world. And not the end of his work either.

Stephens tapped the barrel. The mechanism inside rattled.

'The challenge now is to extract the unbroken bits so that we might make use of them in our next invention.'

'What invention?' said Edgar.

'Who can tell?' replied Stephens. 'But I am sure it will not be long before your Professor or some other University man comes knocking at our door to commission another spectacle.'

Edgar frowned. And what would happen then? Would his father seek him out and kick that apart also?

Edgar sat beside the machine and unpicked the rivets of the barrel hoops. The iron band eased open, the wood relaxed its hold around the glass and the larger, unbroken lens was eased out of its casing and wrapped up in the velvet. Edgar inched the globe of glass step by step up into the attic.

Then the barrel was split apart for kindling, the wires spun straight and, within the space of a couple of hours, it was as if there had never been a magic lantern at all.

At the same time, William was knotted up in a tangle of sheets and quilts, with the stolen gown stowed beneath his mattress, dreaming.

He was back in the Museum, and he was alone.

There was the broad barrel, anchored against the jawbone. The lens cut out a liquid line of light, tunnelling down the courtyard. No illustration adorned the cloth, just a hanging circle of a captured moon. The shattered lens set cracks across the surface, carving valleys and craters upon its face. Beyond its beam, there was nothing but darkness.

'Edgar!' called William.

There was no reply save the echo of the iron.

William walked around the edges of the light, into the shadows. He passed men of stone, the great beast of bone, carvings and columns and the displays of dead things.

The cabinets were turned to mirrors by the reflected light. Again and again William stared into the specimen cases, only to see his own face cast back at him: trapped amongst fossilised fern, or feather-framed by the wide-winged birds.

There was a tap tap tap coming from the west side of the courtyard.

'Who's there?' called William.

No voice except his own called back.

But behind the echo there it came, again, again, the tap tap tapping. William followed it.

As William chased the sound his eyes became accustomed to the sway of the shadows. Inside the cabinets, all the things that William had seen projected were now caught behind glass: creatures with claws, horns and hair stared out of their enclosures as he strode past them, their eyes turned moonglazed by the barrel-light. And there, in the far corner, sat a slender curiosity case, swaying back and forth upon its fixing: pushing out into the gallery, falling back to the wall, beating out a rhythm against the brick.

William went to it. Inside the cabinet, there was Edgar. He was naked, in all his fur-spined glory. His body was curled in upon itself, contorted in confinement. He was hammering against the glass with his fist.

'Hold fast, Edgar!' cried William.

With his cry the barrel-light went out.

All that William had was the cold feel of the glass against his fingertips, and the knowledge that his son was there, impossible inches away on the other side of it. Everything else was blackness.

'Have courage, Edgar!' he cried. 'The Professor will not have you, I promise it.'

William beat upon the glass. He pulled at the wooden edging of the box frame, but it would not give. The more he pulled, the more he felt something pulling at his back behind him. The blackness of the Museum was gathering strength and substance. It was a slick liquid sea. It was seeping underneath him, lifting him off his feet, dragging him down in its wake, catching the skirts of his gown and carrying him away.

'Edgar!' he called, but there was nothing. The black stuff rose up and filled his mouth. He could feel it hardening around him. He would be caught like the creatures stuck in stone, flailing against the pressure of the rock.

Beyond, William could see the black ocean swelling to fill the courtyard, with the head of the giraffe breaking the surface. And beneath, the specimen cases, wrenched free from their fittings, bobbing up and down upon the waves. Somewhere, in the midst of that second sea of winking glass, was his son, shuttered up and impossible to save.

William woke with a great yelp, a drowning man desperate for air. His skin was slick with sweat and his heart was pounding. The blackness of his dream lingered. There was a shadow caught inside his skull. As he fumbled with his bootlaces, he could feel the pressure of it rolling about his head, swaying this way and that.

It gave him a sensation of seasickness as he made his way to the college. As he sat at his watch there was little comfort in it. The shadowed corners of the quad seemed to be leaching out the same waves of darkness, ready to gather William up if he turned his back upon it for even one moment.

Downstairs, Eleanor sewed wire into a corset. Edgar's needles danced along the cloth. The yellow silk opened and closed about her touch like a blossoming flower. A flower run through with veins of silver.

Meanwhile, in the shop, the clocks ticked out the final hours of Edgar's day. He polished instruments and tightened cogs, but there was little satisfaction, after the magic lantern, in bringing even the brightest finish to the inventions of another man. He felt as he had when he had sat in the ashes of the forge, or been trapped in the cage of the scaffold: pushed out to the edges. Edgar remembered his father's words: this Professor would pick him up and put him down again at a whim. There was a great deal of truth in it. This man that would demand a pot, a roof, a lantern, and then cast Edgar away the minute the thing was done. And it was because of this man that his father did not love him. Edgar pulled the screws of the instruments tighter and tighter, twisting his anger into the casings. He was a boy born to make things – had not Mr Ruskin told him so? Well, then, Edgar would claim his birthright. He would not sit behind the curtains, waiting until the Professor came calling. He would do as his mother said: set his mind to a better piece of work. He would commission himself. Standing tiptoe upon the bench, Edgar pulled down the book of designs. He flicked the pages, running all the pictures of all creation in and out of each other, running machine and bone together so that they danced. And there he saw it: a way to marry invention and illusion. To create a thing that would make the name of Edgar Jones famous across all of Oxford.

Edgar raced home. Over supper, he bolted his food, his fingers itching to set to work.

Eleanor watched on from across the table, frowning.

'There is something in the air, and no mistake,' she said. 'This evening your father could not leave the house quick enough. He was up out of his bed before the striking of the clock and went running off down the street with his boots scuffed and his shirt-tails flapping in the wind.'

His father, running from the house like he had run from the Museum. Ashamed to sit beside his son.

Up in his room, Edgar picked apart the floorboards and pulled the bones out from their hiding place: claws, ribs, legs, heads, and all the other bits of animals, covered with the dust of an unrealised revenge. He bundled them into their cloth, tied them to his back and went down the apple tree.

Edgar took his key and unlocked the door of the invention shop. The sky outside the window was studded with stars, and a waning moon – a spur of silver set into the sky. The shelves were stacked with shadows. The telescopes had their eyes all turned towards him as he emptied the bones on to the baize. The ivory glowed iron white in the moonlight as he spread out papers before them, comparing what he had set upon the page with the bits of beasts crouched along the table top. He went up to the attic and filled his pockets with cogs, levers, springs and wires. The bones sat around the edges of the iron, expectant. Edgar unwrapped his pick, his tweezers and all his other miniature instruments. Nothing was forbidden and everything was possible. He took the clockwork trains from the shelf and unpicked the brass skins. There, inside, was a mass of pistons and levers, the innards of the invention.

Time ticked round on the faces of all the clocks. Edgar pieced together bone and metal, threading wire through knuckles and joints. As he did so, all his apprenticeships came back to him. The curve of the ribcage was the roof in miniature. The cogs and the springs he set inside the bone were watchwork. As he softened the wires in the flame of his lamp, a part of him was back at the furnace, watching his master turn grey metal golden in the heat. The skeletons shuffled about on their fixings, claws scuttled across the table top and the grinning heads nodded this way and that as if sniffing the air.

When Edgar was done he took them up to the attic and laid them down to rest.

The winter night was heavy, starless and close. As Edgar walked out into it, it seemed to him that Oxford was a city of illusions. He had the strange sensation that he was back in the barrel of the magic lantern, shuttered up in darkness. The streetlights that marked the top of Broad Street caught the edges of the colleges; the buttress of Balliol looming out of the night seemed a trick of the light, a projection cast out into the black abyss.

The feeling stayed with him as he walked the streets of Jericho. The houses, with their curtains drawn, and the parlour lamps dimmed, were multicoloured lanterns, set along the streets. It took a clever man indeed to know what was real in the world, and what was just a trick of light and mirrors.

The next morning, by the time Mr Stephens arrived at the workshop, Edgar was at his desk, correcting the screws of a telescope. Mr Stephens, moon-faced, grinned large at him through the instrument.

'That's the spirit, Master Jones,' he said. 'Forget the errors of the past and set your mind to the challenges ahead.'

Edgar opened up everything and anything that had to do with magnification. He lined the glass up against bits of mirror and watched as the light danced up the walls. Then piece by piece he put it all back together.

At the end of the day Mr Stephens looked down at the

instruments lined up along the baize, every one of them drawn into a perfect focus.

'Do not exhaust yourself through an unnecessary sense of duty, Edgar,' he said softly. 'You have no need to prove your worth to me.'

But Edgar knew differently. There was everything for him to prove.

He waited until the shutters were drawn, the sign turned and Mr Stephens was whistling his way down Broad Street. The tick tick ticking of the clocks was drowned by the thunder of Edgar's own heartbeat. The sky outside the window was darkening. His canvas would soon be ready. He took the stairs to the attic, set his lamp under the window, and unfolded his papers across the floor. The shadows of his inventions crept up the rafters.

Edgar pulled the lens out from its covering. He took the velvet and a rope, and harnessed the great eye of glass as he had once harnessed himself, swinging it up to the rafters. He dragged the mirror out from the shadows and ran his cloth over the time-tarnished face until it came up gleaming. He set it at a slant by the Broad Street window. He pushed the boxes to the edges of the attic, creating a dusty clearing in the centre. And into the clearing he placed his bones.

Strung through with wire and jointed with cogs, Edgar had created a clockwork menagerie. The stolen pieces were knitted together to make three quite remarkable specimens, creatures from a land that the Professor could never charter: the land of Invention. The Empire of Edgar Jones. There was a cat-dog, with a snarling head, bow-bellied and sharp-clawed. And a shrew-like thing with a sweeping tail the length of its body, wire-curled above its little ribcage, forming a question mark of ivory. And there was a creature that was barely a creature, made up of mismatched bits of beasts. It was snout-nosed, as if its face had been whittled to a point. Its slight body sat upon a set of uneven stump-legs. Its knees knocked inwards. Its front legs were clawed and its back legs cloven. These misfit skeletons were Edgar's best pieces of work, and no mistake. What had Ruskin told him? He had the breath of God inside him. And he knew full well from his father's stories what God could do. He could pull creatures from the sea, He could take a rib and make it a woman. He could give life to lifeless matter, and so could Edgar.

He knelt down beside his animals and wound their springs. Iron creaked against ivory and they stretched their limbs. They reared up, and pawed the air, and turned their heads and looked around them – as if waking from a long sleep. The clockwork ticked inside the bonework and the creatures began to dance. Round and round the attic they went, chasing each other's tails. And Edgar smiled to see them. He was not done with them yet.

He went to the wall and pulled upon the rope that held the lantern lens. The wood creaked, the rope ran across his palm, and for a moment he was back in the Museum again, shivering up in the heights, stuck in white mist and uncertainty. What had the Professor told him? Great plans can involve great disaster? Edgar shrugged away the thought. For the Professor perhaps, who did not have any understanding of the materials he worked with. But not for Edgar Jones. He set his lamp beside the mirror, and tugged again upon the rope. The eye above him swivelled and turned to stare down upon the dancing bones.

And in the meeting of light, and the mirror, and lens, the creatures leapt out of the window. On the street below, the ghosts of bones shimmered in the darkness, uncertain, shadowy shapes. Edgar tugged again, pulled down the lens and everything came into focus.

The lamplight turned the ivory gold, and the skeletons were stretched by the curve of the glass. There was a fieriness to them, as if they had come crawling out of the furnace. Edgar looked out of the window and laughed. It was one thing to draw out an invention on the page, quite another thing to see it dancing its way down Broad Street. He thought back to the Professor's giraffe, slip-sliding its way down the hill on a river of dirt, with no direction at all. Well, this was far superior to that. These flame-ribbed creatures were more terrible and wonderful than the monsters that stalked his father's stories. They were the best specimens a collector could ever dream of. And the Professor would never have them.

Out on the street below, men came pouring out of the tavern, out of the colleges. They were running in and out of the skeleton shadows, trying to catch the creatures by the tips of their fiery tails, the street echoed with shouts and laughter, the joy of the hunt.

This was just the beginning of it, Edgar was certain. He and Master Stephens would be the champions of light and bone and clockwork. They would travel across Oxford and turn the minds of the whole city with their magnificent illusions – a much better show than the Professor could ever set his hand to. The Professor could come knocking at the door all he liked, but Edgar would cast him out of the workshop, as he himself had been cast out of the Museum. Edgar was done with him.

But inside the attic, whilst Edgar was caught up in dreams, there were other animations afoot. As the creatures gambolled down Broad Street, the flames went dancing up the wick of the oil lamp. The hanging lens caught the heat and pushed it back into the heart of the attic. The wind whistled through the open window, playing along the edges of Edger's sketches. As the bones drummed upon the floor, beating out their ivory tattoo, the flame leapt higher and higher. Until, in one moment, wind, light and design all came together. The glass of the lamp shattered, the oil spotted the pages and the paper caught. The flames raced across the floor, jumped on to the velvet and scampered, up, up and up on to the rafters.

Edgar turned and saw a great sea of fire pouring across the attic. It swelled over the boxes of bits, across the floorboards and rose up in a wave. Edgar was back in the forge, being pulled into the furnace; the laughter on the street was Jacob's laughter. It was not just iron that could turn against a man in an instant. So could bone, so could light. The smoke wreathed around Edgar, the fire beat at his back. He would be consumed by his own invention. He threw himself at the open window, launching himself out into the air. He fell, tumbling down to the guttering, gripping on to the ledge, then looked below him.

A river of flame streamed across the cobbles. The men that had laughed at the illusion were now running from it and pointing up at the rooftop. Edgar shinned his way down the drainpipe. He tumbled on to the steet and, as he landed, the last of his great invention collapsed in upon itself. It was as if the world suddenly tipped, the sky flared bright, the street ran dark. Edgar ran and hid in the crowds gathered round the steps of the Sheldonian Theatre. The statues above caught the reflection of the blaze and glared down at him, firece and flame-bearded.

On the other side, the fire raced across the face of the shop, licking up to the thatch and down to the lower levels. The broad bay window displayed a great inferno. Men were running out of the colleges, carrying buckets, racing up to the edges of the fire and throwing the water into the heart of it.

There was a hiss, and then a pop. The men jumped back, and the cobblestones were sparkling with glass from the shattered window. The crowd cheered as if it was a fireworks display put on for their amusement. But Edgar knew how it would be inside. The metal would buckle in the heat, and all the instruments would be splitting apart, the great book of invention would flare bright for a moment and then be nothing but dust and ashes.

More men came, setting ladders against the face of the White Horse tavern and were hauling buckets up the line of it. Water streamed down upon the thatch and huge wafts of smoke spiralled across the eaves. To Edgar's eyes, the clouds took the form of creatures: a rearing cat with a white mane; a smoke-tailed beast. It was as if the spirits of the clockwork bones had been set free by the fire and were up at the rooftops, dancing. The monsters had a life and purpose all of their own: they were set to consume the shop and everything in it.

Then there was Mr Stephens, running up to the door. His cries carried across to Edgar.

'My boy! My boy!'

The men with the buckets pushed him back, but he was flailing against them, ready to run into the great inferno. Not for the sake of his instruments, but for Edgar.

Edgar ran across the street and was tugging at his master's coat.

'Here, sir!' he called. 'I am here, sir, quite safe.'

Stephens threw his arms around Edgar and pulled him close. Edgar could smell the smoke that had leached into the wool of his coat. And in that rough embrace Edgar could feel the man was shaking in his very bones.

'Thank God, Edgar,' said Stephens. 'Thank God.'

Edgar wished that he could pull apart time as neatly as he could pull apart the mechanisms of the pocketwatch. He wished he could set the hours to run backwards, but such a miracle was beyond him.

'I am terribly sorry, sir,' whispered Edgar.

Sorry for every part of it. Sorry for the fact that he set his rage against the Professor above his love for his master. Sorry that all the things his master had ever set his hand to were burnt away. Sorry that he had ever been taken on as the inventor's apprentice.

'It is I who am sorry, Edgar,' replied Stephens. 'For all my talk of keys and freedom I should never have left you. The workshop is a precarious place. There are a thousand combinations of elements that could have set such an explosion in motion.'

Edgar stood silent by his master's side. The fire raged behind them. Up in the attic the bones would turn to dust, the clockwork would melt to liquid iron, there would be no proof, no proof at all.

Before Edgar could say another word, there was a hand upon his shoulder. A strong hand, clamping him down. He turned and, there, towering above him, was the Professor. The flames shadowed his skin.

'Well, well,' he said. 'I saw the inferno from the Museum, and as I came closer the whole street was alive with talk of a parade of skeletons set loose across Oxford. I said to myself, this can be the work of one boy, and one boy only. And here he is: Master Edgar Jones.'

'Skeletons?' echoed Stephens.

The inventor turned his gaze to the shop front. The attic was exposed. The fillings from the wall were tumbling inwards, feeding the fire. The thick-beamed timbers stood flaming. Very like a skeleton.

'It was a trick of light and mirrors, sir,' said Edgar quietly.

'Come, come, sir,' snapped the Professor at Stephens. 'You must know the ways of the camera obscura. It seems that your apprentice took it upon himself to cast the whole mechanism backwards and turn the street into a theatre.'

'Is this true, Edgar?'

Edgar nodded and explained: how he had stolen the bones, how they had lain for a year under the floorboards and how, through the magic of projection and clockwork, he had set them free.

'But whatever for?' said Stephens.

'Just for the trick of it, sir. Just for the invention.'

With the Professor standing beside him Edgar would not speak the truth of the matter: that it was done in revenge and spite, pure and simple.

'And you think that this was the proper thing to do with a set of scientific specimens, did you, Edgar Jones?' snapped the Professor. 'To turn my discipline into a common theatrical illusion, and a badly put-together one at that?'

'Oh, Edgar,' said Mr Stephens softly, 'whatever have you done?'

'Great damage to the University,' barked the Professor. 'And to his own future.'

The fire roared in agreement. There was a cracking of timber and the attic roof fell in upon itself, crowning the shop with a halo of flame. Then behind the tumble of the wood and the spitting of the fire there was another sound: the bells of Oxford, ringing out their seven o'clock chimes. Seven o'clock. The time of the night-watch. Edgar looked out at the crowd. Somewhere, amongst the smoke and shadow, there would be his father. And he would see it all, and he would know that this had been done by his disobedient, disappointing, sinful son.

'I rather think the damage is to my premises,' snapped Stephens.

'Premises that are licensed to you by the University. Set side by side with the colleges, which, if not for the quick response of the scouts, would surely have been burnt to the ground.'

'You cannot hold the boy responsible for what might have been.'

'Indeed, no. But what has been is quite enough. Theft and arson. He must be taken to the University authorities and held accountable.'

Taken to the University. Paraded up and down before his father. Edgar would not have it. He turned and ran out into the crowd, down the line of the street where the bone beasts had danced. But he did not run far. There was a pull at his jacket, and his arm was caught, and there was the Professor, holding him in his iron grip.

On the other side of the street, William stood, frozen. He

saw the Professor holding down his son, and Edgar twisting this way and that, and howling. A creature caught in a trap. Behind them, the great inferno raged. So this is what it had come to. Edgar had set Oxford aflame, and was held in the clutches of the very man that William had tried so hard to keep him from.

The cobbled street was glowing with the reflected fire. It seemed to William a bed of red-hot coals that had been set between himself and his son. And he could not cross it.

PART FIVE

Eleanor was sitting in her workshop, stitching a gown around the body of the mannequin. Sea-blue silk gathered at the waist, with lilies wreathed around the bodice. The cloth sparkled with silver: the sky at night. It was her masterpiece, and no mistake.

There was a bang at the door, and a cold gust of wind blew through the house. She leapt from her chair, unlocked the door and there, standing before the fire, was William. It was William, and yet not William. He was staring into the room before him, like a man stranded in a foreign land. How old he looked, how utterly bent in upon himself. Behind him, the front door lolled open on its hinges, framing a world of darkness beyond.

'Edgar . . .' he said. His voice sounded heavy and strange. As if he was speaking in his sleep.

Eleanor shivered. Something terrible had blown into the heart of their home, she was sure of it. She slammed the door closed, guided William to his seat by the fire.

'What of Edgar, my love?'

'Edgar is lost to us, Eleanor.'

She looked at the clock. Its hands marked out eight o'clock. Caught up in her work, she had not noticed the chiming of the hours. The supper table stood unset.

'Lost?'

Eleanor listened in silence to William's story of bones and clockwork and burning rafters. It sounded to her like a tall tale from the tavern, a fable found at the bottom of a beer glass rather than anything that could have happened to her family. When William came to the end of it, with Edgar dragged off by the wardens, and he unable to follow, Eleanor stood up sharply and began to pace back and forth across the parlour.

'This is a mistake, Will, surely,' she said. 'A great injustice.'

And not just to Edgar, but to them all. To William, who had given the best part of his life and his hours to the University. To she herself, who had turned her back on the tavern, who had carried Edgar in her belly, stitched together all his apprentice clothes, and done her very best to steer their family on towards a better life.

'Edgar is in the hands of the University. There is nothing that can be done.'

'But from what you say, it was an accident. If there is anyone to blame in all of this then it must be Mr Stephens. We signed Edgar away into his care.'

William frowned. He was back on Broad Street, watching Stephens staring up at the burning ruins of his workshop.

'I rather think that Edgar created the whole spectacle without his master's knowledge.'

'You talk as if you think him guilty.'

'I do not know what I think,' replied William in a whisper. 'All I know for certain is that I do not know my son.'

William turned his face to the fire. And there, in the tumble of the logs and the spitting of the embers was Edgar's crime, played out in miniature on the other side of the grate.

Meanwhile, Edgar sat before a constable.

'This is a serious matter, boy, serious indeed,' he said.

Edgar stared back, silent. It seemed that anything he said or did was turned against him. He would not speak another word.

Eleanor sat at her workshop table and penned out letters of appeal, to the Professor of Anatomy, and to the Dean of William's college.

In the room above, William buried his face into the wall of pillows.

The next day Edgar danced across the length and breadth of Oxford. He was caught upon the tip of the cartoonists' pens and captured in caricature, shock-haired, cloven-hoofed, a dark little devil gambolling along the curve of Broad Street whilst the fire burnt behind him. He went skipping across the front page of every paper, and into the drawing room of every house in Oxford. He danced through the main quad of William's college and into the Dean's lap.

When William went to take his place at the gate, Edgar was there waiting for him, splayed out across the table. William had no sooner pushed him aside than the Dean came knocking at his window. The work of a lifetime was undone in an instant. If William could not watch over his own son, then how fit was he to watch over the scholars?

'An Englishman is deemed innocent until his guilt is proven.'

'Come, Porter Jones, you know as well as I that the reputation of the college must be guarded at all cost.'

William stood up, thrust his hat upon his head and walked the streets home. He thundered through the wilderness, up the stairs, and into his bed. He pulled the sheets over his head and there he stayed, with the echo of the black stuff rolling round and round his skull.

It was a day later when the knock came at the cottage door. Eleanor opened it to find a ruddy-cheeked constable and a young man with a notebook standing upon the doorstep.

'Mrs William Jones, mother of Edgar Jones?'

Eleanor nodded.

'I am Captain Sanders. This my assistant, Lance. We have come to search your home.'

Eleanor stared down at his papers. There was her name and William's written out alongside Edgar's.

Eleanor hesitated with her hand upon the doorframe.

'It will be better for your son if you do not obstruct the investigation.'

Eleanor stood aside. The men went straight to the bookshelves and began tossing the volumes upon the floor, delighting in the tumble in the same way that men in the tavern laughed at the fall of a stack of dominoes. The constable took the barograph from the shelf and rattled it. The needle scrawled out exclamation marks of protest.

'These are my husband's possessions. They have nothing to do with Edgar,' said Eleanor sharply.

'Leave no stone unturned, that's the motto of the law,' replied the constable. He twisted the scriptures on the wall, feeling along the backs of them. *The children are the inheritance of the Lord.* It fell to the ground and shattered.

In the room above William was dreaming. He was looking down from above at Oxford in the twilight, as if he were stood at God's shoulder. The city laid out beneath him was a miniature model of learning, streets spiked with spires and battlements and sloping roofs, studded with statues.

The air around William was a grey sea of emptiness, and he was alone at the centre of it. He stretched out his hand. The sky had a stickiness about it, and when he looked at the tips of his fingers they were soiled, soot black. William watched as the greyness turned darker and darker and the streets were swamped with shadow. The city was nothing but scattered blocks of stone, protruding out of the river of blackness.

Then, somewhere high above William, the sky roared, a great bellow that shook the heavens. William felt a gust of burning air at his back. He twisted this way and that, but the sky held him. Then it opened up and rolling rock flaming with fire came hurtling past him and plummeted down down down, and as it fell it grew greater and greater, until it crashed into the heart of sleeping Oxford. It struck against the spire of the Martyrs' Memorial, and wrenched it from its fixture, sending it shattering on to the cobbles.

The sky shook again, and another meteorite came streaming past William, then another, and another. His college tower was knocked asunder; it fell, cracking the roof of the cloisters.

Another burning rock followed, and it was caught by the arms of the ancient oak. The wood sparked and split clean down the middle. It flared bright and was gone. The tree, with all its rings of time, was nothing but a spiralling storm of ash.

The fire below was matched by a fire above. The black sky was threaded through with a net of flame and William was caught within. Below him, the rocks ran thundering through the streets, striking the college walls and sending the whole city tumbling against itself like skittles. They toppled the fences and careered across the meadows and the parks, leaving snaking trails of flame in their wake until Oxford was a levelled land. And the only sound in the world was the sound of walls falling.

William was woken by the sound of things breaking. He tumbled from his bed. Through the floorboards he could hear raised voices. Men's voices. He raced down the stairs, and was greeted by a room full of scattered papers and shattered glass, his wife on her hands and knees, gathering the fragments from the carpet, with two men towering over her. It was the stuff of his dream, and yet not his dream at all.

'What in the devil's name . . .?' cried William.

'Aha!' said the constable. 'William Jones, I presume?'

'The very same,' said William. 'And who might you be?'

'They are men of the law, Will,' said Eleanor softly. 'They are after evidence against Edgar.'

'Men of law!' snapped William. 'Men of law have more honour!'

'You should be more careful in your speech, sir,' said the constable.

William set himself between the men and his wife. 'You

have come here with your mind already set against my son. You visit violence upon my house.'

He pushed at the constable, and the constable pushed back. In one movement, William's arms were pinned to his sides.

'The father resists the investigation. Make a note of it!'

William twisted and turned like a creature caught in a trap.

'This is savagery,' cried Eleanor. 'Let my husband be.'

The constable marched William to the door and out into the garden.

'You will remain here, sir, or it will be all the worse for you and your son.'

William stared back at them through the glass whilst the men pulled apart the room.

Eleanor stood silent, her back braced against her workshop door.

Once he was done with the front parlour the constable strode through the wreckage, to the foot of the stairs.

'The boy's room, if you please, Mrs Jones.'

Eleanor stood by the doorway as the men marched into the room, ducking under the curve of the rafters, too large and too loud for the smallness of the space. The constable wrenched open the wardrobe door. Edgar's Sunday suit hung upon its peg. He pushed it aside and grappled about, striking against the sides.

Lance pushed the mattress from the bed. It sagged and sprawled and thundered down upon the floorboards. The boards bounced with an echo of the fall. The nails danced up from their fixtures and Edgar's hiding place split open. Lance crawled under the bed and thrust his hands down into the dark space beneath.

Out came all of Edgar's secrets. There were the bones that he had left behind: a claw, a head, a knuckle. There was a handful of bent nails. Stuffed in amongst them, scraps of paper aged by time. Eleanor peered over the constable's shoulder. There was an outline of the rooftops of Oxford. And page upon page of bits of animal: beaks, claws and bones.

But this was not enough, it seemed.

Eleanor and William's bedroom was ransacked, covers thrown from the bed, cupboards opened. Likewise the scullery and the kitchen, where china was shoved from the shelves, pots unhooked, bottles uncorked.

Eleanor followed in the wake of the destruction until the men came to her workroom door.

The constable tugged at the handle. 'The key please, Mrs Jones.'

'That's my workroom. It contains nothing concerning Edgar.'

'The key, please, Mrs Jones. Or if you will not assist us then it is no great trouble for us to break down the door.'

Eleanor pulled out her key and tumbled the lock.

The constable pushed past the mannequin and strode into the centre of the room.

The mannequin's belly tipped and Eleanor could hear the rolling rumble of the hidden fortune licking up the sides of the body like a shifting sea. She steadied it with her hand and watched as the constable tugged the cloth from the shelves, pulling apart her world as savagely as he had pulled apart Edgar's. By the table, the other man had his hands deep in the half-finished petticoats and pantaloons, rummaging around in the clouds of lace.

'This is your workroom, you say, Mrs Jones?'

'Yes.'

'And you are in sole possession of the key?'

'Yes.'

'Not even your husband has a copy?'

'No.'

The constable picked up the lace cushion and flicked at the beaded bobbins.

'An interesting arrangement. And tell me, Mrs Jones, are all these bits of finery for your own pleasure?'

Eleanor gathered up the toppled silks and began to shake them out, flaring soft walls of colour between the constable and herself.

'I have commissions. From the ladies of Oxford.'

'And this can be vouched for?'

'It can, but, again, it has little to do with Edgar.'

Eleanor stared out of the window, where William was kicking his way through the wilderness. And for a moment she was back at the start of their life together, with William trampling over bush and bramble with her in his arms, desperate for the threshold. Eleanor turned to find the constable pulling her masterpiece dress from the mannequin.

'What use is this to the court?' she cried.

'No need for emotion, Mrs Jones,' said the constable. 'It is all part of the process. You must trust in the mechanisms of the law.'

'And what shall I tell my client?'

'So you are still at trade?'

'There has been no verdict. And until there is I shall go about my business as I always have done.'

'Is that so?' said the constable, stuffing the silk into his bag, tearing the edges of the fabric. Eleanor felt it as if he were pulling at her very flesh.

'Well, this has been most informative, Mrs Jones.'

The constable hauled his bag upon his shoulder. Eleanor could see the shape of the bones pushing through the leather.

'You will, of course, be notified by the court in due course.'

'Notified of what, precisely?'

'Of the date your son comes to trial, what else?'

The men marched out of the workroom and slammed the door closed behind them.

Eleanor steadied herself against the bosom of the mannequin. The hessian smelt of tobacco and men's sweat, corrupted simply by a touch. On the other side of the window William kicked along the edges of the wilderness, the brambles tangling up in the hem of his nightshirt. All around her the rooms gaped with open spaces and things torn apart. It was as if Edgar had burnt a great hole in the heart of the house, scattering everything into chaos.

The following day, Eleanor received her replies.

The Dean of William's college informed her how, as Edgar had offended against the University, he would be tried by the University and kept within its walls until his day of reckoning. He advised her to consider very carefully the effect that any further missives from Edgar's mother might have upon the standing of his case.

Eleanor's letter to the Professor of Anatomy was returned unopened.

Meanwhile, Edgar continued to pass through the machinery of University justice. He was put in a holding house – an annexe of the University on St Aldates, a small grey-faced cottage with bars set upon the windows. Edgar was placed in a room at the top of it. He was furnished with a bed, a Bible and a piss pot. His door was unlocked for mealtimes, and for an hour in the darkening afternoon, where his exercise was walking in circles in the high-walled yard at the back of the place, with a man in a gown watching over him.

Edgar spent most of his time standing by the window, looking at the fat-thumb tower of the Professor's college, which loomed over him from the opposite side of the road, cut up and quartered by the bars. He spoke not a word to anyone.

Again and again his warden told him, 'Your mother writes requesting an audience with you, Master Jones. It is in your rights to receive her.'

But Edgar shook his head, turned his back to his captors and set his sights upon the skyline.

In the cottage in Jericho the months before the trial were full of empty spaces and words unsaid. It was as if the house, once pulled apart, simply could not piece itself back together again. Eleanor would find herself setting the table with three places, and then standing frozen by the dishes as the grandfather clock ticked away at her back, the lurch of the pendulum an echo of Edgar. She tried to busy herself with her work, but she had lost the trick of putting together the patterns. Whenever she tried to set her needles against the cloth the thread ran wild, gathering up the silk into a fist.

As the days passed it became evident to Eleanor it was equally difficult to put her marriage back together. After years of living at the opposite end of a pivot, in which William's day was Eleanor's night, it was a strange thing to find themselves together, day in, night out. Eleanor missed her own company, she missed her suppertime with Edgar, she missed the bustle of Mrs Simm, charging into her workshop with paper and silks and gossip.

The strangest thing of all for Eleanor was to find herself beached up in the same bed as her husband. They both slept with their backs to the bank of pillows, Eleanor with her face turned to the window. As William thrashed his way through his sleep, Eleanor would find herself gazing into the dark space where Edgar's cot once stood. She thought of the nights when she would wake to find him staring out at her between the bars of wood. She yearned to turn back the years, for her to be once more the mother of a speechless boy who chirruped and sang in his sleep. If she could have her time with Edgar again she would leap from the bed in an instant, haul him out of his enclosure, hold him close to her heart and never let him go. And she would never collude with William in asking him to be anything other than what he was.

Meanwhile, William was equally unsettled by the reversal of his days. In the first few weeks he maintained an outward appearance of respectability. He would dress in his suit and hat and stride out upon the daytime streets of Oxford. He had a purpose still. He had done the one thing that he had promised, on the day of Edgar's birth, that he would never do: he had denounced his own son. He had abandoned him and now Edgar was shuttered up in gaol. He was determined to put it right. He would seek out the best defence in Oxford. What better use was there for the profits from Eleanor's stitchings?

William walked the streets searching out representation. He turned his gaze away from the spires and steeples and focused on the shop-fronts. It was remarkable to William that, once he began to look for them, the golden scales of justice swung out from signs on every corner: the city was pockmarked with offices of the law.

But again and again William would find his case refused. Some men simply would not take on the challenge of a University case. William heard told over and over how the University lawyers could tie a defence counsel up in knots within the turn of a phrase. Other men would not consider taking on a child, as defence was dependent on the assessment of character, and in a child the character was so unfixed, such a slippery thing, that there was nothing to pin an argument upon. And then for many men just the name of Edgar Jones was enough to dismiss the petition. The newspapers had sealed his reputation: he was a wild boy who had stolen from the University and set fire to the city. There was no defending such a crime.

Then, William called on Mr Clark. A lean young man, he could not be more than five years out of college. When William mentioned Edgar's name he clapped his hands together and laughed.

'Edgar Jones, the incendiary boy!' he declared. 'I have read all about his antics.'

'The fire was an accident,' said William carefully.

'Mr Jones, it will be to your son's advantage if you do not press too hard upon me your interpretation of the case.'

'But someone must speak the truth of the matter. Edgar has been shut away from the world entirely. Not even his mother can gain access to him.'

'I do not need to see the boy to give him representation,' said Clark impatiently. 'It is not the truth of the incident that interests me so much as the account of it that I might give.'

William frowned. But the truth was the truth, and that must surely matter? He set out the facts of Edgar's life, the hopes that he had once had for his son, and the way these had been destroyed by his three apprenticeships. Clark nodded and scribbled into his ledger.

'Very good, Mr Jones, very good indeed,' he said with a grin and a handshake. 'This is quite enough for me to begin building a case. We shall make a great tale out of your son's misfortune, and these men of the University will find that they are the ones who are held accountable.'

On his walk home William turned Clark's words over in his mind. A great tale. This did not seem to him to be the language of justice.

Even after finding Edgar a lawyer, William was still restless. But the more he walked the streets, the more he felt that he was stuck in the centre of some vast unknowable mechanism. The justice system of Oxford was invisible to the innocent, but when a man got too close to a crime, the whole apparatus sprang into action. Edgar's shame became William's also. Men who had once bowed to him at the gate would cross the street at his approach. When William came to the door of the bookseller's it no longer opened before he set his hand to it. Instead, the shutters came rattling down. And when William walked past the doors of the colleges they always seemed to be pulling closed against him.

'Pa, why is Oxford so full of fences?' Edgar had once asked.

'To keep common folk like yourself out of the places made for better men.'

How much had changed since he'd spoken those words. Edgar was right: there were an unnatural number of fences set out across the city, marking out a chequerboard of forbidden lands.

William walked the narrow streets that snaked between the colleges, rubbing shoulders with the tradesmen and the barrow boys and the men who took the muck from the gutters. And as he walked, voices and memories followed him.

Turning down St Giles, William was back in the dawn of Edgar's birth, walking through a changed world with stars dancing before his eyes. A snide voice came whispering across the years and down the wind to him, 'Are you sure? Are you quite, quite sure?' Or loitering on the corner of Broad Street, peering at the burnt-out wreckage of Stephens' shop, an urgent voice called at his shoulder, 'Seek it out, seek it!' But the longer he stared at the black skeleton of the timbers, the less certain he was of what he was looking for. Behind him, the walls of the colleges seemed impossibly high, and the gargoyles that crested them all smirked down at William as if all this long while they had been waiting for his banishment, that twisted grin of the Professor repeated and repeated across the faces of stone.

Meanwhile, Edgar sat alone in his locked room, looking out at the same skyline that bore down upon his father. He watched the tumble of the clouds, the pouring of the rain, the passage of the sunlight that charmed the city gold. He watched and waited, waited and watched.

Then, one morning, there was a knock on the cottage door and a man with a letter for William. The golden scales of justice set upon the page trembled in his hand.

'They have set a date,' he said softly, 'for Edgar to be called to account. It is but a month.'

'A month?' echoed Eleanor. 'Well, that is a good thing, surely? Then this whole business will be ended and Edgar will be returned to us.'

William stared down at the paper.

'And then our lives can return to what they once were, Will. You back at the gate, Edgar back to his instruments.' And, she thought silently, Mrs Simm back with her plans and her patterns. Life as it should be, with some colour and laughter in it.

'But that is not all,' continued William. 'I have been called to stand witness, in defence of Edgar.'

'And that is a good thing also,' replied Eleanor firmly. 'You are an honest man, Will, and you have served the University well. Your words will matter.'

William nodded but said nothing. He thought of the stolen gown, which lay hidden under the mattress of their marriage bed.

A week before the trial, Eleanor gained access to Edgar. His refusals were overridden by his warden. It was required that he should be dressed fittingly for court, and who else but his mother could provide such a service?

Eleanor stood in the locked room with her silent son opposite. She pinned up his trousers and the cuffs of his shirt, as if she was setting him out to yet another apprenticeship.

'All will be well, Edgar,' she said softly. 'Your father has found a good man to attend your case. You will be home soon enough.'

Edgar stood impassive, his face turned to the bars upon the windows. Home. He had a home in Stephens' shop, and a key to the door of it, but he had burnt it to the ground. He had once had a home up in the arches of the Museum, but that door would be forever shut to him now. Home. An empty echo of a word.

On the day of the trial, Eleanor woke at dawn in a deserted bed. Looking down from the window she could see William roving around the edges of the wilderness.

She went to stand beside him, and took his arm. His nightshirt was speckled with dew, and the very bones of him were shivering.

'Will,' she said softly. 'It's time.'

William shook his head. 'If I am to speak in Edgar's defence, I cannot sit in the gallery. The University will not allow it.'

Eleanor looked out at the dawn bleeding across the sky. William had promised her, at their beginnings, when he had first spoken of marriage, that it would be the two of them together, following a better path through life. But somewhere along it they had taken different turnings, and now even the very mechanisms of justice were pulling them apart.

'Then I will go alone, Will,' she said. 'A boy needs his mother, no matter how much he might deny it.'

So Eleanor pulled on a grey dress and shawl, placed a veiled hat upon her head and took the road into Oxford.

The court was a stern-faced, grey-bricked building, set at the bottom of St Aldates, at the edge of the city. Inside the rooms were thronging with chatter. Edgar was to be tried in the main hall, and it seemed that all of Oxford had come to watch. The place was a maze of corridors and staircases, and Eleanor found herself running in circles, pushing through the crowds to get to the gallery.

She sat, huddled in a corner. Around her there were scholars sitting shoulder to shoulder with men of trades; newspaper men equipped with pocketbooks and pencils. Up there in the eaves Eleanor heard Edgar's name repeated back to her again and again, as if he was a character from a story: a trickster, a devil, a villain. And not at all anyone's son.

Eleanor looked down into the courtyard below. The space spread before her like the stage of a theatre. There was the seat of the judge, a great throne. There, opposite, were the men from the University, racked up in their jury box, gowns folded around them. There, to the side, the witness box. And standing in the middle of the room, a plinth with bars set around it: the dock. A cage for Edgar even before he had been condemned.

A bell rang, and Edgar was brought in. He barely had the height to look over the bars.

Eleanor shivered to see him, her son, standing stock-still in the midst of this room of men. He was staring at the ground, head bowed. This was not Edgar as she knew him, not the boy who tumbled from the cradle and ran wild through the wilderness. She peered down into the pit of the dock, and she saw, glinting around his hands and feet, iron shackles.

Then the bell rang again, and the room rose up in a wave. A silver-haired judge took his place upon the dais. In his wake, the men who would hold her son up to scrutiny. There was a man who was presented as Mr Ellis, acting on behalf of the University. He was a squat little man, a man who looked as if he had spent his life getting rich on the misfortunes of others. He strode up and down before the court, announcing Edgar as a dangerous entity indeed. This boy, this boy, this boy, he chanted, as if Edgar was not even worthy of a name. He loomed over Edgar in the dock, stabbing at the air between them. This boy might seem like a mere child, but even his stature was a deception. This boy had spent his fourteen years upon the earth building up a career of transgression, thievery and subversion. The crime that Edgar stood accountable for was the culmination of a life corruptly lived.

Eleanor grasped the bar of the balcony in her fist. She may not know her own son as well as a mother should, but this was not the whole truth of Edgar. Not by a long mile.

Then Mr Clark stepped forward. Eleanor frowned down at him from the gallery. This was the man that William had spoken of so highly, but he was hardly a man at all. As he marched back and forth across the court, he reminded her of the college boys that would parade before the bar of the tavern, all garbled speech and nervousness. He spoke of Edgar as a most unusual child. That whilst the facts of the matter seemed clear, that the child had stolen from the University, and indeed burnt down a man's livelihood in property that belonged to the University, these actions arose from a most exceptional set of circumstances, which the jury should be inclined to view mercifully. Mr Clark's intention was to dig deep into the whys and wherefores of Edgar's case and to prove too that the child was more a victim of the University's whims and fancies than the University was the victim of the child's misdemeanours.

Eleanor looked down as Clark and Ellis stood side by side. There could not be two men in the world more different in age and attitude. There was something of the pantomime about the whole event.

Then the bell was rung again. Ellis stepped forward and called the first witness.

'Master Jacob Salt!'

Eleanor watched as a giant of a man shuffled into the box.

He was dressed in a grey suit, which strained at every seam to contain him. In the hanging haunches of his cheeks, in the folds of his neck and in the ridges of his knuckles there were lines of soot, and as he sat upon his stool there was the smell of sulphur leaching through the air. Eleanor could hardly bring herself to look at him. Could this really be the man that she had urged William to sign away their seven-year-old son to?

Ellis took to the stand and folded his arms across his chest.

'Please state your full name and your relationship to the accused.'

'My name is Jacob Isaiah Salt, and I had the misfortune to be the master of Edgar Jones at Oxford Forge.'

'May we ignore the emotion and simply glean the facts?' called the judge.

Eleanor sat motionless as she listened to this sullen man's version of Edgar. How he had shown a determined arrogance even at seven years, marching up to the door of the forge and demanding employment. How he set himself to the bellows and pumped up a great fire, an inferno set at the heart of the workshop, as if his apprenticeship was a rehearsal for his crime. How he would not take his master's guidance in anything, but was always eager to get into smelting work before he had the skill for it.

'So his interest was in the more volatile parts of the industry?' said Ellis. 'The fire and the molten metal and anything that might harm a man?'

'Yes, sir, he was a risk to himself and the forge. I am grateful to the Professor for taking him away before he burnt the place to the ground.'

It was all that Eleanor could do not to cry out from the gallery. The man was a liar and a rogue, that must be clear to anyone. This blacksmith would sell his own soul, she was sure of it, in order to distance himself from her son.

Mr Clark took the stand and tried to prise another version of events from Jacob. But the story returned the same and the same. There was no skill about Edgar, only violence and uncouthness and love of the flame.

The court adjourned. Eleanor found herself walking the rounds of the streets. The bruised dawn had given way to a day of determined rain. It came hammering down the sky, as if the world was weeping for the injustices meted out on her son. She walked through the thick of it, for the feel of the water pounding upon her skin, as if it could wash away her guilt. Had not Mrs Simm warned her from the start, a blacksmith would bring the luck of the devil into her house. And how had she responded? She had laughed at the very thought of it, when she should have done all that she could to pull Edgar away from the fire.

But the more she walked through it, the more the thrumming of the rain calmed her. The trial had only just begun. There was time for the other side of Edgar's story to be heard. There would be more honest men, who would speak in his favour. His other masters would speak of the good in Edgar, and Jacob Salt's malicious testimony would tumble in upon itself.

It was this thought that Eleanor clung to as she watched the Professor take to the stand. She could not imagine a man more different from lumpen, brutish Jacob. He was an ageing man, who walked with a stick and whose hands trembled as he set them on the bar of the witness stand. But he looked out at the court as if he owned it. She smiled to think of William, standing by the fire, dictionary in hand, boasting out this Professor's praise of Edgar. He called their son a champion, and a hero. Eleanor watched as he drew his gown tight around his shoulders. The jury would be more swayed by the testimony of one of their own than the lies of a blacksmith, she was sure of it.

Ellis strode up to the bench and smiled at the Professor as if he was greeting an old friend. He spoke of the Professor's reputation, and the Professor went along with him: he was a forward-thinking man, a man who believed in progress. He spoke of how he first encountered Edgar at the forge, and how the boy displayed an inventiveness that was far beyond his ten years.

'This inventiveness, sir, how did that manifest itself?'

'He had a most unusual way of looking at the world,' smiled the Professor. 'He was full of schemes of how things might be made.'

'And this is what inspired you to take him from the forge?'

'No, sir. I took him for pure necessity.'

Then followed tales of the Museum, of the buckled roof, of the tragic death of Master Thomas and the need of a skilled and agile worker to fill his place. Edgar Jones was simply the only possible candidate. If there had been another boy in Oxford who might have been capable of the work, a more educated and amenable boy, then there was no question that the Professor would have taken him.

'More educated, sir?'

'Edgar Jones came to me illiterate. And he displayed no inclination to better his mind when he was at the Museum.'

Eleanor looked over to the jury ranked up on their stools, smiling and nodding as if they all knew Edgar already. Look beyond the words, she pleaded silently. Look at the body of this Professor, look at the way he trembles in the box. Look at the way he cannot even turn his face towards Edgar. This is a man who would say anything to save his reputation, to free himself of the taint of association with my son.

And Ellis, with his broad smile, with his hand set upon the bar next to the Professor's was doing all he could to fuel the argument.

'And, during this time at the Museum, did Edgar Jones manifest any criminal qualities?'

'Looking back upon it, he did, sir. Or at least the beginnings of them.'

Then there were tales of how Edgar was often found in the Museum before his fellow workers, swinging from a spur, or clambering up a ladder. This was not a crime, this was love of the work, pure and simple; it was just this eagerness that the Professor had chosen him for. But the Professor twisted it all around.

'It was as if Edgar believed the Museum to be his own empire.'

'His own empire, indeed. Then I suppose he was not best pleased when his contract came to an end?'

'Oh, Edgar Jones was dismissed from the Museum before his contract was completed.'

Ellis rocked back on his heels and raised his eyebrows, a pantomime of surprise. 'Dismissed? Whatever for?'

'For flagrant disobedience. For arrogance and insurrection, which could have put himself and his fellow men in grave danger.'

And this was just the start of it. Transgression followed transgression as the Professor told how, the night after Edgar's dismissal, he returned to find his rooms ransacked, his papers scattered across the meadows, and his precious specimens torn apart, a whole wealth of bones missing.

But now the bones returned. A man carrying a silver tray walked the rounds of the courtroom. The pieces that had been found under the floorboards were paraded before the jury. And sitting side by side with them, the blackened remains that had been pulled from the burnt-out shop.

'But, Professor,' said Ellis archly, 'this event was two years ago. Did you not think to report it? Did you not suspect the hand of Edgar Jones in any of this?'

'In truth, sir, I would expect a child to take a more childlike revenge. I thought this the work of more sophisticated men.'

'I am not sure that I understand you, sir.'

'It is no secret that I have enemies, men who would like to see an end to my work with the bones. I thought my room was ransacked by a fellow scholar. To have brought such a thing to the attention of the authorities would only have served to fuel the argument against me.'

'So you say that such thievery is proof of an advanced mind?'

'A mind advanced in cunning, sir. And not just the thievery, the absurd theatrics upon Broad Street was the very stuff that would fuel the superstitious arguments against my work. Edgar Jones plotted and planned this crime over the course of two years, sir, and in my opinion that is proof of a calculating and corrupted soul.'

'Thank you, sir, there is nothing more.'

Calculating. Corrupted. The words echoed through the room as Ellis retreated from the stand. Eleanor felt the fury gathering in her blood. This old man was setting words against Edgar that should surely be set against himself. She watched as he drew the gown around his shoulders, as if it were some kind of armour that gave him protection.

But her anger was not just at the Professor. A part of her was back in the cottage, with William setting the University papers behind glass. If she was at fault for sending Edgar to the forge, then William was equally to blame. He had his mind turned by the sweep of a college gown. If this Professor had come to the cottage she would have sent him away in an instant. He was a greedy man who would set his own interest before all others, that much was clear to her. The way that his voice wavered when he spoke of his bones, the way his fist gripped tighter around his cane when he spoke of Edgar's thievery – well, this was a passion she had seen before, in the trembling of the drunkards' hands upon the edge of the bar. The sign of a man who was led through life by a fierce desire that ruled him. A man who clearly had no understanding of what it was to be responsible for a child.

In the court below, Clark stepped up to the dock and unfolded a piece of paper from his pocket. Eleanor frowned to see it. This was a boy set in defence of a boy and no mistake, someone who must read his argument from a page.

'What would you say is the worth of Edgar Jones, Professor?' asked Clark.

'The worth, sir? I am not sure that I understand you.'

'Do you recognise this document, sir?'

The Professor glanced down at the page and then looked away. 'Of course. These are the apprentice papers of Edgar Jones, assigning him to the Museum.'

'Quite so, and can you clarify for me the exact price that you paid to his master?'

'Two pounds.'

Two pounds. The gallery gave out a gasp, and the jury muttered. And rightly so.

Two pounds, thought Eleanor. The price of a sea of silk. Two pounds . . . she imagined the cascade of coins dropping down the back of the mannequin and gathering in the belly.

'Two pounds!' declared Clark. 'A handsome sum to set against such a difficult child.'

'It is as I have already stated, sir. There was no other boy in Oxford who was suitable for the work. The price I paid for his release was due to the urgency of the task. It is no reflection of his value.'

Value. Eleanor bristled at the word. This Professor talked of Edgar as if he was a thing to be traded, not as if he was a child with a heart and a soul and a future.

In the dock below, step by careful step, Clark extracted the truth of the apprenticeship, trying to put together a more favourable picture of Edgar: of all the things that he had achieved in the Professor's employ; of how the investment had come good for the University.

Eleanor heard tales of Edgar climbing up the broken roof, of him swinging through the sky in his harness. But there was little kindness in the Professor's account: Edgar was disobedient to his master. He would always be getting into places where he had no authority. No matter how Mr Clark tried to steer the questions, the Professor still managed to turn Edgar's achievements to the negative. He may have fixed the roof but he would not take instruction on how to do it; he may have had a skill with the work but his fellow ironworkers neither trusted him nor loved him. He may . . . but he . . . He may . . . but he . . . back and forth, with the bad parts of Edgar always at the fore.

'And yet,' said Clark, striking on the bar for emphasis, 'in spite of all his infractions, you did not exile him completely, Professor.'

The Professor sat silent as Clark paraded the wider evidence before the court – of how the Professor had recommended Edgar to the instrument maker, and of how he had sought him out again when he had need of his magic lantern.

'I put it to you, sir,' said Clark sternly, 'that you had little concern for the welfare of Edgar Jones, one way or the other. You picked him up and put him down according to your need of him.'

Up in the gallery, the air was thick with mutterings. Eleanor smiled. William had put it just as plainly himself.

'On the contrary, sir, I was eager to provide Edgar Jones with the opportunity to be a better man. I rather hoped that being the apprentice to an inventor might provide some discipline and calm the wilder parts of his nature.'

'But you could not be sure of this, and yet you still allowed him to return to the place that, in your own words, he felt was his own empire. The very place that you banished him from, with no thought of the effect this might have upon his volatile nature?'

'I am a Professor of the bones, sir, not of the mind. It is not within my skills to make such assessments.'

'Even when your colleagues expressed grave concern about the effect that your Museum might have upon the weaker minds of the masses?'

Clark unfolded a newspaper from his pocket and read out the account of the Professor's debate: a tale of dramatic spectacle, accusations of blasphemy, and of the unknown clergyman who stormed the stage and ran mad from the Museum.

'I put it to you, Professor, that Edgar Jones is a victim of your philosophies. I put it to you that you collected him for your own purpose, and then cast him out when you were done with him. I put it to you that this is not a born thief that stands in the dock before us but an unfortunate child who took your teachings to heart, and misguidedly animated bones in the hope that it would find him favour.'

'And I put it to you, sir,' said the Professor sternly, 'that if every professor was called to account for the impact of his theories, then the colleges of Oxford would be emptied of their teachers.'

That evening Eleanor walked the streets home with heavy steps. She could not shake the image of Edgar from her mind, sitting in the dock, his hands and feet roped around with chains as if he were a wild animal. She thought of how she bound Edgar up in blankets as a child, to keep him out of her business. She thought of how Edgar had come into the world, urgent, early, and curled up like a tiny fist. Was he destined, from that moment on, to take the road to the courtroom door, no matter what he had turned his hand to?

She came to the garden gate. The house was lit up like a lantern, and there was William, dressed in his porter's suit and hat, standing by the window, staring out into the night in search of intruders.

On the opposite side of the road stood Mrs Simm's house. The drawn curtains were bright banners unfurled against the night. Eleanor yearned towards them. She wished for a bit of conversation where nothing really mattered at all. For sentences that had no hidden meaning at the heart of them. She wished for the simple pleasure of putting together a pattern and making all the pieces fit. But that was no longer the way things were.

She looked back at William. He stood frozen, as if all his thinking had turned him to stone. So this was what her family had come to: a boy in chains and a husband shackled within his own mind. She pushed open the gate, and walked through the wilderness to her door.

The following morning Eleanor took her place in the gallery once again and listened to further evidence against her son. The first witness was the engineer who parroted the Professor, and worse. He said that Edgar was a child who loved danger, who climbed everything that was forbidden, who never took an instruction, who was a risk to himself and his fellows.

'Only a matter of time,' said the fat-faced rogue, 'before he would do great damage to some part of Oxford or another. I am only grateful it was not the Museum.'

Mr Clark tried to pick apart the argument, but the engineer was as strong and determined as the steel that he worked upon. Edgar would be ruled by no man. Edgar brought trouble upon himself.

Eleanor's hand gripped knuckle-white around the banister. Mr Clark should have asked her about Edgar's time at the Museum. Then she would have given him her truth: the truth of Edgar's hands rubbed red raw and flowering with blisters. These were things that he did not bring upon himself, of that she was certain.

But then, the scales of justice began to tip.

Mr Ellis had summoned enough of Edgar's enemies. It was time for Mr Clark to call forth the men who would speak in her son's favour.

The very name of the first witness caused mutterings in the gallery.

'Mr Stephens, erstwhile proprietor of the Invention Shop.'

Eleanor leant over the bar of the gallery to watch as he walked the length of the court and took his place. Unlike the other men, he looked straight at Edgar as he settled upon his seat, and smiled at him. A smile that was full of kindness for her son, the boy who had burnt his business to the ground.

'I am sure, sir,' said Clark, matching smile for smile, 'that you have the sympathy of the court. We know full well that you have suffered more than any man here in the loss of your livelihood under the actions of Edgar Jones.'

'Better the loss of my livelihood than the loss of any life, sir,' countered Mr Stephens. 'A shop can be rebuilt, inventions can be remade.'

'A most generous sentiment.'

'It is my belief that any master should be held accountable for the actions of his apprentice, sir. If Edgar Jones is to blame for the accident, then so am I.'

A gasp went up from the gallery. The jury twisted about upon their perches. Eleanor was almost pitching herself over the balcony. Here was an honest man indeed, a man who cared for her son more than his own reputation. Her blood quickened. Here was hope, after all. If the victim of Edgar's crime did not hold him accountable then how could any other man?

'This is most unexpected,' said Clark. 'Can you enlighten the court to the logic of the statement?'

Mr Stephens could. He spoke with a great passion about the skill that he had observed in Edgar, his enthusiasm for the work, the way that he had turned a great profit for Stephens within a matter of months, his natural eye for invention.

'He was the quickest child that I have ever encountered. He could set his hand to the trick of taking a thing apart in an instant.'

'This is all fascinating, sir, but I still do not understand how such talents shift the blame for the great inferno on to your shoulders.'

Stephens spoke softly about how Edgar was given a key before his time, and free access to the books and the instruments.

'I am afraid, sir, that in my sheer enthusiasm for his talents, I did not consider that I was presenting him with temptation as well as guidance. I should have been more careful in my instruction, and taught him the dangers of invention along with the pleasure of it.'

But when Ellis took to the stand, he turned Stephens' words against Edgar in an instant.

'His talent was in the taking apart of a thing, you say, sir?'

Stephens frowned over the top of his glasses.

'That is the common form of any apprenticeship amongst machines, sir. The taking apart of a thing must be learnt before the construction.'

'And for how long have you been an inventor, Mr Stephens?'

'Twenty years, sir.'

'And in that time you have studied the dangers of your craft closely?'

'Yes, sir, but it as I said. I should have imparted that knowledge to Edgar and I did not.'

'Nevertheless, in your own understanding of these dangers, would you say that the great inferno that Edgar Jones created, if it had gone unchecked, would have had the power to leap from roof to roof and burn apart the heart of Oxford?'

'You cannot hold the boy accountable for what might have been.'

'I am merely trying to assess the danger, sir. Yes or no?'

Stephens cast his gaze to the ground, and then back at Edgar. 'Yes, sir, it could. But it did not.'

But that was all it took: the possibility of destruction. All praise was forgotten, there was just the knowledge of Edgar, a child who could have consumed the city with flame.

Then came a tall man with a mop of red hair. A man of solid stature. Much more of a man than any of those who sat in the jury. Eleanor thought how, if only the whole charade could be decided by a pure show of strength, this man would settle Edgar's fate in an instant.

'Mr Fisher,' said Clark, 'will you explain to the court your relationship with the accused?'

'We were ironworkers in the Museum together, sir.'

'And how did the accused seem to you?'

'He seemed awful small, sir.'

The gallery erupted with laughter. Even Eleanor smiled. She had almost forgotten that such a sound could exist in the world.

'Thank you, sir,' said Clark. 'I spoke in reference to his attitude rather than his stature.'

'He was a brave lad. He would climb upon anything. He had no fear of the work at all.'

'I see. And what about his ethic?'

'I beg your pardon?'

'Was he industrious, or did he slack at the work?'

'Oh, Master Jones could not be kept away from the work. There was nothing he loved more than being at the top of the iron. Why, when our engineer tried to keep him at the lower levels, Edgar made a harness to haul himself up to the heights. And I was his anchorman.'

'His anchorman?'

'The steerer of his rope. It was a good bit of sport, sir.'

Mr Ellis strode up to the box and, as with Stephens, so with Fisher: he threw the argument back at him in an instant. Edgar's love for the work was a love of transgression.

He was a boy who did not keep to the orders of his master.

'And tell me, sir, the Professor asserted that none of the ironworkers held Edgar in his favour. Can you enlighten the court as to why you took the position as his anchorman?'

'It is true. At the start of the work I had little time for him. But he is not a bad lad, sir. A touch proud, perhaps, but not bad.'

Mr Ellis drew a paper from his pocket and spread it across the bar before him. He read, like a man speaking prayers by rote, the pay given to the ironworkers. And Fisher's pay, double that of the others.

'I wonder, Mr Fisher, if you were so enamoured of Edgar Jones, why then did you demand so high a wage to work beside him?'

Up in the gallery, Eleanor twisted her gloves around in her hand, fit to break them. These men, who played with Edgar's reputation as if words were only words. And now it was all upon William's shoulders to set the world straight.

The following morning, Eleanor roused William from his chair and dressed him in his porter's clothes; his trembling fingers could not find a purchase on the buttons and laces.

'There is nothing to fear, Will,' she said softly. 'You are more than a match for this Mr Ellis. He is all slippery in his speech, but you are an honest man and nothing he says can prove you otherwise.'

Eleanor walked with him down to the courtroom. Side by side they went along the cluttered streets. She slipped her arm into the crook of his.

'Courage, Will,' she whispered. 'It will all be done within the day.'

They came to the entrance of the courthouse. There, standing in the alley that bordered the building was a black coach with barred windows. Waiting.

Eleanor steered William past it. Inside the place was thronged with followers of the case. Edgar Jones, Edgar Jones, Edgar Jones was all they heard as they made their way through to the courtroom.

From up in the gallery Eleanor looked down upon her husband and her son set out so far beneath her in their separate boxes. Edgar was twisting about in his shackles, yearning towards his father as if he was a young boy again, watching from the doorstep as his papa went marching down the street away from him. The officer yanked upon the chain, and Edgar was still.

Mr Clark strode across to William. He put his hand upon the rail and smiled.

'William Jones, erstwhile porter of the University and father of Edgar Jones?'

'Yes, sir.'

'I would like to go on record as saluting your courage. It takes a strong man to stand witness for his own family.'

'It would be a weak man indeed, sir, who would not speak the truth of his own child.'

'Spoken like a true father. You are, I understand, a self-educated man?'

'Yes, sir.'

'You came to your college as a kitchen boy and worked your way up to become a night porter, am I correct?'

'Yes, sir.'

'During this time you developed a passion for progressive

literature. We have the records of your purchases from the booksellers.

'Yes, sir, I always had an interest in trying to better myself.'

'And this philosophy of self-improvement was, I take it, a thing that you were eager to pass on to your son?'

'Yes, sir. I attempted to teach him myself, but he struggled with his letters.'

'I see. So instead you had him apprenticed into the practical craft of ironwork.'

'Yes, sir. I was uncertain but my wife assured me it would be to his benefit.'

'And, as we have heard, it was this practical craft which led to Edgar Jones being taken up by the Professor of Anatomy.'

'Yes, sir.'

'And what was your response to this turn of events?'

'I was delighted, sir. There is nothing that could please me more than to see Edgar favoured by the University.'

'So you admired the intellectual pursuits of the University, and were entirely trusting of their system of learning?'

'Yes, sir. I thought there could be no better future imaginable for my son.'

'Thank you, sir, there is nothing further.'

Nothing further? William felt adrift in the centre of the courtroom as Clark receded. The man was a fool. There were plenty of further questions that needed to be asked. Questions about the very nature of the Museum, and the Professor and all the deceptions racked up inside of it.

William frowned and shook his head. There was something black gathering at the back of his skull again. And when he looked up there was Mr Ellis standing before him.

'Mr Jones,' said Mr Ellis softly, 'before we go into the specifics of your son's case, I would like you to tell us about your life before you became a father. Am I correct in assuming that you have spent the majority of your life under the employ of the University?'

'Yes, sir, since I was a young boy.'

'We have heard of your diligence, sir, rising through the ranks of the serving staff until you were entrusted with the position of night porter. This truly is the sign of an industrious and trustworthy man.'

'Thank you, sir.'

Mr Ellis smiled as if he were the one receiving the compliment.

'So during this time you were accommodated within the servants' quarters of the college. That is, until sixteen years ago, on the event of your marriage.'

'Yes, sir.'

'Your marriage to ...' Ellis paused and smiled, 'Eleanor Bradstock, daughter of Harold Bradstock, the proprietor of the White Horse tavern upon Broad Street, am I correct?'

'Yes, sir.'

'An interesting choice for a man who asserts he is always trying to better himself.'

'This is of no relevance!' cried Clark.

'More fact, if you will, Mr Ellis,' snapped the judge, 'and less history.'

William did not hear them. He was a younger man again, sitting on the steps outside the Sheldonian Theatre, with his telescope in his lap.

A voice came whispering to him through the air, urging, 'Seek it out! Seek it!'

He set his eye to the instrument and tilted it up to the sky. There was the ghost of the moon, hovering over the rooftops. He swivelled his gaze, and the spires and the slates all ran into one another. He came to rest on the guttering of Exeter College. There crouching along the ledge of the roof was a row of grinning gargoyles, thick-lipped, smirking. He tilted the telescope and the face of the college was a running river of speckled stone. It was as if he had unhinged the world with his new invention. There was no part of Oxford that he could not peek into. He travelled down the roofs, down, down to the level of the street. Down to a long-slung window, and there, staring straight at him through the glass, was a girl with fair hair and bright blue eyes. She smiled, and the whole world tumbled into disarray. Eleanor.

'Mr Jones!'

Ellis had his face inches away from William's and was tapping impatiently upon the bar.

'Yes, sir!' cried William, with the sharp bark of a man woken from a dream. There was a ripple of laughter up in the gallery.

'I will repeat the question. Am I correct in thinking that after the birth of your son, you continued your vigilance at the gate?'

'Yes, sir.'

'And continued at the night watch?'

'Yes, sir.'

'But this must have been a great cost to yourself and your family. To be away from your wife through the night-time, and to be sleeping through the days.'

'A child has greater need of his mother, sir.'

'Was that your belief, Mr Jones – that your son would benefit more from his mother's company than yours?'

'Yes, sir. But I was most active in his education.'

'As we have heard. And yet you were concerned about the development of your son, were you not?'

'I do not follow.'

Ellis pulled a paper from his pocket and made a theatrical gesture of the unfolding.

'In a letter written by your own hand to a Professor Carter, you describe your son as showing alarming irregularities in character and appearance.'

William faltered in the box. He steadied his hand upon the rail. The blackness in his head was gathering, he could feel it slicking up the sides of his skull. Ellis thrust the paper over the bar to William. There it was, the faded ink running across the page.

'Can you confirm that this is a letter written by your own hand, dated February 1852?'

'Yes, sir.'

'And will you read to the court the second paragraph?'

' "It has come to the attention of both myself and my wife . . ." '

William's tongue stuck in his mouth and the words turned to dust. The room was silent, the air thick with the yearning for the unfinished sentence. Ellis took the paper from his hand and continued.

' "It has come to the attention of both myself and my wife that Edgar has a tendency to violence within his nature. There is precious little in the house that he has not taken apart. In addition, we are concerned about his limited stature and his inability to speak. We are fearful for his future if such conditions were to go unchecked." Do you deny that these are your words, sir?'

William shook his head. 'They were written out of concern for my son.'

'That is not in dispute, Mr Jones. Any educated father would do the same: identify a condition and seek out a cure.'

Ellis folded the letter and handed it to the judge.

'So, Mr Jones, can you recall for the court the essence of Professor Carter's diagnosis?'

William frowned. There was a trick in this, he knew it.

He looked over at Edgar. He had his head down, and his hands clenched around the bars of the box. He looked above him, at the crowded gallery: men and women, bunched together along the benches, peering over the balustrade, as if they were about to launch themselves down into the pit, tear Edgar apart and be done with it. Eleanor amongst them, motionless, with the veil pulled down over her face.

'I do not recall, sir.'

'You do not recall?' laughed Ellis. 'Come, sir, you seek out advice and you cannot recall the essence of it? Do not insult the intelligence of the court.'

'You are under oath, Mr Jones,' said the judge sternly.

William's head swelled and rattled with the pressure of the tumbling black sea. He closed his eyes.

He was back in the study, and there was the porcelain head, and there was Carter's sketch of Edgar, with all the terrible words set around it. And there was the wall covered with diagrams and charts and the red lines running across them, spelling out how nature must advance. And there in the thick of it was Edgar, small, feather-spined, shivering, with the iron claw advancing towards him.

William opened his eyes. There was Edgar opposite him, shackled.

'Professor Carter made much of the importance of influence,' said William softly.

'Influence?' echoed Ellis archly. 'I am not sure that I fully understand you, sir.'

'Perhaps you should ask Professor Carter directly,' snapped William. 'I thought him a charlatan and I have little time for his theorising.'

'I certainly would call Professor Carter to account,' said Ellis, 'if he had not been dead for the past five years.'

There was a small ripple of laughter from the gallery and then it was gone.

'Please, Mr Jones, if you can recollect what you can of this theory . . .?'

'Professor Carter asserted that Edgar might be greatly influenced by the company he found himself amongst. That is why we kept him at home for his schooling.'

'I see. And yet the Professor of Anatomy has told us that Edgar came to him without any understanding of the written word. This is remarkable if he was schooled by such a well-read man as you.'

'He was slow in the written work, but showed a quickness in other talents, sir.'

'As we have heard,' grinned Ellis. 'Tell me, was it under this principle of influence that you decided upon his placement at the forge?'

'Yes, sir. My wife was most convinced that the forge would give him discipline, and provide a place for him to put his energy.'

'So the decision was your wife's, not your own?'

'She swayed the argument, sir, but it was I who signed the papers. I conceded that my wife might have a better understanding than I of the benefit of the practical arts.'

'Thank you, Mr Jones. It is a honest man indeed who admits that his wife might know a thing that he does not.'

Up in the gallery, Eleanor wrenched her gloves around in her lap. There was an argument gathering in the air around her, she was sure of it.

'Now, Mr Jones, I would like to return to Professor Carter's theory of influence. If your wife's assertion was correct then one would suppose that your son would find the better parts of himself through his work at the forge. Was this the truth of the matter?'

'No, sir. Edgar remained unruly.'

'And when he was at the Museum?'

'He went back and forth, sir, sullen one day, saintly the next.'

'So in conclusion, would you say that he is a child who is easily influenced by his setting?'

'Perhaps he is, sir, but the truth of the matter is that Edgar is just a boy, working out his way in the world and he should not be punished for it. If there's any punishment due then it should be to the Professor who took him into that pagan place, turfed him out and dragged him back when it suited him. The mind is a fragile thing in any man, still more in a boy.'

William leant back in his seat and sighed. There. He had said it. He had stood in the courtroom and spoken the clear plain truth of Edgar for everyone to hear. Edgar might be a criminal of a kind, but there was a greater criminal in all of this, who had taken his son from him under false pretences and made him into a boy that he no longer knew. The darkness receded to the back of William's head and licked around the edges like a subsiding sea.

'Mr Jones,' barked the judge, 'you will keep your responses simple. The court is no place for conjecture.'

William nodded and cast his gaze upon the floor.

'I find it a surprising thing in a man of your self-cultivation,' said Ellis softly, 'that you would have such a distrust of the Museum.'

'It is a great trick,' said William. 'A pagan den masquerading as a cathedral to God.'

'And yet a place that you were happy to assign your son to?'

'I was mistaken,' said William. 'The Professor talked so cleverly about Edgar's importance in the whole scheme of it that my vanity clouded my judgement.'

Ellis folded his arms and rocked back upon his heels.

'Would you say this was a tendency in your own nature, sir, to be consumed by a theory rather than see straight through to the truth of the matter?'

William frowned. 'I do not understand your question, sir.'

'To say it plainly, would you say you were a man who was easily deceived?'

William smiled. 'Oh, no, sir. A lifetime spent at the gate has given me a clear way of reading truth and falsehood.'

'Is that so?' smiled Ellis. 'Your Honour, I call in evidence taken from the home of Mr and Mrs William Jones at the time of the investigation.'

The man who had brought the bones came striding across the courtroom with a tray piled up with pieces of cloth. Lace, blue silver-speckled silk, bundled up together.

Ellis shook it out: Eleanor's unfinished masterpiece, unfurled before the jury. He then pulled from underneath it an embroidered set of bloomers, roses curling down from the waistline, following the curve of an invisible woman.

A wave of laughter cascaded over the gallery. Eleanor's hands wrenched at the gloves in her lap, ripping a hole clean through the lace.

'Mr Ellis!' called the judge. 'This is most improper and of no relevance to the case in hand.'

Ellis shook out the bloomers again and the roses danced across the cloth. 'Your Honour, it is my opinion that these articles are of utmost importance in the case of Edgar Jones. They are the heart of the matter.'

'Then make your argument quickly.'

Ellis took the bloomers and the dress, and held them up in front of William. They twisted and turned under his touch, every surface creeping with detail.

'William Jones, do you recognise any of these garments?'

'No, sir.'

'No. And yet they were discovered in your home. In the room that your wife identified as her workroom.'

'Ah!' said William, with a broad smile. 'The workroom is my wife's domain. I do not venture behind the door.'

'You are forbidden from entering a room in your own home?'

'Not forbidden, no, sir, but I do not begrudge my wife her privacy.'

'How very progressive. But tell me, sir, do you have any understanding of what precisely your wife is undertaking within this workroom?'

'She sews dresses for the ladies of Oxford and makes a tidy profit from it. Industry is a thing to be encouraged, sir, even in a woman.'

'I would imagine that would depend entirely upon the nature of the industry.'

'Mr Ellis,' barked the judge, 'make your point clearly or be done with this line of questioning.'

'Mr Jones, do you have any knowledge of the name Miss Rosalind Perch, known to her friends as Rosie? Or of Miss May Fletcher, known as Missy?'

'No, sir, none at all.'

'In September of this year, both women were arrested not two hundred yards from your home, for the crime of importuning innocent men to obscene acts.'

William furrowed his brow.

'Their articles were taken as evidence of their intent.'

Again the man with the tray came striding up to the dock. Again, silks and satins were shaken down before the open court. Forget-me-knots creeping up the sides of the undergarments. A yellow dress with a lace-fringed bodice. No one laughed.

'Mr Jones, you are a man who prides himself upon his observant nature. Let me place the evidence before you.'

The bloomers were draped over the bar before William. The ivory buttons winked up at him from the bindings. For a moment he was back at the beginning of everything, standing by the font whilst the chaplain poured blessings down upon his son, when the lace and the silk ruptured, and there was Edgar, bare-arsed and howling, drawing the whole ceremony into chaos.

'I suggest to you, Mr Jones, that these garments are made by the same hand. That your wife has not been trading with ladies at all, but with common whores.'

A chorus of jeers rang round the gallery. Eleanor pulled the veil tight over her face.

Below, William ran his fingers across the silk. There, in the fineness of the stitches, in the threading of the flowers along the cloth, in this pattern of twists and turns and sinuous running of the leaves and stems there was more than Ellis could ever know. There was Eleanor, perching upon the edge of their bed, pulling up her skirts, pulling at his nightshirt, showing lace and silk and flowers and the flesh beneath them, calling to him, again and again, there'd be no harm in it, Will, no harm at all.

'I put it to you, William Jones, that you have been deceived within your own home. That whilst your wife was consorting with whores, and your son was making plans of thievery, you slept on, oblivious.'

William put his hands upon his temples and pushed at them, as if he could squeeze out the rolling black stuff.

'I put it to you and the jury, William Jones, that if we are to believe this argument of influence, then we need to look no further for the origins of Edgar Jones's insurrections.'

'Mr Jones?' said the judge, 'do you have any comment upon this evidence?'

William looked up at the gallery. There, anchored to her seat like a woman turned to stone, was Eleanor. Her face was shrouded in a veil of black gauze, as if the storm clouds raining in William's head had settled upon her shoulders and taken away all features, all expressions, all that William had ever known of her.

'It seems to me,' said William softly, 'that I am nothing but a fool who has spent his whole life dreaming that the world is other than it is.'

Ellis smiled broadly. 'Thank you, sir. I have no further questions.'

William cast his gaze upon the ground. He could feel the blackness pressing down from inside his skull, pushing him down down into the earth. He was no better than he was when he was left abandoned upon the college steps, shivering, and crying for the family that was forever lost to him. He did not know his own nature, and he did not know his wife's. No wonder that Edgar was as Edgar was.

He wished that the flags beneath him would open up, that time would solidify into a dark expanse of rock and he could slip deep deep down underneath it, pull the stone over his head and sit unseen in the darkness.

Eleanor watched as her husband shuffled away from the box, his spine curved down to the earth as if he was utterly broken.

Whores. The word echoed through the silence of the courtroom. Now it was said, the truth of it was plain. In the cut of the dresses, the size and the shape of them. In the quantity of ripped bodices and severed petticoats. In every word that Mrs Simm said about the ways of men and women and the differences between them. In the sparkling of the jewels set about her throat and her fingers. Even in the skill with which she had twisted Edgar around when he was stuck inside her. If

William only saw the world that he wanted to see, then she, as his wife, was no better.

Eleanor's thoughts tumbled in upon each other as the end of the trial was played out beneath her.

Ellis pulled himself up to his full height and paraded back and forth before the jury as he gave his summation. Eleanor caught only fragments of the argument, but what she caught stuck fast. It was not just Edgar who was now in the dock. She was as good as sitting there beside him.

She heard how Edgar had been given favour upon favour by the University – in his position at the Museum, in the Professor's great care of him, in the Professor's consideration of his future by assuring his placement with Stephens. And yet Edgar Jones had turned each and every one of these favours into his own opportunity for mischief. And how, as he grew older, this mischief had become a flagrant love of law-breaking. Edgar's criminality was beyond doubt. It was Edgar Jones and Edgar Jones only who stole from the Professor; Edgar Jones and Edgar Jones only who turned academic study into a spectacle and burnt his own master's shop to the ground. And yet Mr Clark would have the jury believe that Edgar Jones was the victim in this sorry tale. A victim of what, exactly? A victim of the University's favour? No, Edgar Jones was a victim of his own nature, and nothing more. A victim of his own bad blood. The truth was evident: his mother was deceptive through and through: she had turned her skills to the service of harlots, women who thrived by ensnaring men. And the father had admitted to the whole court that, for all his attempts to better himself, he was a deluded old man who could not apply the lessons of the books he had read to his own life.

'Therefore,' called Mr Ellis, pulling himself up to his full height, 'gentlemen, you must consider your position with great care. It is correct that you should have sympathy for this boy in the dock. He is, after all, a child. But you must express this sympathy in consideration of his future, of the man that he might become. Is it fitting that he should be returned to his parents, whose moral compasses swing so unfortunately wide? Or is it better that he should understand that his wild actions have consequences? That a man's character is like a man's house: if it has been laid to waste it must be built up again from the foundations. It will be a blessing as well as a punishment for Edgar Jones if you surrender him to the care of our corrective institutions where, with the proper guidance, he might be taught how to become a better man.'

A better man. The phrase echoed up the hall to Eleanor. As if Mr Ellis knew the meaning of those words.

Clark followed, with a performance of his own, marching up and down before the jury, but not looking once at Edgar. He raced through his assessment of Eleanor's son, hardly stopping for breath. Mr Clark declared how he knew full well that Edgar was guilty of the actions of which he was accused. Edgar and only Edgar stole the bones and set the fire. But, in the midst of these accusations, there was a question that sat unanswered: why had Edgar Jones committed this crime? Mr Ellis made the case that this was in his nature, and that his nature was a mirror of his mother's. But Mr Clark urged the jury to admit this was a fragile argument if ever they heard one. Would any of them claim that their scholarly understanding, their positions within the University, were a direct consequence of their mother's nature? If Edgar Jones was truly so volatile, so susceptible to bad influences, then the jury must consider where the greater influence lay.

They must decide, where did Edgar Jones truly get his skills and his way of looking at the world? Beneath his mother's skirts or under the guidance of the Professor, who employed him not once but twice for the pursuit of his own glory?

Had not Mr Stephens – he who had lost the most by Edgar's crime – said it plainly: a master must be held accountable for the actions of his apprentice?

The jury shuffled and muttered together upon their bench.

Up in the gallery, Eleanor nodded. This was the truth of the matter, plain for all to see.

'I ask, would Edgar Jones be standing on trial today, if it were not for the ambition of the Professor?'

The muttering grew to a roar.

The judge banged his gavel upon the bench, drumming the room back into silence. 'Mr Clark,' he said sharply. 'Do not forget that it is Edgar Jones, not the Professor who stands accused before us.'

'Indeed it is,' smiled Mr Clark, 'because Edgar Jones has committed a crime, and there is no doubt that he must be held accountable for it. But there is no need to lock him away from the world. Rather, let Edgar Jones be surrendered to a simpler life. The life that he was placed on this world to inhabit: the life of a tradesman, removed from the temptations of aspiration, removed from the colleges of Oxford. Let him start his life again, serving out a simple apprenticeship. Let him be a barrow boy, a hawker, a chimney sweep. A trade without any cunning or invention about it.

'Let father and son return to their place in the world,

chastised but not condemned. And let us pray that William Jones will watch over his son with the same care and diligence that he has displayed at the college gates.

'Let the tale of Edgar Jones be that of a boy who flew too high and condemned his family name to ridicule and servitude. A foolish boy, but not an evil one. There is no need to cage a bird when you can clip its wings.'

Eleanor looked on as the judge and the jury retired, and Edgar was led away, hobbling in his chains. The argument echoed in the air around her. To cage or to clip the wings? Was there any difference at all? It seemed to her just a trick of the tongue. Whichever way the scales of Edgar's life fell, everything was utterly undone.

The passage of the crowds carried Eleanor out of the gallery. She sat alone upon the bench in the corridor outside the courtroom. She looked into the chattering masses for William but he was nowhere to be seen.

Then, after what seemed only a minute but could have been a lifetime, the bell was rung, the doors swung open and there she was, back in the gallery, and there was Edgar beneath her, and there was William, at the back of the room, wrenching his cap round and about in his hands. And there was the jury, sitting upon their perches, and there was the judge, and the paper was passed between them. And there was the question: how do you find Edgar Jones?

'Guilty.'

The room erupted in a great rush of noise. Cheers, applause, and somewhere in the gallery behind her, laughter. And far beneath, squirming about at his stand was Edgar. He twisted and turned and wrestled with his shackles. Pulling at his cuffs, pulling at the waist of his trousers, as if he was trying to wrench himself away from his enclosure.

Again, the judge hammered with his gavel and beat the room back into silence. Then he began his pronouncements. Eleanor could not chase the argument and the justification. Every part of her was in the box with Edgar. And then came the sentence, cutting through everything.

'Seven years,' said the judge. 'And may you emerge from your service a better kind of man.'

Edgar was led away upon his chain, and there was nothing that Eleanor could do to save him.

When Eleanor emerged from the courtroom, the crowd from the gallery was thronging the streets. And there, standing like a statue in the centre of it, William, staring back at the blank face of the courthouse, expressionless, unblinking.

When she put her hand upon his arm he flinched. She held on tight, stepped out into the road and a carriage shuddered to a stop before them. They clambered in and closed the door upon the world.

With every beat of the wheels upon the road Eleanor thought of the other carriage: the black box with bars with Edgar shackled inside it. The strike of the iron upon the cobbles was a pendulum beating out the time. Seven Years, Seven Year. Seven Years . . .

Seven years. Half of Edgar's life again. How would he stand for it? His confinement would take him past his twenty-first birthday. He would come out of the gaol a man. But what kind of a man?

She thought of him as a baby, peeping out of William's coat and laughing at the spinning world. It seemed an impossibly long time ago. She thought of how he recreated the machines of the Museum across the parlour table. She thought of the great grin he gave her as his silver needles tumbled out of their paper and into her hand. She thought of Edgar now, and how he would be for years: shut away from the world, unable to turn his hand to anything. If there was bad blood in him then it would stew and stagnate behind the walls of the gaol. If William was right and the souls of men were eternally in conflict, then Edgar's was as good as lost.

And she and William were lost along with him. Edgar might be the one who had been set behind bars, but from this day on they were all imprisoned: caught within the confines of this moment. Caged by shame and never to be set free.

Eleanor put her hand upon William's. He pushed it away and set his face to the window.

William looked out of the window and watched Oxford retreating. A thick fog was setting in, rolling over the roofs of the colleges, blurring the sunset with a creeping greyness, sucking all the colour from the world. Erasing the city as they passed through it. It was a cruel echo of the day when Edgar and William had walked through the city side by side, marching out to the Museum. The day that William had thought would be the beginning of a great new life for Edgar but now, he could see, had been just the beginning of disaster. William watched as the fog poured down over the doorways of the colleges, portcullises of mist closing off every entrance, snapping shut every opportunity. Spelling out his own fate over and over.

The University had meted out its judgement and William's sentence would mirror that of Edgar. Exile and exclusion. The sins of the son would be visited upon his father.

Never again would he put on his uniform, and walk the streets of Oxford with that sure sense of who he was and where he was headed. It was all lost to him: his place at the gate, with the arch framing the view of the lawns, the city wall, and the tall tower rearing up behind it. Never again would he watch the shifting scree of the lamplights blend into dawn. Porter Jones had lived for forty years, but he lived no more. Now there was only William Jones, father of a criminal and husband of a shameless woman.

When they returned to the cottage William marched straight to the door of Eleanor's workroom and tugged at the handle, wrenching it as if he could pull it from its hinges.

'Unlock it!' he cried.

'There is no need, Will,' Eleanor said softly. 'There will be no more trade from this house.'

'I am your husband and you will do as I say.'

Eleanor opened the door. William pushed past her and marched into a room that was bursting with colour. Silks upon silks hung from the walls and the beams – brash, bright, soft, shining. All holding the shapes of women. The breeze from the door lifted the skirts as William walked past. He came to the table. There were the corsets, winking gold, red, blue, from the table top. Reams of lace were stacked beside them, worming their way across the silk.

He stared back at his wife. She was standing next to a grotesque kind of statue: a woman without arms, a woman with a metal claw of a foot where the rest of her should be.

The blackness in his head pounded. It seemed an impossibility that there had been a room like this hidden in his house for years. It seemed even more impossible that his wife had put it together.

Eleanor hovered by the door.

'I did not know,' she said softly. 'You must believe me, I did not know . . .' But the words sounded hollow and absurd, even to her. Every article set about the room contradicted her.

William looked around the room. Influence, Carter had told him. But it seemed to him now, not that all this luxury had turned Eleanor wanton, but rather these silks and satins and all the other fancies were an illustration of her true essence.

'I should never have taken you from the tavern. I should have left you with your own corrupted kind.'

'But you are my own kind, Will. I am your wife.'

William stood by the window, holding a yellow petticoat up to the light. In another time, this would have been a thing that Eleanor could have laughed at: William squinting down at the folds of it as if it were a script that he could not read.

'We can put this right,' she said softly. 'Did you not say that there was nothing in the world that we could not achieve if we set our minds to it?'

'It seems that I was mistaken.'

William took scissors from the table and cut straight through the petticoat. There was no other sound but the rip of the cloth being pulled apart. Then he set upon the bundles of lace, slicing, stabbing. The pieces scattered across the floor, cobweb-thin flakes of snow falling.

Eleanor looked at her husband, and the blades trembling in

his hand. His eyes were wild. She had seen this William once before: the day that Edgar had pulled apart the clockwork. This man was made of pure anger, not the man she married at all.

'What would you have me do?' she said softly.

'Leave,' he said. 'And do not return.'

William dropped the scissors on the table, the metal sounding dull upon the wood. Then he marched out of the room, out of the door, out past the wilderness and did not once turn to look back at his wife.

Cuffed and confined in the back of the prison coach, Edgar watched as the fog rolled over the rooftops like billowing smoke clouds, as if the fire in the shop were still smouldering, blurring the edges of the buildings, until the angels were limbless cocoons, unformed creatures budding from the rooftops.

Edgar yearned towards the window, pulling at his shackle. The accompanying officer unspooled enough inches of the chain to allow Edgar to press his face against the grille.

'Look well, child,' he said. 'This will be the last sight of the city you have for a long while.'

Edgar watched Oxford fade away from him in piecemeal. The wall that separated the meadow from the road was swallowed by the blurred air. The towers set around the city all dwindled and were lost to the mist.

The journey from the courthouse to the gaol was too short. No sooner had the coach gathered momentum than it stopped again, pulled up by the walls of Oxford Castle. Edgar was hauled from his seat, and taken round the back of the building.

The stone was thick and blank-faced, the windows arrow slits in the façade. The gathering fog gave the impression that the prison was a sheer wall connecting the land and the sky.

The officer knocked at the door and the grille slid open. A dark face appeared in the hatchway. For a moment Edgar was back at the start of his adventures, half his life ago. He was a boy, running away from home. And there was sly Jacob, grinning down from the doorway.

'Who comes?'

'We have a boy convicted of thievery and arson, sir.'

The door swung open, a gaping mouth set into the stone. The officer pushed Edgar forward and he was swallowed.

Edgar found himself standing in a dank hallway. The walls were lined with lanterns, casting shadows up the dull stone. A high desk separated the hall from a long corridor, which stretched off into the darkness. In front of the desk stood a thickset man, clad in a grey suit with a set of keys hanging at his belt and a ledger set in front of him.

'It says something about the world,' said the gaoler, 'when a child is brought to me in chains.'

He came out from behind his desk, crouched down upon his haunches and looked Edgar in the eye.

'So, you have made a career of setting fires and stealing, have you, boy?'

Edgar shook his head.

The gaoler smiled. 'That is the sad injustice of this place. Every room is taken by an innocent man. You will find yourself amongst good company.'

The officers undid Edgar's chains, and stripped him to his breeches. His clothes were cast upon the table top. His suit was a discarded skin, the threadbare pockets turned inside out like peeping tongues.

'The sum chattels of Edgar Jones,' said the gaoler, scratching in his ledger: 'A key and a piece of bone on a string.'

The officer hoisted Edgar's arms above his head. A convict's suit was pulled out from behind the desk and he was thrust into it. The material chaffed against Edgar's skin. It had a familiar smell: dust and dankness, shot through with sweat. The stink of fear and confinement. The smell of a specimen shroud.

Then another set of shackles were fitted around Edgar's wrists and ankles, and looped through with a heavy chain. It snaked behind Edgar like an iron tail. The gaoler tugged upon it, as if Edgar were nothing more than a dog to be pulled to heel.

'From now on, boy, your name is Prisoner 864, and you will answer to nothing else. My name is Mr Morrison, but you shall call me master or sir.'

Edgar stared up at him and did not answer.

Morrison tugged on the chain again, and led Edgar behind the desk. His lantern cast shifting shadows along the corridor beyond. The walls were studded with iron doors, each one very like the door of the forge. They stopped before one, Morrison took the keys from his belt, unlocked it and pushed Edgar inside. All was darkness. Edgar heard the clatter of iron on iron, and felt his shackles pull tight. Morrison held up his lantern and showed Edgar a rusted hook driven into the wall, with the chain wrapped fast around it.

'There is not a man in the gaol who has not been broken by the systems of correction,' he said. 'You will find that there is no place here for proud boys.'

Edgar fixed his gaze on the wall. In the half-light the

pattern of the bricks began to emerge from the gloom.

'Very well,' said Morrison. 'Your silence will cost you your supper. Tonight you will be left in your cell to consider your crime. Tomorrow you will be put amongst your fellow men and we shall see how silent you remain.'

Morrison slammed the door behind him. Edgar sat and waited for the room to reveal itself. There was a grey light leaching through a window at the top of the cell, the misty twilight, etching out the iron bars against the sky. Solid thick bars, cutting up the frame.

A cot was set beside the table, covered by a blanket webbed with holes. The narrow walls wept with mildew, running down rivulets in the rock. Deep-scored lines bunched across the bricks. They looked to Edgar like the kind of things that the Professor would project upon his sheet: the claw marks of creatures. Proof that this was a place where wild animals once roamed. But as he looked closer he saw what they were: scored in sets of sevens, there were days and months and years cut into the walls, a calendar of punishment. And as he sat on the bed, he could hear that the stone held voices, calling out from behind the weeping rock: *Lord have mercy, father, pity, mercy.*

Edgar thought of his own father, standing in the dock opposite him, trembling.

William stumbled down the road, across the bridge and out into the meadows. There was nothing but grass and sky and the chattering of the tumbling river, and the mists rolling across the horizon. It was as if he was standing at the very edges of the world. The blackness in his head rolled and roared, an echo of the churning waters.

Eleanor stood stranded in the centre of the workroom. The breeze from the open door played against the hanging skirts, and the soft silk whispered. 'Shame,' it said, 'shame shame shame'. Eleanor blinked away her tears. And behind the tears, there was anger. White-hot, steely anger. Anger at the men of the court, who would split her family apart with a trick of the tongue and never think twice about it. Anger at William, who would condemn her in an instant. Anger – pure fierce anger – at the way that all her skills had been turned against her. A raging fury at the utter injustice of it all raced through her blood. And she knew where she should take it.

Eleanor marched down the street and through the manicured garden of Mrs Simm. Now she knew what she was looking at, it was obvious. The curves of the hedges, the bright-blossoming roses, the thick velvet curtains that shrouded the windows – every part of this house spelt out luxury.

The door swung open before Eleanor even set her hand upon it, and there was Mrs Simm standing before her, all feathers and finery and glittering glass beads.

'Oh, my poor dear!' she exclaimed. 'I have been so fretful about you and your boy. I was desperate to come and offer you some comfort, but what with your husband standing guard morning, noon and night, well, it was impossible.'

Before Eleanor could say a word she was pulled inside the house and into the parlour. The room was a riot of colour. It was as if Mrs Simm had taken all her attributes – her jewels, her silks, her plumpness – and scattered them about the place. Chaises sat piled high with cushions. Crystal bottles stood on the mantelpiece, shimmering with coloured liquids. A chandelier hung from the ceiling, teardrops of glass. The walls were a forest: paper of green silk, patterned with golden ferns. And on the far wall hung a row of masks. They were oval-eyed, mouthless and crowned with feathers, staring down at Eleanor. Mrs Simm bustled through the room, fetching glasses, smiling at Eleanor as she did so.

'So tell me, is all concluded? And how is the boy?'

'More's the question, how are your girls, Mrs Simm?'

Mrs Simm froze. The decanter in her hand scattered diamond flecks of light around the room.

'My girls? What have my girls got to do with this whole sorry business?'

And out it all came, in a furious torrent of words. The garments taken from the workroom, the bloomers paraded around the court. The accusations of whoring. Edgar shuttered up for seven long years. William, slicing through her work and banishing her from the house.

'I took your work on in good faith, Mrs Simm. And now it has pulled my whole family into disgrace.'

'Forgive me, but I rather think that it was your son who brought the disgrace. At worst, I merely added a little colour to the proceedings.'

'Colour? That's a fine word for it.'

'Mrs Jones,' said Mrs Simm sternly, 'if you had ever questioned me about my business I would have given you an honest answer. I was under the impression that we had an understanding.'

'An understanding?'

'You are a married woman, with your wits about you. I assumed that would suffice.'

Her wits. Eleanor was not sure she knew the meaning of the word. She was a wanton woman who had deceived her husband and lost her son. Her wits, if she had any left at all, were worn thread thin. And here she was, arguing over her lost reputation with the only friend she had left in the world. Her only friend – a woman who dressed girls up in brash silks and sent them off into the night.

Out in the meadows, the fog rolled in across the water. The sky was darkening, turning twilight and, with the mist running through it, gave the impression that the earth and the air were dissolving into each other. Nothing was fixed and nothing was safe.

William stumbled, half blind, back to the cottage. The door was lolling open, the fire was dead in the grate. And Eleanor was gone.

On the shelf at his shoulder, the barograph scribbled out its message as if tomorrow was a thing that could be predicted. The books ranged up the walls, spelling out the ways a man might live. *A System of Logic. Culture and Anarchy. On Heroes.* The more William looked at them, the more his blood ran thick with anger. He had trusted a world of argument and theory, followed every principle of these great thinkers and to what end? Even his books had deceived him. The fury surged inside him in a great wave, and he threw himself at the shelves, pulling down the wall of knowledge about his head, kicking at the falling tomes and splitting the spines until the floor was a sea of scattered arguments.

He went upstairs to the room that he had shared with his wife for all these years, dreaming his way through her deceptions. He pitched the bank of pillows on to the floor, and tossed the mattress on top of them. The stolen gown came tumbling out with it. William kicked at it and ran through his house, out into the wilderness. Into the world that he had always intended to tame.

The brambles and flowering weeds ranged around William on all sides. This was nature, savage, selfish nature. And if the Professor was to be believed, and the patterns of nature showed the workings of God's mind, then God was not watchful and kind. He was a cruel architect. He had made a world full of traps and snares, as vicious as the tangle of the briars. If there was a world beyond this one, where God's great design would reveal itself, then it was not a place that William wished to inhabit.

This very thought gave William a sensation of weightlessness. The anchor that had shackled him to the world since Edgar's birth was tugged free. He had lost his son; he had lost his wife; he had lost his station. He was no one and he was nothing, he was simply another cog in the great machinery of creation. A cog that was surely spinning free from its fixings.

He stumbled along the edge of the wilderness, fell against the trunk of the apple tree and clung on tight. A breeze tickled at his coat-tails. William was beset by the feeling that if he let go he would simply be lifted off his feet and carried up to the clouds.

His porter's suit weighed heavy upon his back. The sleeves of the coat were inching over his hands and his trousers were slipping at the waist, tripping him up and snagging on the creeping briars. The costume of authority no longer fitted him – he who could not even keep his college, his house or his mind in order. Above him the birds wheeled across the sky and roosted in the treetop, looking down at weeping William, curious. They seemed the size of eagles. He stumbled back from the trunk, frightened of the wide-striking span of their wings.

The bracken caught him. William's jacket was snagged in the tangle, his trousers tore as he tried to pull free. The brambles reached up to his waist. Nature was clawing up to claim him. There was nothing to do but go down on his hands and knees and burrow his way out. The briars braced his back as he pushed his way through. His boots fell from his feet, his trousers were lost to the wilderness, and William was left in his shredded shirt, which fell down to his knees. He was losing the last thing he had: his stature. The shrinking that had been chasing him through mind and body was gathering its full force through his blood.

When William emerged at the gate it was an iron barricade stretching high above him. He was trapped. He began to howl, like an abandoned infant. The birds scattered at the sound of it. His tears fell as solid things, drops of molten metal, clattering against the gate, running through the gaps and ricocheting down the street like marbles spilling from the pocket of a child.

In the gaol, the stones echoed William, weeping and wailing with the voices of men. Edgar stared at the days cut into the bricks. The more he looked, the more he was determined. This was another man's fate, not his.

Edgar thrust his hand into his breeches and pulled out a pin: a slender shard of iron, a thing that a mother would use to fix the cuffs of her son's new suit. He clamped it between his teeth.

To know how to make a thing is to take it apart backwards. Thanks to his time with Mr Stephens there was no mystery to his manacles. Their casings might just as well have been made from glass. He clamped the end of the pin in his teeth and fitted the keyhole of the cuffs to the tip. They sprang and fell to the floor.

Edgar laughed. 'Mercy,' called the stone, but Edgar needed none. He was Edgar Jones. He could make his own escape.

He unlooped the chain from the wall. He flung it at the window and the hook that had caught around his cuffs caught just as well on the iron bars. Edgar scaled the wall, up towards the window of mist. He clenched the bars in his fists. They twisted in the rock. He eased them out and flung them on to the bed beneath him. Only one bar remained, anchoring the chain.

Edgar scampered down the wall, and heaped his blanket over the iron. Then he scaled the wall again and set himself against the window. It was the span of his shoulders. He pushed his way through the rock, out into the twilight, out into the mist, gathering the iron tail of his chain behind him.

William threw himself against the garden gate. It toppled before him.

His tears rolled down the street and he chased after. His tears coursed across the cobbles. They glittered as they tumbled like precious stones, or the glass beads of a bodice. If William had been able to catch them he would have seen that they were neither. His tears were solid stone, speckled with iron and quartz, fool's gold. William chased them none the less, and to any observer he was just another stray urchin, gutter-racing.

His bare feet struck against the stone and the earth chimed, as if William's flesh had stronger substance than skin and bone.

And it had. If William had stopped to look he would have seen the soles of his feet were scaled and hard. But William didn't stop. He raced into Oxford, past the ruined shop, down to the crossroads. Across the street the Sheldonian heads glared down from their plinths and all around him the towers and battlements ranged. William's tears rolled ahead of him, down the gutters of Hollywell Street. The weight of his spine pressed down to the earth and he scampered on all fours, like a dog after its quarry.

By the time he came to the gate of the college William was no bigger than the foundation stones. He scurried in the shadows, under the arches and out into the quad, and if the porter at the gate looked up from his enclosure and saw anything scrabbling in the bushes it could only be a feral dog, rooting for scraps.

But it wasn't. Every bit of William was still William and he was going home. He took the turn to the cloisters. The bones of his spine pushed through his breeches. He squatted on the windowledge and felt a great unravelling in his bowels. He pushed and pushed and something sharp and solid went rattling down the wall. William looked over his shoulder and to his amazement there hung a tapering tail. A beautiful thing, the colour of bronze and moss. The rattle and roaring in his head fell silent. There was nothing but the tap tap tap of his tail against the bricks.

Above William the tower stood, a staff of gold, catching the dying light. The gargoyles perched on cornice and gutter. William yearned towards it. He jumped from the window.

And as he jumped the remnants of his shirt fell from his back, scattering in confetti threads. William felt an itching at his shoulder blades. He reached around to scratch, only to find himself stump-armed and claw-handed. He set his back to the cloister wall and rubbed it. There was the sound of a shell cracking. He twisted again, and wings sprouted from his shoulders. And up, up and up went William, outflying the arms of the ancient oak. The gargoyles turned their faces to him in open-eyed surprise. William soared past them and came to rest at the top of the tower. And there, suddenly, the air was full of voices, some cackling, some sobbing, some singing fit to crack the heavens. But above them all, one clear call rang out: 'Place yer bets!'

William turned his head to follow the voice but he found that his neck was set. Bone, fused into stone. He tried to push away from the tower but his feet had been swallowed by the bricks, along with his fine tail. He stretched out his shoulders to beat back his wings, but they were also stuck. He leant forward, struggling against his fixture. And there below him, Oxford spread out in all its glory.

Where William looked he saw not with the vision of a bookbound man, but with animal clarity. His eye was a prism that caught the light and drew a sharp focus. The mist dissolved under his gaze, opening up pockets of vision in the twilight. It was as if William had his telescope set to his eye: whatever he turned his gaze upon he saw it as if it were mere inches away. He looked to the east, and he could pick out the smile upon the statues standing guard by the roof of the library, grinning broad and wide, as if they knew what stone William now knew: the books stacked up inside the walls were a trap; knowledge for the sake of knowledge was no knowledge at all. He looked to the north, and he could see the varied colours of the wings of the birds perched on the Museum tower. He could see the sheen of the leaves of the trees marking the boundaries of the University Parks, and the lithe green life running through their veins.

He looked to the edge of the city and there was the tower of the castle, with its slit-eyed windows and its high walls. With something crawling along the surface of it. William drew focus. He was face to face with the surface of the stone. He could see the scuffing of the sand as the creature scaled the heights. But it was no creature. The swarthy skin, the shock of hair, the sure grasp of the hand upon the bricks, the scrambling up towards the sky – he knew this. It was his son, his Edgar. William gazed upon him with the same simplicity that he had looked upon him in the cradle. His boy with the curious mind, climbing out of the confines of his judgement. And he loved him for it.

William laughed, as he had laughed when he went flying across the ice with Edgar. The laugh caught in his chest and had the weight of rocks within it. William took one last gravel breath and cried with all his might, 'Edgar HO!'

The wind caught his call and sent it flying over the rooftops. But William cried no more. He was stuck: a stone dragon leaning out from the tower, fierce, rampant and forever watchful.

So it was that William joined the ranks of shrunken men set across the skies of Oxford, the great secret etched into the stone. These men of industry and application, these men who loved Oxford more than they loved any place in this world or the next. These men who, when their time came, calcified into the very essence of themselves. These men who had called to William, as if they knew how his fate would play out from the very beginning.

'Place yer bets!' called a scholar from under the arch of William's college. A man who loved the turn of the cards more than the turn of the pages of his lessons, lost his life over a bad debt and came back to Oxford to roost.

'Seek it out!' called Stephens' predecessor, the man who established a shop of instruments and died peaceful in his bed, his hand clasped around a pencil, etching out a thing made of iron and mirrors. He folded himself up under the eaves of Exeter College and spent his days peering into the window, smiling down upon the progress, and destruction, of invention.

'Are you sure? Are you quite, quite sure?' called a shrew-faced Professor of Philosophy, crouched upon the gutter at the front of St John's College, a man who thought himself into such doubt and distraction that he ceased to believe in the workings of his own body and, drop by drop, his blood dried out in his veins.

And William Jones, in his moment of stone-reckoning, no longer a thinker or a husband or a warden of the night, but simply the father of a son whom he loved more than all his theories, who, once freed from the shackles of his expectations, called out to his boy with love and laughter, with the call of one who would pull him up on to his shoulders and haul him about the sky, crying, 'Edgar, Edgar HO!'

Back in the castle, Morrison flicked open the eye in the door. But because man is man and he cannot see a thing that his mind tells him is impossible, when he looked through the peephole, nothing was awry. In the twilight, the window was as sealed and secure as it should have been. The blanket bundled over the bed stuffed with iron was the sleeping form of an unrepentant Edgar.

'We could waste the day in argument, Mrs Jones,' said Mrs Simm softly, 'or we could put together a plan of how to fix this injustice.'

Eleanor thought of the black box of the coach. She thought of the corset in William's hand, split back to the bone.

'I do not think this is a thing that can be fixed, Mrs Simm.'

'Nonsense! From what you say, Edgar is a determined lad. It will take more than a few years in the castle to break him. You mark my words, nothing is as bad as you suppose it to be.'

'It's not just Edgar. William believes I have wilfully deceived him. He will never forgive me for it.'

'You deceived your husband no more than he has deceived you,' replied Mrs Simm sternly. 'He set himself up as a gentleman and now he hounds you out of the house with the scissors, like a madman.'

The room was silent. There was just the soft whisper of Mrs Simms' drink licking up the side of the glass as she turned it about in her hand.

'Perhaps this banishment is a blessing,' said Mrs Simm. 'You are young enough to start your life anew, and have the talent to do it.'

Eleanor shook her head. 'Come tomorrow the whole of Oxford will know my story. My work is ruined.'

'There is always my sister, set up in London.'

'Your sister?'

'Who sent me the dress patterns. She is a seamstress, same as you, my dear,' Mrs Simm continued. 'That's how I recognised your skill the moment that we met.'

Eleanor looked over Mrs Simm's shoulder, at the masks set upon the wall. Beautiful, opulent disguises. The masks stared back at her. Could it really be so simple, to change her own history? To go to the great city of London, and to set up a room of her own? For her only worry in the world to be the piecing together of patterns? To live a life without shame or censure, and without William?

'But I could not desert my husband. We vowed to take the troubles of life together.'

'But you are banished, are you not?' said Mrs Simm. 'He cannot have both sides of the bargain.'

Eleanor felt her eyes prickle with tears. Mrs Simm's handkerchief was upon her cheek. How could she be angry with this old woman, the only person she had ever known who had the wits to speak plainly about the world.

'And what could be better for Edgar,' continued Mrs Simm, 'than for you to start afresh in a city where you are free from any stain, and to build a fortune up for your son?'

'But William—'

'The University will not abandon your husband. The Colleges look after their own. Why, if he runs mad enough they may even make him Professor.'

Eleanor smiled through her tears. 'I must think on it.'

'No, my dear, that is the last thing you must do. You must go home immediately, gather your possessions and return within the hour.'

Eleanor pushed open the door of the cottage and was greeted by a graveyard of broken learning. The books were scattered across the floor, the pages twisting in the breeze from the open door. There was the family Bible, sitting in the centre of the wreckage, the frayed binding poking out of the spine in a crest of hairs. Eleanor cradled it to her and turned the frontispiece. William's name stood proud upon the page, the ink rusted to the colour of blood. But her name and Edgar's name were both ripped clean away as if they had never been part of William's history at all. If she was not the wife who had promised to obey her husband then neither was William the man who had promised her protection. The man she had loved had slipped away and had left nothing in his place but damnation. Eleanor turned her back upon the broken books and walked through to the workroom.

The mannequin stood by the door, naked, faceless, limbless, an amputated judge. Eleanor took the scissors and rammed them into the breast of it, cutting a clean line straight down to the belly. The skin buckled, she tipped it forward and its guts fell to the floor in a cascade of gold and silver. Arabella was pregnant with fortune.

Eleanor sat at the parlour table and counted out her coins, stacking them into two even piles. She took a page from the floor, a woodcut from the Bible: the angel watching over Adam and Eve as they walked hand in hand out of Paradise. She turned it over, wrote William's name upon the back and weighed it down with half her wealth. The other half she pushed into her purse. She returned to the workroom and packed up what she could into a garment bag. A stuffed creature of a thing that stood to half her height. She dragged it across the street and knocked upon Mrs Simm's door.

An hour later a carriage pulled up at the door of the bawdy house. Eleanor was bundled into the back, the driver cracked his whip and it lurched down the cobbles, out round the edge of the misted meadow and into the world beyond. Eleanor pressed her head to the wall and closed her eyes. There was nothing but the clatter of the wheels and the horseshoes, her son's iron carrying her out of the world she knew, and off to find a better fortune. Taking her off to another Mrs Simm.

Over the rooftops Edgar ran, the boy who had slipped the shackles of the city, and flowed like mercury over the spires and the steeples, down the drainpipes, into the shadows. The open-eyed moon looked down upon him, this boy who could not be caught within the net of a judge's argument or kept behind bars of iron. And there in the wind, chasing him all the way back to the door of the cottage, a voice came calling, urging him on: 'Edgar, Edgar HO!'

Edgar returned home to find the cottage cast into darkness, with no lights burning in any window: a house shuttered up against the world. The moon etched out the shape of it against the sky. Edgar picked his way through the wilderness. There, in the heart of it, something flapped and tumbled, a creature caught upon the bracken, a great black bird. Edging closer, Edgar saw it for what it really was: his father's jacket, spiked upon a thorn bush. Edgar hauled it over his arm. Something struck his shoulder. He burrowed into the pockets and closed his fist around his snaggle-toothed skeleton key.

He pushed through the tangled darkness to the front door and turned the handle. In the wind of the night, the papers cast across the floor rose up to greet him. Torn apart arguments, spiralling through the air. Edgar beat them away.

'Mama?' he called 'Papa?'

Unused for months, his voice sounded heavy and strange, no longer high-whistling through the house. The voice of man, not a boy.

'Mama? Papa?'

The house echoed his own cries back to him.

He turned the handle of his mother's workroom. And there he found the guts of the mannequin scattered across the floor, and the shelves studded with bits of making.

He ran up the stairs to his parents' room. There were the tumbled pillows, the mattress set skewed across the floor, and the cleric's gown cast beside it.

He looked at the wreckage and he understood: he was free, and he was utterly alone.

He took the gown, and held it up to the moonlight. It fell down in wings, the folds of authority of the Professor, of the roosting jurymen who had been so swift to condemn him.

He saw how it must have been. No sooner had he been shackled in the gaol than these men had come after his parents, tearing down the walls of books, carrying away his mother's work, chasing them out of Oxford. And when his cell was found empty in the morning, they would come for him.

Well, that was not how it would be. This was not how the story of Edgar Jones would play out. He was quick and he was clever. No man could catch him, no cage could hold him. And neither would he be caught in the tales that jealous men told about him. He would do what Edgar Jones did best: he would invent. And this time he needed no stolen skeletons to do it. He would use himself. He would use his flesh, his bones and the bits of stuff that his parents had left behind. He would stitch himself into the heart of his own creation, and then the Professor, and all of Oxford, would, at last, see what kind of a boy he really was.

Edgar returned to his mother's workroom. There were corset wires cast across the tabletop. Miniature silver spurs. He gathered them until he had a shining fistful of the stuff. There was a needle and thread. There was ribbon and cord. There were the scissors. He took the whole collection out into the wilderness. He shrugged his father's coat upon his back. Then he built up a den of brambles and burrowed into the heart of it. And there, by the dappled moonlight, he began to cut and sew and connect.

Edgar crept out of the wilderness before dawn and made his way down to the Museum. He kept to the shadows, a strange figure, his coat drawn tight around him, and a bundle on his back.

He hunkered down on the opposite side of the street, the place where he had marked out so many hours, watching the men upon the scaffolding, watching the come and go of the carts and the crates. He watched one last time as the wardens made their rounds, and then, as the sky bled through with the dawn, they left their posts and went away back out into Oxford.

Edgar walked across the lawn as if he was a man with authority. From the window above, eyes stared down at him out of the cornice. The monkey had been chipped away, transformed into something else: a bony knuckle-spined cat, scuttling out of a wreath of ivy. Well, it was not just the stone that could reshape itself.

Edgar placed his skeleton key to the lock. It gave.

He walked through the porch where the owls looked down upon him, wide-eyed and curious, he unlocked the second door, and walked into a changed Museum.

Beyond the great gaping jaws, the courtyard was crowded with specimens.

Cabinets stretched between every pillar, a wooden maze of discovery. Edgar could see, beyond, the bones of creatures set out in the far corner, companions to the giraffe. He took the staircase up to the gallery, and there the full spectacle was stretched out before him.

In the giraffe's corner, the skeletons marched two by two upon their plinths. Giant cats, stags, and set beside them things that he could not name. There was the great head that had sat upon the Professor's armchair, now attached to a barrel-body, and it seemed all the fiercer for it. In the adjacent avenue, bones of creatures of the sea were strung from the ceiling – a giant fish, a turtle, with its filigree flippers paddling in the dark.

And it was not just the bones. The wall behind was sprouting with heads. Animals of the forest, captured and preserved in their savagery. Glare-eyed, snarling at the hunt. Their horns were sharp-spiked spirals of polished bone, twisting up the brickwork.

And it was not just bones and horns. On the top of the lines of cabinets, creatures crouched: stuffed. There was a wild-maned lion, a sitting bear, a thing with short fur and a long snout, each stranded on its own wooden island, with all sorts of specimens bottled up beneath. Edgar did not need to get close to see what was racked up in those cases, he knew what he would find: cut-away parts of creatures, whatever bits took the Professor's fancy.

And there, by the wall, the stone men. These great thinkers, looking out from their plinths as if they were lords of all they surveyed. Looking out, but never upwards.

The more Edgar gazed down at the collection, the more he understood. It was for this, this army of dead things that the Professor had denounced him. Well, Edgar was done with the old man and his Museum. To be a specimen was to be set within someone else's story and made an example of. It would not go that way for him.

Edgar peered into the cabinet set beside him in the gallery. It was full of rocks. He unlocked it and pulled out a big black pebble, put it in his pocket and went back down to the courtyard.

In the dawn light the glass roof seemed like a sea of flame, unfurling across the length of the Museum. Edgar clambered on to a plinth of stone, clutched the iron column between his knees and began to shin his way up. He clambered past rivets set by his own hand, up, up and up the trunk of metal, up to the level of the gallery, with its polished pillars and its flowering stone. Then, hand over fist, he crawled up the ribs of iron, up, up and up to the apex, to where the chequerboard roof and the arches met.

Then he took the stone from his pocket and hammered it against the glass. One, two, three times, the Museum rang with the sound of it. A broad-backed beetle caught in the rock was chipped away piece by piece, the rock crumbled and peppered his fingers. Four, five, six, the glass fractured. A cobweb split across the panel. Edgar hit once more and the glass fell away, spiralling down upon the floor far, far below. Edgar stood up on the arch and pushed himself through the gap.

Above the world, the great iron net of the roof spanned out into infinity before him. It was a glacier of ice and fire, playing out in mountainous repetitions, a maze of hills and valleys, glittering with glass. Multiple pathways branched off from one another, webbing out the sky.

Clouds shifted across the sun, and the mountains rose and fell with the reflection. All was fluid. The more Edgar looked, the more he saw: this was a world he knew. This was the land he had seen at the heart of the forge cauldron. This was the place he had yearned to be a part of. And it had been here, up in the sky waiting for him, all this long while, but he had always been stuck underneath it, ignorant. He had forged this world out of iron and courage, and now it was his for the taking. Edgar walked along it, back and forth across his metal land. He took the shining spur that led him to the tower. He anchored his back against it and he waited. Below him, Oxford glowed golden. It was an inventor's diorama, rooted in the hollow of the hills. Edgar spread out his hand. He could pluck out the tower of the Professor's college with a snip of finger and thumb.

He waited as the bells of Oxford pealed out the morning chimes. He waited as the streets filled with the passage of the trades. He waited as the clouds parted and the sky cleared and shone bright blue, like a polished piece of glass.

And there, below, Edgar saw his quarry. The Professor, striding across the grassland, with his claw-tipped cane slicing through the air.

But not just the Professor.

In his wake marched an army of black-cloaked men. They spread out across the lawn like a stain, like the shadowy smoke pouring out from a boiling pot.

Edgar stood up at the base of the tower, took off his coat and shook the hump from his back.

He unfolded it out of itself and there it was: his wings.

Edgar had cut his father's jacket into a tapering canopy, boned through with corset wire. The wire was connected to his fingers by ribbon and the body of the thing was bound to his back by cord. He shrugged his wings on to his shoulders and they rose behind him in the play of the winds, a span of blackness, a thing that Edgar had pored over again and again in that great book of invention. And now he had pulled it from the page and into the world. It was time to take flight.

On the ground below the men stopped their marching. They were turned with their faces to the sky, arms up, pointing at the tower.

'Edgar HO!' cried the sky at his back.

Edgar called back in kind, crying out to the wind and the waiting crowd: 'Edgar HO!'

And he jumped.

The sky slid sideways and the slate-feathered roof of the Museum was at his shoulder. But the edges of the wings caught against the guttering, and he was flung wide. Edgar was falling down the winds and the lawn below was rushing up to greet him, and there was a swarming sea of men, many-headed, arms outstretched to pluck him from the skies, with the Professor at the heart of it.

Edgar would not be caught a second time. He lifted his arms and beat against his fate. The wire cut into his fingers, the cords strained against his waist. But he beat against his fate and stayed his fall. The men clawed at the air but Edgar stretched out and tented his vision with the span of his wings. His broad shadow passed over them as he pushed himself up and away.

Over the roofs of Oxford Edgar flew. Past the forge, looping down across the meadows and back, following the run of the river. He tickled the glasshouses of the Botanical Gardens with the tip of his wings, laughing as he did so. He swooped past the libraries, past the gutted skeleton of the workshop, past the walls of his father's college – circling his own history, the angels smiling at his shoulder as he flew. Then he beat his wings once more, and pushed up, up and up into the sky, and let the winds carry him wherever they would. Over the hills and out into the aerial ocean, in search of adventure.

And as iron gathers to the pull of the strongest magnet, so did Edgar's creations yearn to follow the passage of their maker.

Along the line of the University Parks the railings shifted, their spear tips poking up towards the sky.

The iron arches of the roof opened up their arms for a second, clattering against each other with the subtlest sound of applause.

And beneath them the tail of the giraffe curled up against itself, and fell back in a wink of recognition.

ELIZABETH GARNER

Nightdancing

'Garner writes of myth and landscape with lyricism and sensitivity . . . she is steeped in the gift for being able to control the surreal with startling force . . . A promising and intriguing debut' Amanda Craig, *The Times*

A couple fall in love at first sight – a magical encounter. They search for a home, and soon they are building a charmed life together on the fringes of Wimbledon Common. But when summer arrives, and with it, two gregarious neighbours, their haven is transformed. In the course of lazy days of sunshine and long, hedonistic nights, the boundaries between the two households blur, and the lovers' faith in each other is put to the test. Deep-seated tensions surface, which gradually give way to fears that echo through their days, and haunt their nights.

Nightdancing is an unforgettable portrayal of the transforming power of young love, and the darkness that can be born of an ordinary relationship.

'Sharp prose and bucketfuls of imagination immediately distinguish this highly assured debut novel . . . dark and compelling . . . there is sensuality and power in the language' *Time Out*

'Elizabeth Garner's debut is almost too good at portraying the seeping doubt, creeping paranoia and final, disorientating dread of a disintegrating relationship' *Big Issue*

978 0 7553 0251 2

headline
review

SUE GEE

The Mysteries of Glass

'Unashamedly romantic and sensual, but also so
sparely written that the economy of her writing is
often breathtaking ... a beautiful, redemptive book'
Glasgow Herald

Hereford, winter 1860. Mourning his beloved father's
death, Richard Allen takes up his first position as
curate in a remote country parish. Vulnerable and
lonely, he has ideals of serving his priest and his
parishioners, but there are those who do not welcome
the newcomer, or his views. Then he falls helplessly in
love, and ignites a scandal that will rock a quiet
Victorian community to its foundations.

'Written with the delicate fluency of a storyteller
utterly at ease with her craft ... rippling, sinuous
prose, alive with the cadences of the natural world'
Times Literary Supplement

'The reader is held from start to finish by the mood ...
The Mysteries of Glass casts its own spell, which is the
essential requirement of a novel' *Daily Telegraph*

'Gee's gentle and restrained story celebrates the
sanctity of the ordinary and the beauty of holiness ...
Writing of surpassing beauty brings commonplace
objects into a clear, melancholy light' *Independent*

'This exquisitely written novel transports you to the
simple beauty, poignancy and hypocrisy of the
Victorian era in a way that makes you feel you've been
there. I cannot recommend it highly enough' Katie
Fforde

978 0 7553 0309 0

headline
review

MANETTE ANSAY

Vinegar Hill

'A place for everything; everything in its place. The house is as rigid, as precise as a church, and there was nothing to disturb its ways until three months ago when Ellen and James and the children moved in because they had no place and nowhere else to go.'

When Ellen Grier's husband loses his job, she has little choice but to agree to his suggestion that they and their children move in with his parents on Vinegar Hill. Their new home is more stifling than she feared – a loveless place where dark secrets lurk behind a façade of false piety, and calculated cruelty is routine. Ellen's spirit is close to crushed: how is she to protect her children from their grandparents' bitterness and disapproval? Will her love for little Amy and Bert give her the strength to find a way for them to escape?

'Magical . . . A satisfying journey to freedom . . . Ansay writes in a lovely voice' *Vogue*

'One of the best books of the year' *Chicago Tribune*

'Ansay transcends both feminist epic and midwestern Gothic to achieve, finally, the lunar world of tragedy. This world is lit by the measured beauty of her prose, and the book's final line is worth the pain it takes to get there' *New Yorker*

'A modern-day *Little House on the Prairie* gone mad . . . Manette Ansay is a powerful storyteller with lyrical gifts, and a wry, observant eye' Amy Tan

978 0 7553 3548 0

headline
review

JED RUBENFELD

The Interpretation of Murder

Manhattan, 1909.

On the morning after Sigmund Freud arrives in New York on his first – and only – visit to the United States, a stunning debutante is found bound and strangled in her penthouse apartment, high above Broadway. The following night, another beautiful heiress, Nora Acton, is discovered tied to a chandelier in her parents' home, viciously wounded and unable to speak or to recall her ordeal. Soon Freud and his American disciple, Stratham Younger, are enlisted to help Miss Acton recover her memory, and to piece together the killer's identity. It is a riddle that will test their skills to the limit, and lead them on a thrilling journey – into the darkest places of the city, and of the human mind.

'[Rubenfeld's] portrayal of New York's social divisions, its louche, rumbustious energy, and its skyscrapers reaching higher and higher, have a vivid authenticity . . . an unusually intelligent novel which entertains, informs and intrigues on several levels' *The Times*

'A thrilling, heart-in-the-mouth read . . . Once you start reading, it's impossible to put down' *Scotsman*

'Rubenfeld writes beautifully . . . an intriguing mystery' *Sunday Telegraph*

'Rubenfeld's brilliant conceit is to weave this real-life event into an accomplished thriller . . . a dazzling novel' *Independent*

978 0 7553 3142 0

headline
review

You can buy any of these other **Headline Review** titles from your bookshop or *direct from the publisher*.

FREE P&P AND UK DELIVERY
(Overseas and Ireland £3.50 per book)

TO ORDER SIMPLY CALL THIS NUMBER

01235 400 414

or visit our website: www.headline.co.uk

Prices and availability subject to change without notice.